Marta Maretich is an American writer who lives and works in London. She is the author of two novels, *The Merchants of Light* (Nine Elms Books 2015) and *The Possibility of Lions* (GemmaMedia 2012). Marta holds an MFA from the Warren Wilson MFA Program for Writers. Her short fiction, nonfiction and poetry have appeared in many publications and she has been awarded artist residencies at the Eastern Frontiers Foundation and Yaddo.

Marta was born in Nigeria and raised in California. She has lived in the United Kingdom since 1995. Her husband, Michael Alford, is a painter and they have one daughter.

The Merchants of Light

A Novel of Venice

by Marta Maretich

NINE
ELMS
BOOKS

First published in 2015 by Nine Elms Books
An imprint of Bene Factum Publishing Ltd

Nine Elms Books
PO Box 58122
London
SW8 5WZ
Email: inquiries@bene-factum.co.uk
www.bene-factum.co.uk

A CIP catalogue record for this book is available from the British Library.

Print ISBN: 978-1-910533-06-2
Epub ISBN: 978-1-910533-07-9
Mobi ISBN: 978-1-910533-08-6

Cover design: Kimberly Glyder
Text design: Guy Eaglesfield
Set in Tiepolo and Baskerville
Cover image: *The Banquet of Cleopatra* by Giambattista Tiepolo

Printed and bound in the UK

For Michael Alford

Who taught me everything I really needed
to know about painting.

Contents

PART ONE

Lieutenant John D. Skilton Jr.
Würzburg, Germany, 1945

Würzburg, Germany, 1945

It was raining the day John Skilton arrived in Würzburg. The skeletal walls of the city glistened with water. Little rivulets flowed down mountains of rubble, collected in the tank ruts, and pooled in the impact craters that scarred the roads. *The ruins didn't smoke,* he would say later, *they only dripped.*

That was an understatement — most of what Skilton said after the war was understatement, delivered in a quiet voice laced with cigarette smoke. He always made a point of emphasising that he arrived in Würzburg — indeed he arrived everywhere — after the fighting was over. The Wehrmacht had fled to the east. Hitler had been dead for two months. *My nemesis,* he liked to say in a wry way, *was the Army Corps of Engineers. Those so-and-sos kept stealing my lumber.*

But it was really the rain that was Skilton's powerful, relentless enemy in Würzburg. All through the four months he spent in the city, it pounded down. The local people, huddling in the flooded cellars of their ruined homes, said they had never seen a summer like it. It was as though nature, in some purgative reflex, was trying to wash the last remnants of the shattered city back into the soil. After what Skilton had witnessed since he landed on Omaha Beach almost a year earlier, he could see how it was possible that nature, or even God, might want to scour Europe clean and simply start again. And yet it was his job to pick through its ruins, to see what could be saved: Skilton was a Monuments Specialist Officer. Würzburg was his assignment. When he saw it he felt like turning around and swimming back home.

He first saw the city from the lurching cab of an army truck, pinned between the driver and the young captain who was acting as Fine Arts Officer for the Military Government Detachment. The captain's name was Hauser and he had no idea what Skilton was doing there.

"So how do you rate this, Lieutenant? What do you make of the handiwork?" Hauser was a thickset young man with black hair that was slick with oil or rain. He came from Michigan and before the war he sold tyres, he said. From the sidelong way he was peering at him, Skilton knew he must look all wrong to the younger man, too clerkish, too old for a second lieutenant, with his thinning hair, his tie neatly knotted and tucked between the buttons of his shirt.

"I'm sorry?"

"Did they do a good job?" Hauser jerked his thumb out the window. The truck was passing a handsome three-storey townhouse. Its windows had all been blown out, but its carved façade appeared untouched. As they passed by, Skilton saw without surprise that the building had no roof and no back. The façade rose from the rubble like a theatre set for a different play than the one they were performing. He understood: Hauser was challenging him to be shocked by what he saw.

"They told me you came up the Saar valley with the Seventh Army. How does this compare to down there?"

The driver shifted down, knocking his knuckles against Skilton's knee. The road they were travelling on had been scraped clear of debris, but the side streets were still blocked with landslides of shattered bricks and roof slates. A woman wearing a headscarf picked her way along the base of a rubble mountain, her market basket over one arm. The humid air stank of dank ash, sewage and mould.

Skilton tried to make his answer sound world-weary and matter-of-fact. It was important that he appeared to accept the destruction, the way everyone around him did. It was important that he acknowledge its purpose.

"All the cities are like this," he said cautiously. "I was in Heilbronn, Augsburg. The outskirts are sometimes intact, but the centres are always gutted. I suppose they aim for the centres."

"They did this one in March," Hauser volunteered, tapping the back of his hand against the window.

Skilton felt his heart lurch. "In March? That's very late."

"You're telling me. They didn't even get around to it until the middle of the month, about six weeks before the Nazis surrendered. It wasn't what you'd call a strategic position."

Where had Skilton been in March? What exactly had he been doing when this city was destroyed? His hand moved instinctively to his shirt pocket. There he carried a small notebook, containing page after page of jotted information about Würzburg. It wasn't much, but it was all he could glean on a single afternoon at the headquarters in Paris where he reported to be given this assignment. Yet it was enough to tell him that Würzburg had been a kind of Baroque jewel-box, with exquisite churches, palaces, gardens, an ancient fortress, museums, a university and several notable private collections of art. While he was making his notes, he'd begun to worry that he was ill prepared to handle the task of protecting such a wide variety of cultural treasures. Now, gazing out of the rain-splattered windows of the truck, he wondered if he'd find anything at all left to save.

"Who did it?" They passed the burned-out shell of a German tank abandoned on the side of the road. Even as he asked the question, Skilton knew the answer didn't matter.

The British carried out the bombing, Hauser said. The RAF sent some two hundred Lancasters and probably a few Mosquitoes to drop incendiaries and high explosives. Hauser was a bit of an actor, Skilton observed, a bit of a comedian. He clenched his fists then flicked his fingers wide to mimic blasts. He puffed out his fleshy cheeks to make booming sounds. "It was all over," Hauser said with appreciation, "in about twenty minutes."

"They say the local Gauleiter sat out the bombing in the only air raid shelter in town," he told Skilton. "Then he sneaked off at night with his family. They're still looking for him, and when I say 'they' I mean the people from *here* are looking for him. Know what? I hope they catch him before we do. That would serve him right. He was a *dentist*, of all the crazy things."

"Never trust a dentist," Skilton said, glad to be certain of something.

Hauser grunted. "And just look at this mess they left us." He waved his hand, taking in the wet wreckage of the city. "I signed up to be a soldier, not a janitor."

"I'm guessing you didn't volunteer for fine arts duty, Captain," Skilton said. It was no use admitting to this glossy captain how glad he was for any chance to do some significant cleaning up. So far, his most useful tool for fine arts conservation had proved to be a wheelbarrow.

Hauser growled. "Let's just say next time I'll think twice before I tell my superior officer I like Norman Rockwell." He studied Skilton out of the corner of his eye. "How about you?"

In the hour since he'd arrived in Würzburg it had become clear to Skilton that the captain had no idea what a Monuments Specialist Officer was supposed to do. This was not a new experience for him. No one in the US military seemed to know. He usually found it was better to skip the explanations and just do what he could. But he was going to be working with this captain for some time, so he took the plunge.

"Strangely, this is my field," he said. "I was working as a researcher for a museum when I was called up — the National Gallery, in Washington, D.C. That's why I joined the Monuments Specialist Service. Not that I've been able to achieve much so far. I keep getting hijacked. They had me working as a translator in Civil Affairs until a few weeks ago."

"Is that so?" Hauser looked more suspicious than ever. "Someone told me you speak Kraut."

Skilton smiled, pleased that his reputation preceded him. "That's probably because I speak French," he said.

They came to the Main, a wide ribbon of water flowing through the centre of the city. The Germans had blown the bridge as they retreated and the Army Corps of Engineers had spanned the breach with a construction of iron, strong enough for one vehicle to pass at a time. The truck slowed to a crawl as it joined a line of vehicles waiting to cross. As they waited, Skilton looked across the water at what was left of the old town. The destruction on that side of the river seemed total. Every roof was gone, every window was empty, piles of smashed buildings lay in the street. It was difficult to believe there had ever been a city there to begin with.

They crossed over water dark with silt, breaking in little eddies against the remaining bridge pilings. They continued into town, moving slowly to avoid pedestrians. From time to time the driver had to blow his horn at someone who had strayed into the road. The locals moved sluggishly, like people in shock, and Skilton supposed that's exactly what they were. Würzburg had been spared violence throughout most of the war. Then in just a few minutes the city was reduced to rubble and ash. The people on the street kept their eyes fixed on the ground, scarcely glancing up when the truck passed. Now and then the metallic stink of carrion blew through the vents into the cab.

They inched toward the city's cathedral, the Church of Saint Killian. Skilton saw that its towers were still standing and fought the impulse to call out to the driver to stop. *Later*, he thought, averting his eyes as they jolted past the broken building with a sense of shame, *I'll come back for you later*. He felt like a field medic carrying out triage, sorting through the wounded, identifying those least likely to die. The cathedral was on his list, but it wasn't his first priority.

The truck emerged suddenly from the ruin of the old town onto an immense open plaza. It had once been a parade ground paved with smooth slabs but the bombs had harrowed it into a landscape of crater dells and rubble hillocks. Slender shoots of bright green grass sprouted from every crack, bending sharply in the stiff wind. The driver steered the jolting truck through puddles like round dew ponds toward a horizontal structure that seemed to spread out its arms to greet them.

Skilton leaned forward and wiped the condensation from the inside of the windshield. He felt his heart beating power-fully against his precious notebook. This was the Residence of Würzburg's Prince-Bishop and it was the first item on Skilton's list.

"It looks better than I was led to believe," he said to Hauser somewhat breathlessly. "At headquarters they told me it had re-ceived a direct hit, but I see the walls are intact, the statues are still standing up there on the parapet. This is a nice surprise."

Hauser didn't say anything. He just gave Skilton a strange comical look as though he had said something funny. Then he opened the door into the rain and jumped down into a puddle.

The Prince-Bishop's ceremonial staircase was just like a set in a Hollywood musical. That was Skilton's first, frivolous thought as he entered the building. The pale risers ran up from the dimly lit circular vestibule like a vertical stage and Skilton couldn't stop himself from imagining a troupe of dancers in top hats and tails stepping and kicking down it. His second thought was that the stairs were reasonably dry and clean. The smell of burning hung in the air but there was no trace of water, no large rubble cluttering the stone steps.

He and Hauser began to climb the staircase. With some reluctance, Skilton forced himself to keep his head raised, his eyes lifted, even though he was still afraid of what he might see. He knew that any problem he identified now would be his to fix and no one else's. It made part of him want to keep his eyes shut, but another part of him was carried away by the unexpected joy of finding this part of the Residence still standing. It was incredible. One wing of the palace had received a direct hit. Other rooms had been gutted by fire. Yet this section, the heart of the structure and the part that contained its most irreplaceable treasures, remained standing.

The space seemed to expand around them as they climbed up. Skilton heard the immensity of the hall before he could properly see it. Their heavy boots rang against the stone steps and the noise echoed back at them from above, suggesting a vast, enclosed emptiness. Into this they climbed from the darkness of the vestibule, arriving on a mezzanine that embraced the opening of the staircase. Up there, the windows had been blown in. They were only partially boarded over and rain blew in with cold gusts of wind. The stone floor was heaped with shattered glass and broken window frames. The light was dim, but it was enough to see the contours of the vault arching above them. Skilton unclipped his flashlight from his belt and trained it upwards. He almost jumped with shock. The beam fell on the head of a gigantic dark-skinned woman in a feathered headdress. He played the light down her body — golden ornaments, a powerful, sinuous leg — to find she was riding on a monstrous alligator.

America. Skilton was no expert in iconography, but he recognised the allegorical figure. Playing the beam over the surface of the vault, he quickly located the figures of Asia, Africa and Europe, all giantesses accompanied by their totem animals: a camel, an elephant, a bull. There were gods on the ceiling, too: Venus, her body stretched at full length along the slope of a cloud, Mars in his decorative armor, and, in a blaze of pale yellow sun, a naked Apollo holding a lamp aloft. Girls with butterfly wings restrained white sky horses. River gods lounged on the rim of the dome. Skilton estimated there were about a hundred figures, flying, seated on clouds, parading along the four sides of the room.

A shiver of delight went through him. "The frescoes are still here," he said. "They're still intact."

"So it seems." Hauser was standing to one side gazing through a gap in the boards nailed across the open window. He took a pack of cigarettes from his pocket and held one out to Skilton.

"It's beyond anything I expected," Skilton went on, taking the cigarette. "I thought we might be able to save a few pieces, fragments, maybe a section of the ceiling. But this is incredible. It looks like the entire fresco has survived. I can't believe our luck." His laugh echoed back sharply from the vault above. He felt like dancing, step-kicking down the staircase himself. "And the illusion is extraordinary," Skilton said, aware of Hauser's eyes on him. "Can you see what he's done? Even in this dismal light, my God, it's like looking at a real sky."

As soon as the words were out of his mouth, he knew they were idiotic. The real sky was full of rainclouds, warplanes and smoke from the fires of the displaced. The real sky was the one he had feared to find above the Staircase Hall, leering at him through obscene cracks in the plaster. What he found instead was a false sky, whole, blessedly unreal, adorned with gods and winged creatures and flooded with a serene golden light from elsewhere. *Elsewhere.* The sight of it made Skilton forget why he was there and returned him for one merciful moment to the state of innocence he had enjoyed as a tourist in Europe before the war. It seemed incredible to think of it now, but he and his best friend had spent a whole summer travelling in France, Italy and Germany, drinking in the culture, seeing buildings and paintings and sculptures he had only read about in his Art History courses at Yale. Everything he saw thrilled him. But although he had seen so many beautiful, noble things on his grand tour, he had never seen anything like this ceiling.

"There's more of it," Hauser said finally, holding out a match.

"More?" Skilton reached for his notebook.

"Yeah. It's even fruitier than this, if you can believe it."

Hauser walked him through a pair of doors and into a smaller, square room, half of it in rubble on the floor. They then entered a third room. This was the Imperial Hall, the throne room of the Residence. Skilton had made a note of it back in Paris, but nothing in the records prepared him for what he saw. Once again he had the giddy sense of the ceiling being lifted from the building and the sky flooding in. Above them soared a lofty cupola, its dome pierced with round windows. The light was dimmer here, the boarding was more thorough, but Skilton could just make out a fantasy interior of swirling stucco, marble and gold.

"Astonishing," he said, feeling another wave of wonder that such a delicate human contrivance could have survived the force of bombs. Again, the room seemed largely intact. The beam of his flashlight revealed frescoes framed by huge stucco curtains on either end. One scene showed an emperor on a throne; another what looked like a wedding. A handsome blond girl in a blue dress kneeled in front of a bishop, her bearded groom attentive at her side.

"Well, this has to be some kind of a miracle," he said with a catch in his voice. "We'll never know how it happened but the major staterooms seem to have escaped untouched." He was already thinking about how to rearrange his list. He'd inspect the chapel of the Residence next, which he knew had received a direct hit in the air raid. Then he'd move on to the Cathedral of Saint Killian, then the Marienkirche, then the fortress.

He took another moment to study the ceiling further. It was another piece of painted sky, punched through the top of the cupola and framed with a gilded moulding. The scene showed a golden chariot being pulled through heaven by rampant white horses. In it sat a plump blond girl with a string of pearls around her neck, the same one who was shown getting married in the wall fresco. She had a serene look on her radiant, rosy young face, but her arms were outflung in a dramatic gesture as she rushed to embrace her bridegroom, her future and her glory.

There was something sweetly ordinary about this figure, Skilton thought. In the midst of so much supernatural activity — angels soaring, horses pawing thin air, deities and demigods crowding the margins — the girl in the flying chariot looked like someone he might know, a niece or the daughter of a friend or the teenager that served him his sandwiches in the coffee shop back home. She wore a calm, slightly empty expression, like someone passively enjoying a ride in the country and looking forward to a nice lunch at the end of her journey. The cleverness of Tiepolo's choice made Skilton smile. Putting this robust, pretty, commonplace girl at the focal point of his heaven made the grandiose scene seem far more human and, in a mysterious way, far more real.

Hauser's voice came from the shadows beside him. "Now I feel bad, Lieutenant," he said.

Skilton was still buzzing with relief and gratitude. Gratitude to the RAF for missing something with their bombs, gratitude to Hauser for showing him the thing he most wanted to see: a treasure, surviving. On impulse he put out a hand to pat Hauser on the shoulder, then quickly pulled back, realising such an intimate gesture might be inappropriate. "Why should you feel bad? This is the best break I've had in months."

"I feel like I've played a dirty trick on you," Hauser answered. He sounded uncomfortable. "I didn't think anyone could really care that much about this stuff. Not now."

Skilton felt the grin fading from his face. "I'm not following you," he said.

Hauser took a deep breath and pointed upwards. "Hear that?"

Skilton listened. It was almost completely dark now and his eyes roamed up through the shadows toward the apex of the dome. Into the darkness came the steady hiss of the rain, an uncomplicated sound that any child would recognise. Every so often the wind would lift and the pitch would increase; then it would fall and the sound of the slowing rain would drop to a patter. "All I hear is the rain on the roof," he said nervously.

Hauser shook his head and gave an ambiguous laugh. "You didn't see it when we got out of the truck. But then I guess that's not your fault. The visibility's bad, couldn't be worse. It's hard to get a fix on it. The angle is — "

"What?" Skilton interrupted. "What did I miss?"

"You missed what the RAF didn't miss," Hauser said too loudly. "There is no roof. The bombs that landed on the square, in front? They blew it right off. Boom: flat top." Hauser chopped a hand over the dome of his helmet. "Man, you should see your face right now! I hate to be the one to break it to you, Lieutenant."

"There's no roof." Skilton repeated the words, numb and perplexed. All at once he decided that Hauser was ribbing him. He was just the sort of wiseacre to do such a thing, having a laugh at the expense of the older man, getting his digs in early. Skilton, so often the butt of his comrades' jokes, had mastered the art of being a good sport. He tried to laugh it off. "Oh, you're funny, Captain. You had me going there for a minute. If there's no roof what are we looking at, then? What's keeping the rain out?"

"What we are looking at here is the vault," Hauser said. "Do you get me? *Just the vault*. A few inches of plaster, one or two iron ribs, a lick of fancy paint with nothing on top of it but — nothing. If you don't believe me you can ask the Kraut architect, Bosslet. He'll tell you all about it."

A feeling of revulsion swept though Skilton as Hauser's words sunk in. He'd had the same feeling collecting dead soldiers from the battlefield. Some were in pieces, and that wasn't so hard, somehow, it was honest. But some looked whole when you came to them, untouched, like boys who had died in their sleep. At least they looked that way until you turned them over and found the gaping exit wound. The vault was the same. It looked sound but the truth was that it was doomed and it could come crashing down at any moment, burying him and Hauser alive.

In his imagination, Skilton saw the rain slowly seeping into the plaster, dissolving the painted sky. He saw the ceiling fall, reduced to elemental chunks of gypsum and pigment, revealing a ribcage of blackened iron bones and thrusting the terrible, real sky into the beautiful room. The image shook him to the core. Suddenly, the girl in the chariot, the one who seemed so immediate and so ordinary and so lovely, appeared to be holding out her arms in supplication to him. *Save me.*

Skilton shook it off. The idea was ridiculous, and it wasn't going to help him. Above all he couldn't let Hauser see what this news did to him. He needed Hauser. He took another deep breath and switched off his flashlight as though he had seen enough.

"Well, if that's the case," he said, "we don't have much time."

"Time for what?" asked Hauser.

Skilton didn't answer because he didn't know what the answer was. He walked as calmly as he could to the top of the staircase and started down.

PART TWO

Cecilia Guardi

Venice, 1718

Venice, 1718

When they reached the Campo San Rocco, Antonio's plan for ruining Cecilia's life began to take shape. Despite running all the way through the streets of Venice, they had arrived too late — no doubt Antonio had calculated it — and the procession, the very thing Cecilia had asked to see, had already gone by. The long white sailcloth canopy was in place, bisecting the narrow square like a spinal column, but the Doge and his retinue had passed beneath it and were shut up inside the plain brick-faced church of San Rocco, thanking the leper saint for stopping the plague of 1576.

As soon as she saw this, Cecilia knew Antonio had beaten her. She'd blackmailed him into bringing her to the celebration in San Rocco and from the start he had set out to make the day a disaster. He'd forced her to chase after him all the way from their house in Santa Maria de Formosa to the Campo San Rocco, racing down crowded alleyways, dodging around blind corners, vaulting over beggars and skidding over slippery bridges. Cecilia worried that the *sbirri* would arrest them for thieves but, as she skipped to avoid a one-legged veteran stretched out on the pavement, she realised she hadn't run like this, with her skirt hitched up and her shawl coming loose from her head, for years and years. It was good to be out of the house, good to be rushing down unfamiliar streets, following the gangly form of her brother who ran ahead of her, trying to lose her, laughing. "You can't keep up!" he shouted. "You can't catch me."

She caught him at the Campo San Rocco.

"What an awful shame," Antonio said, gasping for air. He bent over, hands on his knees. She was glad to see he was out of breath from sprinting. "Let's get the Doge to do it all again, just for us." Before Cecilia could stop him, he mounted the church steps and made as if to knock on the church doors.

"Excuse me, Doge Cornaro," Antonio called out. "Could you kindly come out again? Cecilia Guardi missed your first act." One of the guards placed a hand on Antonio's thin chest and pushed him casually back down into the crowd.

To hide her disappointment, Cecilia busied herself rearranging her shawl, folding it securely over her hair, tucking the ends into the waistband of her skirt. When she'd caught Antonio bending their maid, Maria, over the kitchen table, she'd known instantly that she had the power to claim any bribe she asked for, from him or from her: a new dress, a whole bag of cakes or even a boat trip to one of the islands. Instead she'd asked for this outing to the painting exhibition at San Rocco, thinking it was modest and justifiable, thinking it would mean something to Antonio and he would be genuinely happy to go with her. Now, as she glared at her brother, she wished she'd demanded more. But it was too late. She would have to salvage what she could of the day.

"So show me the paintings," she said, attempting to sound commanding. At least Antonio was capable of doing that. "You can tell me something about them, can't you? You're a painter, or so they say."

Antonio unbent to his full height and looked down at her. He was very tall and he towered over most people when he bothered to stand up straight, but not so much over Cecilia, who was tall herself. Unlike her, Antonio was also very thin, which meant that his height, instead of giving him stature, made him ridiculous. His dark hair, never well dressed, had come loose from its tie during their run and strands straggled down the sides of his head. Cecilia had the impulse to turn her brother around right there in the square and fix his hair for him, the way she did for her younger brothers. But then she thought better of it.

He pulled a clown face, pushing his eyebrows up and his mouth down into a frown of mock surprise. "*Am* I? A painter, is that what they say?" He patted his pockets as though the proof might be found there. "Are you sure?"

He leapt off the steps of the church and loped away, threading through the crowd. Cecilia followed him, passing beneath the canopy and moving toward the Scuola Grande di San Rocco, the building that housed the Confraternity of San Rocco, a brotherhood of deep-pocketed Venetians who did charitable works. They sponsored the day's events.

Approaching the Scuola, Cecilia tried to remember why the confraternity did that. It had to do with the great painter, Titian, and San Rocco, the leper saint, the one who had the adorable little dog. How did the story go? The famous painter's death had moved San Rocco to bring an end to the plague epidemic in Venice. In some mysterious way this made him the patron saint of Venetian painters — or was it just painters with the plague? All Cecilia knew was that they had prayed to San Rocco when her father took ill, but it hadn't done any good. Domenico Guardi died slowly, in agony. No saint, not even a diseased one, stepped in to help.

Cecilia hadn't been allowed to go to the celebration in San Rocco or anywhere else since her father's death. She was a little stunned by the crowds and the colour. The square was packed with people who had gathered to see the procession. Bright silk banners hung from surrounding balconies from which well-dressed ladies looked down, sipping iced drinks from fluted glasses. Vendors circulated, hawking cool drinks and nuts and nougat.

The beautiful façade of the Scuola, with its slender columns and discs of coloured marble, was decked for the occasion in garlands of fresh greenery and golden tassels, forming a colourful background for the main event: an outdoor exhibition of paintings by the city's best and most ambitious artists.

There were many paintings on show that day, more than Cecilia remembered from previous years. Framed canvases of all sizes and shapes, depicting all the main subjects — histories, portraits, views — were hung on the façade of the Scuola. The festival of San Rocco provided the only occasion for Venice's painters to display their works in public, so every studio and major artist in the city wanted to be represented there. Paintings dangled from the building's cornices and were suspended from the stone carvings of its capitals. The paintings hung at odd angles, lending the exhibition an air of spontaneity, as though passing painters had decided on a whim to put their best works up in the open air. The pictures looked both vulnerable and unnatural outdoors, with their surfaces raked by harsh sunlight, dampened by the rare drop of summer rain. As a child, Cecilia used to worry about them, but her father had reassured her that a well-crafted oil painting was as tough as ox hide.

Cecilia found Antonio waiting for her in front of a large painting of the Madonna and Child. He stood with his eyes closed as though meditating on deep subjects. "How you do dawdle," he scolded when he saw her there.

"Get on with it," was all she said.

Antonio cleared his throat. "Here is a painting," he said, waving his long arms like a conjurer, closing his eyes again.

Cecilia, suddenly hopeful, prepared herself for the pleasure of listening. Every year her father had carried her through the exhibition on his shoulders, positioning himself in front of each canvas in turn and telling her everything he knew about it: what it meant, who had painted it and, most important of all, who had paid for it. She adored his stories about the figures in the paintings — gods, goddesses, kings, queens, saints, devils — and she loved hearing about the wealthy noblemen that commissioned the works. But the thing she loved most was the way so many people they knew, so many painters, were intimately connected to these celebrities. Ricci, Zanchi, Litterini, Strom, Diziani, Trevisiani, Visenti: her father had worked for many of them. He'd even worked on some of the paintings they saw at San Rocco. Cecilia remembered him standing her in front of a huge history painting and showing her the clump of yellow hollyhocks he'd painted with his own hands. She put out one finger and dared to touch the thick paint, experiencing an intense rush of pride.

Now she gazed up at the image of the Madonna and child, a handsome woman with a fat baby boy on her knee, and prepared herself to listen to Antonio. He assumed a solemn expression. "This painting is made primarily of — paint."

"You clown," Cecilia said. Once again it occurred to her that Antonio was not going to honour his part of their bargain. "That's not what you say."

"It's painted with an instrument called a — brush. Or so they tell me."

"Stop it. Stop it." Cecilia covered her ears. "You are such a fool."

But Antonio wasn't going to stop. He sidestepped along the line of paintings until he was standing under the next one. It was huge, the size of a shed, and it depicted Roman soldiers in shiny helmets and breastplates alongside a rearing mad-eyed horse with a curved neck, hooves lifted to strike. Her father would have told her everything about it: which pigments they used, how they had negotiated such an enormous canvas out of the studio doors. He'd even have been able to tell her the name of the horse.

"Here is another painting," Antonio said, drawling like a

pedant. "It's bigger, you'll notice, and has more paint in it. I can see a quantity of blue paint, with touches of green. And, I'll be, there's some red."

Cecilia decided to try ignoring him and moved on quickly to the next work. She didn't need Antonio. She knew enough about painting and painters to tell herself stories. She placed herself defiantly beneath a painting showing an angel kneeling beside an old man in a loose robe. Both figures were bathed in a liquid shaft of golden light that shone though a barred window. Was it Saint Peter, Paul? Or maybe a more recent saint?

Antonio bounded over, officious, assiduous. "Don't get ahead of me!" he cried. "If you rush you won't get the full benefit."

"Go away," Cecilia said.

Antonio pretended to study the painting. "It appears to me, if I'm not mistaken and I rarely am, based on my long years of experience, that what we have here is yet another glaring example of paintiness and the use of so-called brushes." He turned then and scanned the square in a sort of panic. "My God!" he cried, pointing to the paintings displayed on the other side of the square against the railings of the Frari. "These painted things are all over the place. Who do you suppose left them here?"

Cecilia scowled, pulling her frayed shawl around her face to hide her fury. Antonio dropped his act. "It's not working out for you today, is it little sister? I told you it's no good trying to get one over on your big brother. And by the way, how can you tell Mama about *me* now that I know about *you*?"

"I haven't done anything." She had a bad feeling about the direction the conversation was taking. "Not like you. And Maria."

"Oh no? If I remember rightly Mama forbade you to leave the house without her. There was talk of convents, if I recall. Of shipping off to. I hate to think what will happen when Mama finds out how you made me bring you here against my will."

She saw at once that Antonio was right. He'd trapped her. She couldn't hurt him now without hurting herself even more. To her shame, tears started up in Cecilia's eyes. She retreated deeper into her shawl to conceal them, but Antonio noticed.

Looking far away across the tops of the heads of people in the square he said, "And now she's going to cry."

"What do you know?" she shouted at him, ignoring the crowds of people around them. "Mother will kill me when she finds me missing or she'll kill herself. And all for nothing because you're too mean to do one nice thing even when I *force* you to do it." The injustice overwhelmed her and her reproach dissolved into a sob. Antonio pulled her into a nearby alley, away from the crowd.

"Come on now," he said, continuing to look at the far distance, as though hoping to be rescued. "I was just fooling around."

"You don't know what it's like," Cecilia wailed. "I'm a prisoner in that house. And the first chance she gets, she really will put me in a convent."

"She's not going to put you in a convent," Antonio soothed. "No convent would have you. You're too awful." He fished a dirty studio rag from his pocket and gave it to her. The turpentine on it stung Cecilia's nose but brought her to her senses. "The fact is she doesn't have the money to put you in a convent. And who would look after Nicolò and Francesco? They'd turn into pick-pockets just like that."

"What about your girlfriend Maria?" Cecilia thought of the servant's attitude the day she had caught them together in the kitchen. Maria lay back over the kitchen table with the same dull, patient expression she used when she waited for water to boil. Obviously, this had happened before.

A look of disgust or shame passed across her brother's face. It made Cecilia think of her youngest brother, Nicolò, who was four. He and Antonio shared the same dark eyes and hair, the same delicate blade of a nose and a certain fastidiousness that was hidden most of the time. Cecilia realised that Antonio, at nineteen, was still a boy. He was just sixteen when their father died. Then, everyone said that becoming the head of the family would force him to grow up. It hadn't. He was the same Antonio Cecilia had known all her life: a joker, a slipper-away, reliably lazy and evasive. But she loved him; she loved him because she couldn't help it.

"Show me something anyway," she said, resigned to disappointment. "Anything at all. Then we're quits. I'll find a way to deal with Mama."

Antonio thought briefly. "There's only one really interesting picture here," he said. "But it makes me want to throw myself in a canal."

"Perfect," she said. "Take me to it."

The painting had a little crowd of six or seven people standing beneath it. It was a long, horizontal canvas in a gilded wooden frame. Its supporting string was hooked onto a stone leaf on the façade of the Scuola and it hung at a slight tilt.

There was no need this time for anyone to explain the subject to Cecilia: she recognised it easily. In the foreground of the painting a bearded man stood on a dark promontory clutching a pair of small stone tablets to his chest. Behind him, a group of frightened people huddled and below him stretched an expanse of dark green sea with a wide road cut straight down the middle. Down this pale sea-road came a golden chariot driven by a man in a plumed headdress and, after him, their spears thick as reeds on the seabed, marched an army of soldiers.

Cecilia responded at once to the neatness of the visual conceit, the straightforward strategy of the painting. From the first glance, she knew exactly what she was looking at: the moment just before Moses wipes out the Egyptian army by drowning them in the Red Sea. More than that, the artist had approached the painting in an interesting way. The scene was set in a moment of quiet, a pause just preceding the cataclysm. On the promontory Moses gripped his tablets and pointed at the sky with his free hand, cueing his righteous God. When the hand came down, the sea walls would snap shut and all the Egyptians would die.

With her eyes darting back and forth between Moses' hand and the walls of water, Cecilia held her breath in sweet anticipation of a disaster. None of the Egyptians — not the king in his chariot, nor his thousands of soldiers, not even the horses — seemed to notice the fatal blue-green walls trembling on either side, yet Cecilia, a helpless onlooker, could hardly look away from them.

From somewhere in her memory, Cecilia found the name of the man her father had thought was the best painter of their age. "Who *did* this? Piazzetta?"

Antonio laughed. "If only. At least Piazzetta is someone. You're never going to believe who's responsible for this..." He waved his hands at the painting as if shooing away a cloud of flies. "... production".

She turned to her brother with a sudden, irresistible surge of hope. "Was it you? Did you paint it?"

Antonio opened his mouth then closed it again. His eyes swept off into the distance and she thought she saw him blush. "Yes," he said evenly. "Yes, I did. Can't you tell?"

"Oh, but it's *good*!" She turned to the canvas, delighted. "The perspective works perfectly, the figures are all the right size. The glazes — when did you learn to do glazes that well?"

"I could always do them," Antonio said. "I just didn't feel like it."

"You didn't feel like it!" she said. "But now you see what a difference it makes when you just try, like Papa always said. Just look at the depth you managed to get out of that swipe of viridian layered over the underpainting. And the deep red of Moses' robe and the angels — the angels are drawn perfectly, with those little dabs of lead white popping out on their wings." Her admiring eyes fell on a notice stuck to the corner of the frame. "And, what's this? Can it be? It's been commended! Oh, Antonio!"

Now she forgave him everything. She threw her arms around him and hugged his bony ribcage. Her mother wouldn't care about her sneaking out once she found out about the commendation. Antonio's success was the best thing that could have happened to them all. It meant the family might just survive.

"But we have to go and tell Mama at once," she cried. "She'll be so happy. I'll go and get her and we can show her and..." With her ear to Antonio's chest, she could feel his ribcage resonating. He was laughing. She pushed him away.

"You should see your little face," he said. "It's precious."

This is the face of a murderous sister, she thought, feeling the anger boil up again in her chest. This is the face of the girl just before she attacks her idiot brother with a brick. "I'm going to murder you, Antonio," she said in a low voice.

But before she could attack him, someone else did it for her. From nowhere, a pair of strong male arms appeared and locked themselves around Antonio's neck. The assailant, dressed in a black tricorn hat and a stiff blue frock coat, mounted on her brother's back and rode him as Antonio staggered from one side to the other, trying to shake him off. Shorter than Antonio, the man's big feet dangled above the flagstones, his heels dug into her brother's calves as Antonio flailed beneath him. Cecilia debated whether to put out a foot and trip Antonio so the other man could kill him quicker. Before she could decide, the struggle ended and the two men stood panting and grinning at one another.

"You see? You see?" The short one pointed a finger at Antonio. "I'm too quick for you, Guardi. I told you I'd get you."

"Tiepolo," Antonio said, rubbing his throat. "I will, one day, when you least expect it, find you and slam those stumpy little fingers of yours in the nearest door."

"And then I will have to paint better than you with my teeth. Ha ha!" Tiepolo turned to Cecilia. He swept off his hat and made a little bow. "Your servant," he said. His manners were very correct.

"Oh, very smooth," said Antonio, rubbing the tendons in his neck. "I see they sent you to dancing school too."

"Your servant." Cecilia raised herself to her full height and studied the young man from beneath half-closed eyelids, bringing him into focus through her lashes. His eyes were very large and dark brown. His nose had been broken and sat at a slight angle to the rest of his face, giving it a cock-eyed dynamism. He didn't look like a street thug, much. He looked familiar.

A memory flashed through her mind: a red wall with a picture scratched on it in chalk, a scurrilous caricature of a potbellied dwarf with a big nose and scars from the pox. The *sbirri* rushing up and grabbing the boy artist, a bandy-legged urchin in ragged clothing, before he could run away.

"I know you." Cecilia was genuinely surprised. "You're the boy they caught drawing pictures on the walls of the Arsenal. They dragged you off. I was there."

Tiepolo's big eyes widened still further. "You've uncovered my dark secret, Signorina. It was me."

"Remind me, were they pictures of some senator or someone like that? I was very young, but I remember they were funny."

"They were pictures of our landlord. Unfortunately he didn't find them so amusing." Tiepolo smiled at her, a lopsided, comical smile that made him look like a little boy. It was also a watchful smile, full of intelligence.

"Oh dear. Did they thrash you? We all thought they must have killed you."

"They did something much worse: they apprenticed me to Lazzarini. Lazzarini was the same painter Antonio had trained with.

"That's strange," she said. "I was around that studio a lot and I don't remember seeing you there."

"That's because Tiepolo is so tiny," Antonio said in a hoarse voice. "He used to fall through the cracks in the floorboards."

She watched Tiepolo put his hat back on. Could this really be the same person she had seen dragged away? The boy she remembered was runty, starved. He wore a cut-down man's shirt and shoes that were held together with string — or possibly made of string alone, wound through filthy toes. The clothes Tiepolo had on today were expensive and so new they looked as if they could have been stolen. His square-toed shoes were good quality and had fine silver buckles. None of this fit with her memories and yet — Cecilia looked more closely and saw with some relief that Tiepolo's shoes were splattered all over with fine drops of paint. His hands, too, were covered with it: paint rimmed his cuticles and filled the fine parenthetic creases of his bony knuckles. The pigments were identical to the ones on the prizewinning painting: burnt umber, green earth, lead white, viridian.

She had a sudden vision of Tiepolo slapping the last strokes on the canvas right there on the campo, then hitching it onto the wall of the Scuola still glistening with wet paint. Yes, she thought to herself, the brave, clever, dragged-away boy would be capable of such a stunt. His talent was flagrantly evident when he was only ten and now he was responsible for those trembling, deadly walls of sea and those merciless, sublime angels. It gave Cecilia a strange feeling to find him again, still living, still painting. She realised he'd always been a sort of hero for her, a blood sacrifice to art.

Tiepolo had dragged his eyes away from her. He was asking Antonio about work.

"If I remember rightly," Tiepolo said in a friendly way, "you were painting sets at the opera. How is that going?"

Antonio shrugged. His long frame seemed to sway in the light breeze. Everything about Antonio looked flimsy next to Tiepolo. Her brother's face was framed against the turbulent colours of Tiepolo's painting, defining his features, making him look paler and less substantial than usual. Poor Antonio, thought Cecilia. "It's all architecture. Not hard if you can draw a straight line."

"So, can you?" Tiepolo grinned at Cecilia to show he was kidding. She wondered if Tiepolo were baiting her brother on purpose, then decided he wasn't. He seemed confident, maybe cocky. Probably it was impossible for him to imagine the life of a painter with less talent than he had. But a look of anger passed across Antonio's features like a cloud. Cecilia wondered what his history was with this Tiepolo. Were they friends? Enemies?

Tiepolo seemed to sense he'd blundered and changed the subject. He reached out with one hand and nudged the frame of his painting until it hung dead level. "I wanted to say that I thought it was harsh of Ricci to throw you out like that. He's getting old. He doesn't have the patience to look into things properly."

"It doesn't matter," Antonio said too quickly. Cecilia noticed his eyes flick in her direction.

Tiepolo, not noticing, sailed on. "I don't know if anyone ever bothered to tell you, but they found the packet of ultramarine in the end. Some fool assistant just put it in the wrong jar. Typical."

"Typical." Antonio clearly wanted to silence him. But he didn't need to worry. Cecilia and her mother had already guessed that he'd lost his place at Sebastiano Ricci's studio some months before. The regular money he brought in simply stopped coming and was replaced by sporadic donations, a few coins dumped from time to time on the kitchen table. No one had dared to ask him why. Her mother had stepped up her campaign of begging letters to their rich uncle in Vienna and Cecilia arranged for a neighbour to buy the next-to-last piece of decent furniture, a carved armoire left over from the old days when they were merely poor, not yet destitute.

This thought made Cecilia feel that she should leave the Campo San Rocco at once and get home as fast as possible. When she was at home in the dirty little house near Santa Maria Formosa, she longed to be away; now that she was away, she panicked to think she wasn't at home. She tugged at Antonio's sleeve, intending to ask him to take her back immediately. But just then there was a stir in the square as the doors of the church opened and the nobility began filing out.

First came a group of men in mauve robes wearing long, curly white wigs. As they descended the church steps and moved beneath the canopy, the luminous, nautical shade turned their robes the colour of bruised plums. Next out of the church doors came a man in a black gown carrying the Doge's gilded stool, then another clutching his embroidered cushion. The Doge, Cornaro, came next, in pursuit of his cushion and stool. He was wearing his white satin cloak and his little golden cap shaped like a badly baked muffin. He was followed by a group of men whose crisp black tunics showed off the gold of their many ornaments — these were members of the confraternity, walking with a bit of swagger at the event they organised and paid for. Drawing up the rear came a covey of old men in red robes and white wigs, the foreign ambassadors.

"They all look so hot," was all Cecilia could think to say. She was close enough to see the sweat beading the men's faces as they drifted out of the church in waves, less a procession than the exodus of a sleepy congregation from church. The robed dignitaries travelled only a few feet under the white canopy before dispersing sideways into the crowd. There was no form to it, no magic at all. Cecilia felt the shadow of disappointment. Perhaps processions were for children and not, now, for her.

"Take me home," she said, turning to Antonio. Evening was coming and she was already thinking of the reception her mother was bound to give her. But as she spoke, Cecilia saw the Doge break away from his retinue. He came hurrying over to where she and Antonio were standing, waving one arm like a man flagging down a gondola.

"There you are! There you are!" Cornaro bellowed. "You're just the man I was hoping to see." For one thrilling second, Cecilia imagined he was coming after Antonio. But it was Tiepolo he sought.

The young painter performed a neat bow as the most important public servant in Venice approached him. He looked unsurprised when the Doge took him by the elbow and began to speak to him confidentially, engulfing the lower part of Tiepolo's body in his wide ceremonial robes.

"Wouldn't you know it?" Antonio muttered near her ear. "There's no stopping some people, even when they are too short."

Cecilia wanted to stay to find out what the Doge had to say to Tiepolo. The chief of the city was standing so close to her that she could distinguish the individual threads of embroidery on his cloak, each silken fibre wrapped in minute spirals of gold wire. He smelled powerfully of frankincense from the church. His jowls, falling from a strong chin, wobbled as he spoke. Cecilia saw Tiepolo look up, his dark eyes searching over the Doge's ermine-draped shoulder until he found her face in the crowd. He raised his hand. *Wait.* She thought she saw him mouth the word.

But Antonio was in no mood to wait. "It's time to go," he said, taking her arm and steering her away.

"Hold on," she said. "I'm not done looking."

"You're not done flirting. Oh, Tiepolo, your painting is so wonderful," he mocked. "Oh, Tiepolo, you're already working for the Doge. You wanted to go. Now we're going." Antonio pulled her along almost violently.

"I was just being polite to your friend. You're hurting me!"

"Tiepolo is a dwarf, a hunchback and a social climber. And too lucky for his own good." There was spite in Antonio's voice.

She glanced back at Tiepolo to see if what her brother said was true and caught a glimpse of the young painter, the lower half of his body engulfed by the Doge's voluminous robes. The torsos of the two men seemed to rise from the same golden mountain. Tiepolo's back, as far as she could tell, was straight.

Antonio released her. "Anyway" he said, "I have to meet someone in San Moisé, near the theatre." They were now standing in an alley that ran alongside the Scuola, leading away from the Campo San Rocco.

Cecilia adjusted her shawl, sealing herself safely in. "But you'll take me back home first." It was a demand rather than a question.

"Afterwards," Antonio said airily, turning and striding away down the narrow street.

"But the sun's going down."

"We have plenty of time. You won't want to miss this."

Cecilia imagined herself heading home alone. Antonio was already halfway down the alley, his narrow, dark head standing proud above the crowd. It struck her that she had spent her whole life running after him. From the moment she was able to toddle, she had chased Antonio's thin back toward trouble. For this, she was always grateful to him. Without a little trouble, life was so very boring.

"Our Lady help us," the landlady said when she opened the door and got a look at Antonio. "Not you again."

"I couldn't stay away, my little Dona Giustiniana," Antonio said pushing in the door and sweeping the small woman up in his arms.

"Put me down at once," the woman said. The expression on her face was still and watchful. She shot a glance at Cecilia who was hesitating on the threshold. "You've taken your time. They've been here since lunchtime. He's been asking for you. And so has she."

"At least someone loves me," Antonio said.

"Don't jump to conclusions," the woman said.

He put Donna Giustiniana down. Her hands flew immediately to smooth the stray stands of her reddish hair. She wore a simple dark dress and skirt with a snow-white length of linen tucked into her neckline. Her person was consistent with the entry hall they stood in, plain but scrubbed and well tended. Cecilia had the idea the building belonged to her.

"Who's this then?" she asked, staring at Cecilia.

"I'm his sister," Cecilia said.

"Of course you are," she said. "Who is this, Antonio?" He was already loping up the stairs, taking them two at a time. Cecilia prepared to follow him but the woman laid a hand on her arm.

"You're his sister." It was more a statement than a question. Dona Giustiniana's eyes searched Cecilia's face. "Yes, I suppose it's possible. Even Guardi could have a sister like you. Have you been here before, darling?"

Cecilia shook her head.

"You live with your mother and father, do you, darling? And that no-account brother of yours?"

Cecilia nodded. She didn't like the way the woman was looking at her. Her endearments were mechanical and without warmth.

They were calculated to sound kind, but somehow they had the opposite effect. Yet as she looked at Cecilia, suddenly the woman's expression changed and softened.

"Don't go up there," she said in a husky whisper. "Your brother's friends are foreigners, strange people, and they're all very drunk right now. It's no place for a girl like you."

Cecilia pulled away. "I have to stay with my brother," she said. She heard a door open above; the sound of music spilled out into the stairwell.

The woman stepped back and released her. "Do you really think he'll be going home tonight?" she said in a voice that insinuated that Cecilia knew nothing about Antonio.

Cecilia was annoyed. Who was this woman to size her up and try to tell her what to do? "Are you saying I can't go up there?"

"I'm saying no such thing," Dona Giustiniana said, her dark eyes now very cold. She let go of Cecilia's arm. She had given her one chance. "Let me know how you like it."

Nobody responded when Cecilia knocked at the double doors. Putting her ear to the crack, she could hear a shouted conversation, the clink of cutlery, the stomp of heels on floorboards and, just audible, the sound of a flute and a viol, straining to be heard above the din. Something smashed on the floor. A woman's voice brayed with laughter and there was the sound of a scuffle, as though someone inside were wrestling. Gathering her courage, Cecilia pushed open the door and went in.

She found herself in a long room with high ceilings and a run of tall windows along one side, open to the hot evening air and the sounds of boat traffic on the canal below. The little salon had grey-blue paper on the walls and rose-coloured hangings around the windows. It would have been attractive if it hadn't been in a state of utter chaos. The furniture was shoved back to the periphery and the carpet was bundled into a pile in one corner. A trio of musicians, pinned into a tiny alcove, did their best to play their instruments while a man and two women lurched drunkenly around the empty space in the middle of the floor, laughing and pawing at one another. At the other end of the room, a large table stood covered with the remains of what looked to Cecilia like several meals: dirty plates, half-eaten platters of food, half-drunk glasses of wine. There was broken crockery on the floor and a slick patch on the floorboards where something like gravy had splattered.

There must have been ten or twelve people at the party. Besides the three dancers, several men and women lounged on the sofas or lay splayed across the chairs. All of them were well dressed, the men in wigs, the ladies in bright gowns, red and orange and blue. In them or half out of them. All of the guests were drunk to various degrees. It was the sort of tired, settled drunkenness that had exhausted its first euphoria and was waiting for a second wind. One couple, dressed like twins in matching yellow brocade, sat on the dirty floor in a corner, rolling dice with a cup.

No one had noticed Cecilia come in. She stood with her back to the door, wondering if she should turn and run. She knew immediately the sort of party she'd walked into and she felt a wave of alarm and excitement; it was not the sort of gathering a good girl went to. And yet she felt curious, as though if she stayed she'd finally understand many things about the world that had been hidden from her until now. She might even find Bettina.

She scanned the room looking for her friend's fair hair and somewhat dumpy figure. This was the sort of room she had always pictured Bettina in, when she tried to imagine the life she had chosen — or rather, the life she'd been compelled to choose.

But even as Cecilia looked for Bettina, she knew she could not be there. The room was too fine, the company was too select, and the other courtesans were all too beautiful. Bettina's clients were not nobles, as these men appeared to be. They were labourers and seamen and boys from the seminary. Bettina did not have silk dresses to wear; her life was nothing like this.

Cecilia spotted Antonio's thin legs protruding from under the table. A lady in a sea green dress sat with one foot resting on his skinny buttocks.

"I say Guardi is my hero," the woman said in the lilting voice of a drunken baby. Her dark hair framed a round, doll-like face with rosy painted cheeks. The bodice of her green silk gown was unfastened, revealing an expanse of white bosom and the brown coin of one nipple. "He's the only one of you who will be able to find my thingy. His eyes are so keen. Aren't they, Guardi?" She prodded his buttocks with her foot. Her tiny slipper was made of golden satin, decorated with silver beads. "He's an artist."

"We all know what kind of an artist Guardi is!" shouted a red-headed young man stretched out on a sofa. He had removed his coat and wore only his breeches and an embroidered waistcoat over a crumpled linen shirt.

"That's true," said the woman in green, pouting her red lips. "Still."

Antonio scrambled out from under the table holding something in his fingers.

"My lady, your ornament." He presented it with a flourish, bowing from the waist.

"What did I tell you?" The woman held the trinket close to an unfocussing eye. Cecilia was close enough to see that it was an earring made of fine golden wire worked into a pattern of filigree vines and studded with tiny pearls. "Oh. It's all flattened. One of you stepped on it."

"Never mind," said the redheaded man. "Your ambassador can

always get you another one."

"I loved these earrings." The lady sounded like she had lost her dearest friend. "They came in the most beautiful box."

"Damn your box," someone said. "What's this bundle?"

Cecilia saw the man rise from the sofa and start toward her, still clutching a glass of wine. The wine sloshed onto the floorboards as he approached, his head tilted to one side and his eyes screwed up in an effort to bring her into focus. The first thing that struck Cecilia about him was his suit, which she saw was brand new and made of silk the colour of a ripe apricot. Only foreigners could afford such suits and only foreigners would wear them.

When Cecilia saw the man coming toward her, she knew she should run for it. She had her hand on the door handle, she was ready to fly, but she froze, partly from fear and partly from pride. She watched him as he stepped heavily around the dice players and came close to examine her.

"No matter how much time I spend in this city," he said in an unfamiliar accent. "I will never understand why Venetian girls go around in the middle of summer all wrapped up like a — like a package." He wore no wig and his wavy blond hair receded slightly from a sloping, sunburned forehead. Brown freckles were spattered across his high-bridged nose like the marks on a quail's egg. His pale blue eyes, deeply bloodshot, were set off and made bluer by the orange reflection from his suit. Doubtless that was how the tailor convinced him to pay for it, Cecilia thought.

"Like packages," corrected the red-haired man. His small, clear blue eyes came to rest on Cecilia and he narrowed them. It reminded her of the way a cat looks at a rat just before he kills it. He went on looking at Cecilia with a grimace on his face that wasn't a smile.

"Quiet, Tron. I've had enough of your grammar." The man in apricot silk spoke with a strong foreign accent. "Package, packages. The point is they shouldn't be so wrapped up. In England the girls are not packages at all. They take everything off as soon as the rain stops."

"That would be never," said the man in yellow, looking up from his dice game. He had a different foreign accent, possibly French. Cecilia saw that he was handsome, with long eyelashes and dark hair tied back with a silk ribbon.

"Exactly." The tall man snorted. He smiled at Cecilia showing a set of very long white teeth hedged with plump pink gums. Speaking loudly and slowly as though she were the foreigner, not himself, he said, "What is your name, pretty package? At least I think she's pretty," he said with a glance over his shoulder at Tron. "She's damned tall."

Cecilia looked toward her brother in desperation. Antonio had taken a chair at the table next to the woman in green and was drinking from one of the half-empty wine glasses. He avoided her eyes. He was trying not to look at her because if he did he'd have to take some kind of action. It wasn't right for this foreigner to approach her this way, to pant into her face with breath like a fumigant and ask her personal questions. It wasn't right that he'd brought her to a place like this at all. But had he brought her or had she brought herself?

Across from Antonio, the woman was still studying her crushed earring. Laboriously, she removed its mate from the other ear then dropped it on the carpet and stamped on it.

"There," she said, holding up the flattened product. "Now they're a pair again." She threw both earrings on the table and pushed them toward Antonio. Cecilia saw Antonio slide the crushed earrings off the table with the side of his hand. They landed in his lap and he gathered them up and put them in his pocket. He looked at Cecilia and shrugged.

"The package isn't answering me," the English man said.

"Maybe they cut out her tongue in the seraglio. Let me see your tongue, darling, that's a girl. Tongues are very important."

"Oh, leave her be, Cranleigh," said the dice-rolling gentleman from his place on the floor. "Anyone can see the poor girl's just come for the plates."

"Oh ho!" Cranleigh suddenly exclaimed. "Now I've got it. I know what this is." Wine sloshed from his glass as he gestured at the redhead. "Tron, Tron, you're behind this. You pulled this one on me once before and you laughed about it for a week. The old switcheroo, hey? The boy in a girl's dress? Damn you, Tron, you don't really expect me to fall for that again, do you? I shall defeat you. All shall come to light."

Before Cecilia knew what was happening, the Englishman had grabbed a fold of her shawl and with one violent tug ripped the covering from her head and shoulders. With this, all her shelter was gone. She might as well have been stripped naked. She gave a little scream and wrapped her arms around her chest.

"Ha! You are clever, Tron!" the Englishman shouted. "The top half is convincing. But you can't fool me twice. The proof is in the fundament!" To Cecilia's horror, he made a grab at her skirt, trying to lift it up. She screamed again and sprinted away toward the only protection she had, toward Antonio. The room exploded into laughter.

"Do something!" Cecilia cried to her brother. With great reluctance, Antonio stood up and Cecilia took refuge behind him. Thin and irresolute, he made a poor shelter for her virtue, little better than a dead tree. The whole pretense was ridiculous. He was far too slight to stop the massive foreigner, but even Antonio knew he'd lose what scraps of his honour he had left if he didn't at least appear to try. Fortunately the Englishman wasn't serious about removing Cecilia's skirt. He came to a halt a few feet away and stood blinking at the two of them in confusion.

"Well, that's a cheat," he said. "If she's a boy I'm a rhinoceros."

The laughter surged again. Tron rolled off his sofa and lay kicking his feet on the floor as though he were having a tantrum. The dancers were doubled over and even the musicians were smirking in their cramped alcove. *So this is what it's like to be an actress,* Cecilia thought as her panic turned to rage. *You suffer and the audience feels delight.*

The gentleman in yellow brocade was the first to stop laughing long enough to speak. "Cranleigh, you are such a perfect knight!" he cried. "In you, the great chivalric tradition lives on."

Cecilia was furious now. She snatched a cup from the table and would have thrown it at Cranleigh, but Antonio grabbed her wrist. "Do you want to end up in prison?" he said through his teeth. He was grinning to the room.

The Englishman turned away suddenly and sloped back to the sofa. "I do *feel* a bit like a rhinoceros in this bloody city of yours," he muttered sadly, big shoulders drooping under the rich, sunset-coloured silk. "Always paying for breakages."

"Give me back my shawl," Cecilia said. Her voice was very small in the noisy room. Nobody paid any attention to her. She imagined the cold-eyed landlady listening through the floorboards, patting her hair and smiling to herself.

Cranleigh ignored her too. He slung her shawl over his head and simpered. "How do I look as a lovely Venetian bundle?"

"In that rag you are *bellissima*," said Tron, kissing his fingertips. "Like a fishwife, a true daughter of the city. You smell like one too." He raised his glass first to Cecilia, then, one by one, to each of the other women in the room.

The woman in the green dress had been sitting staring at the table throughout the ruckus as though too sodden to react. Now she seemed to come to life. She lifted her head slowly and turned to look at Tron. "So you're insulting us," she said very clearly with no trace of the babyish lilt. "That must be because you're the only one here who can't afford us, at least not without some help from your friends."

Everyone in the room, including Tron, burst out laughing again except Cecilia and the musicians, who took that moment to launch into a lively number, perhaps because they sensed the party's atmosphere was turning sour. As soon as the music started, Cranleigh began to dance around the room wearing Cecilia's shawl on his head.

"What an animal," the woman in green said with a bitter laugh. Then she turned her lovely painted face toward Cecilia and fixed her with a glazed stare. "He knows nothing about us, does he, darling? Nothing about this city. Look at this girl," she said raising her voice suddenly to address the room. "Look at her. Even in a dirty housedress with all the seams let out, she looks like she stepped out of a painting by Veronese. He should throw himself at her feet. But what does he do? He paws at her like a brute."

Her words made Cecilia blush crimson, not because she had compared her to the blond beauties painted two hundred years before by Venice's most beloved artist, but because they called attention to the poverty of her clothes: her faded blue skirt was spotted with kitchen grease, her linen blouse was grey with use and her faded brown bodice was crisscrossed by darker bands where, as the woman had observed, every seam had been eased to the limit.

"Don't say things like that to her." Antonio's chuckle was unconvincing. He was still standing in front of Cecilia, the flimsiest shelter for her safety. "She's vain enough already. Veronese! There'll be no living with her now."

"You live with her?" said Tron, looking up alertly from his place the floor. His eyes studied her coldly, the rictus of a smile that was no smile. "Did you hear that, Cranleigh?"

Cranleigh wasn't paying attention. He was waltzing clumsi-ly around the room, wrapped in Cecilia's shabby shawl. "I was a poor but honest maid," he sang in falsetto. "Until I met the wicked Tron."

"Lucia is right," said the gentleman in yellow brocade. He had stopped throwing dice and sat looking at Cecilia, his expression mild and full of admiration. "She does look exactly like a Veronese," he said in an excited voice. "And I can say that with some authority since my uncle owns two paintings by him. It's her colouring: the gold sheen of her hair with the pink of her skin. And the way her head sits on the neck like the carved capital of a column." His hand drifted up to his own neck. "That's why Venice keeps me captive. You find everything you're looking for in this city, and you find it in the flesh."

Lucia held out her hands to Cecilia. "Come here to me."

Cecilia stepped over to where she sat and let Lucia take her hands. The other woman's were thin and smooth and cold, as though they were carved of fine stone. Her voice was soothing. "You're trembling, you poor thing. Tell me your name." She rubbed Cecilia's hot, rough hands with her cold ones.

Outside, bells all over the city began to ring: it was sundown. After dark the squares and coffee shops were full of drunken for-eigners in new suits, while the alleys and the wine shops were crawling with sailors on the prowl.

"I have to get home," Cecilia said. She and the woman in green both looked at Antonio, but he had closed his eyes, blinding him-self to responsibility. He lifted someone else's glass to his lips and drank.

Lucia dropped her hands suddenly and said, "Get out of here before they think of you again". That was Celia's cue to run.

Venice, 1718

Cecilia's return home that night was worse than she feared. She was prepared for angry scenes, but the tragic sight of her mother sitting alone in the darkened kitchen, weeping over an empty place setting — hers — almost undid Cecilia. Claudia Guardi threw her hands up to heaven when she saw her daughter come though the door alive. She fell to her knees and thanked God; she made Cecilia get down on her knees and thank God, too. While the two of them knelt on the kitchen floor, she clung to her daughter, leaning her whole weight against the girl, her body heaving with sobs.

"You're all I have!" she wailed. It was true. Even Claudia had realised by now that they couldn't rely on Antonio.

Eventually, Cecilia was able to coax Claudia upstairs and put her to bed in the room they shared. She lay down next to her mother and stroked her back until her breathing became heavy and at last she began to snore her characteristic little snore. Only then did Cecilia shed a tear of regret: she was sincerely sorry to cause her mother such distress. Claudia's imagination was too vivid, that was her problem: in the few hours Cecilia had been gone, Claudia had lived through her daughter's abduction, her rape, the discovery of her battered, bloody corpse floating in a canal. By the time Cecilia arrived home, these horrors were imprinted on her soft brain as concrete facts. There would be a price to pay for all this pain, Cecilia knew. Her mother wasn't as helpless as she pretended to be.

Antonio stayed away that night. When he finally turned up the following day, he was radically crumpled as though his whole body had been compressed by a giant fist and tossed in the gutter. Cecilia smelled him before she saw him. He reeked of alcohol and the fumes of tobacco, a New World vice he'd picked up from sailors. She didn't say a word or even glance at him as he stumbled past the kitchen table where she was serving breakfast to her little brothers.

"Is Antonio sick?" asked Francesco, looking up from his plate. He was six. His dark eyes followed the hunched figure of his older brother up the stairs.

"No, he's just very, very tired," Cecilia said through clenched teeth. "Finish your bread."

"Mama is sick," said Nicolò, four. "Everyone is sick but Cici, Maria, Francesco and me." He sang out this list with pleasure, glad to have an opinion.

"We might get sick," Francesco said. He looked anxiously at Cecilia. He was too young to remember their father's death, but he'd heard the stories. Cecilia couldn't prevent her mother from telling them in front of the little boys.

"No one is getting sick." She tried to reassure him. "Mama isn't sick, either. She just has a little headache."

"She always has a headache," Francesco observed.

"So everything is fine, isn't it? Now it's time to go outside." She got the boys dressed and turned them out into the courtyard to play around the communal wellhead.

Despite the threat hanging over her, Cecilia felt buoyant as she went about her daily work. Her limbs felt loose and her step was quick as her body remembered how good it felt to rush through the streets at a run. Confined to her usual daily circuit of tenement, courtyard and church, Cecilia sometimes forgot she lived in the middle of a vibrant city. She'd been strongly aware of it as a little girl when she was free to roam around the streets with a gang of neighbourhood children, led by Antonio. Back then, she owned the city; its streets and squares were her playground, her school, and her true home.

And then, yesterday, she'd tasted it again, racing after Antonio, mixing with the crowd in the Campo San Rocco, seeing the paintings in the exhibition, meeting Tiepolo again... Tiepolo. The dragged-away boy. She pictured him strangling Antonio and laughed to herself. In fact, apart from that disgusting bordello and the ox of a foreigner stealing her shawl, the whole outing had been a success. The walk home hadn't been a problem. She had even let herself pause at the top of the Rialto Bridge and enjoy the view for a minute, watching the lights coming on down the length of the Grand Canal: little cooking fires glowing beneath the makeshift awnings of the market boats, torches shining in the arcaded balconies of the palazzos, the lamps of gondolas cruising just above the dark surface of the water like fireflies. Cecilia let herself stand and savour the way these lights defined the channel, dancing on its gently moving surface and turning it into a train of black silk shimmering all over with drops of gold.

The thought of gold brought Cecilia back to the present. Going up to the boys' tiny room, she moved aside one of the beds and dug out the family money purse from its hiding place under a broken floorboard. The soft leather bag was light, too light for security. Without counting its contents, she had a precise sense of how much it contained, how long this money would last them, and it was not long.

She counted out a few coppers from the meagre hoard, think-ing of the crushed golden earrings Antonio had swept into his pocket. By her calculation — and she was very good with numbers — the value of the gold in them, if it was pure gold, could feed them all for a year. What had Antonio done with them? Common sense told her that Lucia had not given them to him as a gift but to sell or pawn. One thing was certain: the money was unlikely to find its way into Cecilia's little leather bag.

The memory of Lucia and the other courtesans made Cecilia think again of her friend Bettina. Where was she now?

Bettina had lived with her family on the other side of the court-yard. She was a few years older than Cecilia and her father was a painter like Cecilia's father was, though he was a quaddraturist, a specialist in painted architecture. Cecilia's father and Bettina's father occasionally worked together and the two families were on friendly terms, living parallel lives on either side of the stone well-head. The two girls had been close, popping in and out of one another's houses all day long, and Bettina was sweet on Antonio. She was a gentle girl, with soft brown hair and a tender temperament — she was incapable, even, of strangling a chicken for her dinner. If the world had been a little kinder, she would have made Antonio a loving wife, and, even better, an affectionate, helpful sister-in-law for Cecilia. But one day Bettina's father suffered a fall from the scaffolding and such dreams had to be put aside.

Cecilia remembered it all vividly. She had been present when her father told her mother that the quaddraturist had survived the fall and she was shocked when her mother burst into tears. She sat sobbing, rubbing a hand over her big pregnant belly — she was carrying Nicolò — while Cecilia's father looked on with a grim expression. Cecilia couldn't understand why her parents weren't happier about this news. Bettina's father wasn't dead; surely this was good?

She was too young at the time to see the consequences that must have seemed inevitable to her parents. Cecilia's father and the other painters took up a collection to tide Bettina's family over, knowing it could never be enough. When the quaddraturist finally died eighteen months later, it was Bettina who had to pay for his funeral.

She became a whore not long after the accident. Nobody was shocked. Everybody understood that it was necessary: Bettina was the oldest of five siblings. What else could she do? Among the neighbours there was an innate sympathy — this was a tragedy that could befall any of them. And yet, soon after the funeral, the family moved away and no one spoke of them again, no one seemed to know where they had gone. It was as if they had all died in the fall from the scaffolding. Only they hadn't. They lived on, surviving because of Bettina.

Cecilia didn't see Bettina again for a long time, but she fell into the habit of looking for her wherever she went. Was that Bettina in the veil at the back of the church? Was it her hurrying across the little footbridge with the basket over her arm? No and no. Cecilia wasn't sure what she would say to her friend if she met her again, but she felt certain that they would meet and that, when they did, she'd find some way to show Bettina that she hadn't forgotten about her.

When that day finally came, however, it was clear that Bettina had always counted on Cecilia.

Cecilia sighed and shook a few zecchini from the leather purse, enough to buy food for dinner. Then she closed the bag and hid it again beneath the floorboard.

Antonio clumped down from his room in the attic around dinnertime, looking and smelling a little fresher. He sat himself down in the kitchen where Cecilia and Maria were serving a meagre supper to the boys.

"What's to eat?" Antonio said with forced heartiness, taking pains not to look at either of the women, both of whom had reason to blame him. He slapped his hands down flat on the damp, pulpy wood of the tabletop. Nicolò and Francesco jumped in their seats, then beamed and giggled at him.

"Baby fish," said Francesco. "Tiny baby fish." He picked up a hard curl of batter-fried flesh and showed it to Antonio. Nicolò did the same.

"Mine has an eye," Nicolò confirmed, showing him the black bead in the cooked head.

"I wouldn't look at them too closely if I were you." Cecilia dumped a serving of the contorted sea creatures on Antonio's plate. "They're scrapings from the bilge of the boat."

Antonio began shoveling food into his mouth like a starving man. Cecilia sat down opposite and glared at him, hoping her evil eye might make him choke. She noticed he'd tied his hair back with one of her own hair ribbons.

"What's the matter?" she said finally. "Your friends didn't feed you? Or maybe they only give you the dregs of their wine?"

Antonio took a drink from his clay cup and made a face. "A rich man's dregs beats a poor man's water any day. This tastes like the soles of dirty feet."

"You should know." Cecilia rose and began to clear away the few dishes. She let the boys get up from the table and sent them to play in the light summer darkness of the courtyard. The church bells all over the city began the extended process of striking the hour, starting with Santa Maria Formosa just behind them and reverberating across the city until the sound became a distant clamour.

"Is there any wine?" Antonio yawned.

"Wine? Where would we get wine? From the wine angels that come down bringing heavenly wine from Our Lord?" Cecilia crossed herself, conscious that this was probably some kind of blasphemy. "Of course there isn't any wine. There isn't any money to buy wine."

"How about some olives?" Antonio said. Cecilia threw a wooden spoon at him.

The spoon struck the kitchen wall and clattered to the floor. Antonio ducked like a man who had lots of ducking practice. Maria, who knew what was good for her, left the room in a hurry.

"You had fun, admit it," Antonio said.

"I did not have fun. I was insulted and I ran home in the dark all alone." She lowered her voice. "Some men followed me." She had made this last part up, but it was possible she could have been followed — and worse. "Mama was in tears when I got back. I thought she was going to have a fit. She thinks I'm running wild and you know what that means. You know exactly what she could do to me." Antonio just sat there smirking. "Don't you care how much trouble you've landed me in?"

"It wasn't me who landed you in trouble. I seem to remember it was you who demanded that I take you to San Rocco. Anyway, calm down. I had a word with Mother before I came down."

Cecilia was wary. "You told her what happened?"

Antonio laughed. "Oh, she didn't ask what happened. She asked what I thought we should do with you."

Cecilia threw another spoon at him. "Pig!" Only a lack of vocabulary prevented her from calling him something much worse. She didn't know the right word for what Antonio had become, but if she had known it, she would have used it in multiples.

Antonio was still laughing. "I could still get her to change her mind and then…" He pressed his hands together in prayer and rolled his eyes to heaven. "You know."

Cecilia felt a renewed rush of outrage. "You're the one who should be locked up. Do you think I don't know what kind of people those were last night? And where's my shawl? The least you could do was get it back from that horrible fat foreigner."

"Keep your voice down. Mother doesn't know the details. She could still change her mind."

Cecilia dropped her voice to a whisper. "I don't care."

"You'll care later, in the convent. Now go over there and bring me my coat."

"Get your own filthy coat," she said.

He waited for a moment and when he saw she meant it, he got up and retrieved his coat from the peg. He sat down again and began fishing in the pockets. Finally he brought out a folded piece of cloth and tossed it down on the table in front of Cecilia. At first she thought it was her old shawl. Then she caught a whiff of ambergris.

"That's not mine," she said, her heart beating quickly.

"Lucia sent it for you. I tried to convince her that you wouldn't want it, but she insisted."

Cecilia reached out and unfolded the shawl with one hand. It was woven of creamy soft cashmere, with a garden of flowers worked into the weft using threads of blue and pink and gold. She recognised the rich smell coming from it as the smell of Lucia.

"I can't keep it," she said in a dazed voice. "We'll have to sell it."

"Try it on at least." Antonio said.

"No." She didn't dare. Carefully, she folded the shawl up and laid it over the back of one of the chairs to keep it out of the grease on the table.

Antonio looked disappointed. "Maybe you'll like these better," he said, extending his hand in a fist. When he opened it, two large silver coins dropped onto the table.

It had been a long time since Cecilia had seen a whole ducat, let alone two. With quick hands, she caught the coins before they rolled off the edge of the table and held them in the palm of her hand, turning them so that she could see both faces, one of each. She stared at the coins — one side showed an image of Jesus nestling in an oval, surrounded by nine stars, the other depicted a little scene in which St. Mark handed the Doge a tasselled staff — and then at Antonio. He nodded and she closed her fingers around the coins. They were hard and hot in her palm.

"You see," he said. "You need to have more faith in me. I'm taking care of us."

Venice, 1718

Cecilia pulled the sackcloth shift reluctantly over her head. The rough material rasped her bare skin. It stank of mildew and old sweat.

"Who wore this nasty thing last?" she called out in disgust. The garment was no more than a length of cloth folded in two and whipstitched up the sides. "A real hermit?"

"I suppose you'd prefer a nice clean nun's habit?" Antonio said from the other side of the changing screen. She could hear him dragging something across the studio floor.

She stepped out to show him. "You know, there are better costumes in the box," she said. "There's one here trimmed with fur."

"When I want the Queen of Sheba," Antonio said, eyeing her critically, "I'll ask for the blooming Queen of Sheba. I told you. I need a miserable martyr. That's you." He flicked his finger in her direction. "Shoes."

Cecilia kicked off her old slippers and set them behind the changing screen next to her folded clothes. "I would have done this for you anyway," she said. "You don't have to threaten me to get me to model for you."

"Belt," Antonio said, when she stepped out again.

"What belt?"

He flung a piece of rope at her. She tied it on and he looked her up and down. "It'll have to do. Come here. Over here." He gestured for her to approach a wooden platform he had set up in the middle of the floor. "Hurry up."

She walked sullenly over the floorboards, trying to avoid getting splinters in her bare feet. It was a Sunday afternoon and they were alone in the dirty studio Antonio had borrowed from a pair of art copyists he knew. The room was large, with decent light, but Cecilia saw immediately that this studio was a fly-by-night operation. The whole place had an air of neglect, with dismantled easels stacked in the corners and stepladders strewn haphazardly around the floor. Paint-rimed clay pots and buckets of ferment-ing liquid cluttered the tables, the floor, the sills of the tall win-dows, some with brushes still standing in them. Half-finished can-vases with crude copies of Tintorettos and Palma Vecchios leaned against the walls. The whole place was infused with the stench of rotting animal skin glue, the sour reek of unsized canvas and the stink of rancid cooking oil wafting up from the café downstairs.

Cecilia stepped up onto the dais and entered a shaft of light. Dust motes floated in its brightness, giving the light a body of its own. "Are you going to tell me who I'm supposed to be?"

"No," Antonio said. He went to his seat by the window and took up his drawing board. With the glare behind him all Cecilia could see was his angular silhouette, a bent knee, an elbow, the clear-cut rectangle of the drawing board. "Just stand with your arm out," he said.

"Like this?"

"No, not like that. Pointing, gesturing. Like that."

"Oh, you mean like a signpost," she said mockingly, pointing one hand in the direction of the door. "Your instructions aren't very helpful, you know. Papa always used to give me an idea of who I was. He'd say, you're a servant girl in the house of the king, or, you're a little shepherdess standing on a hill looking down on your flock. Didn't he do that with you? Didn't he say, you're a pageboy in the court of Alexander the Great, or something like that? I remember that time he dressed you up in a towel and had you hold that huge shield. But that was after you'd started your growth spurt so you were just too skinny and looked like a skeleton. He had to get a fatter boy." She giggled and heard what she thought sounded like a snicker from the quarter of the room where Antonio was.

"Is there someone else here?" she asked.

"Of course not," Antonio said. "Shut up and change pose."

"Already? You can't be finished with your drawing yet. You were never that fast."

"Don't argue with me. Fall to your knees, like you're in despair."

She did as he asked with deep sigh of ennui and a show of reluctance. "I am in despair."

"What's that supposed to be?" Antonio shouted. "You look like you're about to scrub the floor."

"Someone *should* scrub this floor. It's a disgrace."

"You can do that afterwards," Antonio growled. "Now, supplicate!"

She clasped her hands in prayer and raised her eyes toward heaven, trying to look like a saint in extremis. As she settled into the pose, she began to remember some of the modelling techniques she had learned as a child. It was always useful to run up and down the street for a few minutes before you started, so your legs were less twitchy. It wasn't a good idea to drink too much water beforehand, because then you had to stop to pee and artists didn't like it. And it was essential to clear the room of flies: flies loved a model more than they did a donkey.

Antonio hadn't bothered to do this and there were a number of fat bluebottles buzzing drunkenly around the room. One came and landed on her shoulder. Cecilia closed her eyes.

The best way to hold a pose, she'd learned, was to empty your mind, to think about nothing. But it was very hard to think about nothing, so she came up with the idea of picturing a very small, very familiar object, like a button, and imagined it getting smaller and smaller. When it disappeared, she was thinking of nothing. She could hold a pose, then, for as long as she wanted.

Cecilia formed the image of a button in her mind. It was very pretty, made of mother-of-pearl. She added a red rosebud painted on the centre for interest and immediately began to wonder where a person could buy such buttons. Before she knew it, she found herself planning to put aside money, buy six of the pretty buttons and sew them all down the front of her best bodice. Now she was thinking of a row of buttons, curse it! Things were moving in the wrong direction. Suddenly, she heard a loud yawn.

"Are you bored, Antonio?" she taunted. "I know I am. Or maybe you're just hungover. Again." The acoustics were odd in the studio, she thought. The yawn had seemed to come from the shadows behind her brother where a series of large canvases on wooden stretchers stood slanted against the wall.

"All done!" Antonio said with a flourish. "Time to change again."

"What? That was fast." Cecilia shook out her arms. "You're not done already?"

"Close your mouth. Now stand up and balance on one leg," he said.

Cecilia rose and faced him with her hands on her hips. "What are you doing, Antonio? You can't change the pose every two minutes."

"I can if I want to." Antonio's voice sounded nervous. "I'm the master here. I'm in charge."

She fought the impulse to answer back. There were so many mean, true things she could say to her brother. Instead of saying any of these things, Cecilia said, "I want to see."

Before Antonio could stop her she had jumped down from the dais and padded over to stand behind him. Peeking over his shoulder at the tattered sheet of grey-blue paper pinned to his drawing board, she burst out laughing.

"Oh Antonio! Those are *terrible*."

"What do you mean by terrible?" He sounded strangely pleased to hear this.

"They're a mess!"

He frowned down at the tangle of red chalk lines. "They're

sketches. Sketches are meant to be loose."

"Even so, what would Papa say if he saw these?" She pointed at his scrawls. "Look at my head, it's in entirely the wrong place. And my hand; it's more like a flipper. For heaven's sake, little Francesco could do better than that. You're just not trying at all. Here." She wrested the chalk from his fingers and added a few strokes, sketching a tapered hand just the way their father had taught them. "You see? You know how to do that as well as I do, so why don't you do it?" She thought she heard a muffled snort from the shadows. "What was that sound?"

"It's just the rats," Antonio said. "They caught wind of you and came running from the port." He snatched the chalk from her hand. "Now get back to where you belong, and stop telling me what to do."

"I was only trying to help." She said this with sass, looking over her shoulder as she returned to her spot. It pleased her to nettle Antonio. Or was he nettled? Actually, he seemed delighted by her criticisms. She thought she heard a stifled snigger as she walked away. She whirled around.

"Are you laughing, Antonio?"

"Of course I'm laughing," he said seriously. "Or maybe it's the rats."

"If I was producing scribbles like those, I wouldn't be laughing, I'd be crying." She reached the dais and sat down on it, confident, comfortable. "Ah. That's more like it."

"Oh no," Antonio said in commanding voice. "None of that. No slouching around for you, penitent. On your feet."

He got up and fetched a stepladder. *Now I'm in for it,* she thought. Antonio set the ladder up in the patch of light. He grinned at her. "Well, what are you waiting for? Up you go. No, wait." He sped off again into the shadows of the studio and returned with a large brass tray.

"Oh no," she groaned. She knew what was coming. "Not a tray."

"Oh yes, a tray." He put it in her hands and she found it weighed as much as a small child. She narrowed her eyes at Antonio, who capered back to his stool and took up his drawing board, humming as he did so. Grimly, Cecilia started to climb the ladder with the unwieldy tray banging against her leg. She should have known Antonio would make her do ladder work. Paid models charged extra for elevated poses because they were so strenuous and uncomfortable. Even dancers, who had an easy time holding most attitudes, hated them. So did Cecilia. Whenever she saw a ceiling decorated with joyful nymphs or angels sporting in the air, all she could think about was vertigo, numb limbs and muscle cramps. When she reached the penultimate step of the ladder, she looked down at Antonio and weighed the pros and cons of spitting on him.

"Don't just stand there," he said, beaming up at her. "Offer it nicely now."

With one foot on the step and one on the top of the stepladder, she balanced the tray on both hands and held it up above her head and to one side, as though presenting it to someone on a higher plane than herself. A god, presumably, or God.

"Lift it higher," Antonio commanded her. "Higher, on the tippy-tips of your fingers. Now look down at me."

"I'm looking at you all right," Cecilia said. "I'm mesmerised by the bald patch on the top of your head." In fact, she couldn't see a thing. The afternoon sun was sliding down a slot between two buildings and shining straight into her eyes.

"At least tell me what's on my tray." It was difficult to speak with her torso twisted, her lungs squeezed by her ribcage. But she wasn't about to oblige Antonio by keeping silent. There was nothing he'd like better than that.

"Your own breasts, of course," Antonio answered gaily. "I've decided you're Saint Agatha now." He was referring to the innocent girl saint who was roasted over coals and had her breasts cut off by an emperor. "It's a good thing you're so naturally flat-chested," he said.

"You make me sick," Cecilia said with hauteur, offering the tray up fiercely. "You can't draw and you're foul minded. What would Mama say if she heard you talking in that disgusting way? I know what she'd say. She'd say you were learning such filth from the bad company you're keeping." She heard a snort of stifled laughter. "You won't be laughing when you end up in hell," she added primly.

"Do you really and truly think I'll go to hell?" Antonio asked. His tone was curious, sincere.

"You know you will if you keep living like you are. Do you think I don't know what sort of ladies those were the other night?" she countered.

"No, what sort of ladies were they?" he asked in an innocent voice.

"Bad ones. Obviously." Cecilia found she had to keep her words to a minimum. The awkward pose was really beginning to bite now. Both her shoulders ached, each in a different way. The tightness in the tendons of her neck was rapidly turning into a fiery pain. The small of her back clenched with the effort of holding her arms above her head.

Antonio seemed determined to keep her talking. "You thought they were bad, you say?" He sounded incredulous. "Whatever made you think that about them?"

"*Please.* It was obvious from the way they dressed. Your best friend Lucia had her whatsits practically dangling in the soup."

"Her whatsits?" Antonio echoed.

"Her you-know. What they cut off Saint Agatha."

"Oh, you mean her *breasts.*" Antonio persisted. "In the *soup* you say? Is that what makes a woman bad? Would it have been better if they had been dangling in the fish course? How about the ices?"

"Stop making fun of me," Cecilia said.

"I couldn't possibly do that now," Antonio said in a serious voice.

"Then I'm not going to talk to you anymore," she groaned. The pain was excruciating now, but she was determined not to show it. Struggling to suppress a whimper, she conjured the image of an ugly brown button as big as the tray she was holding. In her mind, she shrank the button slowly, determinedly, with pure concentration, while her body's murmur of protest gradually turned into a scream. She closed her eyes for a moment, and felt herself swaying dangerously in space.

"I need a break now," she said, capitulating. There was no response. "Antonio?"

Opening her eyes, she saw his stool was empty, his drawing board was lying on the floor. Antonio standing by the window lighting a clay pipe.

"Just having a little smoke," he said casually, breathing out a cloud of fumes. "It's good for my technique."

Cecilia lobbed the tray at him then. Given that her arms were half dead and her shoulders were rigid with cramp, she was astonished at how good her aim was. The tray sailed across the room, flashing in the sun as it went, and caught Antonio on the shoulder with a resonant gong. He doubled his long frame over and cried out in pain as the tray clattered to the floor at his feet.

"That'll teach you to leave me up a ladder!" she said furiously, towering above him with her fists on her hips. "Next time I'll take your head right off."

In her fury, Cecilia gradually became aware of a loud gale of male laughter. It wasn't coming from Antonio. Cecilia watched in confusion as one of the stretched canvases leaned slowly away from the wall and then fell with a loud slap on the floor, raising a cloud of dust and revealing the forms of two men. One was the red-haired aristocrat from the night before. The other was the fat Englishman who had taken her shawl. Both men were laughing helplessly, hanging on to one another for support.

Cecilia couldn't even look at Antonio. She didn't wait for explanations. She was off the ladder, down the studio stairs and out the door before anyone could stop her.

J ust two days later, they came for her.

Cecilia was sitting on an upturned bucket outside the kitchen door, sewing up a hole in one of her blouses, when she saw two well-dressed gentlemen come into the courtyard. As they ducked under the low lintel of the passage that led into the street, she instantly recognised the shorter one as Tron, the redheaded aristocrat who had been hiding behind the canvas in the studio. For a moment, she thought that his tall companion was the Englishman, or the rhinoceros as she thought of him. But she quickly recognised the slender figure of the other foreigner from the party, the handsome French nobleman whose uncle owned Veroneses. She didn't wait to learn more. Cursing Antonio, she bolted into the house.

"If any noblemen come calling," she said to Maria, rushing past her and up the stairs. "Tell them I'm out."

"I'll be sure to do that," Maria said with a sarcastic snort. "Noblemen!"

There was a knock on the door and Maria's head swiveled toward it in alarm.

Cecilia hid herself in the boys' room. Through the thin floors of the tenement she could hear the low, cultivated murmur of the men's voices and Maria's nervous, high-pitched replies. Her heart

THE MERCHANTS OF LIGHT

beat so powerfully that she wondered if everyone in the house could hear it. Why in heaven's name had they come? And how on earth had they found her?

It crossed Cecilia's mind that they might have come to see Antonio, but something inside her made her certain that they were actually there for her. Dread filled her being. They would tell her mother about the other night, that was certain. They would accuse her of stealing something — Lucia's earrings or her fancy shawl or maybe the two ducats Antonio had brought home. And then the *sbirri* would arrive and drag her off to the Wells, the prison beneath the Doge's palace, where she'd spend the rest of her life chained to the wall, submerged at low tide, with rats swimming up to nibble her earlobes and her nose. Her only comfort was the idea that Antonio would be chained to the wall next to her. Whatever happened now, she'd make sure of that.

Shortly, the maid came thumping up the stairs. Cecilia poked her head out onto the landing. "Tell me they've gone!"

Maria looked as panic-stricken as Cecilia felt. Her eyes were wild, and her hands fluttered around her like trapped bats. "They've gone, but they're coming back! Are they friends of yours?"

Cecilia grabbed the maid's wrists and pinned them, partly to contain her own rising sense of panic. Looking into Maria's face was sometimes like looking into a badly silvered mirror. Only a few years older, the maid came from the same small mountain village as Cecilia's parents. She had been with them since her childhood and was some kind of distant relation. The resemblance between the two girls made Cecilia wonder, for one fleeting, evil instant, whether she could convince the *sbirri* to take Maria away instead of her. As quickly as the thought came into her mind, she knew it had been sent by the Devil and she pushed it out again.

"Never mind that. What do they want?"

"They asked for Antonio and when I said he wasn't here they said they'd talk to your mother. They're coming back in an hour. Oh, sweet Maria! Could they be after the back rent? I have to tell your mother."

Cecilia's only hope was to stall. "Mama has a headache," she said. "She doesn't want to be disturbed."

Maria set her jaw and again Cecilia saw shades of her mother's face and her own in the maid's stubborn expression. "She wants to be disturbed if it's work for Antonio. They said something about a commission for your brother. Are you going to stop me from telling her that?"

Reluctantly Cecilia stepped aside and let Maria knock on the door to her mother's room. The maid entered the room and, after a brief pause, flew out again like a stone shot from a catapult.

"I'm to go and borrow some coffee and biscuits from next door," the maid whispered urgently, flying by. Her hands were flapping again. "You're to get in there and help her get dressed."

Cecilia pushed open the door to see her mother struggling to emerge from alluvial deposits of grey sheets. She wore only a linen shift that fell loosely around her large body. Her thick blond hair, streaked with grey, was rucked up at the back of her head where it had knotted on the pillow. Claudia blinked repeatedly, seeming bewildered, as though she'd just woken from a complicated dream, and yet she was moving with a sort of animal determination that surprised Cecilia and worried her.

"Get my striped dress from the cupboard," she commanded in a hoarse, faint voice. "Quick."

Cecilia didn't argue. With a sense of fatalism, she dragged the dress from the cupboard and helped her mother put it on.

"My hair," her mother said, gesturing vaguely at her head. Cecilia began tidying Claudia's tangled mass of hair, kneeling behind her on the bed they shared. The bed was an heirloom and the only decent piece of furniture left in the house, the only thing they hadn't been able to bring themselves to sell. Its headboard was decorated with the Guardi family crest, a shield divided into quarters, like little pens, two of them containing gryphons, two containing ducks.

As she teased out the knots in her mother's hair, Cecilia looked at the painted crest on the headboard and asked herself a childhood question: was she, Cecilia Guardi, a gryphon or a duck? Some days she felt like a gryphon, magical and winged, some days she felt like a duck, ordinary and ridiculous. Today, for certain, she was a duck, with her neck stretched out on the chopping block.

"Trust important clients to turn up here on the hottest day of the year," her mother said. Her voice was beginning to sound more normal. "How do I smell?"

Cecilia sniffed her. "A little — musty," she admitted.

"Get me that cloth, and a little water from the jug."

While Claudia ran the cloth over her armpits and under her breasts, Cecilia finished pinning her mother's hair off her sticky neck. She was still looking for a way to divert her. "I think it's rude of them to think they can just drop in on us," she said. "We should tell them to come back another day."

Claudia shook her head. "When the work comes in, you have to be there, darling. You have to look ready, even if you aren't. That's how I used to help your father and that's how we're going to help Antonio." She sighed deeply. "He's such a clever boy and such a good painter. All he needs is a chance to prove himself."

Cecilia felt an almost overwhelming urge to tell Claudia everything she knew about Antonio, but she kept her mouth shut.

Soon, her mother's hair was neatly dressed and topped with a lace cap. Claudia heaved herself onto her feet and sailed out the door and down the stairs with an energy Cecilia hadn't seen for months.

The aristocrats returned when they said they would. By a miracle, the Guardi women were ready for them. They ushered them into the tiny front room, sat them on mismatched chairs borrowed from one neighbour and served coffee and dry almond biscuits borrowed from another. Claudia herself had carefully unpacked and washed the four remaining porcelain coffee cups from the set she'd been given for a wedding present. They were tiny and translucent, rayed with dark blue stripes that ran from the base to the gilded lip. The cups were the only things that looked as though they belonged in the same room with Tron and the Frenchman.

It astonished Cecilia how big the two men looked inside their house. Tron, who wasn't tall, had to duck when he came into the room. The Frenchman — his name was Count Deboisville — was taller and was forced to incline his head to avoid hitting it on the beams. Cecilia saw him put a hand to his dark wig to make sure it hadn't been knocked awry. The two men seemed at ease, however. If they were shocked by the poverty of the house, they made no comment. They were complimentary about the coffee; they ignored the mouse that emerged from a crack in the wall and ran along the baseboard until it reached a second crack, where it ducked inside. They chatted to Claudia and both of them avoided looking directly at Cecilia who sat silently watching with her hands folded in her lap.

Tron did most of the talking. Cecilia noticed that he was much cleverer when he was sober, but he still made a bad impression. He came from one of the noblest families in Venice, an ancient clan whose name was in the Golden Book, yet he still had the air of a common tradesman. Cecilia had a feel for the marketplace; she could tell when someone was angling for a bargain, even if they were trying not to be obvious about it. And that's what Tron was doing as he talked to her mother. He was saying he wanted one thing, a painting by Antonio, when he really wanted something else. He was trying to get a feel for Claudia's price; he was discovering her weaknesses.

Claudia didn't seem to notice. As the visit progressed, she became more animated and more relaxed, or possibly just more alert, and she began to joke gently with the men. Her strong mountain accent came to the surface and the subject turned to the Val di Sole and the mountain village of Mastellina, where the Guardis originally came from. Claudia told them how she and her husband had travelled first to Vienna, where he completed his apprenticeship, and then on to Venice. "When my husband met me," she told the men, "I had never so much as drawn water from a well. I had never seen a well! In Mastellina, we had only a river, the Noce. Can you imagine?" She didn't mention the fact she had always hated the city of Venice, that she had kept the toddler Antonio literally tied to her body with a cord for the first two years they lived there for fear that he would fall into one of its abominable canals.

Claudia's conversation appeared guileless, but Cecilia could see her mother was doing her own bargaining. She sold Antonio relentlessly, crudely, telling her visitors how talented he had always been, boldly inventing commissions for work that he had never done. It wasn't clear whether the visitors knew that Claudia was lying. There were times when Tron seemed surprised to be reminded that Antonio was actually a painter at all. But he went along with it for reasons of his own, following Claudia's leads, sipping the coffee slowly with thin, pale lips.

Cecilia studied the Count, too, who seemed to be thinking thoughts of his own. He appeared much younger in her parlour than he had in the brothel. Looking beyond his imposing wig and fine clothes, she saw a man of no more than twenty-five, with an open face, an easy laugh and seductive green eyes. His hands, emerging from lace cuffs, were slender and achingly beautiful. He didn't say much but when he did he spoke Venetian well, with only a slight accent. He came from Paris, and was happy to tell Claudia all about that city, but he loved Venice, he said. Cecilia remembered what he had said on the night of the party, that in Venice you could find anything you were looking for, in the flesh. Unaccountably, it gave her a thrill to think of the Count pronouncing the word *flesh*.

Later that afternoon, a package arrived at the house. It was from the Count and it contained a small round cheese, three yellow apples, and a bag of walnuts. It came with a personal note to Cecilia's mother. "Remembering the delicious Val di Sole," Deboisville had written, or someone had written for him, in a slanted, swirling hand.

"Maria, Maria," Claudia breathed with reverence, fondling the contents of the package. It wasn't clear whether she was talking to the servant or the Virgin. "It's a *casolet* cheese, from Val di Sole. Wherever did they manage to get one?"

She began to cry. Without saying a word, Maria took the cheese and chopped some of it into cubes, cut up the apple in the same way, and tossed the pieces in a bowl with shelled walnuts, oil and salt. She found a slice of lemon somewhere and dribbled its juice over the top. Then she placed the bowl in front of Claudia who ate the strange dish with her fingers in a kind of ecstasy.

When Antonio came home that evening, he found a bowl of cheese salad waiting for him, the chopped apples browning at the edges. He attacked the food with his usual gusto, but seemed to lose his appetite as he listened to Claudia's version of the visit from Tron and the Count. At the end, he pushed the bowl of salad away without finishing it.

"If they come again," Antonio said, "don't let them in. Do you hear me? They can take their business elsewhere." His eyes found Cecilia's with a look she couldn't interpret.

Claudia gaped at him. "What are you saying, son? Are you crazy? They were very good to come to see you in your home. It shows how serious they are. And, do you know, they weren't the least put out when they found you weren't in."

"I'm sure they weren't." He shook his head, his eyes still on Cecilia.

"Why are you looking at me?" she said. "They're your friends. I didn't send for them." Cecilia gave him a glare that let him know she blamed him for everything. And yet there was something in his reaction that made her think again. Unless her brother was a better actor than she thought, the news of the nobles' visit came as a surprise to him. He even seemed worried by it.

Her mother, on the other hand, was happier than she had been in months. She couldn't stop talking about how she'd had a visit from two noblemen.

"The Count reminded me of Giovanelli when he was a young man," she went on as she finished the rest of Antonio's salad. "Giovanelli was a great patron to your father. There was no end to the paintings he needed: portraits, all kinds of battle scenes, little bitty saints for the bedrooms." She sighed, dabbing the oil from her lips with the edge of her apron. "We lived well back then."

Cecilia took her time putting Francesco and Nicolò to bed, lingering over a story she was in the process of weaving for them about two little boys who took a journey to the savage lands of the New World. She inevitably made the story too exciting, adding dragons and lions and gryphons, and then she had to talk them calm again with long passages when the ship sailed and sailed over glassy, clear seas.

It was almost dark before she climbed up the three flights of stairs to Antonio's room in the attic. His tone was urgent when he asked her to meet him there, saying they needed to talk, but she had no qualms about making him wait. She went up when she was good and ready. A glance around the cramped, squalid space where her brother slept, half storeroom and half garret, told her Antonio was waiting for her outside on the *altana*. The door was ajar and she pushed it open and stepped out onto the ramshackle wooden platform built out over the roof tiles on pilings. Antonio was there, sitting on the edge of the rough plank floor, feet dangling into space, smoking his little clay pipe.

"If we had a hundred ducats to our name," he said without turning around, "he would have sent two cheeses and a whole bag of apples." He blew a cloud of blue smoke into the air.

"I don't know what you're complaining about," Cecilia said. "Mama was thrilled with the Count's gift."

Antonio half turned and she could see his face in profile silhouetted against the dirty white wall of the next door building. "You and I both know that present wasn't for Mama."

"No?"

"Mama is just a wide public thoroughfare that leads them straight to you."

Cecilia felt herself blushing. "How odd that you're annoyed about that," she said, "since you obviously sent them here."

"I didn't send them. They figured it out for themselves: dead father, buffoon of a brother, mother as soft as a pastry. You're fair game, Cecilia. Nobles do this all the time."

Cecilia felt her anger rise again. She stamped her foot, shaking the flimsy structure beneath them. At that moment she didn't care if she shook the *altana* into the canal. "I blame you for this, Antonio. You took me to that house. You brought them to the studio and let them look at me wearing nothing but a sack. Why did you do that? Are you their pimp now as well as their stooge?"

Cecilia prepared herself for a spirited comeback from her brother, for insults, repartee, even a slap. Instead, Antonio actually hung his head. "It was just a joke," he said quietly. "I didn't think they would actually — come for you."

"Well, now they have."

"Yes."

Contrition was the one thing she never expected of her brother. She stepped carefully toward him and felt the makeshift structure shake under her weight. The *altana* was rotting, just like everything else about the house. There were places where whole boards were missing, and Cecilia didn't like to walk on the rickety platform any more than she had to. She came up when she needed to hang out the laundry but never otherwise. Yet the view from up there always thrilled her. On clear days she could see the mountains on the mainland through a chink between two of the taller buildings. Tonight, the heat haze limited the view to a landscape of segmented red tile roofs, pale walls and brick chimneys flared at the top like fans. The moon had just appeared over the rooftops, a smudged, silvery crescent. Cecilia could see other people leaning on the rails of their balconies, watching it rise.

She moved to where Antonio was sitting and lowered herself down next to him. Removing her loose slippers in case they fell off, she let her feet hang over the edge of the platform. There was a long pause during which they listened to the sounds coming up from the street, and the buzz of the little black bats as they cut through the evening air.

"Do you think I could hit that man down there with my shoe?" Cecilia said finally.

Antonio lifted his head. "You were always a crack shot. But then how would you get your shoe back?"

"The Count could buy me another pair. One with gold threads and silver beads. Now that would be a high class weapon."

"True," he said. "Go ahead, then."

She made as if to fling her slipper down into the alley. Antonio mimed the actions of a man getting hit in the head by a shoe: perplexity, fury, fist-shaking. Suddenly Cecilia glimpsed the old Antonio again, funny and easygoing. It was like seeing a close friend after a long absence. If they were just a little bit richer, she thought, Antonio could go back to being that way again. It wouldn't matter that he wasn't serious about work. No one would expect him to keep them all alive or blame him for not being more successful. And wouldn't that be good? Wouldn't it be good for all of them? Her mother's whole being lit up at the sight of a decent cheese. That's where the family had arrived, an unavoidable consequence of her father's death. And things weren't going to get any better, she realised, if something didn't change. Her mother wasn't changing, and neither was Antonio. Perhaps it had to be her after all.

"Tell me about how it is for them," she said.

"For who?"

"For those girls. Like Lucia. She's a friend of yours, isn't she? You don't — you aren't her lover?" As the words came out of her mouth, Cecilia felt the risk in them.

Antonio snorted. "I'm not answering that one. As if I could be. My God, are we really having this conversation?"

Cecilia persisted. "I've heard all about these women from Father Bernard, how they burn in hell and have all kinds of diseases. And we know Bettina — we knew her. But I don't really have any idea about courtesans or actresses or whatever you want to call them. You on the other hand must know lots of them. I suppose you meet them when you're painting sets at the theatre. So you must know all about them. For example, you must have some idea how much they earn."

Antonio looked genuinely horrified. "Cecilia, for God's sake! You can't ask me things like that. How much do they earn!"

"Who am I to ask then, Father Bernard? Mama? Deboisville? You're the only person in the world who can give me a straight answer without automatically turning me into a whore."

She chose her words carefully, and when she uttered the last one, she watched Antonio wince as if she'd slapped him. This satisfied her: if her brother was going to expose her to these worlds, he was going to discover that she was prepared to be more honest about them than he was.

"I just wonder if they think it's worth it."

Antonio was agitated. He tapped out the bowl of his pipe on a rotten plank. "You're asking yourself if it might be worth it."

Cecilia shrugged. "I'm sure it beats making rope in the Arsenal." That's what honest, poor women, women who were not young or beautiful, ended up doing to keep their families alive. The workday started at dawn and ended after dark, the pay was a pittance. The hemp fibres destroyed their hands and their lungs. Breathing them in shortened their lives even if it gave them a little more time than starvation did.

Antonio looked her in the face. She was pleased to see he was sincerely horrified. "You're not becoming a whore, Cecilia." His voice shook as he said this. "Not while I'm alive. It would kill Mama."

She drew herself up straight and smoothed her skirt. "I don't know about that. It wouldn't kill Mama any faster than this life we're living now. I'd buy her chocolate and new dresses. Cheeses galore. I'd get the furniture back so we'd have something to sit on. I'm sure that would more than make up for my mortal sin."

"I'll beat you to prevent it if I have to." Her brother's voice trembled. He sounded as if he might cry. "I'll lock you in."

"Really? You feel that strongly about it? Shame. In that case we'd better think of something else." She smiled. "Why don't we sell you to the Turks as a slave instead?"

Antonio looked at her sideways, then laughed. "You little monster. You think you're funny."

"Serves you right," she said, pleased.

Cecilia had no intention of selling herself to the Count or anyone else. She had her own reasons for this, but she couldn't tell Antonio what they were. They had to do with the last time she'd seen Bettina. After months of looking for her, Cecilia had bumped into her in the street one evening. Even though it was dark in the street and Bettina was wearing a large cloak with a hood, she recognised her friend instantly and threw her arms around her.

Cecilia had so many questions for Bettina. But now, face-to-face, she could only think of one. "Where are you going?" she asked.

Wordlessly, Bettina drew a bundle from beneath her cloak and held it toward her. Cecilia saw it was newborn baby wrapped in a pale scrap of blanket, sound asleep. "To the Ospedale," Cecilia said, supplying the answer Bettina couldn't bring herself say out loud. Bettina nodded and started to cry.

Cecilia didn't ask Bettina any questions after that, though later she wished she had. It didn't cross her mind to go get Maria or her mother to help. What could they do? Instead, she took the sleeping baby from Bettina and together the two girls walked to the Ospedale della Pietà, which wasn't far away. When they got there, they stood for a while in the shadows, watching the people coming and going on the Riva degli Schiavoni. As soon as the street was empty, they approached the building and found the right window. It was wider than the others, and placed lower down on the façade at just the right height for its purpose. Cecilia handed the baby back to Bettina and watched her place it inside the window on a wide marble ledge that was more like a threshold than a sill. Almost at once, like a trap being sprung, a wooden hatch opened behind it and a pair of hands, thin and bony, with wrists like dried twigs, reached out of the darkness and dragged the baby inside.

They stood for a long time in the darkness and Bettina wept. It was then Cecilia understood the tragedy of being a whore. It wasn't the sin of what you did with men or what men did with you. It was the loss of your children, the only precious things that ever really belong to a woman. The Ospedale wasn't a bad place for a bastard child to end up: the nuns taught the girls to sing — the music master Vivaldi's choir was famous — and they sent the boys to farming families in the Veneto. But the memory of the disembodied hands reaching out to claim Bettina's baby produced a kind of panic in Cecilia. It made her run to find Nicolò and Francesco and put her arms around them and subject them to kisses.

She couldn't explain any of this to Antonio. Instead, she reached into one of her pockets and pulled out a folded piece of paper. "You'd better take a look at this. He sent it today."

The Count's message to Cecilia was brief but it dripped with flattery and struck an intimate note. When she received it, Cecilia's first thought was how rich the Count must be to use so much paper to convey so few words. They were pretty words, though. "That arrogant, scheming bastard," Antonio growled as he read.

She watched Antonio tear the paper into tiny fragments and toss them into the air above their heads. A gust of wind carried them into the open space between the buildings and from there they drifted down toward the canal and rained like apple blossom onto the dark surface of the water.

"We have to get rid of him," Antonio said in a hopeless voice.

Cecilia considered. "You could tell him what you told that friend of yours that used to like me a few years ago," she suggested. "That I bite my toenails and bleach my hair with baby piss. That certainly put him off."

Antonio was grim. "That won't work with Deboisville and Tron. They have reputations to uphold. They'll have told their friends about you by now. They've probably rented a room for you already."

"A room!" Cecilia echoed in disgust. "So they think that if they buy me a pretty shell they can just expect me to crawl into it like some kind of miserable little crab?" She thought of Lucia, flushed and luscious, with her bodice open to the navel. And of Bettina, her pale, stricken face and empty arms in the flickering light of the torches on the steps of the Ospedale. "They don't know anything."

She took a moment to look once more at the view. The *altana* was like a shipwreck's life raft riding over the roofs of the city, she thought, and she and Antonio were castaways, praying for the sight of land. Halfway up the darkening sky, the moon shone smaller, brighter now and sharp-edged, like the curved blade of a scimitar. For no good reason at all, maybe just because of the moon's clean slice, Cecilia suddenly felt very calm and very certain. She knew what she needed to do and that certainty made her feel happy. She tried to memorise the feeling to use later when, she was sure, she was going to need it.

Later, Cecilia would ask herself why she chose Tiepolo. She knew other young men, and some of them had shown more than a passing interest in her, like the one Antonio told about the baby piss. These were nice boys with reasonable prospects, decent looking, not criminal. Some of them were painters like Antonio and her father, which is to say painters who worked for painters who owned studios, painters whose contribution laid beneath the visible surface, in the substrate of the gesso ground or the dull, necessary foundation of the underpainting. It was respectable work and it could keep a family alive provided the man stayed healthy.

Off-hand, Cecilia could think of four or five young men who fit this bill, any one of whom would have made a reasonable husband for her — because that's what she needed now, a husband to put an end to predators like Deboisville and Tron. So why did she fix her sights on Tiepolo? Was it his looks, his voice, the fact that he was strong enough to strangle Antonio?

After thinking about it for a long time, she decided the thing that drew her to Tiepolo was her memory of the caricature he'd drawn, so long ago, on a wall of the Arsenal: the potbellied, beak-nosed dwarf of a landlord, so ugly and so apt. While it was true that any little boy could scribble on the walls, this particular one had transformed that scrawl first into an act of open defiance and then into a future for himself. That was talent. The authorities dragged him away for it. They punished him, they beat him, and then — then, because they were Venetian after all and knew what it meant when an untutored boy was capable of doing a thing like that, they surrendered to the inevitable and turned that boy into a painter.

It demonstrated something Cecilia believed in her heart: that talent was a form of power. In a world where wealth and status were things you had to be born with, talent was a way — maybe the only way — to beat the odds, to put a rude finger up to fate and triumph. All painters lived off talent. Her father hadn't possessed much of it but he had taught her to recognise talent and she had spotted it immediately in Tiepolo's painting of Moses drowning Pharaoh's army. She didn't need the Doge to confirm it for her. She didn't need to know the painting had won a prize. It was talent Cecilia wanted to marry because, from talent, everything else flowed.

A nd so the day after her conversation with Antonio, Cecilia went to find Tiepolo. She wasted no time — she knew she could only put Deboisville off for so long. She asked around and learned where Tiepolo's studio was. Then, not knowing how else to begin with him, she took herself straight there and offered herself as a model.

His reaction wasn't what she'd hoped. Tiepolo didn't seem to remember her at first. Once she'd reminded him, he looked her up and down in a confused way. "Did Antonio tell you I was looking for models?" he said. He seemed shorter than he had in the Campo San Rocco. He was dressed for the studio in a workman's tunic and a pair of loose trousers. On his head he wore an odd cap made of striped fabric, turned back at the edges to reveal a napped reverse. A number of little tassels hung down from the crown. These swung from side to side when Tiepolo moved his head.

Cecilia drew herself up to her full height and contemplated that silly hat, wondering if she had made a mistake. "Painters are always looking for models," she said. Embarrassment made her voice sound flat and bland.

They were standing in the doorway of the studio, Tiepolo's first, which he was renting with a loan from one of his patrons. It wasn't a large space and it was so crowded with easels and equipment that it was hard to move without bumping into something. But Cecilia could see that everything was ship-shape: not clean, because studios were never really clean, but organised, logical. A sole assistant moved somewhere at the back of the room. She spotted the portrait of the Doge Cornaro on an easel, the face and cap already completed, the red and golden robes still only sketched in. There was no sign of the painting of Moses parting the Red Sea. Cecilia presumed Tiepolo had sold it and felt a sense of confirmation and loss.

Tiepolo stepped back two paces now and took a good look at her, sizing her up. She hadn't expected a critical evaluation. She'd assumed Tiepolo would realise right away that her offer of modelling was just a pretext for seeing him again. But if he did, he was being deliberately obtuse. "Do you have any experience?" he asked.

"What a question!" she said, frustrated and slightly outraged. How could a man be so dense? She put her hands on her hips and cocked her head to one side. "My father was Domenico Guardi," she pointed out. "A painter. My brother is Antonio Guardi, also a painter."

"Of sorts," Tiepolo said, and smiled at her for the first time. Something about the outlandish hat made him look very young, like a child dressed up for a part in a play. At that moment his battered nose and a pair of sparse, fuzzy, reddish sideburns were the only features that made his face seem at all manly.

"Antonio is a painter," she said. "And if you came from a painting background, which I'm guessing you don't, then you'd know that everyone models in a painter's family. It's free labour. Real models cost money."

"As I know all too well," Tiepolo said. "So what's your rate?"

"What?" The question caught Cecilia off guard. She hadn't actually thought about being paid.

"Your rate? What do you charge painters who aren't members of your family?"

"Pay me what you paid your last girl," she said and blushed, thinking how such a statement might be misinterpreted. But Tiepolo didn't notice the innuendo or her flushed complexion. To her astonishment, he hired her.

Things went very badly at first, at least from the point of view of seduction. As far as modelling was concerned, though, things went very well. Tiepolo was working on commissions for several large history paintings and he was doing preliminary drawings for all of them at once. He employed several regular models, men and women, some old, some young, and there were times when the little studio was crowded with figures in robes. He kept Cecilia busy. She posed for him in Levantine dress and clothed in burlap, like a shepherdess. She knelt at the feet of an old, bearded man — an ex-sailor — with another woman, in a family group. She pretended to play a mandolin that had no strings. She held a tall terracotta amphora on her hip throughout one long, warm afternoon.

Tiepolo knew just what he wanted from his models. He drew quickly but could spend hours working on a single figure or group. He had them change positions often, sometimes getting up on the dais to demonstrate a pose. Cecilia and the others would laugh at the sight of the young painter with his hands spread wide, his face a mask of martyr's resignation, or on his knees receiving a visit from an angel, but at least they knew what he was after. He was fair with them when it came to paying. He used an hourglass to keep track of their hours and he settled with everyone in cash at the end of each week.

The first time Cecilia received her pay she could hardly believe it. This was another thing she hadn't anticipated. She ran home all the way and proudly added the few zecchini to the moneybag under the floorboards. For a few hours she buzzed with happiness, imagining that this could be another way of solving their problems. Then a messenger came with a note from Deboisville and she was reminded that her pitiful earnings were nothing, a mere distraction, and that time was running out.

But Tiepolo was proving impervious to her charms, if they really were charms, and Cecilia didn't know what to do about it. If he saw the blond beauties of Veronese when he drew her, he didn't give any clear indication. He treated her like all his other models; never touched her, never tried to speak to her alone. It wasn't that he was unfriendly toward her or that he seemed to dislike her, it was that he wouldn't come near her. And even though she spent long days with him, Cecilia didn't know what to do to move things forward. She had imagined that he, the man, would do more of the work. One day, she thought, he'd come to her with his shining eyes and ask her to take off her clothes and pose as a nymph or a goddess and then she would know he loved her. Wasn't that the way it worked? But it never happened. Sometimes she caught him looking at her with an expression that could have been interest or curiosity or mere bafflement. "What is it?" she'd say, the colour creeping into her cheeks.

And he'd say something strange like, "your skin is looking very green today" or "your face breaks down into perfect quarters." What was she supposed to think of that?

So the weeks went by and the drawings of Cecilia and the others multiplied, filling up the pasteboard folders and leather rolls stacked on the shelves of the studio. They were beautiful drawings, full of the talent Cecilia was searching for. Tiepolo had captured her in those drawings and now, even if he didn't realise it, she belonged to him.

Yet Deboisville was circling closer and closer the way they said sharks circled shipwrecked sailors before they started to eat them.

Cecilia began to panic. She tore up his notes without answering them, but it was pointless: his campaign was working just fine on her mother. He sent Claudia chocolate and dropped in for chats. Cecilia had to sit there silently and listen to them, avoiding Deboisville's passionate sideways glances while her mother giggled and simpered and behaved as if she were the one he was after, not Cecilia. Was it possible that Claudia didn't see what was happening? Could she be that naïve, or was she ready to sell her only daughter in exchange for a better life?

Antonio was no help. After their conversation on the *altana*, he seemed to lose his nerve completely and began staying away from the house for days at a time, dodging responsibility for what was about to happen. Any day, Cecilia knew, Deboisville could decide he'd invested enough time in chasing her. Then all the cute little games would stop and he would tell them plain what the transaction was to be. Aristocrats, she knew, always set the terms. Cecilia had the feeling that some moment of truth was fast approaching.

Cecilia knelt on a cushion on a raised platform in Tiepolo's studio with Maria's head resting in her lap. "I'm not sure about this," Maria whispered out of the side of her mouth. "You never said anything about me being in it."

"Be quiet," Cecilia whispered back. Her hands cradled Maria's wide face, fingertips lightly touching her cheeks. Her head was bowed low over the servant's with an expression that should have been compassion but which, at the moment, was more like exhaustion. She hadn't slept well for several days.

It was dawn. Tiepolo had asked her to come in early because he wanted this particular quality of morning light for his drawing. She brought Maria with her for company but when they got to the studio, Tiepolo put her to work, too. Now Cecilia knelt on a cushion while Maria lay with her head cradled in Cecilia's arms. Maria was supposed to be the Virgin, fainting after seeing Christ taken down from the cross. Cecilia was supposed to be the other Mary, or perhaps Martha, consoling her.

Maria fidgeted. "But are you sure it isn't sacrilege to pretend to be Our Lady?" she hissed.

"Stop worrying," Cecilia said. "He's not even going to draw you. It's just so my pose looks right." She patted Maria's cheek roughly. The model for Mary had failed to show up. Cecilia had a choice of holding Maria in her arms or a sack of stinking sheep's wool. "Just go to sleep."

For a long time the only sounds were the scratching of Tiepolo's pen and the throaty throbbing of the pigeons stirring under the roof tiles. Cecilia felt the maid drift off to sleep, her body becoming heavier and softer as though she were gently expanding and her bones were dissolving. Her own pose was reasonably comfortable, but she wasn't sleepy. It was a perfect opportunity to think, but she wasn't enjoying her thoughts much.

The evening before, Deboisville had found her alone. She'd sensed this was coming, but nonetheless she was surprised when he suddenly materialised in front of her. She was on her way to the bread stall and it was the first time she'd ever run into him in the street. She knew instantly that he had planned it and that it meant he knew all her movements and could reach her any time he felt like it.

Deboisville was accompanied by two other men Cecilia had never seen before, both as handsome and well-dressed as he was. The three young aristocrats blocked the narrow street with their large bodies, forcing other pedestrians to squeeze against the walls to get past. They didn't seem to notice or care that they were taking up all the space. Deboisville was as charming as ever. As he talked, his beautiful hands sculpted the evening air and the lace at his wrists wafted the scent of a rose garden. Deboisville invited Cecilia to take a meal with him and his friends and, when she said no, he accepted her refusal without any resistance. But as the three men moved away, Cecilia realised she was shaking.

Being careful not to move her head, Cecilia studied Tiepolo through half-closed eyes. He was a familiar figure to her now, sitting as ever on a stool at the edge of the platform with his drawing board across his splayed knees. This morning he was wearing a motheaten knitted cap of maroon wool — he seemed to have a collection of odd hats. His big eyes darted back and forth between her and the paper as though he were transferring her image there with his gaze alone. She couldn't see his hands. He lifted his chin and made a moue with his mouth, squinting his eyes into an intent, pursed expression that would have been funny on stage but in the calm of the studio was only a sign of his pure concentration.

Tiepolo compared badly to Deboisville in most ways. He was always paint-spattered, he smelled of turpentine instead of roses, he was short (though not hunchbacked, as Antonio had said) and he had a weakness for wearing bad hats. But worst of all, unlike Deboisville, Tiepolo was out of Cecilia's reach. She was sure about that now: his family had arranged for him to marry the daughter of a lawyer, a girl who'd bring him one thousand ducats' worth of dowry. That was a lot of money, more than enough to set up a much bigger studio, hire more assistants and begin the real work of spinning his raw talent into gold. When she learned this, Cecilia knew she was defeated. Even if Tiepolo desired her, he'd be crazy to choose her over a girl with that much money.

She thought of Antonio. He was the same age as Tiepolo, he'd received exactly the same training in the same studio. From that perspective, they were like two eggs laid in the same nest. But Antonio would never be his own master. He would live and die an assistant, just like Cecilia's father had, because the talent, the cursed talent, wasn't there.

Talent was a matter of fortune, Cecilia thought, something people couldn't control. And life was a sort of gambling house, a great *ridotto* where you made wagers with your talents and won or lost according to luck or calculation or the tilt of the table. And was beauty a sort of talent? She asked herself this question because it seemed pertinent to her situation. No, she decided, it wasn't. Because beauty didn't belong to the person other people thought of as beautiful — she knew this for sure. It belonged to the people who saw the beauty and desired it. Beauty was the talent of the beholder.

So in life's *ridotto*, Cecilia had nothing to play with, no way to get into the game. Antonio had next to nothing and in some ways that was worse, more disappointing, because the possibility was there, but winning was impossible. It meant the Guardis would shortly sink into poverty, disappearing like bright coins thrown into a canal. That was how it went: Cecilia knew families this had happened to, Bettina's family, and others. You see them for a moment as they sink beneath the surface, they flash, they fade. Then they vanish in the cloudy green water, settling out of sight into the bottom sludge. Where were they now? Scattered. Gone. Sunk.

And now it was going to happen to them. The rent was three months overdue. She had sold the good bed to a neighbour, but hadn't had the heart to tell her mother yet. Modelling alone couldn't keep a roof over their heads. They were out of options, unless Cecilia went to Deboisville. The trouble was, she couldn't do it. She was too proud.

Cecilia focused on Maria's sleeping face, fighting the awful feeling of powerlessness that was stealing up on her. Maria, with her blond hair and pink colouring, resembled Cecilia's mother.

The sight of her features, relaxed in sleep, forced Cecilia to think of Claudia. It was Claudia who would suffer most from their ruin. She had hardly survived the shock of becoming a widow; becoming indigent would surely kill her. Cecilia imagined her mother, old and dirty, sick, rotting away in some filthy charitable hostel or living in a doorway like some poor hags did. Claudia was too gentle to be like the aggressive street crones who survived by begging and doing nasty odd jobs. She would die in misery and squalor and fear, clinging to the last striped cup from her delicate coffee set. Cecilia, unwilling to take the necessary steps to prevent it, would have to watch this happen.

And her brothers, the little boys Nicolò and Francesco, Cecilia couldn't even think about them. She thought again of skeletal hands pulling her babies, the ones she hadn't had yet but which she could feel like a crush of seeds in her body, into the darkness.

At this point, she gave up her struggle. Pity overcame her. She had fought against it for a long time because pity for Claudia, for her little brothers, even pity for Maria who would share their fate, was really pity for herself and that kind of pity paralysed her. No matter what she did, she could not separate her life from theirs. They might not understand, but she knew there was no use trying to escape into a life of sin and luxury. It wouldn't work. She wasn't capable of it. It would mean living an illusion, in denial of the way things really were. It was better for her to open her heart and embrace the reality; that they were all doomed, together. There was nothing she could do — would do — to save them.

Up until this moment, Cecilia had fought this ugly truth with everything she had, with hard work, with cunning, with mockery and blame, even with spite. But in the still atmosphere of the morning studio, she let herself sink into it like a coin in the mud of a canal. It made her feel hopeless, and strangely at peace.

"Cecilia."

She heard her name and looked up sharply to see Tiepolo standing at the edge of the platform. She hadn't heard him get up or move across the floor. He was staring at her with those big eyes of his. His face wore an odd expression like a man who has just seen an amazing conjuring trick and can't quite believe it.

"I'm sorry," she said, suddenly aware that tears were running down her cheeks. "I'm sorry." She was embarrassed not only for the tears but for her thoughts about him, for her wish to use him. Her fate would not be Tiepolo's fault and he could not be her saviour. She could not make him be that.

"What were you thinking about?" he asked. His voice was unsteady as though it were difficult for him to ask this simple question.

She tried to shrug it off. Nothing, she told him. She couldn't look him in the eye. He reached out and cupped her chin in his hand and turned her face to his.

"Your expression changed," he said. "Very gradually, it grew so tender, as if it was melting into sadness." There was a question in his eyes, but Cecilia wasn't sure what it was. In her lap, Maria breathed heavily in her sleep. Folded beneath her, her feet tingled as though they were being nibbled by shoals of tiny fish.

Cecilia wiped her cheeks on her sleeve and tried to think of some explanation. "I was thinking about the Virgin," she said. "And the girl who tries to help her. I was trying to feel what they would feel." As she said this, she was aware that, on some level, her words were true.

"And what was that?" Tiepolo asked.

"I felt that we are all lost," she said and started to cry again.

"Yes," Tiepolo said, continuing to hold her chin in his hand. Then, without warning, he leaned forward and kissed her. His lips were thin and hard with purpose. They were very warm.

They were married in the autumn in Tiepolo's church, San Ternita. It was a secret ceremony, held on a weekday without fuss. No public notice was posted, no banns were read. The rites were muted and the priest hurried through them like a man late for his lunch. It was the sort of wedding usually performed when the bride was obviously pregnant, which Cecilia wasn't, or when the couple were marrying for a second time; a rushed, necessary rite with no poetry and few promises. The only witnesses were Claudia, who cried throughout, Antonio, and the little boys. No one from Tiepolo's family dared to come.

Cecilia had been prepared for this. Tiepolo's mother, Orsetta, had objected to her son's choice of a bride. In fact she objected at the top of her lungs over a number of days and it was said that the washing lines around the Tiepolo family home were still vibrating with her shrieks of outrage. The problem was the dowry: Cecilia brought the family nothing and, in Orsetta's eyes, this meant the wretched girl had cost them all one thousand ducats.

Gossip about Orsetta Tiepolo's rage had quickly spread around Venice and reached Cecilia in Santa Maria Formosa. She understood Orsetta's view and she accepted that it might have the power to change Tiepolo's mind about her. So when Nicolò had come running to tell her that a messenger had arrived from Tiepolo, she had braced herself.

The messenger, Tiepolo's young assistant, put a small, untidily wrapped package into her hands. But instead of an apology or an excuse, it contained a tiny bag of orange silk. Inside was a string of small pearls with a golden clasp. Instead of a note there was a drawing, hastily sketched on a quarter sheet of blue paper. The style was comical and reminded Cecilia of the first Tiepolo she had ever seen. It depicted a scruffy little man in an outsized tricorn hat kneeling alongside a beautiful woman at the altar. The groom mooned at the bride with big goggling eyes; his huge hat was almost as big as his body. He had a broken nose and there were splashes of paint on his suit. The bride, a goddess in profile, resembled Cecilia. Around her neck Tiepolo had drawn a string of pearls the size of fat plums.

On her wedding day, Cecilia wore hand-me-downs and borrowed garments: a pale yellow dress of her mother's hastily cut down to size, a stiff cloak of sky-blue wool borrowed from a friend, new linen bought on credit. As she fastened the string of pearls around her neck, she marvelled at the precise way the necklace encircled her throat, just resting in the soft angle where the column of her neck flared out to her collarbones. Using nothing but his naked painter's eye, and without letting Cecilia know that he was doing it, Tiepolo had estimated her neck's circumference with perfect accuracy. No other man, she thought with pride, could have judged it so perfectly.

On their wedding night, Tiepolo made her keep the pearls on when he undressed her. He ran his fingers over them, his tongue, his teeth. It was then that Cecilia understood that the pearls weren't hers alone. From now on all the treasures belonged jointly to both of them.

PART THREE

Cecilia Tiepolo
Venice, 1719–1724

Venice, 1719-1724

There were countless jokes about newly married couples and the things they got up to in bed. These had always embarrassed Cecilia, but now that she was a newlywed she understood why people made them. It was partly curiosity, partly prurience, but mostly it was pure longing. Cecilia pitied the jokers. If they were old, they'd lived what she was experiencing and lost it. If they were young, they didn't know what they were talking about. Everyone in the world seemed to share the longing — and so the joking — except she and Tiepolo. They no longer had to make jokes and they couldn't spare the time to make them.

Their room was on the third floor of the house near the bridge at San Francesco della Vigna. From their window they could see the church and watch the gondolas docking at the water gate of the Contarini palace. Ambrosio, Tiepolo's oldest brother, and his family shared the house. Orsetta, still fuming over the lost dowry, occupied the best bedroom. Tiepolo had his studio on the second floor, which was very convenient for the young lovers. Cecilia would never have wanted to prevent her husband from working.

It was amazing, the islets of time a person could find for making love. Tiepolo and Cecilia mapped them like navigators. There was one before the day started, in the grey hour just before dawn. Cecilia opened her eyes and felt Tiepolo's body pressing against her back, cleaving to the curve of her spine and pressing into the warmth of her buttocks. They slept locked together all night but now his hand stirred and squeezed her waist, folded over her breast, his leg slid over hers. She twisted toward him and found his face, his mouth. He put his lips against her ear, clamped a hand on her soft hip, steadying her, and went deeper.

These details were never in the jokes but Tiepolo informed her there were picture books that showed them. "But how can that be?" Cecilia asked, pressing him for details. She wondered how any artist could show the reality of love: the pressure, the wetness, the heat, the burst of brightness at the end. "These are things that happened inside us," she said, "things no one can see. And where would a person stand to draw them?"

Tiepolo rolled on top of her, nestling his hips between her thighs. He touched his off-centre nose to hers. "Right here," he said.

"You're too close," she said. "Where's your vanishing point? Where are your lines of perspective?"

"I'll give you lines of perspective," he said.

Yet Tiepolo had his ideas, like all men do, and Cecilia sometimes wondered if they came from the books he mentioned. After lunch, when there was another one of those islets of time, Tiepolo pressed Cecilia up against the bedroom wall. He was stronger than she would have thought possible. He could hoist her by the thighs and hold her pinned with her backside against the cool plaster, skirt around her waist, bodice open, while he moved inside her. When the pleasure came, Cecilia closed her eyes and saw a magnificent ship in full sail. She told Tiepolo about it later. "Does that ever happen to you?" she asked him.

"Sometimes," he said. And then he thought about it for a moment. "Yes, it does sometimes. That's funny. Maybe it happens to everybody."

"And what do you see when you see things?" Cecilia thought he might say *You, I see you, Signora Tiepolo*. But he answered honestly, which she preferred.

"I see colours," he said. It sounded as if he was discovering this for the first time.

"Which ones?" She laid her head against his chest. His heart beat very steadily, very slowly.

"All of them," he said. "Even the ones that aren't yet colours."

It was difficult to imagine what it would be like to see colours that weren't colours, yet she believed him. "How lovely," she said.

He liked her to wear her pearls even when she stripped naked. He took them in his mouth like a bit. They made tiny clicking sounds against his teeth. Once, he put them on himself. His neck was much thinner than hers and they slid over his Adam's apple and hung comically among the little hairs at the top of his chest. "Gorgeous," she teased.

Night was an archipelago of moments, stretching across the hours until dawn. They would make love, sleep and wake to make love again until they were both exhausted and chafed. They weren't sleeping enough, and Cecilia felt stupid and languid during the day, like a young bride in a joke. She did silly things like leaving the rice on the fire too long, or letting a shirt flutter into the canal when she went to hang it on the line. But after a few weeks, practice made pleasure almost effortless for her and Tiepolo, the inevitable result of putting their two young bodies together, and they both began to relax. Any awkwardness or resistance they felt at the beginning disappeared. Sleep was sweet, and waking up together felt like a triumph.

This was marriage, Cecilia concluded. Not the ceremony in church, but this gradual fusion of bodies connected by tenderness. It put something to rest for her. Where her life had seemed small and pinched before Tiepolo, now she felt there was an abundance of everything. She couldn't explain it, but she knew she and he made this abundance between them. Now, together, they could get on with business.

And there was plenty of business. Only now that she lived with Tiepolo did Cecilia begin to understand what success meant for a painter. Life with her father and Antonio had given her no clue.

For one thing, it meant that work was constant and took up all the available space in the house. In his new studio on the second floor, Tiepolo carried on two, three, four paintings at a time, only limited by the number of easels he could stand up in the space. His workshop was on the ground floor. There, he and a small team of labourers hammered together wooden stretchers, trimmed canvases or prepared boards for painting. Tiepolo's brother, who, like their father, had a business fitting out ships, kept some of his wares there, but Tiepolo's gear occupied most of the space because Tiepolo was making most of the money. Upstairs, Orsetta waged a continual battle to keep the studio mess out of the family living quarters. Pots and brushes and pieces of scrap paper with partial drawings seemed to drift up the staircase and settle like ash in the dining room or the parlour or even the bedrooms.

Success also meant the house was like a public square: there were always people coming and going, milling about, showing up at all hours. With more work coming in, Tiepolo hired two more assistants and, for the first time, took on a number of drawing students, who drifted around with dreamy expressions, carrying huge portfolios under their arms. There were always people dropping by, too: aristocrats, merchants, churchmen, clients and curious foreign tourists, or other painters who came to gossip or negotiate or simply spy on what Tiepolo was doing.

"Don't you find all those people distracting?" Cecilia asked him one night.

"What people?" he said in a sleepy voice. It was hard to keep Tiepolo awake after they made love. Cecilia persisted. She'd been waiting all day to speak to him.

"All those people who come to the studio. You know, like Dolfin today. He stayed for hours. I thought he would never leave." Dolfin was an aristocrat and an important patron of the arts. He'd bought Tiepolo's painting of Moses and the Red Sea for an excellent price. Now he was discussing other commissions.

"Dolfin buys my paintings," Tiepolo murmured, as if that were enough to excuse any crime. She could just see his face in the moonlight shining though their window. His irises glittered slightly beneath lids that were only three-quarters closed, but she knew he might be dreaming already: Tiepolo slept with his eyes slightly open, a habit he said he learned during his apprenticeship so he could nap secretly while appearing to do other things. Cecilia poked him in the ribs.

"They keep you from working," she said. "You should tell them to go away, tell them you're busy. Or let me tell them for you."

Tiepolo smiled without looking at her and squeezed her close to him. "Will you fight them off for me, my little dragon wife? Will you stand at the door of my studio waving a sword? I think I'd like to see that. Oh yes, I would. You'd look beautiful with a sword, like Judith or Salome. Now that's an idea...Judith, Salome..." His voice trailed off and his lids dropped over his eyes again.

"I'm pregnant," she said and watched the lids snap open, the eyes turn to find her face in the moonlight.

Cecilia posed for Tiepolo at four months wearing nothing but a bed sheet. This was something she could do because now she was his wife and there was no one who could tell her otherwise. She was supposed to be Europa.

"Are you thinking about a button?" Tiepolo asked her from behind his drawing board. She had told him her trick. She had told Tiepolo everything.

"I didn't think they had buttons back then. Did they?" It was fine to be alone together in the studio. It was wonderful for her just to sit and do nothing while the excess fluids of fertility pumped through her body.

"Then what are you thinking about? You're thinking about something."

"Ices. I have a craving for ices. Does my face look innocent enough for you when I think about food?" Europa was supposed to be a virgin. They had discussed the story before she sat down to model. Unlikely as it seemed, Europa didn't have any suspicion that the bull she was sitting on (Cecilia sat on a pile of cushions; Tiepolo would paint the animal in later) was in fact the god Zeus in disguise, plotting to ravish her. Girls from antiquity were always having these kinds of problems, Cecilia reflected with disapproval. They had to be mentally defective not to see what was coming.

"Your face looks innocent," Tiepolo said. She couldn't see his mouth behind the drawing board he held on his knees, just his big eyes peering at her over the top, but she could hear the smile in his voice. "I don't know about the rest of you."

"You have only yourself to blame for that," Cecilia said. Pregnancy was swelling her all over. Her breasts were the size of summer melons and as hard. The plain white sheet draped over them without hiding their contours. It skimmed the bump of her belly, now just beginning to show.

"Are you going to put Zuane in this painting?" she asked. Zuane was the young black servant they had hired as part of their strategy for making peace with Orsetta.

Tiepolo put the board down and looked at her. "I hadn't

thought of that. Do you think I should?" He sounded interested in the idea.

Zuane had been with them for several weeks and Tiepolo kept staring at him and praising the unique shape of his head, like a long black olive, he said. Zuane was polite about his master's strange compliments, but he was polite about everything. Orsetta, for example, excited herself with the notion that her young servant was some kind of pagan savage. She lectured him about the blessings of baptism until, with the delicacy of a diplomat, Zuane gently explained that he had been baptised as a baby back home in the dark heart of the Dorsoduro district, just on the other side of the Grand Canal.

"Your mother thinks you hired Zuane for her," Cecilia said. "Wait till she finds out you hired him for yourself."

"Don't you be the one to tell her."

"I'll tell Zuane. So he'll be ready for you."

"You'd better teach him your button trick." Tiepolo squinted at her and picked up the board again. "Relax your hand on your thigh."

"You relax your hand on my thigh," she said. She inched up the sheet to expose her leg. Tiepolo stared at her with his big eyes popping. He put the drawing board down.

They named their first child Elena, after Tiepolo's favourite sister. To their second, they gave the name Anna Maria. Cattina, Ambrosio's wife, gave birth to a son around the time Anna Maria was born. She and Ambrosio named him Domenico, after his grandfather, the defunct Domenico Tiepolo, and put him into the general baby pool. Suddenly the house near the bridge was full of Tiepolo babies. Cecilia and Cattina and Orsetta ran after them from morning until night, not always sure which one they were cleaning or feeding or changing or comforting. Claudia came over to lend a hand, bringing Nicolò and Francesco, who added their boy energy to the mayhem. Tiepolo put his young brothers-in-law to work around the studio to keep them out of the way. It was one of their jobs to fly the babies in the putto sling.

You could never have enough putti in your sky, Tiepolo always said, quoting one of his teachers, Sebastiano Ricci. You could have too many clouds, too many overbearing angels, too much architecture blocking the view. But fat babies fluttering around on pigeon wings — these an artist could never overdo. Putti were adorable, classical. Nobody minded baby nudity. And they were funny: What other celestial being could you show peeing off a cloud? But most of all, they were versatile. You could put a putto anywhere and give him any job in a picture from rolling back the dawn to delivering a holy relic. A good painter needed to be able to paint putti well — there were many examples of beautiful pictures ruined by ugly, ungainly or badly drawn flying babies. Tiepolo's remedy was to go back to the source: real babies, his own.

"So that's why you're always wanting to make them," Cecilia said.

"That's why," Tiepolo said.

Tiepolo thought the perfect putto was about the age a human baby was when it learns to walk. Elena, their eldest child, was the first to walk and so she had the honour of being the first to fly. She went in the sling when she was eleven months old, held aloft by her young uncle Francesco. Cecilia improvised a sling arrangement out of three linen bands, one looped around the baby's chest and one around each leg, each wide enough not to dig into her doughy flesh. Elena cried the first time she was lifted aloft — she was naked, the studio was chilly — but Francesco rocked her gently back and forth while everyone in the room praised her. She soon began to enjoy herself, kicking her fat legs while Tiepolo and two of his most serious students sketched her. Cecilia watched from the sidelines holding the infant Domenico in her arms, to make sure nothing went wrong. Francesco tilted Elena's body upwards, as though she were ascending toward the rafters, then down, as if she were stooping to pluck a feather from the surface of the canal.

There was no doubt about it, having a family was improving Tiepolo's work. His putti were more attractive, more anatomically convincing, his women were more beautiful, blonder, plumper, more like Cecilia. He hung up his painting, *The Rape of Europa*, in the Campo San Rocco that summer and people commented on how much the ox-eyed young girl sitting on the bull resembled her. Antonio reported this to Cecilia, who was too busy with the children to attend the exhibition.

"There's a sort of myth brewing about you, you know." Antonio was holding a lamb cutlet in his fingers, chewing the meat off the bone. Her brother had a habit of dropping in around lunchtime, often staying until after dinner. Although so much had changed for Cecilia, little had changed for him.

"Do I have time for mythology?" Cecilia said, spooning rice into Elena's mouth while she held Domenico on her knee.

Antonio licked his fingers. "They call you his muse," he said. "What do you think about that?"

"Muse my eye," Cecilia said. "Just tell them my husband's too cheap to hire real models." Inside, she felt a sensual pride. It wasn't about muses. It was about freedom. Tiepolo was her husband and he could paint her any way he wanted: wearing a sheet, stark naked, standing on her hands with her rear in the air. He could paint their babies flying. That was their private family business. Nobody could say anything to him or to her about it now.

She surprised herself by wondering if Count Deboisville had

seen the painting of her sitting on the bull. It had been three years since the day he and his friends had cornered her in the street. Back then she had been a child, now she was a woman with wide hips and arms grown strong from lifting heavy babies. She was proud of the way she had grown and the things her powerful body had brought into being: healthy children, a satisfied man, a whole houseful of happy Tiepolos. Even Orsetta seemed content. With plenty of money coming in, the thousand-ducat loss was rarely mentioned. Her chief delight these days was to dress up in black taffeta and stroll in public places, attended by Zuane in yellow livery, making a display of her wealth and her leisure.

All this was a result of Cecilia's handiwork, and Tiepolo's. Together, they were making money and babies and prosperity for those around them. And for themselves. Sometimes Cecilia caught one of Tiepolo's young drawing students looking at her with naked longing and she understood: it wasn't just her body the young artists desired, it was more complicated than that. They wanted everything their master Tiepolo had and everything he had the power to create. They wanted her, Cecilia, because to them she was Tiepolo's creativity made flesh, the symbol and totem of his success. She was a prize that became more valuable every time it was seen by others, which is to say every time Tiepolo used her image in a painting.

But this wasn't what made Cecilia happy. She didn't believe in herself as a symbol — she didn't believe in symbols at all. She wasn't really the woman Tiepolo put into his paintings in so many guises, so many costumes. Others might believe it, but she knew better and so did Tiepolo. She modelled for him because it helped him and because it saved the family money. If she were honest, she also did it because she loved to be with him in the studio: painting was in her blood, in her background. She'd spent her childhood running in and out of studios. The minute she set foot in one, she felt at home. There were times when she felt closer to Tiepolo in the studio than in bed, or she felt a different kind of closeness that was just as intimate and just as satisfying.

"How did she find out?" Cecilia asked Zuane as he helped her waddle down the stairs after her incensed mother-in-law. She was so pregnant with their third child that she could hardly walk.

"Signora Cattina," Zuane said with displeasure, keeping a firm grip on Cecilia's arm.

"There are days when I would gladly wring that woman's neck," Cecilia muttered. When Cecilia first met her sister-in-law, she thought Cattina childlike and shy; she lisped when she talked and avoided eye contact. In fact she was several years older than Cecilia and had a grudging nature and an unhappy talent for stirring up trouble with Orsetta, especially when Ambrosio was away on business.

When they reached the studio, they saw Orsetta confronting Tiepolo before a large canvas propped on an easel. A quick look at the two of them told Cecilia this was serious. Orsetta's eyes, so like her son's, all but popped out of her head. Her mobile face twitched and her mouth worked, showing the gaps where she'd lost front teeth. Her face was flushed red, and the wattle under her pointed chin trembled.

"I forbid you to show this obscenity to anyone!" Orsetta cried. She was dressed like a lady in a day gown of black silk with a short cape over her shoulders and a white lace cap over her grey hair, but the sound of her voice could still make the washing lines vibrate.

During the first months of marriage to Tiepolo, Orsetta had waged more or less constant war against Cecilia, throwing mur-

derous glances, muttering criticisms under her breath and referring to Cecilia in the third person even when she was speaking
directly to her. "I suppose She will expect roast chicken again"
or "So She's decided to grace us with Her presence at last" or
"She seems to forget I hear every single word She says". Every
so often Orsetta's rage would break out into violence and she
would throw pots and slam chairs and bark orders like the tyrant
she was. When this happened, Cattina cowered and Orsetta sometimes struck her as though she were a servant, slapping the girl
with an open hand on the back and shoulders.

When this began, Cecilia stopped whatever she was doing and
stood up tall and still where she was, facing her mother-in-law.
She tried to remember that Orsetta's life had been hard and it
had hardened her. She'd lost her husband young, then lost her
inheritance to crooked lawyers — it was a familiar story in Venice.
But instead of caving in like Cecilia's mother had and letting herself sink into poverty, she'd spent two decades fighting: fighting
for justice in the courts, fighting to keep her five children from
starving, fighting to secure an apprenticeship for her talented
baby, her special darling, her hope: Tiepolo.

Holding on to this knowledge gave Cecilia calm in the face of
Orsetta's rages. Perhaps for this reason, Orsetta never dared to
strike her.

Gradually things changed for Orsetta. The babies came, and
the money came, and then Zuane, who, for Orsetta, was a living
sign to the world that she was now a woman of means. Little by
little the old lady started to turn more of her domestic duties over
to Cecilia (never to Cattina, whom she considered to be dull-wit-
ted) and spend more time out of the house. Yet Cecilia knew the
harpy in Orsetta was only resting. Now she observed that, yes,
Orsetta's hooked nose was very like a beak. Her arms, flapping
beneath her short black cape, resembled wings.

"I don't care how much Don Hoopdeehoopdeehoo paid you for it," she shouted. "It is not leaving this house. Everyone who sees it will know!"

"What will they know, Mama?" Tiepolo stood beside her, looking down at the canvas in question as though it were a harmless basket of puppies. His face wore an expression of forced neutrality, but no trace of agitation. Tiepolo wasn't afraid of his mother. The assistants, on the other hand, were terrified. They had fled the studio when she came sweeping in and Cecilia guessed they were cowering downstairs in the workshop.

Zuane found Cecilia a chair and she gratefully lowered herself onto it, preparing to watch the way Tiepolo dealt with his mother. After four years of marriage, she was still learning this art. Tiepolo's air of innocence was a good tactic, for starters. Orsetta was slightly deflated by her son's mild reply. "What will they know?" she said in a slightly quieter voice. "They'll know Tiepolo painted it."

"But surely that's what we want," he said. He pointed to a spot in the corner of the canvas. "See, I even put my name on it." Tiepolo allowed himself a humourous glance over his shoulder at Cecilia.

"Don't you mock me, little boy. I may be old but I'm not blind." Orsetta poked her finger at the picture. "I can see as well as you can that it's *Her*. Sitting there stark naked with all those men standing around with their tongues hanging out. Soldiers! It's disgusting. It's wrong."

"Her?" Tiepolo looked puzzled. "Who's 'her'?"

"Your wife!"

"Oh, that's not me," Cecilia chimed in. She was still slightly breathless from her trip down the stairs. "How often do you see me lounging around like that?"

Orsetta seemed to see her for the first time. "Ha!" she shrilled and pointed a crooked finger at Cecilia. "Listen to Her. I see Her lounging around plenty, plenty. Like right now." Orsetta glared at Cecilia who settled more comfortably onto her chair and smiled, running a hand over the grand dome of her belly. "There She sits."

"But you're mistaken. It's not me, Mother," Cecilia said. "Is it, Tiepolo?"

"No, no." Tiepolo maintained his air of blamelessness. Cecilia remembered it from the day the *sbirri* caught him drawing on the walls, a look of open innocence behind which there was a world of knowing. She smiled: her husband was so clever.

Orsetta put her hands on her hips and squared up to her son. "If it's not her, then who is it?"

Tiepolo seemed to think. "I can't remember her name. It's a strange one. Starts with a C." Tiepolo blinked his big eyes.

"Campaspe," Cecilia said.

"That was it. Yes. Campaspe."

"Never heard of her in my life," Orsetta said. "You're making it up."

Cecilia tried to explain. "The story is that an artist, Apelles, was commissioned by Alexander the Great to paint his mistress, a girl called Campaspe. When he saw the portrait, Alexander the Great was so bowled over by Apelles' genius that he gave Campaspe to him. It's a popular subject."

"Ridiculous and scandalous!" Orsetta stamped her foot. "Trading a woman for art. It's nothing short of pagan!"

Cecilia was inclined to agree. But such a transaction would never happen under any circumstances. The patron would just take the painting and the woman, while the painter would be lucky to get paid on time. She had said as much while she was sitting for Tiepolo, with her shift sliding off her shoulder and her body twisted at an uncomfortable angle to hide her big belly.

Tiepolo shrugged. "A commission is a commission, Mother. I don't invent these stories, I just paint them."

"So that naked woman isn't Her?" Orsetta said suspiciously. She could tell they were humouring her.

"How could it be?" Tiepolo said.

Orsetta changed tack. She crossed herself and said, "Merciful God, that means you had some polluted actress sitting naked down here. In our very own home. And you've dragged poor Zuane into it. Look, there he is, right there, leaning against the easel, and his soul barely saved. Shame on you!"

"There was nobody in here but the master and me!" protested Zuane. "What does she take me for?"

"Don't worry," Cecilia whispered to him. "Tiepolo will handle it — oh!" She felt a sudden pang deep in her body. It was a familiar feeling by now, after two babies. She judged its intensity and guessed she had a few more hours. There was no need to rush.

Tiepolo leaned in toward his own picture, narrowed his eyes and said, "Does that really look like Zuane to you?"

It was obvious to Cecilia that Tiepolo had amused himself with this painting. It was full of his little visual jokes. There was Zuane in yellow leaning comfortably against the easel, his olive-shaped head in profile. And there was their noisy little black and white dog, Gabbiano, at Zuane's feet, staring straight out of the frame, wearing a little red bow around his neck and looking as though he might trot up and beg a treat.

Cecilia recognised herself, of course; Tiepolo had decorated her body, placing a jewelled diadem around her hair and a gold circlet on her stout upper arm. One of Tiepolo's usual models, an out-of-work actor, sat for the figure of Alexander, wearing a red cloak from the studio property box and a crown of bay leaves borrowed from the kitchen.

But the real giveaway, the thing that told Cecilia that this picture was for fun, was the figure of Apelles, the painter. It was obviously a self-portrait of Tiepolo. He sat at the easel, looking over his shoulder at Campaspe, wearing a furry oriental hat. Tiepolo hadn't disguised or flattered himself when he painted his slantwise nose, his big goggle eyes and his scruffy studio clothes. Apelles gawped at Campaspe, whose bare breast was turned away from the viewer, toward him, with a look of desperate lust. In his hand he held a brush, its tip tumescent with pink paint, poised near the canvas to define her rosy nipple. Cecilia knew this look so well she could have painted it herself.

The comedy of the painting infected her. She began to feel giddy. "My objection is that hat," she said out of the blue. At the same moment, she felt another pang in her gut, stronger than before. For reasons she couldn't have named, she began to giggle uncontrollably. "My husband can never resist a silly hat!"

"The hat?" Tiepolo looked at her curiously. "What's wrong with the hat? It's classical. I was thinking of Rembrandt."

Cecilia rocked with laughter. It helped with the pain. "It looks like a silk-lined dead cat!" The chair tipped with her weight. She felt Zuane put his hands on her shoulders to steady her.

"Signora?" Zuane said.

Orsetta glared at her. "What's the matter with your wife?" the old lady asked accusingly. "Is She laughing at me?"

Cecilia couldn't stop. "Where's Rembrandt's cat?" she cried. "On Rembrandt's head!"

"She's unhinged!" Orsetta stormed. "She's lost her reason!"

Tears rolled down Cecilia's cheeks and something inside her seemed to surge upwards, then break. Liquid flowed between her legs and pooled on the seat of the chair. She was laughing so hard she had to close her eyes and didn't see the others scrambling to help her.

The midwife came but they couldn't get Cecilia up the stairs in time. She delivered the baby boy in a storeroom off the studio. The child was big, but he slid out like a fish down a chute and it occurred to Cecilia that she was getting good at this. They called him Domenico, despite Cattina's protests that her boy was already called that. Cecilia pointed out that her father had been called Domenico as well. There were two grandfathers named Domenico so it followed that two Domenicos in one house was not too many. Cecilia thought she might name all her sons Domenico, just for fun. It would make it so easy to call them in for meals.

When the smallpox epidemic swept through the city, Cattina's Domenico was the first to die.

His illness followed a pattern known to every Venetian. The two-year-old complained of a headache in the morning and by midday the fever came. After two days, the fever abated, and poor little Domenico sat up again and seemed better. Cattina, still pretending, brought him downstairs to eat in the kitchen. By that evening, the blisters began to appear on the toddler's face and the adults could not pretend anymore not to know what the sickness was. After that the oval blisters rose like hard bubbles to the surface of the boy's soft skin, tiny and few at first, as in a pot of water set on the fire, then faster and larger until, after three days, the child's body was boiling with pustules. When these slipped over his lips and broke out on the wet pink membranes of his mouth, his throat swelled closed and he stopped breathing.

Cattina's Domenico died on the fourth day. Cecilia's Domenico died three days later. He was three months old and went quickly, mercifully. Two weeks after that, Elena, Cecilia's airborne girl, died after a long struggle.

Only Anna Maria, her middle girl, held on. Cecilia sat by her little daughter's bed day after day in a kind of trance. Anna Maria was the only one left in the children's bedroom now, but her tiny, suffering body seemed to fill the whole house. She seemed enormous to Cecilia, magnified by sickness until there was nothing left in the world but Anna Maria and her pain. Like a woman in a dream, Cecilia watched the blisters invade her daughter's skin, gathering force, growing larger, reddening, breaking open, weeping, releasing the sharp stink that penetrated every room in the house. When the girl's small body was one great red dry crust of scabs, like that of a child flayed and left in the sun, Cecilia prepared herself for another death. But one day Orsetta came in, took one look at the little girl and announced, "She's going to live."

Cecilia stared at her. "No," she said. "She can't live."

"She will, I tell you. Have I been wrong so far?" Here she paused and studied Cecilia's face. "Why are you looking at me in that accusing way? You should be thanking God."

But Cecilia didn't feel thankful. She didn't know if thanks were due.

Six other children died in their street that autumn; across the city about a quarter of the children under five succumbed. Orsetta made this calculation and declared it to be better than you could expect from an outbreak. In other years, smallpox had claimed two-thirds of the city's children and scarred the other third for life. The priest's view was that children shouldn't be given names until the smallpox had come through and done its work. People felt the loss less, he said, when the little ones died nameless.

Teresa, Luca, Giacomo, Paolina, Elisabetta, Jacopo. Cecilia knew the names of all the dead children and recited them to herself in a litany. Children were common property in the street near the bridge. She had held every one of them in her arms, picked them up when they fell over, wiped their snotty noses and sat with them while their mothers ran to the baker's. Her neighbours had done the same for her children. Teresa, Luca, Giacomo, Paolina, Elisabetta, Jacopo, Domenico, Domenico, Elena. The names rang in her head. Such beautiful names, such beautiful children. Had she forgotten any? Had any died nameless? Cecilia vowed to remember the children but she could hardly bring herself to look at their mothers now, or at Cattina, who stumbled through the rooms like a sleepwalker. When they passed one another in the street, the other mothers avoided each other's eyes like women who have been shamed in some terrible public humiliation.

The cold weather set in. The fog crept across the city, dulling the outlines of the buildings and cloaking distant views. Zuane burned the children's clothes and the sheets from their sickbeds, tipping the ashes into the canal. Cecilia brought Anna Maria downstairs for the first time and sat her on a woven mat in front of the fire. The little girl couldn't bear clothes on her raw skin, and so they kept the fire burning hot and they let her sit there naked, playing with the dog. She smiled at the sight of Gabbiano, her first smile in weeks, cracking the scabs on her cheeks. She clutched him passionately to her chest, then pushed him violently away with a cry because the contact hurt. Orsetta crouched down to examine the scabs.

"Well, she's still with us," she pronounced expertly. "And she always will be." She crossed herself and chucked Anna Maria under the chin. Anna Maria flinched at her touch.

Cecilia knew what her mother-in-law meant. Smallpox survivors were a common sight in Venice. Cecilia had seen them often, some so scarred they looked like people whose clothes had been set alight. It was mostly the men you noticed because they didn't bother to conceal their scars. Girls went out veiled, if they went out at all. The worst cases hid away at home or in convents. They never married. Cecilia looked at her surviving daughter and instead of feeling joy, she felt a wordless rage. It wasn't over. God had not delivered Anna Maria from anything. Her suffering was just beginning.

When the children fell ill, Cecilia moved out of the room she shared with Tiepolo and went to sleep in their room. Nobody questioned this. At night she curled her tall body up on the cramped child's bed next to her daughter's and lay listening to Anna Maria's ragged breathing. She longed to reach out and run her hands over the little girl's ravaged skin, smoothing it the way a potter polishes a jar until its surface is like glass. Isn't that the way she had shaped her children to begin with? Stroking and squeezing and kissing their sweet bodies into perfection? But Anna Maria slept badly and no longer liked to be touched or cuddled. The slightest disturbance roused her to a loud half-conscious wail that could take hours to quiet.

Cecilia didn't sleep; her breasts hurt her. Her babies were dead and her mind knew this, but her stubborn, animal body didn't know it for a long time. Without babies to drink her milk, her breasts were like aching, silken sacks packed with stones. She bound them with linen and laid cool damp leaves on her nipples to ease the pain. But when a baby cried anywhere in the night, the sweet liquid cascaded down, soaking her shift, leaving stiff patches where it dried on the fabric. She had the impulse to get up and walk the streets until she had found the hungry baby and offered it the little nourishment and comfort she had left to give.

While the children were dying, Cecilia hardly saw Tiepolo. There was nothing strange about this; women usually looked after the sick while men went on working. He was present at the important moments. He stood beside her at the burials and watched the tiny bundles containing their ravaged children lowered into a common pit where their playmates already lay. He didn't cry

— or Cecilia didn't remember him crying. She didn't cry either.

Afterwards, he was patient with her, or at least he didn't make any demands. Now that Anna Maria was gaining strength, she should have returned to her own bed, but Cecilia made no move to do so. Tiepolo became a man she heard rather than one she saw or touched.

She listened for him when he went to bed at night, moving up the stairs and pausing, just perceptibly, just for a moment, in front of the door to her room. She heard him get up in the morning and go thumping down the stairs to the kitchen with his characteristic tread, so heavy for such a small man. She imagined the kitchen girl giving him bread and a cup of chocolate, his one daily luxury. Then he would go straight to the studio on the second floor and put on his dirty coat with the mangy fur lining, the one Cecilia had forbidden him to go out in, when she cared about such things. He'd place some kind of hat on his head, thinking of Rembrandt, and have the assistant lay a small fire in the stove to dry the air and keep the paint from freezing. What was he working on now? Cecilia had no idea, and no interest in knowing. It had been weeks since she had gone down to the studio to see what was happening. None of that had anything to do with her now.

Gradually, the thought of Tiepolo working began to gnaw at Cecilia. He hadn't missed even a single day in the studio, not when the children were dying, not when they were dead. It was what Cecilia would have expected of him, what, indeed, she would have urged him to do under normal circumstances. But now she convinced herself that this dedication to work proved Tiepolo was heartless: he thought business was more important than children; he thought children could be replaced. They often joked about how much he liked making babies. Obviously he thought the answer to losing your children was just to make more of them.

One morning, two months after the children died, Cecilia heard Tiepolo singing as he went down the stairs. She sat up in bed and listened for a moment. Then she sprang to the door and yanked it open, catching him halfway down the flight of stairs.

"Can you be quiet," she hissed. "Anna Maria hardly slept."

He froze and stared up at her, wide-eyed, startled, hurt.

She went on. She couldn't stop herself. "I can't believe you're singing! In the morning!" She wanted to scream at him, *Don't you know our children are dead? I can't even remember what music sounds like!* "What's the matter with you?"

"I'm sorry," he said. "I wasn't thinking."

"And try not to stomp down the stairs. It shakes the landing." She closed the door again and turned back into the room. Anna Maria sat up in bed and looked at her before unleashing a bad-tempered wail.

As the days passed, the little girl grew stronger. She was like a starving bird, her mouth always open for food, her hands reaching to snatch biscuits and bits of cheese. Everyone in the household indulged her, passing her little treats and devising games to make her smile, which she did rarely, and mostly at the dog. All eyes were on her, willing her to be gay, to bring happiness back into the house. But the more the adults coaxed her, the more sombre Anna Maria became. Cecilia thought of the Venetian sailors who returned home having suffered torture or served as galley slaves or been badly wounded in battle. They were empty-eyed, unsmiling, hollow-seeming. They had lost something essential of themselves and it never came back. Anna Maria, returning from her own ordeal, was like this, a diminished creature whose natural joy had been damaged by disease, then cut away in order to save her life. In the raking winter sunlight, her cheeks resembled pink peaches eaten by insects. When Cecilia put her arms around her, Anna Maria pushed her away. That made sense to Cecilia, since mothers, for children, make the world. This was the world Cecilia had made for Anna Maria.

About this time, Cecilia began to make herself invisible. It was a gradual process that started with her slipping away when no one was looking. With the children dead, there was much less to do around the house and on quiet afternoons she'd put on her cloak and go out alone. The first few times she carried a basket over her arm so that she could claim to be running errands. But nobody challenged her and later she left the basket behind.

She walked like a woman in a hurry, but she had nowhere to go. It was mid-winter and there were few people on the streets. She pressed through cold white fog or rain sheeting down between the buildings. The wooden soles of her winter pattens clattered against the wet cobblestones. Sometimes, the wind and tide drew the cold grey lagoon water up out of the canals, flooding the pavement and turning the *campi* into shallow pools that had to be crossed on wooden duckboards.

Even when the water was high, Cecilia went out, moving instinctively, taking turns at random. She tended to head westwards because she knew that the city stretched farther in this direction, so there was farther to travel. Their house was in the *sestiere* of Castello, near the tail of the fish-shaped city. Cecilia navigated in the direction of the head — Dorsoduro — ending up in strange squares, in front of churches dedicated to saints she had hardly heard of. She came to dead ends at canals where the bridge had rotted away or been moved elsewhere. Without warning, she'd emerge onto the wide, paved quay facing the sea and, with the freezing wind hitting her square in the face, she'd stare out at the green, agitated water of the lagoon where a multitude of ships rode at anchor, their masts naked of sail.

One freezing day, a client of Tiepolo's recognised her. She was far from home, near the Rialto Bridge, when he caught sight of her and tried to speak to her. She fled. After that, she bought herself a mask to cover her features. This was a second-hand *moretta*, a round, black velvet shell that covered the face completely the way a lid covered a pot. Cecilia had never owned a mask before and she was surprised to find this one had no straps or fastenings but stayed in place by means of a button clamped between the teeth. The second-hand clothes dealer she bought it from told her that the button was there to keep girls from speaking, which made them more attractive. When Cecilia took the bit in her mouth for the first time she tasted stale garlic, old fish, the ghost of the lunch of the girl who owned it before her. What had happened to that girl? Cecilia decided she must have died. She loved the way the mask curved to fit her face, blocking out her individuality and giving her privacy. When she put it on she felt a sense of security she hadn't known in a long time.

When she got home, she'd hide the mask under the mattress of her bed in Anna Maria's room. In the night, the thought of it there comforted her, a soft velvet hole into which it was safe to crawl.

One day, Cattina caught Cecilia hiding the *moretta*. She appeared suddenly, standing in the doorway. "What's that?" she said.

"Nothing," Cecilia said, pretending to arrange the bedclothes. "Do you need something?" Cecilia could still taste the bit of the *moretta*; it tasted of silence. It was an effort to open her mouth and produce words.

Cattina hesitated. Recently she had begun to act as though she were afraid of Cecilia. "No. It's just that your brother came to see you while you were out."

"Did you feed him?"

"Of course." Cattina shrugged. Cecilia observed the way her

sister-in-law had changed since the children died. Her sallow face had never been pretty but now it was haggard and exhausted. There were smudges beneath the eyes so dark they looked like bruises. Her curly hair, pulled back tightly from her forehead, was sparse and dry. There were new lines etched across her wide brow. Cattina looked old, Cecilia realised. So, certainly, must she. Perhaps they should all be wearing masks now.

Her body shrank. The winter air was heavy with mist, the streets were saturated and walking often became wading, but Cecilia herself was drying up like an apricot in the sun. Her milk stopped flowing. She was sad to see it go. She never felt more sufficient than when she was feeding one of her children but the milk, the sufficiency, went when they did; she never expected to see either return.

The new year came. Ambrosio, Antonio, Tiepolo, and two of Tiepolo's students got drunk on some good red wine one of Tiepolo's clients had given him. They sat up late in the parlour, playing cards and making noise. Sometime during the night, Cecilia woke to find Tiepolo standing in the doorway of the room where she slept with Anna Maria. *How predictable,* she thought, her heart beating quickly. He called her name. It crossed her mind that she should put an end to this; she should go to him. She should take his hand and accompany him across the landing. She should stretch out in her comfortable marriage bed and press the length of her body against his radiant male warmth. For the first time in months, she felt a stirring of desire. Willfully, she crushed it.

"Go away," she said in voice that sounded like it belonged to someone else. "You're drunk. It's disgusting."

Husbands beat their wives black and blue for saying things like that. Cecilia wondered if Tiepolo would strike her now. She imagined the whole house waking to the sounds of his violence. The rest of them would back him up — Orsetta, Cattina, Ambrosio, the maids, Zuane, even little Anna Maria — they were all sick of Cecilia's moping. But Tiepolo just closed the door and retreated across the landing.

Alone in the dark, she began to wonder why he had given up so easily.

One freezing afternoon Cecilia saw Tron arm in arm with Deboisville, strolling across the Campo San Polo. She stopped in her tracks and stared at them out of the vacant eyeholes of her *moretta*, wondering if she were dreaming. The two men wore splendid brocade coats lined with fur. The fog beaded like drops of mercury on the felt of their black hats. They passed within a few feet of Cecilia without sparing her a second glance. She had the impulse to run after them, to tear off her mask and go with them wherever they felt like taking her. What would it matter now if she gave herself to them? What did she have to lose? She could take another name, a whore's name, and claim the life she had refused when she became Tiepolo's wife. Putting your babies in a basket and pushing them through the hatch at the Ospedaletto could not be worse than watching them die of smallpox. Perhaps that was why whores always seemed so carefree. There were certain kinds of suffering they never had to live through.

Tron and Deboisville turned a corner and disappeared and with them went the idea of moving backwards in time. Now Cecilia could only move forward. The trouble was, she couldn't imagine what might lie ahead.

On the Molo, the long commercial quay facing the lagoon, Cecilia watched the merchant ships unload their goods. When she was small, this sight made her heart race with delight. Sailors and merchants swarmed over the wharf. Men threw bundles, casks, baskets, bolts of cloth wrapped in hemp sleeves, leather trunks and coils of rope from the boats, lobbing them through the air in precise arcs, timed to be caught by other men standing on the quayside. Like all Venetian children, she knew the ships were unloading the riches of the world — silk, perfume, lace, wine, pearls, porcelain, fragrant wood, chocolate, pigment, finely made swords. These treasures came from Constantinople, the Lebanon, Armenia, as far away as China. Because of the ships, the world's wealth flowed through Venice like water and, as a child, Cecilia had always felt a rapacious thirst for it. She longed to unpack all the bundles, to pry the lid off every barrel, to unroll every bolt of cloth, to unlock every trunk and to possess every single thing she found inside.

But now as she watched the activity on the quay, she wondered how people could want these things, how they could bear to go on piling them up in their houses, cramming them in their mouths, wrapping them around their bodies. They should ban the ships, she thought wildly, burn the fleet, shut the port. They should allow Venice to rest, just rest, in its green lagoon, starving itself back into purity. And once it was purified, they should dismantle the city, pulling down the palazzos and the tenements and returning every stone to its quarry, extracting each deep, dirty piling as though it were a blackened tooth and letting the canals flow together, free of their channels, merging into swampland, reed-choked, home to tiny fish and flocks of marsh birds. No people should be permitted to live there anymore, that was the main thing; no people to love and hope and suffer.

Claudia came to see Cecilia. She came alone, without the boys, and Cecilia knew her mother had been sent for, probably by Orsetta, to see what she could do with her surly, disappearing daughter-in-law.

"Have you come to take me back?" was the first thing Cecilia asked her mother when they were alone. Claudia had proposed a trip to the bakery a few streets away where they sold the little nut cakes she liked so well. Anna Maria trundled along between them, one small hand held by each woman.

Claudia looked guilty. "What a thing to say!"

"It wouldn't surprise me." Cecilia said, watching the eyes of passers-by to see if they stared at Anna Maria's scars, ready to challenge them. "Everyone knows Orsetta is an exacting lady. If a piece of merchandise doesn't come up to scratch, you can be sure she'll march straight back to the shop and get her money back. It must be obvious to everyone by now that I'm faulty."

Claudia looked at her wordlessly. In the new red cloak Cecilia had given her for her saint's day she looked a different woman from the one who cried over the Count's salad. Cecilia's marriage to Tiepolo had transformed Claudia's life. The rent was always paid now; Francesco and Nicolò both had apprenticeships, and Cecilia was blessed — that was the word Claudia always used before the children died — beyond all expectations.

"My sweet girl," Claudia said. "It hurts me when you speak to me so harshly." Her eyes filled with tears.

"Oh, here we go." Cecilia wanted to prevent her mother from saying whatever it was she had been coached to say. Cecilia guessed Orsetta had been to see her and the two of them had mapped out the problem of Cecilia. Both ladies had much to lose if Cecilia failed them now. "We've had enough tears to last a lifetime. You don't see me crying, do you?"

Claudia shook her head. "No. You're not crying. But…"

"Then what am I doing!" Cecilia almost shouted. "What am I doing that's so bad?" She knew the answer. She wondered if her mother would come out and say it. Anna Maria looked up at her with a worried expression.

Claudia noticed the child's look. "How about a swing, Anna Maria?" she suggested. "Come on, my darling, take my hand and your Mama and I will swing you like a bright little bell. One, two — three!"

They swung the little girl all the way to the bakery and through the door. The kind baker made much of Anna Maria and they bought six of his sweet cakes. They sat outside on a bench in the minute campo while Anna Maria played around the wellhead, chewing her treat. It was a cool day, but the sky was clear and the air was soft. A swallow dipped low over a roof. Spring was on its way.

"I'm sorry," Cecilia said watching the swallow tuck itself under the eaves of the building opposite.

Her mother sounded hurt. "You think I've come to lecture you. But when did I ever lecture? Even when I should have, I never did. Maybe it's because I don't speak this language so well." She sighed. "What can I say to you, my darling, clever girl?"

"Nothing. Please. I can guess what you'd say anyway."

"Oh, then that spares me the trouble of saying it." She reached out and squeezed her daughter's arm. She clucked her tongue. "Too bony! Have another cake." Cecilia took the cake and placed it in her mouth.

"Do you remember Iseppo?" her mother asked suddenly.

"Iseppo who?"

"Our Iseppo. You were two when he was born, four when he died."

Cecilia swallowed with difficulty. "I don't remember him."

"That's all right. You were very small. Do you remember Angela? You were six when she was born. No?"

Cecilia shook her head, fighting a pain that rose up from deep inside her, a very old, dark hurt.

"That surprises me. You were very upset at the time. Those were hard years. But then we had Francesco, and then Nicolò came along. Though I was always sorry I never got another lovely little girl." Claudia reached up and stroked the side of Cecilia's face. Cecilia pulled away abruptly from her mother's touch, but it was too late.

It had been weeks since Cecilia had actually cried. The tears seemed to be forced out of her eyes by a choking pressure in her throat. "I thought I was doing so well," she babbled.

"You were," Claudia crooned. "So well. And you can do well again. These things happen."

"No," she shook her head. "No. I used to think we could just go on having them, that we could have as many as we wanted. But I can't do it — I can't go on. I can't ever do that again."

She felt Claudia move closer to her and slide her arm around her shoulders. "My sweet Cecilia. My beautiful dove," she said. "I'm not going to say you have to be strong. Look at me. I'm not strong at all. I was no good to anyone after your father died and you know that better than anyone. But that was different. When you lose a child, you lose part of yourself. When you lose a husband, you lose your whole world."

Celia stopped crying and sat up abruptly. "What do you mean by that? What did Orsetta tell you?"

Claudia looked embarrassed. "She told me you are still sleeping in the children's room."

"She told you that?" Cecilia stood up. Fighting the impulse to turn and rush away, losing herself in the city, she faced her mother. "That is nobody's business but mine. How dare she discuss such a thing with you!"

"She's worried about you — your future. She's worried about Tiepolo."

"Worried! I'll give that woman something to worry about!"

"Darling! Keep your voice down."

"She's happy to see me brought down. She's always hated me."

"That's not it, Cecilia. That's not it at all!"

Cecilia caught sight of Anna Maria peeking at them from behind the bulging stone body of the well. The child looked worried. Cecilia waved at her, then lowered her voice. "What's wrong with you old women? I've watched my children *die*."

Claudia was quick to answer. "So have we. Me and Orsetta, too."

"Orsetta?"

"Two of them. Just like you, just like every woman in this filthy, disease-ridden city." A righteous tone crept into Claudia's voice. "Father Bernard says he hardly has a woman in his congregation who hasn't buried at least one child. Some have buried all of them."

"That's supposed to shame me, is it? Humble me?"

Claudia reached up to her. "It's supposed to help you."

Cecilia pulled away. Her mother set her mouth in a determined line. "Just so long as you realise a normal young husband won't wait forever. Eventually they make — other arrangements. You know what I mean. Then everyone ends up in hell. Him, her, whoever she is, and you." She threw up her hands as though the game was up. "I'm sure you don't want that."

Claudia's warning planted a seed in Cecilia's mind. Whenever Tiepolo left the house, Cecilia followed him with her eyes, wondering where he was really going. *Other arrangements*. Claudia meant other women. God knew women were plentiful enough in Venice, not only prostitutes but fairly respectable women who would happily take a lover like Tiepolo. His fame was growing; he had plenty of money and if he wasn't good-looking he was certainly young and vigourous. More vigourous than any of them would suspect, Cecilia guessed.

As the spring warmed into summer, people shed their cloaks and strolled in the squares, sporting their best clothes. Flower sellers appeared on the street and the canals began to send up their characteristic pong. Cecilia was forced to put away her *moretta* — nobody in the city wore masks after Lent. This put an end to her long rambles. She stayed at home and took more of a hand in the housework. Cattina was pregnant again — Ambrosio had come home from the sea for long enough to make sure of it — and struggling through the first months of nausea. Her early morning retching sounded like a reproach to Cecilia. She held the bowl for her sister-in-law when she vomited and with her free hand gathered Cattina's dark curls away from her face to keep them clean. She was aware of Orsetta watching her, so she kept her face perfectly still, revealing nothing.

After that one midwinter night, Tiepolo had made no serious attempt to coax her into bed. Sometimes, at meals, she caught him looking at her with an expression she couldn't read. She knew it wasn't lust. Was it pity? Was it disgust? She supposed she had grown ugly; her body had dwindled until it was smaller than before she was married. Her belly was a bowl curving inward from her pelvic bones and her clothes hung slackly from her shoulders, like clothes belonging to another woman. She took no trouble over her hair or her hands. She washed infrequently. This was part of being absent, although she was still there.

She speculated that Tiepolo might be afraid of her. Orsetta thought Cecilia had lost her reason and said so to anyone who would listen. All of her mother-in-law's resentment against her seemed to re-awaken now and Cecilia overheard Orsetta tell Cattina that, when the baby was born, they would send Cecilia away so that she "wouldn't be tempted to harm it". A year before, Cecilia would have flown at her mother-in-law for saying such an evil thing. Now, she merely accepted it as the consequence of not doing everything they wanted. Orsetta had an idea about the criminal envy of childless women. She wasn't alone. It was possible that Tiepolo saw her this way too, that now he thought of her as a kind of witch, dangerous to have in the house.

One warm day, as Cecilia was going downstairs to return a bucket to the studio, she unexpectedly met Tiepolo on the stairs, coming up.

"Cecilia," he said huskily. He had never liked using her Christian name and it sounded strange coming out of his mouth. "I thought you should know."

"What?" She looked down into the wooden bucket she was carrying. It was lined with dark leather, still wet from the scrub water.

"I'm going to be away for a few weeks."

"Oh."

For the first time in a long time, she caught a whiff of him, his working smell. It was a strong mixture of male sweat and turpentine, chalk dust, linseed oil, and the mineral, chemical tang of pigments. Cecilia had often found this scent transferred to her own body. There had been times when she made a point of letting it linger on her skin, a mark of Tiepolo's ownership. Just now, it smelled like danger.

"Did you hear what I said?"

"You're going away for a few weeks. I assume it's a job. Is it far?" She felt as though she couldn't breathe; he was standing too close.

"Not far, just at the Corte dell'Albero , off the Grand Canal. I'm painting a little ceiling for the Sandis."

"That's no distance," she said flatly. Questions arose in her mind: *Why do you have to go there? Why can't you work from home?* and, *Why don't you help me get out of this?* She pressed her lips together to prevent herself from speaking, or kissing him, thus undoing the work of months. Tiepolo was leaving her. Wasn't that what she wanted? She saw no other remedy.

"Won't you miss me?" The childlike note in Tiepolo's voice took Cecilia by surprise. The two of them had never been given to lover's talk. Tiepolo didn't tease or flatter or pretend to be wounded when he wasn't. Likewise, Cecilia had never required him to stoke her vanity with words. So she knew how much it cost him to ask her this question and what he risked from her answer. Out of respect for him, she remained silent, staring into the empty bucket.

"All right," he sighed. He backed against the banister, holding his body as far away from hers as possible. She passed him without looking at his face.

That was when she knew Tiepolo had given up on her. She was twenty-one and her career as Signora Tiepolo was over.

W as that her? Cecilia craned her neck to see a pale woman riding in a gondola, her pale, powdered face seeming to float in the darkness of the cabin.

Or was that her? Cecilia evaluated the pretty girl hawking water scented with pomegranate syrup in the shade of an awning.

All summer long, everywhere she went, Cecilia saw Tiepolo's mistress. She spotted her at the market, shoveling summer beans into her basket, fine tendrils of hair curling against her long neck. She saw her in the campo, wafting her flushed cheeks with a sandalwood fan. At mass, she spotted her kneeling in a front pew, wearing a dark lace veil that left only her chin and her pink mouth visible. Her full lips moved as she begged God's forgiveness for loving Cecilia's husband.

Once Cecilia had allowed herself to conjure up the other woman, she found her rival was legion, like the demons in the Bible story, shape shifting, everywhere. She had brown hair, blond hair, even grey. She was tall, short, skeletal, or corpulent. She dressed well; she went about in rags — these things, Cecilia knew now, had little importance for men. Her skin was white, pink, black, brown, pocked, or smooth. She put on peasant clothes and danced the *furlana* for money in the street or she worked as an acrobat, wearing white stockings that showed every inch of her plump, sensuous legs.

Some things were certain about the other woman: she was never sad or difficult. She was joyful, replete with charm, unharried. Cecilia heard her laughter echoing down the narrow streets and ringing in the curved spaces under the bridges. She smelled her perfume on the breeze. The sweet sound of her singing drifted down from open windows. Cecilia concluded that there was a fatal amount of beauty in Venice. It was only a matter of time before Tiepolo reached out for some of it, if he hadn't already.

In the end, impatient, Cecilia's imagination chose the right woman for her husband. She knew that none of the ordinary women she saw were good enough to be Tiepolo's mistress. Tiepolo's woman would never be seen in the streets. Rather, she would be one of the special, invisible women, a privileged noble lady, rich, who never went out in public. In Cecilia's imagination, this woman had auburn hair and a bed covered in dark blue satin. She lived in the Corte dell'Albero and her bedroom looked out over the Grand Canal. All morning, she preened her satiny loveliness in the cool shadowed rooms of her palazzo. Servants tended her hair, her feet, while the best cooks prepared a feast of Tiepolo's favourite foods: whitefish in orange sauce, summer berries, pale Friulian wine.

Cecilia knew her husband; this was part of the problem. She tortured herself with the knowledge, envisioning exactly how Tiepolo would eat and drink and then throw himself into making love, happily and gratefully taking every pleasure the woman had to offer. The man wasted nothing you gave him. No one could know that better than she. Afterwards Tiepolo and his mistress would lounge on the bed and watch the ribbon-like reflections from the canal racing across the ceiling.

As Cecilia elaborated this scene in her imagination, the ceiling gradually became the one Tiepolo had gone to the Corte dell'Albero in order to paint. What was the subject? Mentally, she extemporised a design of blue sky and fat golden clouds, each one the bed of a sleek goddess sprawled in a lascivious position. Each goddess had auburn hair and wore an expression of carnal satisfaction.

A week passed. Two. Tiepolo stayed away and, though messages went back and forth from the studio to the job site, no word came for Cecilia. Now she was certain: she had been replaced. It was so easy for men to do — and who would blame Tiepolo? As long as he provided for her and Anna Maria, no one in the whole world would protest.

She experienced a new kind of pain, different from the one she felt when her children died, but continuous with it, like a new room built on an old house. She had willfully sent Tiepolo away and this was the inevitable result. Claudia and Orsetta had both warned her. It was done now. She told herself that this pain she felt was the last requirement, the final sacrifice. All she had to do was get through it and the problem of Tiepolo would go away just as abruptly as it had arisen, that day so long ago when Antonio took her to the Campo San Rocco and she met him displaying his dangerous Red Sea. That was the past: gone. What was her future to be without him, then? Where would she go?

Cecilia shocked herself: the first place she went as an abandoned wife was straight to the palazzo at the Corte dell'Albero.

She didn't plan to do it. One sultry day in August, her little brother Francesco poked his head through the kitchen door. He had come from the worksite at the Corte dell'Albero in a boat with Tiepolo's assistant, Vincente. He was covered with fine, white dust, like a sweet brown bun powdered with sugar. She kissed his warm cheek and tasted gypsum. "When did you get so tall?" she said.

"You always say that," he said, sliding out of her grasp. "Where's the medium-sized ladder? Down in the studio they said you had it up here."

Cecilia helped her brother look for the ladder and they found it in a third floor bedroom — Orsetta had lent it to a workman fixing tiles on the roof. Together she and Francesco eased it around the turnings of three flights of stairs. Cecilia asked Francesco how the work was going.

"Hard," he said. "They're making me mix all the plaster and it's making my hands crack. Look." He held one up. The fingertips were pulpy and raw. "I don't like fresco painting. When I have my own studio, I'm going to do everything on canvas."

Cecilia stopped halfway down the last flight of stairs and looked at her brother along the rails of the ladder. "Tiepolo is painting the Sandi ceiling in fresco? Why would he do something like that? He knows fresco just rots in Venice."

"Don't know." Francesco shrugged his shoulders. "Vincente says it's a kind of mania."

"Vincente said that?" Vincente was Tiepolo's main assistant. He had come with him from Ricci's, leaving the older painter to help Tiepolo start his business. "That's disrespectful."

"Oh, Tiepolo agreed with him," Francesco said. "He says it's crazy, but not to tell the clients. You won't tell?"

"I won't tell."

As they manoeuvred the ladder out the street door, Cecilia caught sight of the boat bobbing in the canal with Vincente waiting in it.

"*Ciao*, Vincente," she greeted the assistant. He was a man in his thirties with a face that looked like it had been chipped from stone, all planes and angles, with a pair of small eyes set beneath a low brow. In his red cloth cap and his painter's jerkin, he looked out of place in charge of a boat. He was standing on the stern of a *batela*, a medium-sized working boat, holding the oar with both hands and looking ill at ease, like a man who has suddenly found himself riding a large wild animal.

"He doesn't know how to row," whispered Francesco along the rails of the ladder. "We almost got run over on the way here."

When they reached the boat, Francesco scrambled in and Cecilia handed the ladder down to him, rung by rung. She watched her brother settle the equipment athwart the seats of the *batela* as Vincente prepared to cast off.

"I didn't know you were a sailor too, Vincente," she said, suppressing a giggle. Vincente had managed to tangle the line around his ankle.

"I am a painter not a sailor, Signora," he said in a dignified voice. "Tiepolo is not satisfied with my work as an assistant. Now I am forced to become his gondolier."

"Poor Vincente." Cecilia hadn't asked Tiepolo any questions about the job that day when they met on the stairs. Then, she thought she knew the answers, but learning that Tiepolo was doing the Sandi ceiling in fresco had made her think again. Most painters in Venice were in agreement that fresco was too vulnerable to the city's damp climate, liable to moulder and crumble and collapse. What, she wondered, could have led him to take this step?

"Wait," she said and began to lower herself down the slippery stone steps. "Wait." The boat rocked dangerously as she stepped in and manoeuvred to a place next to the ladder.

"Signora…" Vincente looked worried. Cecilia wondered what he knew.

"What's the matter? Do you want me to get back there and row for you?"

"You'd row better than him," said Francesco from the bow. "Your arms are much stronger."

"What are you doing?" Cattina was suddenly above her, standing on the quayside, gazing down. She had a shopping basket propped against her pregnant belly and Anna Maria clinging to her hand.

"I'll be back soon," Cecilia said automatically, for Anna Maria's sake. She was aware that what she was doing must seem a little crazy. The little girl looked at her in the boat, then looked up at Cattina for reassurance.

Cattina screwed up her small eyes in concern. "It's too sunny," she said. "Take this."

She removed a straw hat from her head and gave it to Anna Maria who came down the steps to hand the hat to her mother. Cecilia took the hat and put it on her head while Anna Maria watched her gravely. It was strange: everybody was acting like she was setting off on a long journey, perhaps one from which she wouldn't return. What *was* she doing? She was going to confront Tiepolo; to see for herself the terms of her abandonment.

Her heart raced as Vincente took his place standing at the

stern, set the oar noisily in its lock and began rowing. Francesco made a show of pressing his hands together in prayer before settling himself in the bow. The *batela* moved off unsteadily, leaving Cattina and Anna Maria looking after it from the quay.

Cecilia settled herself on the hard bench as the boat passed smoothly underneath one bridge, then another. The wooden walkways rattled as people crossed above their heads. The tiny ghostly crabs that lived only under bridges ran to tuck themselves in crevices. It was low tide and the *batela* rode far down in the channel, sliding past walls coated with dark mussels and red algae. After the third bridge, Vincente turned left into another canal, then right again.

Cecilia marvelled at their speed. In the time it took to thread your way from one campo to the next on foot, the *batela* crossed a quarter of the city. In this water-filled metropolis, she had rarely had the opportunity to travel by boat. Water travel was for the rich and for those with jobs to do on the water. Cecilia wondered who the *batela* belonged to: Ambrosio was the only member of the family who owned a boat, and his was a much longer, wider *caorlina*, which was rowed by four standing men. He used it to move merchandise around the city and across the lagoon.

"Whose boat is this?" she asked Vincente.

"Client's," Vincente answered, concentrating on his rowing. It crossed Cecilia's mind that she might be sitting in a boat owned by Tiepolo's mistress.

They passed through Cecilia's old neighbourhood, behind the house where Claudia and the boys still lived. Francesco shouted up at the windows, but no one looked out. They made another turn, slipping through the shaded canyons between the buildings, now and then navigating bars of light where the summer sun slammed through a gap, striking sparks from the green water and penetrating the surface in white shafts that were lost in the murk.

The boat slid under a much larger bridge, covering them with a veil of cool shade. As it pulled away, Cecilia found they were floating in open water, merging with the traffic on the Grand Canal.

"Do we have to cross it?" she shouted, looking with alarm at the crowded waterway. The side canals had been smooth as glass, but the water of the Grand Canal was lifted into a chop by the wind blowing off the Adriatic. A sharp gust caught at Cattina's straw hat and Cecilia clutched it to her head while, with the other hand, she held the ladder to keep it from sliding sideways as the boat rocked. Vincente, just then struggling inexpertly with the oar to keep their boat from running into another vessel, didn't reply. Cecilia let go of the ladder and crossed herself surreptitiously as they began to make their way through the dense traffic on the canal.

Heavy seagoing barges, *trabacolo*, loaded with goods, their cargoes covered with canvas, cruised along slowly with their sails furled, rowed by several oarsmen. Sleek black gondolas darted in all directions with curved metal prows rearing up from the water like axe blades, some with shiny black cabins for passengers who preferred privacy, some with seats open to the weather. There were many other small working *batele*, too, like the one they were riding in, competing for space on the water with nimble, needle-prowed *sandoli* and larger boats used for cargo and transporting goods, *caorline* and *peate*.

With great difficulty and some oaths, Vincente navigated their craft around a group of sailing barges anchored together in the channel. Their great, flat rudders had been lifted clear of the silty bottom, their sails had been stretched over barrel-shaped frames to serve as awnings and their stripped masts pointed at a blue, wind-scoured sky. The conjoined decks of the barges served as a floating marketplace where merchants, sailors, customs officials, and stevedores swarmed. As they passed near their pitch-black hulls, Cecilia could hear the voices of the merchants as they bargained, the chink of money changing hands, the scrape of heavy goods being dragged across the decks.

They left this frenzy as abruptly as they had entered it, turning into a narrow canal. The water here was glassy and calm. There were no other boats in sight. They shortly drew up to a wide water gate with steps leading upwards to a set of double doors, standing open. Francesco helped Cecilia out onto the landing, taking her hand as she climbed the wet stone risers.

This was the Palazzo Sandi in the Corte dell'Albero. Cecilia had prepared herself for grandeur, intimidation, and the hauteur of overpaid servants looking down their noses at her. But as she stepped inside the ground floor entry hall, what she found was a building site. The wide, low passage was cluttered with raw materials: milled lumber stood in stacks against one wall; sacks full of rubble lined the other. A selection of lime-caked buckets, a greasy winch, and a tarred coil of rope cluttered the floor. At the far end of the passageway, silhouetted in the light coming from another pair of double doors, Cecilia could see the forms of men kneeling on the floor. As her eyes adjusted, she saw they were laying red and white tiles in a checkerboard pattern. Hot air blew along the passage, sucking gritty marble dust from one end to the other. She removed Cattina's hat to prevent it from being snatched back through the doors into the canal.

Vincente and Francesco swung past her with the ladder. "Tell Tiepolo I'm here," she said running her hand over her hair. "Have him come down. I'll wait." She watched them disappear up a wide, plain marble staircase, tilting the ladder upwards to manipulate it around the bend.

She stood at the bottom of the staircase in semi-darkness and felt the dust settling on her skin. The trip in the boat, the chaos of the Grand Canal and the surprise of finding the palazzo in this stripped-down state, had thrown her. What did she hope to discover here? Clearly, there would be no russet lady, no bed hung with silk, at least not in this palazzo. Workmen were this palazzo's only tenants, that much was obvious. But she wasn't about to give up. She'd learn something new about Tiepolo here today, she told herself. She'd catch him out.

She heard him before she saw him, his heavy tread pounding down the stairs above, the leather soles of his shoes slapping the hard marble. He seemed to be descending at a run. He appeared suddenly on the landing above her, skidding a little on the smooth floor.

"So you are here," he said. "I thought Vincente was pulling my leg." With his body wrapped in an old jerkin, a labourer's cap on his head, and a tear in one knee of his breeches, Tiepolo might have been a mason or one of the men who carried sacks of rubble. He was coated in the same powdery dust that had covered Francesco.

"Are you surprised to see me?" she said, drawing herself up to her full height and looking him in the eye. One of the men cutting tiles whistled, one clear note that echoed in the passage.

"This is my wife here!" Tiepolo bellowed without breaking eye contact with her. "Let's show some respect!"

"Pardon." The voice reverberated down the hall. "No offence." Cecilia smiled bitterly to herself. Who else were they expecting?

Tiepolo smiled back at her, friendly but slightly wary. "I am surprised to see you."

"In a good way?" she asked.

"In a good way." He walked down the last few steps slowly until he reached the bottom one. He stopped there, his head exactly level with hers. She noticed he hadn't been shaved in several days. His eyes roved down over her body and Cecilia thought for a moment he might embrace her, rubbing that rasping male chin against hers. Instead he asked, "Am I in trouble?"

"I'm not sure. That depends on what you're doing."

He gave a little laugh. "You know what I'm doing."

"No, I don't," she said and crossed her arms.

"But I told you — "

"You didn't."

"Only because you weren't interested." He sounded exasperated. "Do you care?"

"Of course I care."

Tiepolo opened his mouth to say something, then changed his mind. "Come and see," he said and took her hand.

He led her up two flights of stairs. They were rather narrow, hemmed in by unpainted plaster walls that coated Cecilia's sleeves with dust when she brushed against them. The marble edges of the steps were razor sharp, with no softening of wear. Everything about the palazzo was newly minted and raw, as though everything in it had recently been quarried from the earth or pulled red-hot from the forge. The lead casing of the high windows supported thick round lenses of glass that distorted the view into a small garden next door.

"Is anyone living here?" she asked as she followed Tiepolo up. His hand in hers felt rough and unfamiliar.

"Just us and some labourers," he said. "We commandeered a room on the third floor to sleep in. Straw pallets on the floor, but it saves time."

"I don't think I want to see that," she said, trying to hide her curiosity. "What have you been eating?"

"There's a place that does cooked food around the corner. It's foul, as you'd expect."

"As you'd expect."

They came out on the *portego* on the second floor. This was a long room that ran right through the palazzo from the canal side to the facade facing the street. It, too, was more modest in scale than Cecilia had imagined for a palazzo, like an expanded version of the *portego* in their own house, though the ceilings were higher and several large doorways led to other rooms. Like the rest of the building, this room was still undecorated. The air smelled of wet plaster and freshly sawn wood. The only other signs of life were a carpenter and his young assistant hanging a pair of doors in the entrance to one of the rooms.

"Don't watch them," Tiepolo said in a low growl, shaking his head in disgust. The assistant strained to support the heavy door while the carpenter worked out the position of the hinges. Suddenly, the boy lost his grip and the door tilted out of position. The carpenter swore viciously and threw down his measure. The door slammed to the ground. Cecilia jumped.

"I see what you mean," she said.

Tiepolo made a contemptuous sound. "Useless. They hung our door yesterday. It's like watching a pair of clowns, only not very funny. This way." He led her to the far end of the long room, approaching another double doorway, its door in place, the wood primed but not yet painted.

"It's still not right," Tiepolo said, showing her how the door scraped against the floor, drawing a large arc in the thick dust and digging into the soft marble. "I may just rehang it myself."

Cecilia had stepped into the room and stood silently gazing around her. This chamber spanned the width of the building and was fairly large and rectangular in shape. Filtered light entered through three tall windows, all pushed open to admit the humid air and the smell of the canal below. The four walls were of bare pinkish plaster, newly rendered and pristine. The room was empty except for a scaffold tower, which stood on the left-hand side. This was a rustic structure made of poles lashed together with rope and leather thongs. Unplaned planks were laid loosely across the top of the tower to make a working platform. At the top of it, Cecilia caught sight of Francesco, like a boy sailor in the rigging of a ship. Vincente was climbing up the crossbraces, trying to drag the stepladder behind him. Tiepolo hurried across the room to give him a hand, boosting the ladder from below.

Cecilia stepped into the room and began to study the ceiling. It was high and gently vaulted and about half of its surface was already covered with painted scenes. Her eye scanned the work swiftly and her heart began to beat faster.

To hide her agitation, she said, "It's fresco."

"Yes it is." Tiepolo came to where she was standing. "What do you think?"

"I think your clients should get their money back," she said, feeling breathless. Her heart was hammering against her ribs so powerfully she wondered if he could hear it. "You can get away with fresco on the mainland, but in Venice, never. Wasn't it you who said that? It won't last ten years."

She saw Tiepolo frown and felt a spiteful sense of satisfaction. Without making any special effort, she had put her finger on exactly what was worrying him about this project. He muttered something about new techniques and giving the client what he wanted.

"Your client didn't ask for fresco," she said on a hunch. "You know very well you talked him into it."

Tiepolo's reaction told her she was right. He raised his eyebrows and pursed his lips. Suddenly he looked like a little boy caught doing something forbidden. "I did it for the sky," he admitted. "You know how I love a nice deep sky. I wanted it big," he threw his hands out wide, grasping space. "Profound. Luminous. A summer sky, or like the sky where it meets the sea at the horizon. You know what I mean: that's fresco sky. There's no other way to get that effect."

She tilted back her neck and gazed up at the ceiling. "Well, you've got sky all right," she said. The sky of Tiepolo's ceiling looked as though real swallows could fly in it. "And you've got a whole lot of other things, too."

She pointed above her head to a swirling vortex of cloud. At the top of this vortex, in an oval pool of pale yellow, sat a remote figure wearing a plumed helmet and a lavender robe. Not far away, another figure tumbled, wings on his heels, wings on his helmet, holding a staff twined with a serpent. These gods were caught in a kind of stacked cone of colour, surrounded by bands of darker yellow, ochre, then saffron-coloured cloud that punctured the limpid blue of the sky.

The effect was very convincing, Cecilia thought, and very disconcerting. It was as if a hole had been punched in the roof of the Sandis' nice new palazzo, admitting the summer sunlight and a small shower of gods. She wanted to say it was brilliant, she wanted to say she loved it. Instead, wanting to distract Tiepolo from the sound of her heart hammering, she probed for another soft spot.

"But what's the story?" she asked. "Is there a theme of some kind? I see Minerva and Hermes, but who's that boy with the lyre? Why is he wrecking that city?" She pointed to a figure that stood on a rocky outcrop, wearing a short tunic whipped by the wind. He was holding the instrument on his hip and picking its strings in a distracted way while bricks and blocks flew off the top of the city wall and tumbled in the air. Cecilia pointed to another corner of the ceiling. "And what's going on here?" She pointed up at a figure mounted on the rampant winged horse. He was levelling a sharp lance at a diminutive, lion-headed, snake-tailed monster. "I understand that it's someone riding Pegasus, but what's that thing he's killing? I can't make head or tail of any of it."

She saw at once her words had hit their target again. Tiepolo was already explaining, eager to tell her.

"Tommaso Sandi is a fine man, a good client," Tiepolo was saying. "But he likes books."

"And that's a bad thing?"

"In certain ways." Tiepolo took her back several months, giving her an account of the commission, the early discussions, the contract negotiations. Cecilia listened. This was the kind of conversation she and he used to have in bed, with his hand on her breast and her head on his shoulder, before the children died.

"I go over to Sandi's house, yes? There, in the middle of the room, is a huge table covered with books. Vast ones, books as big as trunks, with leather and gold all over them. And in each book Sandi has a little leather marker, stuck between two pages. He starts opening the books up where the markers are, saying he's going to explain to me what he wants on his ceiling. I'm thinking, perfect, wonderful, he's going to show me pictures. But does he show me pictures?" Tiepolo was animated now, playing up. He wagged his finger comically. "No! None of it! He opens up his books and starts reading to me."

He mimed his client hunched over a tome, running his fingers along lines of type. He mimed himself, standing looking up at the ceiling, scratching his head. "Amphion builds the walls of Thebes with music, he reads. *Eh? Who?* I say. Bellerophon does something or another with Pegasus. *Huh?* Hercules enslaves his enemies with his *tongue.*"

Here, Cecilia laughed. She couldn't help it. "Sweet Maria! How does he expect you to show *that?*"

Tiepolo pointed his thumb over his shoulder toward the wall where the scaffold tower stood. Above the platform Cecilia could just make out the heads and shoulders of her brother and Vincente.

"We're giving Hercules a very long tongue, aren't we, Vincente?"

"Like unto that of a serpent, boss," Vincente mumbled, his mouth full of tacks — he was nailing a paper pattern to the wall. "That'll teach them."

"Sandi says it's all about the power of eloquence," Tiepolo told Cecilia. He threw out his hands in a gesture of resignation. "I suppose that's what you'd expect from a lawyer. Let's hope Sandi's friends have read the same books as he has or they won't understand a thing."

"Surely it can't be that bad. How about this side?" Cecilia took three paces into the room and turned to look at the scene on the ceiling just above the entry door. She stopped short as she took in the figures of a half-naked man with his arm around a half-naked woman.

"Ah. This side," Tiepolo said.

On the curve of vault above the door, the couple wrestled on the brink of an abyss. The man's right arm, clutching a violin, was flung back stiffly behind him, while with his left he clutched the semi-naked woman in an attempt to keep her from falling into the void. The man's body was muscular, powerful, like the body of a sailor or a wrestler: his skin was a strange, dark ochre. He wore leaves in his tumbled hair and an orange cloak whipped around his muscled torso like an untethered sail in a storm. By contrast, the body of the woman was soft and pink and utterly yielding. The line of her haunch, thigh, and calf traced a smooth, serpentine curve that ended with a tapered foot pointing into the smoky abyss beneath her.

"Don't tell me," Cecilia said, putting up a hand to shush Tiepolo. "I know this one."

Cecilia noticed how, even in this moment of peril, the man tucked his fingers beneath the woman's scant mantle, making contact with the creamy flesh of her hip. A three-headed dog, straining on a chain fastened to a fiery darkness, lunged at the pair of lovers — they had to be lovers. Beyond the three-headed dog, a clutch of figures sat in shadow, observing the struggling pair without pity. The man glared back at the sinister group with large, defiant eyes. In contrast, the woman wore a dazed, distant expression. She seemed oblivious to any danger. Her gaze focused on nothing.

Now Cecilia was sure. "Orpheus," she said, "and what's-her-name. His wife."

"At least that one's a story people know," Tiepolo said, a little nervously. "The violin was Sandi's idea. His daughters are learning to play."

Cecilia tilted her head from one side to the other, scrutinising the painting. Her heart began to slow as a new feeling crept over her. "The man seems familiar," she said. "His face, his messy hair, his big feet." Cecilia looked down at Tiepolo's feet and then straight into his eyes. "Is he someone we know?"

"Oh, I just made him up." Tiepolo was caught. His Orpheus was recognisably a self-portrait.

"And what about the woman?" Cecilia persisted. "Do we know her?"

It was strange to see a grown man blush, the skin reddening beneath a three-day growth of stubble. There was no denying that his Eurydice looked like Cecilia. Not the Cecilia of now, thin and angry and half-crazed, but the blooming, full-bodied Cecilia from the days before she had buried her children.

She watched her husband's reaction, doing her best to keep her own face still, masklike. She had expected to discover another woman at the Corte dell'Albero; instead, she found a stolen version of herself.

"It's a good thing your mother can't see this," Cecilia said finally. "She'd have an absolute stroke."

She thought of asking Tiepolo how he had managed to paint

this image of her without having her sit for him stark naked at the top of a ladder. The fresco's perspective was steep, the figures foreshortened in ways that seemed impossible to fudge, even for a draughtsman like him. For Orpheus, he had evidently drawn himself standing over a mirror. But Eurydice? How had he worked out the tricky angle for her torso, her half-kneeling position? And that otherworldly expression? This certainly wasn't the placid girlishness of Europa or the full-blooded sensuality of Compaspe. Eurydice wore a look of blankness and bewilderment that Cecilia had never seen before in any of Tiepolo's pictures of her. The only place she had seen it, she realised suddenly, was in the mirror over her washbasin.

So this was how she looked to him over the past months, she thought, like a dead woman. Dead but guiltless and, to him, still beloved. Why had he never said so?

Had Tiepolo hoped she would come here and see this? Cecilia was certain he had never thought of it. He hadn't invited her. He had no reason to believe she'd show up the way she had, on a madwoman's whim. And it wasn't Tiepolo's way to spell things out, certainly not in pictures. Only inferior painters did that.

No: Tiepolo had simply devised the ceiling using the tools he had to hand, solving its technical problems the best way he knew how. That was all. This didn't surprise Cecilia. What did surprise her was that, until now, she hadn't realised that she had become one of her husband's tools. He'd absorbed her image, given her a permanent home in his painter's imagination. He could see her, and paint her, even when she wasn't there, even when she believed she had disappeared.

It was wonderful — and a little like robbery, Cecilia thought, looking at Tiepolo with amazement. "You're a robber!" she felt like saying to him. "You've kidnapped my form, my image." Only in this case she had to admit that the thief took better care of what he stole than the original owner did. Tiepolo was a generous crook and he loved what he stole, stole what he loved. He turned his loot to good account, sharing his wealth. At this point in her confused thinking, something in Cecilia's heart gave way.

"Don't worry. I won't be the one to tell her," she said, meaning Orsetta. "She doesn't understand these things."

She moved closer to Tiepolo and laced her arm around his waist.

There was something else she had noticed. There were three putti in the fresco. The largest one, close to Eurydice's out-stretched hand, was blindfolded and pointing a finger toward the sunlight. Far above, two smaller ones receded into the heavens, disappearing in a tangle of baby limbs. Cecilia had counted them — two going; one, damaged, staying behind. She had even named them — Anna-Maria, Domenico, Elena — but she knew for certain that Tiepolo had not named or counted them. He had simply painted the number of putti he thought the ceiling needed, two there, one here. And it was perfect. He had cast himself as Orpheus and endowed himself with a hero's body, powerful enough to save a lost wife. He had not thought about this either. He just used the tools he had to hand.

"I can't remember how the story of Orpheus and Eurydice ends," Cecilia said after a pause. She laid her head on Tiepolo's shoulder. "Does he save her?"

"Of course he does," Tiepolo said heartily, happily, surprised, holding her close to him. "Look at them."

PART FOUR

Count Francesco Algarotti
Venice, 1743

Venice, 1743

Francesco Algarotti lay curled on the floor of his old bedroom, his handsome cheek pressed against the cool tiles. His head was on fire; his gut clenched with periodic spasms. In a delirious vision he saw a maid with muscular forearms twisting his intestines like a dishrag, smiling a sadistic smile. Francesco contemplated dragging himself to the chamber pot again, but the gesture would be pointless. He was entirely voided and empty, a husk so light he might blow away in the breeze.

It was finished. He was dying. The journey from Dresden had killed him.

"*Addio*," Francesco said aloud. It was his goodbye to the world, which had always been so good to him. The inside of his mouth tasted bitter as he whispered, "*Addio*, sweet world — and thank you." He closed his eyes for the last time.

He opened them again when he felt someone kicking him gently in the rump.

He turned his head and saw a pair of embroidered house slippers. In them was a pair of big feet, which looked familiar, as did the skinny ankles and calves. Literally familiar: Francesco had the same bladelike shins, which he took pains to conceal in the best silk stockings. His brother Bonomo had no shame about his ugly shins. The beautiful world had to take them as it found them.

"The servant came to tell me you were dead," Francesco's brother said in a voice that sounded much too loud for the room. "I wanted to make sure."

"I am dead," Francesco confirmed, rolling over on his back and crossing his arms over his chest.

"That explains why you're on the floor and not in the hygienic new bed I've had specially prepared for you at huge expense."

"Beds are wasted on the dead."

"Is that a saying or did you make it up? It's pithy. It should be a saying."

"Posterity is all I have left," Francesco said, flourishing one hand weakly. "It's all that counts. Said the Count."

Bonomo groaned. "I'm so glad we sent you to that expensive university in Bologna. It did wonders for your puns."

He sat down on the high bed, which creaked under his considerable weight. Francesco noted that his older brother was getting fat, taking on a shape like their father's, a big square torso teetering on spindly Algarotti gams. It was a sign of his prosperity, for which Francesco had reason to be thankful. He put his hands on his own slender midriff, checking for bulges. Finding instead nothing but declivities and jutting ribs, he moved his hands quickly away.

"Aren't you afraid of catching what I have?" he murmured. "Your servant hardly comes near me."

"You know I never catch anything," Bonomo said, picking up a glass by the side of the bed and sniffing its contents. "What is this? Some medicine from that quack?"

"Rose water and white wine. It's a French concoction. Treats all ills." He watched Bonomo take a swig, feeling his stomach curdle. "Help yourself."

"Not bad at all. It tastes like a flower garden. Vittoria will like it." Vittoria was Bonomo's vivacious wife, who had a tendency to kiss Francesco more often than was strictly necessary for a sister-in-law.

"Vittoria hasn't been to see me once," he moped.

"Are you joking? My sweet Vittoria won't set foot in a sickroom, especially not one occupied by a man that's come from abroad. Don't take it personally. She sets no store by the quarantine. She thinks the diseases just bide their time for forty days, waiting for their chance to strike as soon as they come within range of the children. She sends her love, though."

As he talked, Francesco's brother studied him carefully with shrewd merchant's eyes that missed nothing. Bonomo had a solid grasp of reality; Francesco counted on it. During the last few days, there had been times when he felt so awful he wondered if he actually might die. If Bonomo had registered any serious sign of worry at the sight of him laid out on the floor, Francesco would have known he was in trouble.

Bonomo drained what was left in the glass and smacked his lips. "Well, give us a holler if you do finally make up your mind to die," he said in a bored voice. "Cousin Nannetta has her beady eye on these rooms, you know. We had trouble fending her off while you were away." He hoisted himself off the bed, came over to where Francesco lay, and looked down on him from beyond the curved horizon of his stomach. His face reminded Francesco of the sun. His expression was quizzical.

"I don't need anything else," Francesco said, reassured by his brother's solar lack of concern. "Really. I'm on the mend."

"Glad to hear it." Bonomo gave him another nudge with his foot. "By the way, I had them put your correspondence on your desk. You're a popular boy. I don't get that many letters in a year."

Bonomo stomped out, shaking the floor with his confident tread. Within a minute, the reluctant servant appeared with a basin of warm water. He helped Francesco back onto the bed, washed him with a rough cloth, put him in a clean shift, and renewed his rose water and wine. As Francesco settled back onto the pillow, he thought, why did I stay away so long?

Two days later, Francesco was well enough to sit up and eat a few mouthfuls of a soft rice dish his sister-in-law had prepared with her own hands. He had the servant bring a mirror and discovered he looked precisely as bad as he felt: sunken eyes, hollow cheeks, a week's growth of beard. He shuddered. It would have been all right if he'd looked ethereal as a sick man. Ethereal could be attractive. But in fact he resembled a hungry young Judas or a galley slave. So much for his legendary allure.

And yet it was high time, Francesco thought, attempting to be stoical, high time that he laid aside the pleasures of youth and dedicated himself to something serious. Obviously he was supposed to lose his looks at this point in life because he no longer needed them. There was no requirement for scientists, men of letters — respected men — to be handsome. Think of Socrates, hideous and brilliant. Ravaged looks were a confirmation that Francesco was turning a corner in his life, finally becoming the man he had always wanted to be, instead of the man other people desired.

This high line of reasoning didn't entirely convince Francesco. He stirred to call the barber who came quickly to scrape away the ugly stubble and smooth his cheeks with almond-scented cream. The hairdresser arrived not long after and did what he could with Francesco's dark, tangled locks. When they had gone, he felt restored to civilisation, if not to beauty. He put on a dressing gown and staggered to his desk in the adjoining room.

He found it neatly laid out, ready for him. On it were good quality paper, ink, pens, and blotters. His letters were stacked in a pile, arranged by order of receipt.

Francesco sat down and began to leaf through them, an activity that usually made him feel happy. His correspondence came from all over Europe, from Paris, London, Saint Petersburg, Rome, Naples. The letters were written by great and famous men and women: aristocrats, *philosophes*, *bels esprits*, heretics, freethinkers and proponents of the latest ideas in science and literature and mathematics. Among them was a long missive from Voltaire — Francesco recognised the sarcastic thrust of his friend's descending pen strokes — and another from Lady Mary Wortley Montagu, whose heart he had broken, but only with her eager consent. These were people who respected Francesco as a man of the Enlightenment. A fair few of them also wanted to get into his pants.

Normally, this evidence of worldly success cheered Francesco. Today, he felt too fragile to enjoy it. He rifled the pile, searching for a letter that was not there. How could it be? Frederick wasn't writing to him anymore, and he wasn't writing to Frederick. This had been Francesco's wish, to which Frederick had conceded with a kingly flourish. He always liked to appear magnanimous, damn him. It was one of his most annoying personal traits.

He pictured Frederick in his campaign tent in Silesia, sitting by a rough table with maps spread out on it. His eyes, tracing the maps' topographic contours, were the same shade of blue as the uniform he always wore, a profound, saturated colour, a colour of sadness. Frederick was thirty this year, just like Francesco. They had reached life's crossroads at the same moment and each had taken a different path. Francesco's took him to Dresden, then to Venice in search of independence. Frederick's took him to Silesia, to fight his brutal father's war.

Francesco lay his head down on his desk and tried to stop daydreaming about Frederick and think clearly about his own situation. He was thirty — already. It was hard to believe. Time had passed so quickly and he'd wasted so much of it. His social and amorous success in the courts of Europe had made him no richer. His little book, *Newton for Ladies*, so much praised, so much discussed, was a financial flop. His membership of the Royal Academy, though highly prestigious, brought no remuneration. His title — Count Algarotti — was nothing more than a love gift from Frederick, a mere ornament that couldn't be sold or traded or otherwise converted into coin. Life had surprised Francesco. Things that had once seemed unattainable had come to him too easily while things he had thought were his birthright — respect, secure status, a decent living — proved impossible to get. His talents had turned out to be other than he first thought they were. Whatever they amounted to, he really had to make something of them now. Otherwise, he'd grow old living on his allowance from Bonomo — a humiliating prospect — or be forced to go back to Berlin and spend the rest of his life playing Frederick's pet while what little reputation he had earned for himself drained away.

Fortunately, or perhaps hazardously, he had a plan. Having already been many things in his lifetime — a scholar, a scientist, an author, a courtier, a royal lover — now, like some shape-shifting demigod in Ovid, he'd transformed himself into an art agent for Augustus the Third, the Elector of Saxony, King of Poland. Like all his previous metamorphoses, this transformation was Francesco's own idea, but he took the step with reluctance and only after he'd exhausted every other avenue to fame and fortune. It meant falling back on a freakish talent he'd long taken pains to hide: his perfect memory for images. Francesco's mind was an archive of every painting, drawing or etching he had ever seen. It was a God-given ability (or curse) — he could never quite decide.

For him, this made his expertise in the field of art (unlike his mathematical and literary skill, which were hard won) no better than a party trick. Yet there was no question that it impressed other people and now it was his best hope of gaining some kind of a living. Francesco had worked hard on his plan for expanding the king's famous painting collection at Dresden — then even harder selling it to Augustus and his canny, tightfisted minister, Count Brühl. Now he found himself, back on home territory, in the role of consultant, art expert and agent to a king. He had to deliver. He knew it was his last chance.

He thought again of Frederick, who, for all his power, had not been able to solve Francesco's problems. Friends still wrote to him with news of the king. They reported that he played the flute for an hour every morning before riding into battle. They said he composed exactly one lyric poem per week, between skirmishes, to keep his hand in. Francesco wondered if Frederick ordered them to write these things about him in their letters — he was capable of that. Then he decided it didn't matter.

"Long may Frederick continue to practise art in the theatre of war," he said out loud. Perhaps one day the two parts of his divided soul would fit together like the ends of a well-made buckle. By that time, if it ever came, Francesco might have completed the circuit of his own soul and become a man with his own living. Then everything would be different.

The next morning Francesco rose, dressed, and drank two cups of strong coffee. Buzzing like a bee and waving off the solicitations of his sister-in-law, who doubted he was well enough to go out, he summoned a gondola and set off to see his first picture dealer. He carried his brief in his leather document case, complete with the royal seals of Augustus to flash in front of his contacts, to impress them. This was Wednesday. By the end of a week, he had been to see all of the major dealers in Old Masters in the city and had met and commissioned two of the living painters on his list.

"There you go," he bragged to Bonomo, waving the contracts under his brother's nose. "That's how easy it is to bring art into the world. Out of my head, into their hands, onto the canvas. *Presto.*"

Giambattista Pittoni and Giambattista Piazzetta had both welcomed Francesco with open arms. Flattered to be patronised by the King of Poland, apparently pleased with the subjects Francesco had chosen for them, both painters had agreed terms on the spot. "It's very satisfying to hire such talented painters to create the pictures I dreamed up," he said. "It's better than painting them myself. And so much cleaner."

Bonomo laughed at him. "So you think commissioning a painting is as easy as ordering a new coat from your tailor, do you?" Francesco had barged into the room that served as his brother's office, but Bonomo seemed glad to have his workday interrupted. "You walk in, they measure you, stitch it up and you collect the finished garment at the end of the month?" He shook his head.

Francesco flopped down into a comfortable chair and pushed off his smart, tight shoes. "Why not? Venetian artists never fail to deliver. They're true professionals."

"Exactly," Bonomo said. He leaned back in his chair and folded his hands over his broad stomach. "Which is why it's not as simple as that. They have their own ideas, you see, their own ways of doing things. They aren't just puppets to be manipulated to suit your taste. They know things we don't know."

Francesco made a sign to the servant. He needed coffee. "You talk as if you think I don't respect them! I honour them. I revere them. That's what I'm doing here."

Bonomo eyed him astutely. "Yes, but you don't seem prepared to listen to them."

Francesco was annoyed by his brother's air of superiority. It was true that Bonomo, unlike him, had some experience in the art trade. He even collected on a small scale. But Francesco didn't like his tone. "It's early days, Bonomo. I realise that. At this point, they aren't saying anything to me but yes Count, certainly Count, thank you very much Count. They're glad of the work."

"Maybe," said Bonomo. "Who are you seeing next?"

"Yet another Giambattista: Tiepolo. Have you ever noticed how many Venetian painters are named after Jesus' cousin? I suppose naming your baby Jesus would be too much."

Bonomo's face lit up, not at his poor joke. "Tiepolo! Ah, Tiepolo, our own Tiepoletto! So small but so mighty."

"You sound as if you might burst into song. Go ahead. Don't mind me."

Bonomo delivered a few phrases of a popular tune in his deep baritone. "You should be singing yourself, you lucky dog," he said. "Commissioning from the great Tiepolo. He's a genius. There hasn't been anyone like him since Veronese. Can I come with you? Can I carry your case?"

"No, you'll ruin my entrance. But you'll be pleased to know I'm commissioning three paintings from him." Francesco held up three fingers.

"Ambitious." Bonomo gave an evaluating frown. "What kind of terms are you offering him?"

"Terms?"

"Come on: money. How much?"

"Bonomo, you are such a *merchant*." Francesco had nothing to hide from his brother and he was proud of his work on the budget because it demonstrated his flair for mathematics and his practicality. He'd had spent long hours developing three sets of prices for each of his artists: a low figure (hopeful), a median one (realistic, or so he thought) and a high one, for dire emergencies. He told Bonomo his middling offer for three Tiepolos.

Bonomo snorted. "You must be joking."

"What's wrong with that? Piazzetta was happy enough with the equivalent. Surely Tiepolo won't expect more." He felt suddenly worried.

"Oh, my little brother," Bonomo said. "You've been out of town too long. Have you ever heard of Count Tessin?"

Francesco drew himself up straight and answered down his nose. "I've more than heard of him. I met him in Paris a couple of years ago."

Tessin was a Frenchified Swede, a diplomat and connoisseur, very charming, extremely cultured. He'd talked to Francesco about his enthusiasm for the painter Watteau who also happened to be Frederick's favourite artist. People said Tessin was sleeping with Madame Boucher, the painter's wife, and this was seen as a further confirmation of his commitment to the arts. Francesco wasn't in the mood to relay this choice gossip to Bonomo, whose know-it-all attitude was irritating him.

"Oh yes? Then I suppose you already know Tessin came here a few years ago and tried to commission Tiepolo to paint the royal palace in Stockholm. Note my careful choice of words: *tried.*"

"Are you saying the agent of the King of Sweden failed?"

"Is our little Tiepolo in Stockholm now, or is he down the canal in San Silvestre eating peas and rice every day? He turned Tessin down flat. It seems the king couldn't pay him enough to make it worth his while."

Shit. The coarse word flew into Francesco's mind unbidden. The more he learned about Tiepolo, the more pictures he saw and recorded in his retentive mind, the more he realised that this short-legged son of Venice was the most exciting painter working in Europe. Others, it seemed, had come to the same conclusion. So obviously had Tiepolo. "Do you know how much he wanted?"

Bonomo shrugged. "Too much. I heard Tessin quoted as saying the amount he asked was 'impertinent'." Bonomo chuckled while

Francesco suffered a spasm of dread. "It didn't stop him from buying a few Tiepolo pictures for himself, though, so I guess there were no hard feelings. They were little ones. About so big." With his hands, Bonomo framed a rectangle to show just how small a picture Tessin could afford. It was about the size of a child's footprint.

T he next day, Francesco arrived early at Tiepolo's house. He'd come in full battle dress, wearing his best lace, a green silk coat and the new wig he'd had made for him in Paris. The elegant effect, he felt, was ruined by the cumbersome document wallet he had been forced to carry with him. When he'd asked Bonomo to spare him a servant to carry it for him — or at least to make good his own offer to carry it — Bonomo had laughed in his face. So Francesco would have to appear before the great Tiepolo like a builder carrying his plans tucked under his arm. This wasn't helping his nerves. His palm left a faint damp mark on the wallet's fine brown leather covering.

It was easy to find Tiepolo's house. He lived only a short distance from Bonomo in an attractive building that faced onto the piazza of San Silvestre, just a step away from the Grand Canal. It was bigger and grander than the houses of his main artistic competitors, Francesco noted with an expert eye. Its size and situation spoke of more than success, they spoke of wealth. This sent a powerful message to potential clients: *you are approaching the home of a peer.* Yet, like most Venetian painters, Tiepolo worked out of his dwelling place. His busy studio occupied the two lower floors of the building, while his family lived up above.

Francesco knocked on the street door. It was opened by a Moorish servant in a yellow coat. The man regarded Francesco impassively as he explained the nature of his visit.

"Are you sure Signor Tiepolo is expecting you?" he said running his eyes across Francesco's fine lace jabot.

"We do have an appointment," Francesco replied, a little put out. His reputation as the king's agent was spreading in Venice. He was used to being shown more deference than this.

But the black servant, well fed and well-dressed, with exemplary white teeth, underscored the message of Tiepolo's success, for such servants were fashionable and expensive to maintain. This one was particularly distinguished since he spoke Venetian flawlessly and had an elegant bearing. His face seemed somehow familiar to Francesco — perhaps he had seen him in the street. A handsome Moor like him would stand out wherever he went.

Eventually the servant seemed convinced by Francesco. "It's just that the master didn't mention it. But that's not unusual when he's busy. Follow me." He turned and led the way up a flight of stairs.

"And is your master very busy at the moment?"

The servant laughed. "The master is always busy," he said. They had reached the first floor. The servant threw open a pair of double doors and Francesco found himself in Tiepolo's studio, a place he'd long dreamed of visiting.

Bonomo had tried to warn Francesco about Tiepolo's popularity. He had delivered a sort of précis of the painter's current commissions, reeling off a list that included an extensive series of frescoes for the Villa Cordellina near Vicenza, a set of ceiling panels in oil for the Scuola Grande dei Carmini, a noble portrait or three, a ceiling fresco for the Scalzi, altar pieces, etchings, drawings, history paintings… Francesco had stopped listening at some point, sure that Bonomo was exaggerating. No one painter, he told himself, could be doing all that work at one time.

Now, looking into Tiepolo's studio, he knew Bonomo had been telling the truth. The brightly lit room seethed with activity. The servant led him past a pair of assistants, one crouched on the floor, the other mounted on a pair of steps, working the high and low extremes of a large canvas perched on a tall triangular easel. At another easel, a man transferred a charcoal drawing to canvas. A little team of lime-spattered boys hopped here and there like chalky monkeys spreading gesso over a series of canvases leaning against a wall. At a table, three teenaged girls were busy scrubbing and shuffling innumerable clay pots of different shapes and sizes. When they caught sight of Francesco, all three stared openly, then started to giggle.

The hectic scene came as a shock to Francesco. The other artists he had visited in Venice had stilled their studios for his visits. They had donned their most elegant clothes and put their stinking materials away and lined up their workers, scrubbed, sober, and obedient. The idea was to convey the false impression that their workshops ran like efficient machines and that painting itself was a clean, orderly business, like making cheese in a good dairy. The result was that Francesco saw nothing happening in them. By contrast, at Tiepolo's no effort had been made to conceal the process from him.

Francesco felt the spirit of inquiry stirring in his heart. It had been a long while since he'd felt it this strongly, so distracted had he been by love and love's bitter opposite and the boring necessity of making a living, but there had been a time when science was his only passion. As a university student he had made a study of Newtonian optics, a work that brought him fame and, in almost equal part, humiliation. Yet he had never lost his curiosity about the visual. As Frederick had once pointed out to him, the ability to remember pictures was Francesco's unbidden gift. It was only natural that someone born with this bizarre capability should try to understand the mechanisms of sight.

The Moorish servant led him through the bustle. "I'm sure he's here somewhere," he said irritably. "Hey, where is the boss?"

"Back there," one of the painters replied, jerking his thumb toward the far end of the room. "She's with him."

They finally located Tiepolo tucked away in a small storeroom deep in the recesses of the studio. The painter was surprised to see him. "Count Algarotti! Was it today we were meeting?" He pushed his way out of the tiny room, which was really more like a cupboard, and greeted Francesco formally. A tall blond lady in a blue dress emerged from the storeroom after the painter and stood eyeing Francesco inquisitively. "My wife," Tiepolo explained.

Francesco bowed to her, wondering what Tiepolo could have been doing in a cupboard with his wife in the middle of the morning. Was the lady a touch disarrayed? She curtsied to him calmly and murmured a greeting. She had an oval face with black eyes, pink skin and fair hair done up in a bun. Her only ornament was a string of small freshwater pearls worn around her neck, which was particularly fine and white for a lady of her age. Her broad bosom was covered with a white linen scarf. As with the Moorish servant, Francesco had the odd feeling he had met her before.

"Signora Tiepolo," he said boldly. "I feel sure we're acquainted." She blinked her dark eyes at him as though trying to adjust to a very bright light. Francesco's good looks often had that effect on ladies.

"People are always saying that to me," she said. She had a lilting local accent. "I have one of those faces." Signora Tiepolo stared him in the eye and he felt more than ever that he knew her from somewhere. Sadly his memory for human faces wasn't as perfect as his memory for pictures.

The servant left them and Tiepolo led Francesco toward an area of the studio where there were several chairs and a large wooden table. "For meetings," he explained, clearing the table of a stack of drawings. He pulled out a cane chair and bade Francesco to put his portfolio on the table and sit down. Francesco did so, enjoying the informality, hoping it meant that the painter regarded him benevolently.

"What can I do for you, Count Algarotti?" Tiepolo said, plumping down on his chair at the table. He was a short man, solidly built and strong looking. He had large brown eyes, an off-kilter nose, and a slender chin. Francesco had glimpsed the painter around town before and then he had been wearing very good clothes, as fitted his level of success. Today he was dressed like a workman in a pair of loose trousers and a brown tunic that crossed over his chest. He wore an eccentric hat, tight across his brow like a nightcap, almost red, somewhat purple, with a sort of flap or gusset at the crown. It was something like a labourer's cap, but then it wasn't. The hat delighted Francesco in its ambiguity. He couldn't stop looking at it.

Francesco expected Signora Tiepolo to leave them alone as soon as the meeting began. He was surprised and irked when she sat down at the table with them. The presence of a woman in the room made meetings less businesslike. He feared Signora Tiepolo would interrupt, or make him explain things in terms that were too simple to be meaningful. But Signora Tiepolo remained mercifully silent and even seemed to be thinking of other things. Eventually, Francesco forgot that Signora Tiepolo was in the room and talked to Tiepolo as though she were not there. That proved a mistake, though he didn't realise it until later.

Francesco began his approach with flattery, as always. He had done his groundwork on Tiepolo, as he had on all his artists, furnishing his inner gallery with as many images of the artist's work as he could arrange to see. For this reason, the flattery he produced was of the highest quality, consisting only of true and heartfelt observations based on knowledge. It was a technique

Francesco had used to splendid effect in salons and courts all over Europe. It worked on queens and, of course, on kings. It worked no less well on Tiepolo.

Like the good agent he was, he spoke for his employer, for Augustus, telling Tiepolo that the king had the highest regard for his ingenuity, his lively line, his brio, and his wit — all qualities that Francesco himself most admired about the painter. Tiepolo listened appreciatively without contradicting him. He made no attempt to be humble. Clearly, he was a man capable of basking in the admiration of others. Francesco took this as a hopeful sign and forged on.

"Our aim is to establish the greatest art collection in Europe," he explained, delivering the neat formula that had taken him so many months to develop. "One that spans the history of painting and contains works by the Old Masters and also those by the most illustrious artists of our own time."

Tiepolo was amused. "So you're in the market," he said, "for paintings by the living as well as the dead. Myself, I always like working for patrons who appreciate the fact I'm alive. That's how I stay that way! Isn't that right, Signora?"

As he said this, the painter hunched his shoulders toward his ears and shimmied them in helpless mirth at his own joke. He looked merrily at Signora Tiepolo who rolled her eyes just perceptibly but said nothing. Things were going very well, Francesco judged. He moved on.

"The king would like to commission three large history paintings," he told Tiepolo, producing a sheaf of notes and sketches from his portfolio. "The first will be a scene drawn from Procopius' *Arcana Historia*."

Francesco launched into his narration. He'd observed that painters, being simple artisans, responded well to enthusiasm and drama, and so he took pains to make his approach as entertaining as possible.

"This painting will depict the moment the soldier recognises his old general, the great Belisarius, who has been blinded and is living as a beggar. Central is the figure of Belisarius, an old man, broken in body, racked with remorse, but at the same time muscular, heroic, with the traces of brute power still discernible in his diminished frame. He's dressed in a ragged shift and his eyes stare sightlessly so it's obvious he's blind, but I beg you to paint the general with irises — blank white eyes are so repellent, don't you think?"

"Certainly," Tiepolo agreed. "But —"

Francesco sailed on. "Belisarius stares into the distance with blind but not horrid white eyes. His mind is a tumult of hope and pain and resignation and shame and anger, as he hears the familiar voice of his old comrade in arms crying '*Belisarius!*'" Francesco threw out his arms and shouted. "'*Oh, Belisarius, my general. Can it really be you?*'"

Tiepolo looked impressed. "Who did you say the writer was?" the painter asked in an awed voice.

"Procopius," Francesco affirmed, satisfied with the reaction he'd produced. He'd always had a flair for acting. "I can lend you my copy if you don't have it in your library. But I'm sure you do." He pointed out that the plan provided lots of scope for painting architecture. He produced some etchings of particular buildings in the Roman Forum that he'd like to have included in the painting. Then he rifled through his papers and brought out a different sheaf.

"The second work," Francesco announced, "takes place in a tent. I always thought you'd jump at the opportunity to paint a scene set in a tent, Maestro. It's Achilles' tent."

Tiepolo seemed pleased. "A scene from *The Iliad*. What a good idea. We could have the lovely Briseus in attendance, the armor fashioned by Hephaestus piled in the foreground..."

"Oh, but don't you think that's been done to death?" Francesco said quickly, his excitement getting the better of his manners. "The scene I've chosen isn't the one painted by absolutely every-one in the past. This scene is rare, special, fresh-picked just for you."

"Oh?"

"I want you to depict the moment when Priam, the King of Troy, bursts into Achilles' tent to plead for the body of his son, Hector."

"Priam. Another old man," Tiepolo remarked, looking at the etching. "And no lovely Briseus?"

"We have no need of Briseus! No one paints the faces of old men the way you do, Signor Tiepolo," Francesco said. "You're better than Rembrandt. I really mean that. And this Priam will be modelled on this portrait of Augustus the Strong, the deceased father of Augustus the Third." Francesco placed an etching of a portrait of the dead king from Dresden on the table in front of the painter.

"Ah," Tiepolo said.

Then he showed Tiepolo some rough sketches he had done himself of various pieces of armor in Augustus' collection. "It's very important," Francesco stressed, "that all the trappings in the tent and especially Achilles' armor are authentic and correct in every detail." King Augustus had a passion for ancient history and owned a vast collection of antique armour and weaponry.

Here, Tiepolo put up a hand to stop him. "Count Algarotti, I don't have to tell you that ancient Greece happened quite a long time ago. I don't think anybody really knows what they wore in battle or anywhere else."

Francesco took this patiently, reminding himself that Tiepolo, for all his talent, was not an educated man. He couldn't be ex-pected to follow the latest discoveries coming out of places like

Herculaneum, couldn't know the huge advances being made in the field of ancient history. He reassured the painter that he could advise him on all the fine historical details, providing models for the armor as well as for the view of ancient Troy that would be clearly visible through the open flap of Achilles' tent.

"Now, the final subject." Francesco had saved this one for last because he knew it was his most brilliant. He grinned at Tiepolo. "I think this will inspire you."

The scene came from Judges, Book 7, he explained: Gideon saving the Israelites from the Midianites. The story went like this: Gideon and a handful of Israelites faced annihilation at the hands of the armies of the enemy tribe. They were badly outnumbered, so God devised one of those clever Old Testament tricks to deliver them. First, he equipped all three hundred Israelites with trumpets and empty pitchers with torches concealed inside. Then he instructed them to surround the enemy army in the dark and, on Gideon's signal, break the pitchers and blow their trumpets all at once, creating the din of a huge attacking hoard. The plan worked. The Midianites took to their heels, and the Israelites were saved.

"Everything about this theme plays to your pictorial strengths," Francesco told Tiepolo. "Best of all, no other painter has ever tackled it before."

"No," Tiepolo said. "There may be good reasons for that..."

"Precisely," Francesco agreed. "It's because no other painter possesses your skill at depicting moments of great drama. I'd like you to capture the precise moment when the jars shatter and the light streams forth." He rose from his chair and began to act out the scene. Holding an imaginary pitcher handle in one hand he mimed a smashing action. Then, putting an imaginary mouthpiece to his lips, he made a loud bleating sound.

"As the shards of pottery fall to the ground," Francesco fluttered his fingers downwards, "the dark valley blazes with light, the light of Wisdom and Justice and Reason!" He threw his hands wide. "Gideon, with the face of Augustus (I've brought a little portrait of him for you but, between you and me, you'll have to slim his cheeks down to make him look more — biblical) blows the trumpet while the Midianite general shelters his face with his arms." (Francesco sheltered.) "The terrified soldiers freeze, their faces transfixed in expressions of horror." (He aped panic, paralysis; he clutched at his head.) "In the sky overhead, a host of angels blows heavenly trumpets. I want people to *hear* this painting, Signor Tiepolo. I want it to be *deafening*."

Francesco looked down at Tiepolo whose big eyes were fairly popping. The painter's mouth hung open a little. In the studio, all work had ceased as the assistants and labourers stood and stared. He felt gratified: obviously he had made his impression.

A woman's voice broke the spell.

"Let me see if I understand you correctly," Signora Tiepolo said. "Are you asking Tiepolo to paint *sound?*"

"Signora, you are very perceptive. You have understood me perfectly. I know if anyone can do it, Tiepolo can."

The lady frowned and opened her mouth as if to say something more, probably something complimentary. Tiepolo laid his hand on her forearm to stop her.

"Your commissions are very…very intricate," the painter said quickly. "I can see all the thought and planning that have gone into them. Certainly they are very original." Francesco bowed with humility and pride. All these things were true. "We'll have to see what we can do."

Tiepolo stood up and offered his hand. Francesco took it, feeling a little let down. Had he expected Tiepolo to leap to his drawing board and commence the work immediately? Well — yes he had.

"Wouldn't you like to discuss the contractual details? I think you'll find the financial arrangements generous." He had decided to offer his top price at the outset. There was no point beating around the bush with this artist. But Tiepolo brushed aside the suggestion, saying he was sure the terms would be satisfactory. Similarly, he deflected Francesco's suggestion that they devise a schedule for the work, assuring him they could do this at a later date.

Back on the piazza, blinking in the sunlight, Francesco's being hummed with anticipation. He had conquered Tiepolo. It would only be a matter of weeks before his visions became reality. Or so he thought.

With his work well underway, Francesco let himself be swept up in the life of the city. Summer was in full swing and everywhere he turned there were happy distractions: music, dances, plays, entertainments on the piazzas. Venetian society welcomed him back with open arms and he received invitations daily to gatherings of various kinds. Francesco had always been popular, but now everyone was dying to see the new, cosmopolitan Francesco, freshly returned from distant lands. Everyone wanted to take the measure of his clothes and observe his manners and hear his astonishing stories of life abroad. They relished the pleasure of addressing him, whom they had known forever, as *Count*, then laughing at the ridiculousness of it all.

No one was unkind enough to mention what had happened the last time Francesco had returned to Venice: the disaster of his failed demonstrations was old news. This time around, he was a huge success everywhere he went. He was even a little bit famous, which pleased him more than he liked to admit. To a small coterie of the city's educated young men, he was a hero. His polymathic life was an inspiration to them. And he was living proof that the advances of science and philosophy could take hold even somewhere as deeply conservative and devotedly frivolous as Venice.

Tight groups of these eager young men often sought Francesco's opinions on matters of science and philosophy. They asked him to read their awkward little papers and resolve their disputes, which he did graciously and gently (they were often rather vulnerable).

For this reason, when one day a stranger approached Francesco in the street, he thought nothing of it. "Count Algarotti?"

He turned to see a young man dressed in an extravagant costume.

"I am in rather a hurry," he replied, at first taking the youth for a busker. The young man was wearing a sort of pantomime military uniform consisting of a shiny white coat of cheap material and midnight blue vest, both smothered in abundant coils of false gold and silver frogging. Gilded epaulettes the size of dessert plates teetered on his shoulders, dripping long fringe to his elbows. The outfit was topped by an enormous hat with a black cockade stuck to one side. Even Francesco, with his limited knowledge of military matters (and his even more limited interest) could tell this uniform belonged to no regiment in existence.

"Forgive me." The stranger swept off his hat and bowed low. Underneath the silly costume, he was a handsome youth of about nineteen with dark skin and hair. "I couldn't let the opportunity p—pass to pay my respects to the most brilliant man in Venice."

"Have we met, Signor?" Francesco studied the young man, trying to guess who he might be. His speech and manners were certainly refined. They were in San Moisè and there were many theatres in the vicinity. Francesco guessed he was some sort of actor.

Before he could come to any conclusions, the youth began to

talk at great speed, burying Francesco in an avalanche of hero worship. Whoever he was, he had done his homework. He knew of Francesco's book and his demonstrations, he knew of his friendship with the Abbé Conti and Lodoli and the other leaders of thought in the city. He was well informed about his travels, his laurels, and the reason he had returned to Venice.

"Your example has led me to pursue a life devoted to literature and science," the young man concluded, quite breathless.

"Enough about me," Francesco said. By this time he'd grown quite fond of the stranger. "Tell me about yourself. I see by your uniform that you are some kind of a military man?" He smiled a little as he said this, inviting the youth to make excuses for his costume.

"I am not really a s—soldier," the youth responded with a slight stammer that re-emerged once he'd finished the rehearsed part of his speech. "This is just temporary. I used to be an abbot, you see, but I found that profession con—contradictory to my temperament."

"An abbot?" Francesco smiled more broadly. "Somehow you don't strike me as a religious person, Signor."

"Not in the least," the youth said, lifting his chin. "It's against my beliefs. So I am doing what I can to get into a new way of living. The military seemed a promising avenue, but this is only for now." He plucked at his splendid frogging with some distaste. "My real ambition is to travel, to meet great men, to speak languages. And then to write, like you. I've already published a poem, in Naples."

Francesco congratulated him sincerely — nothing felt as good as your first publication — and yet there was a quality about this young man that suggested he wasn't going to succeed in living the life of the mind. Partly it was the silly uniform, which still had no real explanation and which, Francesco was certain, the youth had invented for himself. Partly it was the young man's demeanour. There was something exaggerated about him. His eyes shone, though he was not drunk. All the sinews of his body were taut, like ropes holding a running sail. He seemed simultaneously ridiculous and dangerous and Francesco concluded that he was the sort of person you should either mock or run from, but never trust. To be on the safe side, in order to make checks on him afterwards, he asked the youth's name.

"Giacomo Farussi," the gallant replied with another flourish of his hat. "Your servant. And I really mean that. If you should ever require the slightest service — "

Francesco interrupted him. "Farussi? Are you by chance related to La Farussi, the actress?"

The youth paused, his hat held in midair. "She is my mother," he said in a flat voice that spoke volumes of shame.

Francesco was intrigued to discover the unexpected connection. King Augustus kept a troupe of good Italian actors at court and La Farussi had long been a valued member of its company. "But what a coincidence. I know your mother well. In fact, I've seen her perform innumerable times in Dresden."

"Dresden is where she has lived for many years," Farussi said with a proud, pained expression. "Her children were raised here in Venice."

That explained everything: the young man's theatricality, his weird taste in clothing and the impossibility of placing him socially. Such a creature could only be the offspring of actors. Francesco tried to recall whose mistress La Farussi had been the last time he saw her in Dresden — she was no longer young, but remained popular with mature lovers of the theatre. He assured young Farussi that his mother was much admired in the court of Augustus the Third, which was perfectly true.

"Thank you for saying so," the young man answered. "But for reasons you will understand, I intend to use my f—father's name in my literary life."

Francesco did understand. The only thing more disreputable than an actress was the son of an actress. The chances were slim, however, that this young man had any idea who his father actually was. "And what will that be?" he asked indulgently. "So that I can look out for it?"

"Casanova," the youth said. It rang no bells with Francesco. "Giacomo Casanova."

"I will look forward to reading your future works," Francesco said and made his escape before the strange youth could find a reason to latch on to him permanently.

T o please Venice, Francesco did his best impersonation of a young man whose only concern was to look good and be amusing. In private, however, he maintained the sort of rigourous work regime that Frederick would have approved of. He kept his clock set in accordance with the strict English system for keeping time, resisting the temptation to adopt the elastic Venetian mode, which was based on the ever-changing interval between sunrise and sunset. He fitted work into the dull hours between social engagements. After lunch, while Bonomo and his family dozed, he splashed cold water on his face and took advantage of the quiet to write letters, jot notes, check and double check his budget. He made lists and ticked items off them:

Zuccarelli: commissioned a pair of landscapes, one based on Virgil, the other on Cicero. *Tick.*

Amigoni: accepted commission for classical scene out of Xenophon. *Tick.*

Major picture dealers in the city — met with them all (?). *Tick.*

He paused and considered this tick mark critically, then scribbled over it. Meeting the picture dealers of Venice was nothing

— the hard work would be getting them to produce suitable paintings for Augustus at an affordable price. The king and his ministers had no idea how difficult this could be. They seemed to think that valuable paintings could be found littering the streets of Venice, and that all Francesco had to do was go around with a handcart, shoveling them up. Entering into negotiations with the wily art dealers was more like walking into a cage of lions, in fact. You had to keep a whip in one hand and a chair in the other, or else they'd eat you alive.

Right now, the lions were all telling Francesco the same thing in a universal roar, that there were few Old Masters on the market and that the competition for them was fierce. Francesco had received this news calmly, understanding that they were softening him up to pay inflated prices for inferior goods. So far, as he anticipated, he'd been shown a few piddling-sized paintings by second-rate artists — derisory offerings, which he'd treated with derision. One or two were obvious fakes, which abounded in Venice. It was a good thing Augustus had sent a native Venetian to do his collecting for him, he reflected. Anyone else would end up walking away with a handful of worthless yellow prints and a Palma Vecchio forged the week before and dunked in a filthy canal to make it look old.

He sighed. It was a shame he had to spend so much time on dead painters. He loved his dealings with the living ones and was more convinced than ever of two things: first that the accident of being dead didn't elevate a mediocre artist to greatness; and second that bad paintings didn't improve with age. In this way, painters were unlike saints and paintings were unlike cheese. He smiled at this *aperçu*, reminding himself to put it in his next letter to someone or other.

Francesco turned to the frustrating question of Tiepolo. He'd failed to arrange a second meeting and now the painter had gone out of town, to Vicenza, where he was frescoing the walls of a villa. He'd be there for several weeks, taking advantage of the dry weather so essential to the success of the technique. Francesco, on the case, had written to him, trying to sound affable while probing for a firm commitment. Tiepolo had replied very cordially, writing in flattering terms about how nice it was to meet someone so knowledgeable about painting etc. But Francesco wasn't fooled. A past master at such charming evasion, he felt himself being fobbed off. The pleasant, empty letter confirmed his suspicion that Tiepolo, far from being safely in the bag, was yet to be snared.

He considered his next move. If there was one thing he'd learned from his days spent at various royal courts, it was that when you want to win a man (in any way) you must take a three-hundred-and-sixty-degree approach to him. If you need him to fund your opera, for example, you learn about his love of China roses. If you want him to bankroll your book of verse, you offer his favourite dessert. "Sometimes," Francesco had once boasted to Bonomo, "you can spot the key to a man's sympathy in the eyes of his horse." Francesco had won Frederick with music. The first time they met, they sat down and wrote a sonata together. Within a year, Frederick had made Algarotti a count and brought him to Berlin. With this in mind, Francesco decided to try a lateral approach to Tiepolo and pay his respects to the signora.

"Petition T's muse," he wrote on his list. Thinking again, he crossed out the word *muse* and replaced it with *wife*. He'd been called a muse himself while he was living with Frederick and he didn't care for the title. Muses, he well knew, were never taken seriously. He jotted a courteous note to the lady, roused Bonomo's surly servant, and had him take it directly to the house in San Silvestre.

Francesco prepared himself carefully for his call on Signora Tiepolo. He sent gifts ahead: a large box of chocolates and a copy of his book, *Newton for Ladies,* with an inscription. He did his groundwork on her background, too, and this proved very interesting.

The painters of Venice were a tight-knit community. Many of them were related to one another through marriage or other more intricate forms of kinship. Some of Francesco's contacts had known both Tiepolos since they were children and were happy to gossip about them. Francesco learned that Signora Tiepolo was the daughter of an immigrant painter who had worked in many studios and specialised in the depiction of flowers. Her father was long dead and long forgotten, but she had no fewer than three brothers still working as painters in the city. The oldest, Antonio Guardi, was something of a character in the painting community. He lived — happily, it was said — like an indentured servant in the palazzo of the war hero Marshal von Schulenburg, painting reproductions of works by better artists for two zecchini a pop: dirt cheap by anyone's standards. Then there were two much younger brothers, Francesco and Nicolò. They were marginal, jobbing artists known for painting views, a lowly genre that paid badly and left its practitioners in obscurity.

Signora Tiepolo had humble origins, but then so did Tiepolo, who didn't come from a painting family at all. His father had been a shipping merchant and had died young, leaving the family destitute. Tiepolo had risen to prominence through talent alone, but it was his marriage to Cecilia Guardi, daughter and sister of painters, that cemented his place in Venice's painting community. Popular mythology had it that Tiepolo spotted his future wife on the street, declared her the living incarnation of Veronese's ideal woman and proposed to her on the spot. "*Veronese only has you in his dreams,*" he was supposed to have said, "*I am determined to have you in my bed!*"

Friends scoffed at this story: the fact was Tiepolo needed Cecilia Guardi as much as she needed him. Apart from her good looks, she'd proved a useful wife: healthy, fertile and canny with money — just the sort of wife an ambitious painter needs. And then, of course, Tiepolo used her constantly as a model. Look at any Tiepolo painting, they said, and there she was: Venus, Maria, Cleopatra, Judith, Armida, Rachel, Europa, Helen, Salome. That fact alone must have saved the painter thousands of ducats over the years. No wonder the Tiepolos were so rich.

When Francesco heard this last observation — that Signora Tiepolo served as Tiepolo's main model — he knew he'd been an idiot as usual. Once again, he'd been distracted by the bright glamour of his own talent and failed to see what had always been directly in front of his eyes.

Determined to remedy this failing, he took himself straight home and locked himself in his room. He pulled down the blinds, lay on his bed and took himself to his inner gallery.

Francesco was only a boy when he discovered his perfect memory for images. His father, an enthusiastic lover of the arts, noticed it first. He used to trot little Francesco out at parties and have him demonstrate his talent by describing every painting and print hanging on the walls of a palazzo he had visited only once. Guests were astonished and tickled: they challenged the little boy with tricky questions about the works, which he answered with no difficulty. His recall was so complete that it recorded pictures the owners themselves had forgotten they possessed and captured minute details that everyone, except possibly the artist, had overlooked. It was during these performances that Francesco began to think of himself as a prodigy, a belief that helped him greatly later in life.

Yet, like every excessive talent, Francesco's recall proved to be a mixed blessing. By his teens, his memory was clogged with images. For a while, they seemed to take up all his thinking space and he struggled to concentrate on his studies. He took refuge in science and mathematics, disciplines relatively free of the visual. That helped to an extent. Unfortunately, he moved among the rich, the educated, the noble, whose walls were always thick with pictures. Short of blinding himself, there was no way to avoid seeing them and, in consequence, mentally storing them whether he wanted to or not. So as a means of coping, he hit upon the idea of constructing a sort of gallery in his head. If he couldn't avoid remembering pictures, he reasoned, he might as well make his memory orderly.

In the beginning he gave his inner gallery the only form he knew, arranging it like an art collection in a rich man's palazzo with pictures crammed together on the walls, ceiling to baseboard, in a full frontal display of wealth. Like the rich, Francesco placed important works most prominently at eye level, with lesser ones positioned high or low, where they attracted less attention. Like them, he gave no thought to lighting and chose the pictures to match the décor, rather than the other way around.

For a while, this sufficed. His inner gallery benefitted from a sort of spatial logic that helped him keep it under control. Yet over time, as Francesco travelled the world and expanded his learning, he began to feel dissatisfied with its layout. There were, he reasoned, important differences between his mind and the salons of the wealthy. His mind, for one thing, was infinite. There was no need to limit the amount of space devoted to art. He could extend his inner galleries ad infinitum and arrange the images as he liked, by artist, by date, by subject, by colour, even by size.

Lying awake at night, he began to toy with the design of his inner gallery, giving it forms he had never seen in reality. His refinements had now led him to a point where every work of art hung precisely at his own eye level. They were widely spaced on imaginary walls and each individual picture was bathed in even, natural light. Each picture was plainly framed, labelled and positioned near works that were related to it in some logical way — by period or artist or nationality or technique — so that the pictures spoke to one another and of one another.

There was a ritual approach to the inner gallery and Francesco followed its path each time he went there. First he imagined himself descending from a carriage and approaching a Palladian building fronted with smooth, simple Doric columns. Then he ascended a set of wide stone stairs and passed through a grand doorway into an open vestibule with a checkered parquet floor. Flights of stairs rose like wings on either side of the vestibule, leading to different parts of the collection. Francesco chose the one on the right, following the faint scent of orange blossom.

Tiepolo's gallery was a long, wide, rather austere hallway lit from above by glazed skylights such as those Francesco had seen used to luminous effect at Sir John Soane's house in London. The walls were covered in printed paper of a deep yellow colour that provided an ideal background, Francesco believed, for all Tiepolo's works. At the far end of this corridor was a set of French doors — Francesco had never quite understood what they were doing there but he liked them, so he left them where they were. They opened onto a sunny balcony that overlooked an orange grove in full bloom. The scent of orange blossom wafted into the corridor, flooding the entire gallery with a pure, irresistible sweetness that created the perfect ambience for appreciating Tiepolo's artworks.

Francesco began to review the works. He'd begun to build up his Tiepolo collection as a boy in Venice, involuntarily, long before he understood its importance. On the walls of his mind were early, dark examples of Tiepolos from the Ospedaletto and from Doge Cornaro's palace, where his father had once taken him on business, all hastily but permanently stored in his young memory. He had dug these Tiepolos out at the start of the Dresden project and placed them in a small temporary room in his mind while he decided whether to commission Tiepolo or not. As he developed his brief for Augustus, he added more images to his gallery: etchings, prints, illustrations from Venetian books, altarpieces, the frescoes at Udine and the Scalzi. Once he was convinced that Tiepolo had to be part of his project, he conjured the yellow hallway to house the artist's works and moved the collection to its new site.

Now as he proceeded down the hallway, looking at each image in turn, Francesco's irritation with himself grew. Because — here she was. Sometimes Mary, sometimes Eurydice, Rachel, Salome, Venus, Pharaoh's daughter. Whoever she was supposed to be in the story, Tiepolo's woman was always physically the same woman, a lush, lazy beauty with a pink flank, a straight leonine nose, a soft chin and a neck like a column of marble: Signora Tiepolo. It was glaringly obvious. How had he failed to see it?

Francesco opened his eyes, feeling suddenly apprehensive about his upcoming visit. He had met many celebrated beauties in his time and many, many women — queens and strumpets, scullery maids and educated ladies — who had served as models for famous paintings. But he had never before met one who was the single source and origin of all female beauty for a great artist, as well as being his wife. He tried to summon up an image of Signora Tiepolo as he had seen her the other day in the studio, but all he could recall was a pair of dark eyes, a string of pearls and an ordinary blue dress.

He took his time choosing his clothes on the day of the visit, settling at last on a coat and waistcoat of Venetian tailoring, hoping the outfit made him look elegant but at the same time familiar and slightly needy. He made his way to the house at San Silvestre along a now-familiar route. The street door was opened by the black manservant, Zuane, who was expecting him this time. He led Francesco up two flights of stairs, passing the doors of the studio, which were tightly shut. Finally he admitted him to the *piano nobile*, where the Tiepolo ladies sat in tense readiness for him.

All three jumped up from their places as he entered, like automata set on springs. Francesco's own heart was beating strongly as he came for the second time into the presence of the woman who was the inspiration for his now-favourite painter. The first time he'd met her, he had committed the classical sin of failing to recognise her — in antiquity mortals were eternally punished for such slights, turned into trees or natural features or animals. He knew he was lucky to have a second chance. Determined to put things right, he rushed into the room with his hand outstretched, eager to touch the goddess and pay her court.

Unfortunately, the goddess was in hiding. In place of the dazzling immortal he hoped to meet, Francesco was confronted, again, with an ordinary woman, the very same one he had met in the studio, but dressed up for his visit. Today she was wearing a lace cap over her hair and what anyone could see was her Best Frock: green and lilac stripes, not flattering. Her clothes were expensive, she wore numerous golden rings stacked on her fingers, yet something about her appearance made Francesco think of a maid wearing her mistress' finery. Her note inviting him to coffee had been surprisingly assured — it wasn't every day a Count paid a visit to the wife of a painter — but now, face to face with him, Signora Tiepolo seemed shy and gauche. When he kissed her hand, she withdrew it gracelessly and removed herself to safety several feet away.

They all sat down stiffly on a set of brand new sofas. A maid brought in a tray, and Signora Tiepolo plied Francesco with coffee and sweets as though she had nothing else to offer him. In one of the thickest local accents Francesco had ever heard, she asked about his health, his parents' health, Bonomo's. He answered the rote questions politely, wondering if the woman could read the disappointment on his face. Perhaps she was used to it: he can't have been the only fan of Tiepolo's to be let down by Signora Tiepolo's stubborn, everyday reality. Francesco felt the sadness of a myth dying in his hands.

She introduced him to her two daughters. Anna Maria, the older girl, had a face coined from her father's, with its narrow chin and sharp-bridged nose, hardly ornaments for a girl of twenty. Her cheeks were scarred with smallpox and her demeanour was sour, as though she had no interest in pleasing anyone. She sported a pair of frown lines like little cart tracks between her eyebrows and Francesco interpreted them as a sign of bad temper and intelligence, which so often went hand in hand. The girl made an attempt to smile but her expression lacked naturalness, as if smiling were an unaccustomed chore for her.

Elena, the other daughter, was a few years younger than Anna Maria and very silly. She gasped our loud when Francesco kissed her hand. "He's so elegant!" she cried ingenuously, wriggling like a puppy. Francesco identified her as one of those enthusiastic girls who drops like a stone into the lap of the first cavalry officer she meets — he'd run across them often in the past. (Sometimes these girls had done their damnedest to drop into *his* lap, with limited success.) Yet Elena's fresh young beauty soothed Francesco a little. With her dark golden hair and oval face, she was like a half-divine heroine, only a muted echo of the lost goddess mother, but still lovely. If he squinted slightly, he could almost see her stepping out of one of her father's frescoes to squeeze herself into her uncomfortable pink dress. He gazed into her smiling face, drenching her with charm, making her turn a fetching shade of rose. It occurred to him that this looked strange because Tiepolo's women never smiled or blushed. It also occurred to him that Signora Tiepolo had invited him for her unmarried daughters' sake. Knowing he was bound to disappoint them all, he sighed and prepared himself to endure a futile hour.

Later, Francesco couldn't remember all he said at this awkward encounter. The conversation failed to flow and he worked hard to rescue what seemed like a lost cause. He filled the air with compliments the way a fiddle player fills the air with music, because that was his job. He praised Tiepolo. Later, he remembered remarking somewhat desperately on the décor of the room, which had been recently refurbished. Its greenish-grey walls and pink curtains were pedestrian. They bore no trace of the owner's amazing artistry. Casting his eyes around for things to admire, Francesco noticed a little plaster roundel on the ceiling above them and had an idea.

"Why, Signora," he said to the lady, "this ceiling is calling out for embellishment by your husband. A scene in fresco here would be the crowning glory of such a fine room."

Up until this point, Signora Tiepolo had been sitting silently in her chair, playing with the innumerable rings on her fingers. After the initial pleasantries, she responded to his comments with single sounds, like a woman who isn't entirely comfortable with human speech, preferring to let her daughters answer for her. Francesco decided she must be like the wives of so many artisans, passive and uneducated, illiterate if not a little stupid, devoted to her family and deeply religious. These women were the polar opposites of the fashionable, witty ladies he kept company with in the salons in Paris and London and Saint Petersburg. Francesco supposed that ambitious men like Tiepolo married them for refuge. You couldn't talk to them about science or art, but you could certainly relax in their presence.

Now, however, Signora Tiepolo seemed to come to life. She glanced overhead. "A scene in fresco?" she said. "Here? D'you think?"

"I do," he said. "This roundel is the perfect spot for a painting on a classical theme — or a sacred subject," he added, remembering, perhaps too late, that he was talking to a Venetian woman of a certain age and class.

His instinct was correct. Signora Tiepolo shot him a critical look. "Oh, definitely a *sacred* subject," she affirmed. For a moment her eyes rested on his. He'd noticed that they were dark brown, but now he realised with a kind of shock that Tiepolo, in every image of this woman, invariably painted them blue.

Feeling a sense of dislocation, he asked, "And what sacred subject would be your choice, Signora?"

"San Rocco, of course." Francesco could have guessed the answer. San Rocco was the patron saint of painters. Yet inwardly he grimaced: the derelict saint with his running leprosy sores, made an abysmal motif for interior decoration.

"I find San Rocco's little dog so touching," he said.

Signora Tiepolo shifted in her chair. She cocked her elbow at a sharp angle and placed a fist on her hip. "It's all the same," she said. "Tiepolo'll never really do it. I've been after him about it for ages. Do you know, in more than twenty years of marriage, I have never managed to convince him to put so much as one dab of paint on our own house?"

"No!" Francesco said.

"No. I tell you I have to hire decorators for everything. And you know what decorators are like." She slapped open her fan deftly.

It was a finely made thing with carved sandalwood blades and a screen painted in the oriental style. Francesco could smell the fragrant wood as she stirred the air. Her enigmatic eyes watched him over its moving arc.

There was a pause during which Francesco duly absorbed the message that Signora Tiepolo had no influence over what her husband painted. At this point, he began to plan his exit seriously. Yet he judged the occasion demanded one more attempt at conversation before he excused himself.

"I wonder if you received the book I sent you," he asked. "Along with the chocolates," he added, thinking that the chocolates probably made a greater impression than the book.

Signora Tiepolo's response was instantaneous and unexpected. The lady snapped her fan shut and looked down at the carpet as though tracing her thought in its frenetic pattern.

"We did," she said sadly, shaking her head. "We did."

"Oh?" Francesco gazed around the room in confusion.

Anna Maria cleared her throat and chimed in. "My mother wasn't able to read your book." Her words sounded rehearsed. Looks passed among the three women. They had obviously pre-arranged this response.

Signora Tiepolo tilted her head to one side and spoke to Francesco as if he were a three-year-old. "Forgive me, Count. I didn't feel I *could* read it. Because, as you know, it was banned by the Church."

Francesco felt like kicking himself. What had he been thinking? His book on Newton might be the right thing to send a countess, a princess or even an actress. But how could he have thought it was the right gift for the wife of a painter? Wrapped up in his fantasies about Signora Tiepolo, he had forgotten who she really was. Respectable Venetian matrons were pious. They didn't read banned books.

Fearing now that his gaffe would damage relations with Tiepolo, Francesco hurried to explain that, though the previous pope had indeed banned his book, the current one, Benedict, had lifted the ban.

Signora Tiepolo blinked at him with eyes the colour of coffee. Her fan opened, resumed its movement, forward and back, like the beat of a heart. "Can His Holiness do that?" she asked in a tone of interest. "Un-ban a ban?"

"Signora, he could and did." Francesco felt sweat break out on his neck beneath the linen collar of his jabot. "Like most educated men, Pope Benedict is a dedicated Newtonian."

"Is that a fact?" Signora Tiepolo said. He saw the corner of her mouth twitch slightly in what might have been the beginnings of a smile. Instantly, the fan's painted screen passed over it. Was it his imagination, or was Signora Tiepolo making fun of him? "Anna Maria," she commanded, never breaking off her gaze.

Anna Maria spoke up. "*I* read your book," she said again in the same rehearsed voice. He noticed for the first time the familiar brown cover of *Newton for Ladies* in the girl's hands. Where had she been keeping it? Perhaps she'd been hiding the book in a pocket. "Mama asked me to read it for her and tell her about it."

"Oh. Well — thank you very much."

"Anna Maria is the clever one," Signora Tiepolo explained. "Say something about Count Algarotti's book, Anna Maria."

Anna Maria obediently opened the book as though it were a lesson she'd prepared. She cleared her throat. "It was good. We all liked the picture. And now we know it looks just like you."

She held out the book to him as though he might have forgotten any of its beloved details. The "picture" she referred to was the frontispiece, the book's only illustration. It showed the lovely Marchioness and the handsome Chevalier walking together in the villa garden. Francesco had commissioned the engraving himself, from Piazzetta.

"I did in fact pose for the figure of the Chevalier," he admitted. The model for the Marchioness was his brilliant friend, Émelie du Châtelet, Voltaire's mistress, who had encouraged him to write *Newton for Ladies*. "Did you like anything else about the book?" he asked, surprised at how pathetic his question sounded.

Signora Tiepolo nodded to Anna Maria, who obliged him. "I like the Marchioness, she's funny. Whenever the Chevalier's explanations about science start to get boring, she livens things up by teasing him." She leafed through the pages. "For instance, here. When the Chevalier is jawing on and on — that is, *talking* — about Sir Isaac Newton's demonstrations she says, 'We may affirm that as everything which Midas touched was transformed into Gold, so everything that Sir Isaac Newton touched was turned into a Demonstration.' That's funny. It's a way of getting him to be quiet."

"I intended the book to be entertaining," Francesco said, feeling himself blushing. "Like a play."

"Well, it was. Sort of."

"And did you have any questions about the — ah — science?" he asked tentatively. It had been years since he'd felt so vulnerable. "I'd be more than happy to answer them."

The girl looked scared for a moment. Her eyes darted to her mother and the cart tracks deepened on her forehead.

"Blended light," Signora Tiepolo prompted. "You remember, darling. Mixed paint?"

"Oh yes." Anna Maria seemed to recover. "If light is made up of all the colours blended together, right, then why isn't everything in the world just plain white? And why, when we mix all the paints together, does it produce a horrible mud colour, instead of white?"

Francesco was tickled with her questions. It was one thing to have educated ladies in Paris read his book, but to make any kind of impression on the mind of one of Tiepolo's daughters, right here in Venice, was like a sweet dream. He decided Anna Maria was a genius. He imagined spending the rest of his time in the city teaching her science and mathematics. He launched into a lecture about reflection and refraction. He took out his notebook to make Anna Maria clarifying sketches of light bouncing, light absorbing, light blending, with long arrows shooting here and there and wavy lines undulating across the page. He explained about mineral pigments and the difference between coloured material and the pure bands of coloured light produced when white light passes through a prism. He could have kept going like this for longer, but Elena interrupted him. Fed up with being ignored, she said she had a question, too.

"Formulating questions even without even reading my book?" Francesco said suddenly remembering he was there to be charming, not pedantic. "That is remarkable."

Elena flushed again but continued. "Where is the Marchioness' husband? She spends all her time with the Chevalier and her husband is never around. Wouldn't he be jealous?"

"I was wondering the same thing!" said Signora Tiepolo, sitting up with sudden energy and then seeming to think better of it. As she subsided back into her chair, Francesco had a clear mental image of all the Tiepolo ladies sitting there beneath the empty roundel, eating cookies and listening to Anna Maria read his book out loud. Why was the signora pretending ignorance?

The question stumped him, however. None of Francesco's readers, male or female, had ever asked it before. He was reminded once again that he was no longer in the salons of Paris or London where everyone knew (because they knew Francesco) that the husband of the Marchioness had nothing whatsoever to fear from his wife's companion. Naturally, he was unable to explain this in plain terms. Instead he made up some tale about the husband overseeing the instalation of fountains in the villa gardens and being too busy to worry about what his wife was doing. This seemed to make sense to the female Tiepolos.

While he was talking, he couldn't help being aware of a series of loud noises coming from the lower floor. At first it reached them as an irregular pounding, now heavy, now lighter, accompanied by a high-pitched whine such as the sound sometimes produced by experiments with pressurised steam.

"Good heavens. What could the assistants be up to in the studio?" he asked.

"It's not the studio," said Anna Maria in a voice dripping with sarcasm. "It's the precious darlings."

Doors slammed, there were near-human shouts. As the sounds came closer, the racket reminded Francesco less of an industrial process than of the sound made by a stampede of panicked cattle. Finally it evolved into something like the noise produced by a team of acrobats in suits of armor throwing one another up a wooden staircase.

Elena looked like she might cry. "How can they act like that!" she wailed. "Don't they know we have company?"

"Oh, they know," muttered Anna Maria. "They know."

The door to the salon flew open with a bang and in rushed a small boy of about five clutching a little black and white dog. Hot on his heels were two older children, a girl and a boy, roaring like savages and clawing the air with their hands. The boy with the dog screamed and launched himself at Signora Tiepolo.

"Mama! They're going to cook him!" Clutching the little dog under one arm, he started to scramble up Signora Tiepolo's wide silk skirt. Francesco saw her wince as the little boy's boot heels dug into her legs and belly, but she made no attempt to stop him.

"Lorenzo," she murmured as the boy trampled her dress and thrust the animal in her face. "What is all this about?"

Tearfully the boy explained that his brother and sister were threatening to roast his dog and eat him. Signora Tiepolo soothed him, saying that, no, his brother and sister would never eat little Fleabag (or whatever he was called); they loved him every bit as much as Lorenzo did.

"They love to eat him," Lorenzo said surveying his brother and sister with hostility.

The dog rested passively in the boy's arms. It was hideous, with a ferret-like face and shiny, bulging eyes. It extended a pink tongue and moistened its own nose, not frightened at all. Meanwhile, the two older children had paused a few feet away. Not sure what to do, they stood clawing the air and roaring from time to time, but their ferocity lacked conviction. They shot little glances in Francesco's direction. He knew this performance was for him somehow, and he tried to oblige.

"Who are these terrifying beasts?" he cried, a little too loudly. He'd never had much of a feel for children.

"You think they're terrifying?" Anna Maria murmured in his ear. "Wait until you meet Angela."

A tall girl with a pimply, sullen face appeared in the doorway and lurked there.

"Angela is thirteen," Anna Maria said in a conspiratorial whisper, letting all that this implied remain unspoken. Francesco was beginning to love this acerbic, clever Tiepolo girl.

"Just how many of you are there?" he whispered to her, hoping to confirm her as an ally.

"I've lost count," she said, disgusted. But she obliged him by performing a quick inventory on her fingers. "There's me, Elena, Domenico — who works with Papa — Giuseppe — he's at the seminary of Santa Maria della Salute — Angela, Antonio, Orsola and Lorenzo: eight. Ten, if you ask Mama, but she counts the dead ones."

Eight children, Francesco thought with a sense of awe. What do you do with so many? Tiepolo's paintings, he'd noticed, were often full to the bursting point with babies and little children crowding in at the margins, filling up the dead space around the central drama. Now he thought he recognised some of the faces in the lively crowd in the parlour. Perhaps their father was always, in his mind and in his pictures, looking for places to put them.

The civilised coffee morning dissolved into family chaos. Francesco said his goodbyes as quickly as he could and returned home with the feeling he'd wasted his time. Signora Tiepolo's vacant roundel was, he thought, the emblem of this meeting: having gone to discover the goddess at home, Francesco had found nothing, Giotto's O, all empty. Tiepolo the man might live in that house, but Tiepolo the artist certainly did not. The goddess had eluded him again.

The weeks passed. Francesco was goaded by a pair of silences. One came from Tiepolo. He knew the painter was back in Venice, yet he hadn't heard anything from him. It was clear now that this was deliberate. His evasion made Francesco feel humiliated, and it made him want Tiepolo all the more. It was funny how that worked. He was used to being on the other end of that equation.

The second silence came from Frederick. Every day when letters arrived, Francesco looked for one bearing the seal of Prussia, a spatchcocked eagle pressed into red wax. Every day, it wasn't there.

After several weeks, when the silence became too much for Francesco, he did what he had promised himself never to do again: he went to his trunk and took out the heavy bundle that contained Frederick's letters.

He knew before he untied the ribbon that this was a mistake. The mere sight of Frederick's handwriting gave him a physical jolt. Frederick's script was so like Frederick: slapdash, sometimes brutal and only superficially refined, but impelled by a fine forward energy that drove its content directly into the mind. The language of the letters was French and Frederick's spelling was awful, though his grammar was sound, his overall style manly and direct. His message, in contrast, was often petulant, especially toward the end. *Inconstant*, Frederick called Francesco. *Flighty*. The tone was teasing, but a royal fury boiled beneath the words.

About the time Francesco had gone to Dresden, Frederick was making preparations to march off to Silesia with his surly generals to "fix the face of Prussia", as he wrote coquettishly, whose features were "too irregular" for his taste. Francesco had seen this move coming barely in time. His departure for Dresden was a weak response to something he had no power to influence, but it made him look at least slightly purposeful, at least slightly in control. Frederick, shocked by his flight but too proud to make a scene, lent Francesco the coach that would take him away.

Working hard in Dresden, Francesco let himself be reassured by the affectionate tone of Frederick's early letters from the battlefield. At first they were imbued with the king's longing for the finer things they both valued: for music, for intelligent conversation, for the presence of *"my swan"* — Frederick's nickname for Francesco. From time to time the king even sent Francesco lyric poems on the subject of himself: *"Ô mortel trop charmant! Ô mortel trop amable! / Sacrifiez pour moi les schah, les Chouli-kans…"*

It was very sweet, so like the Frederick of the old days, before he'd become king and taken to wearing a military uniform all the time. But it was dishonest too. Frederick had misjudged his tactics. Francesco didn't want sonnets from him, he wanted some measure of truthfulness. He would have preferred to hear more about

Frederick's military progress, to share his real preoccupations, his ugly daily concerns. Instead, Frederick delivered evasions trussed up in pretty silk ribbons and garnished with vivid red seals. From his billet in a captured villa, the king sent Francesco his views on the property's interior decoration and contemplated redesigning the garden. No mention that his presence there meant its owner was dead, or in prison, or busy signing, with a sabre to his throat, some treaty of total capitulation to Prussia.

In his responses — he naturally kept copies of them — Francesco had matched lie for lie, evasion for evasion. He had danced around Frederick's thwarted desire and rage with verbal choreography honed by years spent in the company of the cleverest people in the world. Caesar and Sparta, Dacians, Parthians, Graces all mixed up with Grenadiers. Flattery and reason, science, poetry, flirtation and rebuke: Francesco threw it all into the pot, everything he had, fully aware that he was avoiding the issues and this would only make Frederick madder. He called Frederick *Votre Majesté*, a French feminine honourific that grammatically forced him to address the king, for page after page, as *she*. It was an old joke of theirs. In light of what had become of their relationship, Francesco winced when he read it now.

After months of this pointless dance, both men lost patience. The last straw came in the crude form of a quarrel over seventeen ducats. Francesco asked to be reimbursed for some minor travel expenses; Frederick, always stingy but never more so than when his feelings were wounded, told him to come and collect them in person if he wanted them so much. Francesco recognised this as a final offer and he rejected it with hauteur. Instead, he went to Venice in a hurry, afraid Frederick would send troops to stop his carriage and drag him back. He had to admit he was a little disappointed when they failed to materialise.

Yet, sitting at his desk, Francesco missed Frederick. He was sure Frederick would enjoy Venice, a place he had never visited; a place he would now never go to, unless he decided to invade it. He would have appreciated its antiquity, its deep, diverse culture, and even its hint of corruption — there was nothing Frederic liked better than enjoying, then condemning, any kind of corruption. He'd relish the opportunity to dress up in a black domino and mask and go about incognito, drinking in inns like other people, gambling at the Ridotto, going to the theatre — it had always been one of his fantasies to move about unrecognised and that was possible only here, only in Francesco's home city. Why did he refuse to come?

And Francesco would have liked to have Frederick with him in Venice. He longed to regale him with his adventures in the art trade. The antics of the picture dealers would have made the king laugh his most cynical laugh, a sound Francesco loved to hear. Frederick would have relished the scandal as well as the fact that Francesco was giving him confidences at the expense of Augustus, of whom he was very jealous. Before the war, the two monarchs had vied for the honour of being Europe's greatest enlightened patron of culture. Once Francesco and Frederick had dreamed together of creating entire cities devoted to art and music and science. Now Frederick was compelled to spend all his money on artillery instead of art. Augustus had won the competition.

Poor Frederick, Francesco thought, imagining him sitting in his draughty tent surrounded by the bulky, stupid aristocrats who served as his officers — a wall of depressing dark blue uniforms. Francesco had witnessed with his own eyes how isolated Frederick was in their company. When the king made jokes, the military men blinked in confusion, their faces grew red, then, after an awkward pause, they laughed with compressed lips, as though in response to an order. Yes, Frederick was all alone in his war. And Francesco was all alone, even surrounded by the beauties of

Venice. How had this come about?

With a sigh, Francesco gathered up the letters and bound them together with the blue silk ribbon. The thought of Frederick reminded him that he still had much to prove.

Francesco stood in glittering company in the main reception room at Palazzo Balbi holding a glass of finest stemware from Murano. It was filled with warm, brown, flat English beer. He sipped; he winced. It was a piquant juxtaposition — the swirled stem and gilded lip of the glass containing the earthy foreign brew — and today it was not to Francesco's taste. Out of ingrained politeness he brought the glass to his lips one more time as he listened to Vittoria, his brother's wife, describing their summer travel plans. As she talked, the taste of the beer filled his mind with images of England, its damp wheat fields, its smoky rooms, its boiled cabbage, and the continual, melancholy presence of seagulls even far inland, which had, during his time there, so reminded him of home.

The palazzo he stood in belonged to an Englishman, Joseph Smith. Smith was a wealthy merchant who'd lived in Venice for forty years and his palatial home reflected an unusual life path. Smith had bought it as a ruin and made it grand again with an expensive new frontage designed by his friend Visentini. Then he filled it with an eclectic mix of Venetian art and English furniture. The paintings on the walls were local — Smith was an avid collector and promoter of the arts. The furniture was very English: squat and highly varnished with twee flourishes to make it appear "refined". The food Smith served was similarly idiosyncratic. The beer in crystal was example of his host's taste in miniature. There was a time when Francesco would have drunk it without complaint. But now he had been to England. In England, he reflected, no one had ever compelled him to drink bitter beer against his will. As a servant passed with a tray, he put the glass on it and asked him to bring some wine.

Out of the corner of his eye he caught sight of Smith working his way across the crowded room. His host was beautifully dressed in a pale pink coat and a fashionable wig carefully constructed to make his close-set eyes seem more widely spaced and take the emphasis away from his heavy brow. He was an old man — Francesco guessed he must be at least seventy — but he carried himself very upright, as instructed, no doubt, by some dancing master.

"Smith's looking well," Francesco commented to Vittoria.

"Is he?" Vittoria squinted blindly across the room. She was a very pretty woman with fair hair and greenish eyes and a small pink bow of a mouth. But she was very nearsighted. Francesco guided her chin until her face was pointing in Smith's direction. "I still can't see him. Has he got a new coat on?" she asked.

"From the looks of it, I'd say yes."

"Then he's looking for a new wife," she said. "The old goat."

"Is Catherine Tofts, then — Has she finally — ?" Catherine Tofts was Smith's wife. He'd married her when he was practically penniless and his fortune was built entirely on hers. She had been a famous soprano in her youth, but had lost her mind when their only child died in infancy. She had lived ever since confined to the top floor of Smith's palazzo.

"Has she died? The poor woman, I wish she had. Her cousin tells me she's clinging on, just," Vittoria told him. "*He* seems to think it won't be long, though. Look at him. Is he kissing someone now? For heaven's sake."

Francesco observed Smith incline his head to nuzzle the peachy cheek of a very young girl and felt a sense of revulsion. He'd been coming to Smith's since he was little more than a boy, as had all the other young men of good family in the city. Even as a youth, he knew Smith's patronage wasn't personal — not even he could predict which of the notable young Venetians would end up on one of the councils one day, or even become Doge. Yet Francesco was aware that he had benefited hugely from Smith's calculated generosity and he didn't forget it.

"Surely, after all this time, he must take his comfort where he finds it," Francesco said in an attempt to cover his distaste with a show of loyalty.

"Comfort!" His sister-in-law pursed her rosy lips and snickered.

Francesco felt a tap on his shoulder and turned to find Smith grinning at him with precarious teeth. "My boy," Smith said, and embraced him, engulfing him in a powerful cloud of scent. Smith's pomade, sea captains swore, smelled just like the tradewinds to the lee of Ceylon. "Or of course I should say, my dear Count." Vittoria shot Francesco a significant look, then edged away before Smith caught sight of her.

Francesco returned his bow. "My esteemed Consul," he said in English.

Smith responded in English. "Not yet, Algarotti, not quite yet. I mustn't count my chickens before they're hatched."

Francesco smiled at this folksy turn of phrase. Chickens had nothing to do with Smith finally receiving the consulship from the English government, a post he had been ruthlessly, expensively, pursuing for two decades. Everyone knew Smith really had his eye on the Residency, a more advantageous office for making money, but Smith wasn't popular back home, despite trying very hard. The word back in England was that *pigs would fly* before he got it.

"But surely they are securely engaged in the process of hatching?" Francesco said, showing off his command of Smith's native tongue. "That is what my most trusted sources have given me to understand."

Switching back into Italian, a language he spoke flawlessly, Smith said, "Your grasp of Newton's mother tongue has improved. Add that to your French and your superlative Latin and I'm sure you are able to converse with all the brilliant gods of our time, gods of science, gods of literature, even, they say, the *gods of war*."

Here, Smith winked at Francesco, who was forced to look away. The thought of discussing Frederick with Smith made his stomach turn. Fortunately Smith was far more interested in finding out how Francesco was getting on with his work for Augustus. He pelted him with questions.

Francesco answered him frankly. There was no point in trying to hide anything from Smith, who had a finger in every pie when it came to the Venetian trade in art and antiquities. A rapacious collector of gems, prints, antiquities, paintings, coins, and books, he also acted as a broker, opening up new markets for artists across Europe. Giovanni Antonio Canal was a prime example. Twenty years before, the artist called Canaletto had been nothing but a painter of theatre backdrops. Now his views of Venice hung on the walls of mansions and palaces from Saint Petersburg to Bristol. Francesco had seen them for himself. These days the painter was so overbooked with foreign commissions he almost never left his studio. Knowing this, Francesco hadn't even bothered to put Canaletto on Augustus' shopping list.

All this was Smith's doing. He had been the first to hang Canaletto's views on the walls of his salon, to the confusion of Venetian visitors who scorned the very notion of view painting as high art. Locals carped about the way this glorified scene painter used optical devices to bend and stretch his perspectives in order to crowd more tourist attractions into the frame. They dismissed his technique as basic, his vision as pedestrian, lacking poetry. His runaway success with foreigners bewildered them. Only Smith, the immigrant, understood what no Venetian could: how much the rest of the world would pay to own even a tiny, distorted piece of Venice.

Now Smith listened intently to Francesco, no doubt corroborating what he was telling him with what his sources reported. He picked up on the mention of Tiepolo with a kind of twisted pleasure.

"So, the little genius is proving elusive," he said slyly. "That doesn't surprise me one bit."

Francesco murmured some excuse.

"The thing you have to understand about *that* one," Smith said, avuncular and cruel, "is that he is never too busy to do a commission he actually wants to do."

"Oh?" Francesco tried not to flinch. Smith wasn't usually so unkind and the barb reminded him how much things had changed between them since he'd been abroad. In England, he'd discovered Smith's secret: in Venice, Smith pretended to be Venetian, stuffing his palazzo to the rafters with Venetian art, throwing Venetian-style entertainments, patronising important Venetian people. But his game was and had always been to sell Venice to the English. Palazzo Balbi, which seemed so cosmopolitan when Francesco was young, now looked to him like what it was, a showroom for English customers with invisible price tags dangling from the fine paintings, the stems of the glassware and even some of the more attractive guests.

Since he'd returned to Venice, he'd noticed a change in Smith's attitude toward him. The old man was far warier, far more guarded. When they met, Francesco felt him prodding and testing, trying to find out how much he knew, who he'd been talking to in England. Perhaps he sensed Francesco's regard for him had faded. Or perhaps he recognised Francesco as one of his own kind, a transitional man who acted as a bridge between Venice and the rest of Europe. That made him competition. Francesco had the impression Smith would have liked to crush him.

Smith reached out and patted him on the shoulder, pleased. "Don't look so downcast, Count. You're new to this business. You know artists as a connoisseur knows them. Dealing with them as a businessman is another story. The good ones are always busy. You have to know how to jump to the front of the line. With Tiepolo, there's only one way."

"And what is that?" He expected Smith to say *money*, then to laugh crudely.

"You have to excite his imagination," Smith said thoughtfully. "And then let it run free."

"I'm not sure I understand."

Smith paused and seemed to reflect. "Let me give you an example. You know England well now, you've spent quite a lot of time there, you speak the language almost perfectly. Almost. Tell me, how many Tiepolos are there in England?"

Francesco consulted his inner gallery, mentally hurrying down a series of well-lit hallways decorated in the English style. He passed English Amigonis, Dorignys and Canalettos by the score. But there were no Tiepolos.

"None," he said, quite certain. "Unless I missed one."

"You missed nothing. You never do. In the places you went, you certainly would have seen them if they had been there. They are not. I know this. No altarpieces, no oil paintings, and certainly no frescoes, since we know that Tiepolo doesn't like to travel. Now, you and I agree Tiepolo is the greatest living painter in Venice, possibly the greatest working in the world today. So why would that be? Why would the English not be lining up to buy him? Why don't I have a single Tiepolo painting in my own collection? Haven't you ever wondered?"

Francesco had always assumed this was because Tiepolo wouldn't work for the low prices Smith notoriously paid. Artists endured his gouging in the interests of developing a relationship that would lead to the sale of their works abroad. Tiepolo, with an abundance of more open-handed local clients, could dispense with Smith's expensive patronage.

"It is mysterious," he said. "Now you mention it."

Smith went on. "Let me tell you what happened the one time Tiepolo was commissioned by the English. He did an altarpiece for their embassy in Madrid, *Saint George and the Dragon*."

"Certainly a suitable theme for him," Francesco said, eager to show his expertise.

"Ideal. And of course Tiepolo did a fine job with it, as always; all by his own hand, no sketchy bits churned out by apprentices, good ground preparation, top quality pigments from Negozio Scotti's. The lot. I saw it myself. It was exquisite. You and I would have given an arm to own this painting." He clutched Francesco's arm passionately, as if ready to wrench it off and exchange it for Tiepolo's luminous Saint George.

"But?"

"The English rejected it."

Francesco was astounded. He'd never heard this story. "How could anyone reject a good Tiepolo?"

"That's what I wanted to know. So I asked around my contacts in the diplomatic service, my correspondents in England. I can usually get to the bottom of things if I try," Smith said ingenuously. "The answer, when I finally found it, was not really that surprising if you think about what's been going on in England and the rest of Europe in recent years. You of all people should be able to guess, with your knowledge of the progress of intellectual life. And of course, your knowledge of the English character."

He looked at Francesco with his hoary eyebrows suspended high on his forehead, crowding his wigline, expecting an answer. At a loss, Francesco begged him to explain.

"But I've already told you, son: imagination. They did not like Tiepolo's little touches of play and wit and make believe. His iconography was all over the place. Saint George's armor was wrong. The horse was the wrong kind of horse. Saint George himself, they said, just didn't look English enough."

"But the historical Saint George came from North Africa," Francesco said.

Smith scowled at him. "The point is that the English can appreciate Tiepolo's talent, but they'd prefer he exercised it in a more rational manner. They're all in love with Reason these days. And where on earth are people more reasonable than England? Even the young ladies are keen natural scientists. It puts you off, some pretty little Mary or Anne going on about planets and precipitates and gasses and what not. They all know history too, and Lord won't they tell you all about it! They're *steeped* in the classics, if not stewed in them. No sooner does someone dig up an artifact at Herculaneum than the massed marquises of London want it represented in every painting concerning Roman history. Do you see?"

"I do." Francesco was beginning to wonder how much Smith had heard about his programmes for Tiepolo. Had Tiepolo himself been telling Smith about Francesco? Had they been laughing at him together? The idea was awful.

"Tiepolo is a real Venetian," Smith was saying. "Unlike the educated ladies and gentlemen of England, he sees no significant difference between the past and the present. Oh, he loves history's decorative and theatrical potential — no painter produces a more thrilling classical scene than he does — but he can't be bothered to fuss over fiddly details of then and now. For Tiepolo, everything happens in the moment: Mary ascends to heaven in flocks of angels, Pompey loses his head, manna falls from heaven, maybe not right *here*, but right *now*, just down the road or across the lagoon in Treviso, perhaps. For the English, it's an intellectual disaster. For God's sake, those people invented time!"

Francesco rallied to Tiepolo's defence. "But surely with the proper guidance, the proper preparation, Tiepolo is more than capable of producing work that suits the modern sensibility." Even as he spoke these words, he knew he was playing into Smith's hands.

"You think so?" Smith eyed him with amusement. Now Francesco was sure he'd been talking to Tiepolo. "I remember standing right here with an English earl of somewhere or another, you probably know him, and he summed it up in that way the English aristocracy have of dismissing things forever. He said, 'In Signor Tiepolo's paintings, there are always too many objects in flight. It makes a tall man want to duck.' That's why I don't have any Tiepolo in my collection. I don't believe I can do anything at all for the man, brilliant as he is."

Francesco was disturbed. On the one hand, he was sure Tiepolo would laugh if he heard Smith talking like this, as would most of the artists in Venice who had ever had dealings with the cunning English dealer. Doing for artists invariably meant enriching himself or furthering his own reputation with his countrymen, something at which Smith had only been partially successful despite trying very hard. Francesco remembered his clever friend Lady Mary Wortley Montagu delivering a comic impression of Smith that captured exactly his sidelong glances, his false bonhomie and the moment when his social veneer cracked, letting the raw rapacity of the man shine through. On the other hand, he knew what Smith meant.

Smith's eyes darted over Francesco's shoulder indicating he was preparing to move on to other guests. "You and I share a love of Tiepolo, regardless of his flaws," he said. "That's because we are both Venetians and we understand his state of mind, even if we no longer live within the same limitations. I'll tell you what. I have a treat for you. Go into the library and ask my servant to show you the new publication by Anton Maria Zanetti. I won't say anything more than that there are some etchings by Tiepolo in there that you of all people need to see."

The path to Smith's library was familiar to Francesco. He and Bonomo and all the other young men of their generation had spent many instructive hours there reading Smith's beautiful books. The place had always been a treasure trove, the best private library in the city, and it still was, for Francesco, a well-furnished piece of heaven. It was in Smith's library that Francesco first felt the physical thrill of holding books written by the sort of man he hoped one day to become.

The book in question was easy to locate. Smith always displayed his new acquisitions on a large table at the centre of the room. Francesco found the volume of etchings there, along with three or four other works of philosophy and verse. He opened it and flipped rapidly through the pages. Most of them were occupied by etchings by Zanetti, perfectly respectable but dull copies of works by Parmigianino. Francesco kept going until, near the end of the volume, he found what he was looking for, the pages contributed by Tiepolo.

There were just ten images, one per page, skillfully printed in black ink. Out of curiosity and a vestigial desire to be agreeable to Smith, Francesco prepared to give the etchings a glance before returning to the party. No matter what Smith believed, there was nothing he didn't know about Tiepolo already, nothing he wasn't prepared to accept.

Francesco ended up looking at the etchings for an hour. Then he fled Smith's palazzo like a man pursued by wolves.

There's a human head in the campfire. The magician points it out, but there's no need: the burning head is the focal point: literally, the place where the fire is. The scene is a scrubby hillside littered with the traces of a shattered civilisation: smashed, tumbled statuary; broken monuments carved with words in a forgotten language. A crowd has wandered out from the town to witness the ritual. They stand in profile like ranked militia, their expressions bored and neutral, like the faces on so many coins. The day is cold: the magician wears a thick skirt and a patterned shawl. You'd guess he was the one responsible for what's happening — the fire, the head. Doesn't it look like a ceremony, like magic being conjured? Yet everything about his reaction tells us that he is more surprised than anyone else present. He points, he gapes, his fat turban works loose in his agitation, coming unwound. The naked boy standing next to him looks on with no expression. The young man seated on the ground simply tends the fire. The head might be speaking; it's not clear, nothing is clear. No one makes a move to touch it.

Francesco shut himself in his room alone while he struggled to comprehend the images he'd seen at Smith's. There were only ten of them. At first glance they had looked much like other Tiepolo etchings he had seen. His practised eye easily picked out the hallmarks of the artist's hand; his preference for certain directions of hatching, his elastic, sportive line. There was no question of them being another man's work — that would have made things easier. Tiepolo had called the images *capricci* — caprices, fantasies — inviting everyone to take them with a grain of salt.

But Francesco couldn't do that. He would have liked to deny the Capricci, to pretend he had never seen them, but that was impossible now. In the hour he had spent in Smith's library, they had forced their way through his eyes and into his retentive brain, claiming their own chamber in his inner gallery. It was one of the secret ones, on the topmost floor, up a winding staircase, behind a locked door. Its walls were covered in silk the colour of coal. The only light came from candles. Francesco would never be able to forget the Capricci now, or dismiss them.

Skeletal pines lean on a diagonal. Owls perch on them in broad daylight. Thin sheep stand and stare. Three magicians huddle together in the wasteland. Their costumes speak of foreign lands — or the dressing-up box. They might be actors or they might have come from far away, travelling by ship or by camel or both; the Magi following a star. But there is no infant Messiah waiting at the end of their journey. Instead, from flames burning on the flat surface of a tree stump, a little viper rises, a tiny Leviathan emerging from waves of fire.

A skeleton reads to a group of well-dressed people from a large book. His news stuns them.

Hook-nosed Punchinello instructs a group of townspeople: magicians, soldiers, a woman. What does he say?

What did Tiepolo expect people to make of these weird scenes? They weren't biblical or classical or even historical and yet they suggested stories so cunningly that Francesco's trained mind laboured to find meaning in them. Were the magicians good or bad? Were they witnesses to these phenomena, or had they caused them? And the crowds of onlookers, were they implicated? His mind groped for meaning. It was like reaching for an object in its usual place — a brush, a shaving bowl — and finding that some malicious person has moved it. He came away with handfuls of nothing, a sense of rage and confusion. Tiepolo was playing games with him, with all of them.

Take the iconography. Francesco knew his iconography as well as any painter. He'd made it his business to study the lexicon all painters used, Cesare Ripa's reference book, the *Iconologia*, in which the standard meanings of objects and figures were clearly spelled out. And while Smith was right to say that Tiepolo could be whimsical in his use of iconography, there was no doubt the painter was perfectly trained and knew how to use it correctly.

Yet objects in the Capricci refused to obey the rules. Owls, for example, should indicate wisdom, or a portent, or maybe the presence of the goddess Athena. But when Francesco tried to apply such interpretations to the owls in the Capricci, he came up with nothing. They were everywhere in the ten prints, sitting on uprooted trees and broken monuments, blinking at scenes that had no explanation. Yet no matter how hard Francesco tried trap Tiepolo's owls and pin them to a meaning, their meaning evaded him. He was forced to conclude that they signified nothing: they were nothing more than owls. The same was true of the many suggestive objects that littered the landscape of the Capricci — quivers, horns, sextants, books, cow skulls, human skulls, shields, swords, sheets of music, helmets, scrolls, axes, calipers. None of them meant anything.

Francesco struggled to get his mind around what Tiepolo had done. Smith thought the etchings were evidence of Tiepolo's Venetian addiction to fantasy. For Francesco they were far more troubling than that. Tiepolo had gathered all the symbolic objects he could find and piled them in the foreground of his Capricci without reference to symbolism. He had included figures that could not be identified and arranged them in scenes that had no story attached. In doing this, he had abandoned the central principle that pictures *should mean something*. In essence he was making fun of his own art, sending up his own genius and revealing it to be nothing more than a set of tricks and tropes and attitudes.

Francesco writhed at this thought. Was this what had been going through Tiepolo's mind while he, Francesco, was describing his ideas? Did his painstakingly researched commissions amount to no more for Tiepolo than a heap of objects, a gesture or two, a few stock figures making up a scene? The Capricci suggested it was all the same to Tiepolo whether the hero was a soldier or a skeleton, whether he held in his hands a sword, a cross or a piss pot.

But even that wasn't the most troubling thing. The most troubling thing was that Francesco loved the Capricci more than anything he had ever seen by Tiepolo. When he saw them in Smith's library he had the unsettling feeling Tiepolo had somehow extracted the images *from his own imagination.*

This was very bad. This meant Francesco's expensive education had been for nothing. His studies had equipped him with method, with reason. They had given him the tools to kill and dissect magicians just as quickly as he could catch them. But none of it was any use. He was still a man driven by dreams and feeling and superstition: he was still a Venetian, labouring under the weight of the Mystery. And yet, he wasn't a good Venetian either. He couldn't submit to the Mystery, the way Tiepolo could, he couldn't enjoy it. He had to pick at it, prod it, try to channel it into some form that at least looked reasonable: he couldn't leave the Mystery alone. This, he realised, was the reason why Tiepolo would never work for him. This was the reason why he was still, after everything he'd learned and achieved, a complete buffoon.

At this low moment, Francesco's eyes fell on the two prisms standing on his windowsill. They were pretty things with silver filigree casings and tiny bubbles, like champagne bubbles, suspended in the glass. Now they caught the afternoon light and threw scrambled patches of colour on the whitewashed wall, taunting him. *You never learn*, they seemed to say. *You've done it again.*

These were the prisms Francesco had made for himself in Murano on his return from his first trip to England. He had come home to Venice full of swagger and scientific confidence, flaunting his membership to the Royal Academy, with a plan to teach his fellow citizens about the science of light. Venetians were backward, scornful of science, ignorant about the Enlightenment, but Francesco thought he could change all that by replicating in his home city the Newtonian demonstrations he'd carried out so successfully in England.

The trouble had been the Muranese prisms. They were exquisite, with little handles of worked silver bound around their triangular bodies with silver bands. They'd come from the glassworks nested in a carved casket lined with white silk and were altogether much lovelier than the prisms he'd used for his demonstrations in England. Those had been made by dour, utilitarian manufacturers of watch crystals and were no-nonsense by comparison. They worked reliably, however, throwing clearly defined spectra of light onto a screen, demonstrating that white light is really made of bands of different coloured light and proving Newton's theory.

The same could not be said for the Venetian prisms. Pretty they might be, but they turned out to be unschooled in the physics of light. In place of the clear red-orange-yellow-green-blue-indigo-violet spectra produced by the plain-Jane English prisms, they produced idiosyncratic rainbows with some colours missing, red or green omitted, and others misplaced. Francesco eventually realised that this was due to impurities in the glass, the champagne bubbles producing tipsy, irresponsible rainbows. But by that time it was too late; his demonstrations were a fiasco and he was a laughingstock. His attempt to teach Venice the value of science had the opposite effect. It was said in every salon that Francesco had proved that an Englishman's physics applied only in England. Light in Venice, it was obvious, would never submit to boring northern rules.

Francesco hung his head in his hands. He had failed with Newton, failed with Frederick, and now he was going to fail with this final test, winning a Tiepolo for Augustus — for this had now become the mark of success to him. All this failure derived from the same cause: Francesco's intellect was divided. For all his learning and his efforts to make himself into a man of the Enlightenment, he remained torn between reason and feeling, science and magic, war and art. Every time he tried to bind himself to one side, the other drew him back, traduced him, undermined him and caused him to fail. Because of this he was fated to be ridiculous and contradictory, a man of no real substance, like his prisms, decorative but intrinsically flawed and worthless except as an ornament.

Francesco didn't want to be an ornament. He stood up and opened his window, seized the prisms and threw them into the dark green water of the canal.

Francesco needed to get out of town. Smith invited him to his villa on the mainland, where he stayed for a few days enjoying card games and gentle walks in the country lanes of the Veneto and supper parties at Smith's good table. Then he moved on to a cousin's villa to meet Bonomo and his family. Together they enjoyed the same amusements all over again, this time with a view of the Brenta canal. Other guests came and went. They were all people Francesco saw regularly in Venice. The things they said and did, the rhythm of the days, the food, the servants who brought the food, the music, were all just as good as they were in town, which is to say they were just the same. There was a magnificent invariability about it, Francesco thought gloomily, that was very Venetian. He did his best to find it reassuring rather than maddening.

The third week found Francesco near Vicenza on business. One evening he was invited to supper at the Villa Cordellina where his host, a wealthy lawyer, could hardly wait to show off the frescoes Tiepolo had done for him earlier in the summer. When he saw the paintings, Francesco flushed like a spurned lover who catches sight of his darling in the arms of another. Tiepolo had produced a peerless series of works for the lawyer including a ceiling with an allegory of *Intelligence Triumphing Over Ignorance* and two magnificent historical scenes: *The Continence of Scipio* and *The Family of Darius Before Alexander*. Not only were the frescoes astonishing in their quality, they were also full of figures Francesco recognised: children who looked like Tiepolo children, black servants who looked like Tiepolo's majordomo, youths whose russet good looks recalled the features of Tiepolo's son and assistant, Domenico, and even ugly black and white lapdogs that looked like Fleabag. In every painting there was at least one figure that resembled Signora Tiepolo; sometimes there were several, a flock of blond sisters, each looking in a different direction. It seemed to Francesco that everyone was included in Tiepolo's history — even the lawyer had his portrait in the picture — everyone except him.

When he saw this, Francesco experienced an unwarranted rush of feelings: hurt, resentment, jealousy, but overall a painful feeling of exclusion, of being left out and slighted. He knew that this was mad, but he couldn't help it. He fled the paintings. For the rest of the evening he strove to stay in other, Tiepolo-less, parts of the house. He told himself to give up on Tiepolo.

Summer and autumn passed. Winter slid over the city. Francesco stood surveying the late crowd at the Ridotto through the eyeholes of his mask. The main gaming room was packed as usual at the end of the evening. The gamblers clustered around numerous small tables, men and women, aristocrat and citizen, all bent to their luck. Most were dressed in the traditional Venetian disguise, the *bauta*: black tricorn hat, black lace domino covering head and shoulders, white half-mask. Here and there an unmarried girl went with her head uncovered, a round black *moretta* blotting out her features like an inky thumbprint. Foreigners, who came to the Ridotto for the spectacle as much as they did for the gambling, sometimes found the scene sinister, suggestive of a black mass or a flock of carrion birds feeding with sharp, pale beaks. But the mood in the Ridotto was gay despite the dark costumes. Conversation flowed among small groups of black-clad figures loitering between the tables. A woman's laughter spilled over from a distant room like a peal of bells and, from somewhere in one of the alcoves, a quartet of musicians played a pretty tune.

Francesco hummed along for a few bars, strolling around by himself. He slipped his glass beneath the beak-like upper lip of his mask and sipped, aware that he was stalling. He didn't really enjoy gambling. A natural gift for mathematics had ruined it for him when he was still a child: he could never take pleasure in the near-certainty of losing. He knew he might as well throw his purse into the canal and go straight to bed and get a good night's sleep, but the prospect outside was bleak. Christmas had gone by, Lent and Carnival were still weeks away. The city hunkered in its cold lagoon, surrounded by skeleton ships bobbing at anchor, lashed by rain and wind. His little purse was the price of admission to the one place in the city where life could be found in the depths of winter. The Ridotto was a refuge from the dead season. Everyone in Venice came there.

It was a safe bet that that every single person Francesco knew or wanted to know, everyone he loved, hated, or was curious about, would eventually appear in the Ridotto crowd, easily recognised although draped in disguise. Francesco mused that the gambling house was itself a study in probability. It might possibly offer the only sure-fire wager in the city.

And yet he was very surprised when he spotted Cecilia Tiepolo tucked away in one of the small side rooms, playing faro at a quiet table lit by a pair of tall candles. At first Francesco doubted his eyes. He passed by the table once, twice, studying the woman, unable to decide if she were really the painter's wife. A black tricorn, domino, and mask entirely concealed her hair and face and yet he was certain it must be her. *How?* He asked himself. *How can I be sure?*

He watched Signora Tiepolo fling a drape of her black lace domino back over her shoulders, revealing a flushed bosom and arms tightly encased in sleeves of glossy yellow silk. They were Armida's arms, Juno's, Thetis', powerful as those of an oarsman, yet feminine and soft, tapering to a fine hand. He'd seen those arms a hundred times. He'd preserved them in his gallery. There could be no doubt it was she.

Acting on impulse, Francesco approached the table and picked up one of the little booklets of betting cards, called a *livret*. He wasn't sure exactly why he did it. He'd made himself give up on Tiepolo back in the summer, to save himself more heartbreak. Yet he was curious to find out what Signora Tiepolo was doing in the Ridotto. It certainly wasn't the sort of place you'd expect to find a pious housewife of the artisan class. All he knew for certain was that he wanted a chance to watch her, to see her in this new context.

He nodded at the banker, whom he knew slightly. He was a young nobleman who went by the nickname of Il Gobbo, the hunchback. Despite the slight irregularity of his spine, Il Gobbo was handsome and managed to look almost dashing in the long white wig and black cloak that were required as part of his role as banker. He had his requisite sack of gold in plain sight at his feet.

"Place your bets," Il Gobbo said.

Selecting a card from the *livret* at random — a five as it happened — Francesco placed it on the table and laid a small wager
on it. He watched Signora Tiepolo place a series of bets, reaching
out with her mythic arms to position the coins on several different cards. She moved methodically, cocking her head to one side,
pointing the white beak of her mask down at the cards, then up
at Il Gobbo, like an intelligent bird. Francesco could tell from her
manner she was a practised player of faro, and he was surprised
again. Of the many games played in the Ridotto, faro was by far
the most risky. The stakes climbed sickeningly with every hand,
eventually becoming so high that vast fortunes could be wiped
away at the turn of a single card. Faro had destroyed so many aris-
tocratic families that the playing of it had been banned in France.

As she placed her bets, Signora Tiepolo displayed no sign of
nervousness or even excitement. Gone was the flitting fan, the
habit of twiddling her rings. And with these ticks, Francesco realised, went her air of inconsequence. It was like a clever piece of
stagecraft: she was transformed by her own air of concentration.
For the first time, Francesco glimpsed Signora Tiepolo as he had
seen her in Tiepolo's paintings: calm and monumental, impassive
and strong, carrying a weight of womanhood that acted on him
with magnetic force. He felt a little thrill run down his spine.

The game continued. Il Gobbo drew an eight for the bank and
a jack for the players. There were several people betting at the
table. The croupier efficiently collected the losing wagers and
covered the winning ones. Francesco's bet was not affected and
he let his wager stay where it was. Signora Tiepolo had bet on the
eight and lost the turn. The croupier collected her wager with the
usual flourish. Immediately, she placed a stake on another card.

There was a lot of money on the table in front of her now.
Francesco scanned the coins and did a rapid calculation: he
guessed the sum was about the price of a nicely finished Tiepolo

drawing. The idea made him nervous — it was always fatal to ascribe material values to wagers while gambling — but he calmed himself, remembering that, unlike many of the aristocrats milling around the Ridotto, Signora Tiepolo knew where her money was coming from. The Tiepolos were, he reminded himself, so wealthy they had no need of Francesco's commissions.

He noticed something else about the lady: she was cribbing. She had a little slip of paper pinned to the table with one elbow. On it, he could just make out a list of cards and a tally for how many times each had appeared in the deal. Francesco also took note of her position at the table. It was customary to offer the few seats in the Ridotto to ladies and allow them to sit beside the banker. But Signora Tiepolo was sitting unusually close to Il Gobbo, so close that he bumped her breast with his elbow as he dealt. She made no move to give him more space. Attentively, she watched every movement of his hands. Francesco remembered that Il Gobbo had a shady reputation and had been accused of running cheats in the past, though nothing was ever proven.

The tension built rapidly and the stakes climbed steeply with every successive hand. Signora Tiepolo won the next hand, and so did Francesco, a thing that always thrilled him despite himself and made him determined not to lose what he'd already won. To keep his stake, he indicated he wanted to wager only his winnings by folding his *livret* card in half and standing it, like a little bridge, on the table — faro was a game of subtle symbolism, using metaphors and signs to indicate intent. Signora Tiepolo crooked up one corner of her *livret* card to show that she wanted to wager both her winnings and her original stake.

Il Gobbo drew, left and right. Francesco lost his winnings and gathered up his stake jealously, alarmed by the possibility of losing more. But then realised he had to risk his money in another hand if he wanted to continue standing at the table, watching Signora

THE MERCHANTS OF LIGHT

Tiepolo. The lady had won the turn, tripling her original stake. Serenely, almost languidly, she reached down and made a small notation on her sheet. Then she crooked up a second corner of her *livret* card to show she was staying in the game.

"The lady is lucky," said Il Gobbo, all charm, eyeing her. Signora Tiepolo's only response was a tiny gesture of the hand that seemed to say, *Get on with it.* The turn was *quinze-et-le-va*. If she survived it, her winnings would be fifteen times her original wager. Il Gobbo turned the cards, right and left. Signora Tiepolo won again.

Francesco watched her make another mark on the little slip of paper with her tiny silver pencil, exactly like a scientist noting results. Then she crooked up a third corner of her *livret* card. Francesco felt himself begin to sweat on her behalf. This turn was *trente-et-le-va*; now Signora Tiepolo was playing for thirty times her stake.

A small crowd had gathered around the little table, as it always did when the stakes got this high. On many occasions, Francesco had seen educated marquises and clever duchesses lose their heads at this point, abandoning any pretext of strategy and throwing themselves hysterically into the jaws of fate. Not the painter's wife. She sat rocklike and calm, ignoring the onlookers, as though her steadiness had the power to keep Il Gobbo in line and bring out the cards in her favour.

Seeing that Signora Tiepolo's money was still in play, Il Gobbo started to look more cheerful. He knew the lady's chances of winning plunged with every hand, while his, the banker's, climbed correspondingly. By now, Francesco had no doubt in his mind that Signora Tiepolo was making exactly the same calculation, and probably more accurately than Il Gobbo, who had a difficult time keeping track of the interest on his own considerable debts. The banker turned a pair of cards and one of Signora Tiepolo's appeared on the left-hand side: a winner. The banker's air of cheerfulness evaporated.

"That's more like it," Signora Tiepolo said under her breath. Now she began to move, sitting back in her chair, pulling her black domino over her shoulders, rummaging in the folds of her skirt for her purse.

"Signora…" Il Gobbo's face was pale under his long, white sheepswool wig. The word *fleeced* sprang into Francesco's mind. "Signora, you are extremely lucky tonight." Francesco could hear the effort he was making to keep the desperation out of his voice. "Why not stay? There's *soixante-et-le-va* coming up, you'll win sixty-three times what you wager. Clearly, tonight is your night."

Signora Tiepolo seemed not to hear him. "Croupier!" she called and beckoned the man over. "Why don't we count the money out over here where we won't be in the way?"

Il Gobbo grudgingly nodded to his man who hefted the bank's sack of coins onto the table and begin to count out Signora Tiepolo's winnings. Francesco counted along with him. The amount was a little more than what he had offered Tiepolo when he tried to commission *Gideon Defeating the Midianites*. He watched Signora Tiepolo count her coin a second time. Outwardly at least, she seemed unmoved by her win, a serene goddess of the gaming table whose secret was that she had no need of games and no fear of losing them. She nodded then, slid the pile of coins into her purse and rose to go.

Removing his mask, Francesco stepped forward to greet her. "Signora Tiepolo." Again, he had no plan in mind. He just felt he had to speak to her.

The lady hesitated before turning reluctantly to face him. "Well, this is a surprise," she said without removing her mask. "What a pleasure to run into you here." Her voice was as common as ever. Her tone was polite but he could tell she wasn't pleased to see him.

Francesco spoke too quickly. "Forgive me for intruding, but I've just witnessed your triumph at the table. I'm thoroughly impressed, Signora. It is never easy to beat Il Gobbo at his game and you did so splendidly."

Signora Tiepolo sighed then and seemed to give in. Loosening the strings that held her mask in place, she pulled it away from her face and settled it on the brim of her hat like a white bird in a black nest. Her face was flushed pink, as well it might be following the excitement of winning a small fortune. There were little beads of sweat caught in the fine blond curls at her hairline. She dabbed her face with a handkerchief and surveyed Francesco with level brown eyes. He glimpsed the goddess again. The deity was watchful.

"I was lucky tonight, thank God," she said.

"That wasn't only luck," he said. "I couldn't help noticing you were keeping a tally of the cards. That's a very sophisticated method."

"You are very observant." She looked at him shrewdly. "It's not forbidden, to my knowledge."

"Oh no. I wasn't suggesting it was wrong to count the cards," he hurried to say, afraid he'd offended her again. "I just was thinking that most people wouldn't take such pains with the odds. And, even if they did, most of them wouldn't have the slightest idea of how to use the numbers to improve their chances. I salute you as one mathematician to another." He bowed to her.

"A mathematician! Well, that's something coming from a man like you. I'll tell Tiepolo you said that."

This was the opening Francesco had hoped for. It saved him the trouble of directing the conversation to the subject of Tiepolo. "And is your husband here with you this evening?" he ventured. "And your lovely daughters? I expect they've inherited your mathematical talents as well as your beauty. They'll be nearby, I'm sure, systematically stripping these crooked bankers of their gold."

Signora Tiepolo looked at him with disapproval. "My dear Count Algarotti," she said, "surely you can't believe I'd bring my daughters to the Ridotto. It really isn't the atmosphere for young girls." Here again, Francesco saw the goddess stand aside to make way for the matron, protective of her brood. Confused by Signora Tiepolo's rapid shifts of being, he tried to backpedal. But suddenly the matron disappeared and the goddess returned, smiling, teasing, provocative. "I am joking with you, Count," she said. "I bring them here all the time, of course. How could I leave them at home? They'd never put up with it. Tonight, though, they both have stinking colds. You should thank me for not bringing them. As for Tiepolo," she sighed, "he's out of town and anyway he doesn't like to come. The only thing my husband really loves is work."

For some reason, it occurred to Francesco that Signora Tiepolo might not be telling the truth. Tiepolo might be standing beside them right now, disguised in a white mask and black domino, quietly listening to everything they were saying. If this were true, then he had nothing to lose by being honest with the lady.

"I'm reassured to hear that," he said. "I've been trying to arrange a meeting with your husband for weeks and I was beginning to think he's avoiding me."

"Oh, Tiepolo wouldn't do that," Signora Tiepolo said. "Why would he do that?"

Having set off down the road of truth, Francesco had no choice but to go on. "I was hoping to have him complete at least one commission for King Augustus the Third, but he's been swamped by other projects ever since I arrived in Venice. We've spoken on several occasions; we've corresponded many times." He was aware that a begging tone had crept into his voice. "Many other painters have gone to work for me. And yet I cannot persuade your husband to paint our pictures. I begin to suspect he doesn't approve of me."

There followed a pause. Signora Tiepolo nodded and pursed her lips. "Of course he approves of you," she said at last. "He likes you very much. And he thinks you're quite clever about painting for someone who isn't actually a painter."

For some reason, Francesco felt these words like a blow to his heart. They were said innocently enough, yet never had he felt so summarily dismissed. Placing a hand over his wounded heart, he said. "I think you are trying to be kind to me, Signora. You're trying to let me down gently. But if what you say is true and Tiepolo thinks well of me then why won't he accept my commissions? Why won't he take my money? Perhaps you know the reason, Signora. I would be so grateful if you would tell me even if it were painful to me. Tell me I'm gauche. Tell me I'm a fool. Tell me I'm too pushy, that my ideas are idiotic, but please, please, tell me how to get Tiepolo to work for me."

Signora Tiepolo seemed surprised to hear him speak like this. She looked around to see who was standing near before answering him. "Is that why you came to the house the other day? To ask me that? You silly boy, why in heaven's name didn't you say it straight out? Why spend the afternoon talking about Isaac Newton and heaven knows what else when what you really want to talk about is business?" The lady laughed then, a youthful, raucous laugh. She reached up and gave his cheek a playful but firm slap. "You are a very clever young man," she said. "Maybe a little too clever. Am I wrong?"

Francesco's cheek stung. Now the lady had struck his heart and his face. He wondered where her next blow would land. Wherever that was, he would stand there and take it because there was no doubt he deserved it. She had cause to strike him: first he'd overlooked her, then, despite long acquaintance, he'd failed to recognise her. Finally, he tried to use her in the crudest way to get to her husband. Yet his success with Tiepolo really did depend on her, he realised now, not in the way he'd first thought, but in some deeper sense that had to do with his own worthiness, his ability to grasp the nature of the works he was so eager to have Tiepolo make for him. To know Signora Tiepolo in all her avatars, as an ordinary housewife in a pink parlour, as a naked divinity recumbent on a cloud, as a heroine from mythology, as a goddess flipping the cards of fortune — as an icon and as a woman — was to touch the heart of Tiepolo's genius and catch a glimpse, just a fleeting, momentary glimpse, of the place where art comes into contact with life, throwing sparks. Why had he not seen that before?

Looking straight into his eyes, Signora Tiepolo now brought her hand to his face and caressed the cheek she had slapped. "What are we to do with you then, young Algarotti? My daughters are in love with you, you know. Both of them, though Anna Maria won't admit it, of course. Elena just lies around staring at that picture in your book and doodling little arrows because they make her think of you. I suppose the world must be full of girls who are in love with you. I was saying to Tiepolo the other day, I don't think I've ever seen such a handsome man in my life."

He opened his mouth to reply, but she went on, continuing to cradle his face in her hand. "But beauty is really no good to a man, is it?" she said. "It's more of a liability. It confuses everybody. I said that to Tiepolo, too. And do you know what he said?"

Her fingers felt cool in the overheated atmosphere of the gambling house. Signora Tiepolo's gesture was more provocative than maternal, yet they were standing in a public place, in the middle of the crowded Ridotto, with their masks pushed up, their faces on display for all of Venice to see. None of this seemed to bother Signora Tiepolo in the slightest.

"What did he say?" Francesco was afraid of the answer.

She let her hand drop and shrugged. "Nothing."

"Nothing?"

She shrugged again. "He'd fallen asleep. His days are very long, you know. He's working much too hard. What I'm saying…" She leaned closer to him and dropped her voice. Francesco thought she was going to proposition him and he prepared himself to say yes, yes, yes to anything Signora Tiepolo wanted. "What I'm trying to tell you," she said, "is that Tiepolo's excuses aren't excuses. He really is as busy as he says he is. Domenico, on the other hand, is freer, more available."

"You mean your son?" Francesco hadn't expected this sudden shift from seduction to pragmatism. He felt disappointed.

"Who else?" she said. "Now I really must be getting home. It will be morning soon and all the robbers will be able to see me." She laughed and gave her purse a little shake to rattle the coins in it.

Francesco watched her lift her mask from its place in the brim of her tricorn hat and settle it back over her face. "Please, let me accompany you," he said, feeling the moment had somehow slipped through his fingers.

"There's no need," she said. "My servant is waiting for me at the door. Good night, Count. I'm sure we'll see you soon."

First thing the next morning, Francesco sent off a message to Tiepolo. The answer came in the afternoon. As soon as he received it, Francesco was out of Bonomo's house like a shot, barely pausing to put on his heavy cloak. It was raining steadily that day, but he practically skipped across the greasy pavements, dodging spouts of water cascading from the gutters. At San Silvestre, he hurried up to the studio where he found Tiepolo bent over a table with one of his assistants, leafing through a pile of drawings.

"Maestro." He presented himself with a bow. Water dripped off his cloak and formed a small puddle at his feet.

"Did you swim?" Tiepolo said, looking him up and down with amusement. Francesco smiled. The disturbing things he'd seen in the Capricci had made Tiepolo seem unapproachable. The meeting with Signora Tiepolo in the Ridotto had left him uncertain. Today Tiepolo had on his usual working clothes with a once-grand coat pulled over the top. On his head he sported a hat that looked as though it might have been fashioned from the skins of water rats. Looking at him, Francesco tried to forget about the other Tiepolo, the mysterious, evasive, unpredictable one whose imagination lived in a wasteland populated by magicians. *This* was the artist he understood: funny and capable, reasonable, accommodating, a consummate professional.

Joining in with the spirit of fun, Francesco shook himself, throwing a spray of water around him the way a wet dog might do. An assistant came and took away his sodden coat.

"I was pleased to get your note, of course," he said. "But curious. You've never sent for me before."

"I haven't?" Tiepolo led him over to the benches, their usual place for talks. "Well, that's my loss then. We never really get enough time to chat, do we, Count? I so enjoy our talks. But time goes by and I'm running around and we don't bump into one another. I'm reduced to listening to gossip about you."

"Gossip? That sounds bad."

"Oh no, Count. Only the good kind of gossip. They say you've nearly completed your collecting for Augustus."

"It's true," Francesco said, sitting down. His wet stockings itched against his shins. "I'm making my first shipment to Dresden in two weeks."

"You made short work of that." Tiepolo reached under his hat and scratched his scalp thoughtfully. He seemed to be thinking and Francesco felt his hopes rise. Perhaps this was the moment when Tiepolo would finally commit. It still wasn't too late.

"So I guess that means you'll soon be out of a job," Tiepolo said with a twinkle in his eye. Francesco laughed. "I suppose it does. Why? Are you looking to hire a labourer?"

"That's funny." Tiepolo laughed louder than before, then sighed. "But seriously. Domenico will be here in one second. I really wrote for his sake, to put him out of his misery. Before he gets here I wanted to take the opportunity to let you know how much I appreciate what you're doing. It will be his first commission. I expect you know that. It will mean a lot to the boy and I can promise you he's ready. You won't be disappointed."

Francesco blinked. In his message to Tiepolo he'd said only that he had a further business proposition to discuss. He made no mention of his plans to commission Domenico. "No — Of course. But how did you know about…?"

"My wife of course. If you want to keep secrets you certainly can't entrust them to her," Tiepolo said with a wave of his hand. "Women are constitutionally incapable of keeping secrets. Especially mothers in matters where their children are concerned. Signora Tiepolo told me at breakfast; she couldn't keep the news to herself. And she told Domenico. You should have seen his face! He didn't quite believe it. But we said, why shouldn't Count Algarotti commission you? He's a man of discernment. He knows good work when he sees it."

"I hope I do," Francesco said, a little stunned. He had hoped for an intervention by Signora Tiepolo, but this wasn't the one he'd expected. He caught sight of Domenico hurrying across the studio toward them.

The boy approached and delivered a deep bow. "Your servant, Count Algarotti."

"Young Tiepolo," Francesco said. "Your father tells me that your mother has let the cat out of the bag. You probably know more about my commission than I do now. Go on. Tell me what your gracious Mama reported."

Domenico looked uncertain. He glanced at his father who sat with his arms crossed, face neutral, giving no hints. The boy stood up a little straighter.

"Forgive me, Count. My mother only said that you were interested in commissioning some drawings. I don't know if that's right. I apologise if it isn't. But that's what she said."

Francesco was relieved. For a moment he'd worried that Signora Tiepolo was proposing that Domenico paint the paintings for Augustus, an arrangement he could not agree to. Drawings were a more modest proposition, entirely suitable for a young artist just starting out on his career. Francesco had to admire Signora Tiepolo's sense of appropriateness.

"Your mother is a very naughty lady," he said. That much was certainly true. "But entirely accurate," he added.

They began to discuss the terms of the commission, reviewing the young Tiepolo's artistic strengths. Domenico produced examples of his work and Francesco observed that he'd been flawlessly trained and possessed, possibly, the first glimmerings of talent. Francesco had already been through his inner galleries, looking for suitable subjects for the young artist to copy. Two paintings stood out: a Palma Vecchio and a Titian, both hanging in a palazzo not far away, in Ca Renier, where Domenico would be able to study them. Francesco suggested these and they agreed on the medium — red chalk — and a price. If only commissioning the father had been so straightforward.

From his place on the bench, Francesco watched Domenico return to work. The boy seemed to glow with happiness and pride. *Well, that's something,* thought Francesco. A good deed. Part of him was amused by the way Signora Tiepolo had turned the tables, taking advantage of him before he could take advantage of her. Still, he wasn't sorry. Commissioning the young Tiepolo was an idea he really should have come up with himself. One day Domenico would inherit his father's studio and be, from the looks of it, quite as famous.

Tiepolo had drifted away during his negotiations with Domenico. Now he reappeared at Francesco's side. "All settled?" he said.

"I think so." It crossed Francesco's mind to raise the issue of his commissions one more time. By manipulating him into this contract with Domenico, Signora Tiepolo had provided him with an opening. She would have expected him to take it — *she* would have done so. But Francesco let the moment go. If Tiepolo had agreed to paint him a painting on the spot, he wouldn't have known what to ask for. Belisarius, Priam, Gideon — they were all dead subjects for him now. In Tiepolo's eyes, they had never possessed any life.

Francesco stood up and prepared to leave Tiepolo's studio for the last time. Tiepolo stopped him. "Before you go," he said.

"I'm never leaving her," Bonomo said in rapture. "I'm going to have a bed brought in here and sleep beside her. I may die here at her feet."

Francesco's brother spread his arms to embrace the painting. It was a large picture with an expanse of canvas the size of a bed sheet and, even unframed and propped at a casual angle against the wall, it dominated Bonomo's salon. It depicted a scene set in an open-air loggia flanked with fluted columns. In an atmosphere of oriental luxury, a beautiful lady entertained a pair of gentlemen at a small table, surrounded by an exotic crowd of onlookers. Inquisitive dwarves, skinny dogs, impassive soldiers, bearded necromancers, and a pair of identical Moorish pages: Cleopatra's entourage invaded Bonomo's house and the painting's vivid pigments threw the rest of the room, which had been recently decorated, into relative shadow, making everything look tawdry and dusty and dull by comparison.

This was Francesco's Tiepolo, the one he had never asked for and never imagined: *The Banquet of Cleopatra*. He'd had Tiepolo's men deliver it to Bonomo's in order to share his triumph and he was pleased the painting was having exactly the same effect on his brother as it had on him when he first laid eyes on it in Tiepolo's studio.

"I'm in love," Bonomo said. "I want to marry this painting." He had been all for stripping all his own paintings from the wall, sending for a carpenter and hanging the Tiepolo properly, but Francesco thought that was too dangerous. The painting was only his for a few days, after which he would have to crate it up and send it on to Augustus. He imagined having to wrestle Bonomo for possession. He always lost to Bonomo at wrestling.

"I told you'd I'd get one," Francesco said, and giggled like a little boy, pouring himself another glass of prosecco. Bonomo had ordered up a bottle in celebration and now it was nearly empty.

His brother swept over to him, put a strong arm around his shoulders and squeezed Francesco powerfully. "You told you'd get three, you knave. But I'm not going to quibble. Tell me again how you pulled it off."

"Oh, it wasn't me." Francesco unfurled a finger from his glass and pointed it at the figure of Cleopatra. "It was her."

"The Queen of Egypt?"

"In a manner of speaking."

Tiepolo's Cleopatra was a handsome, full-bodied blond dressed in a gown of pale orange silk, its hem thickly embroidered and studded with jewels. She presided confidently at her modest table, which was covered with a white linen cloth and had little on it but an ornate dish with some fruit in it. She sat with one arm akimbo, its fist planted saucily on her hip, its elbow jutting out. The other arm was stretched out across the table, the hand hovered in midair over a slim, fluted glass full of reddish liquid. Between the thumb and forefinger of that hand, Cleopatra held a large white pearl shaped like a teardrop.

"I can always tell when you're hiding something from me, Francesco. But I'm too happy to care. To the queen!" Bonomo said.

"To Cleopatra," Francesco said, raising his glass.

"And to Tiepolo." Bonomo raised his glass and the brothers touched rims with a delicate clink.

"To all the Tiepolos." *To Cecilia Tiepolo,* Francesco thought. *Mathematician, mother and strategist.* He still didn't know how she had persuaded Tiepolo to let him have the painting, but he was delighted to give her all the credit. He owed it to her. He had underestimated her importance; he'd patronised her and tried to use her. All the time she'd been making her own decisions about him — and influencing Tiepolo's. He knew the instant he saw *The Banquet of Cleopatra* that the queen — and she was a queen — was sending him a message of reconciliation and a reminder of her power.

"Please don't feel obliged." Incredibly, those were Tiepolo's words to Francesco as he had the labourers carry *The Banquet of Cleopatra* out of a storeroom into the light of the studio.

"I'll take it," Francesco said, or at least that's what he tried to say. It was difficult to formulate words just then. His head felt light, his heart was pounding like a machine. He fought the impulse to leap forward, seize the painting and run away with it.

"You'll recognise the scene of course," Tiepolo said. "I think it comes from Pliny."

"Yes. Pliny the Elder." Francesco knew the passage well: Mark Antony tries to impress Queen Cleopatra by wagering that he can squander more on a single banquet than anyone in the world. Cleopatra is not overwhelmed by the lavish banquet he presents. She bets him she can do better and then, with devastating style, she does.

"In obedience to her instructions," Francesco quoted, "the servants placed before her a single vessel filled with vinegar, a liquid whose sharpness and strength is able to dissolve pearls. At this moment she was wearing in her ears those choicest and most rare and unique productions of Nature; and while Antony watched, she took one of them from her ear, threw it into the vinegar and, after it was melted, swallowed it down."

Francesco had seen and stored in his inner gallery other painted versions of this popular scene. He'd even been a witness when a certain scientifically minded English lady undertook to repeat Cleopatra's stunt, approaching it as an experiment in Pliny's veracity. The pearl, though dulled and damaged, failed to dissolve over a period of weeks, proving, the lady said, that Cleopatra must have used something more caustic than vinegar to win her wager. But then, what would you expect of the Queen of Egypt?

"I started this painting for another client," Tiepolo was saying. "But he's had to let it go. It's a slightly awkward situation."

Francesco gazed rapturously at the painting for another few seconds then said, "Joseph Smith."

Tiepolo was surprised. "You're a very perceptive young man. Was it the fruit dish? He was very particular about having antiquities from his collection included in the scene. Or perhaps he spoke to you about the commission, as one dealer to another?"

Francesco laughed at the idea of Smith confiding anything to him. "He's never said a word, Maestro. It's just a very good likeness."

He pointed to the canvas. There were three figures seated at Cleopatra's table: the queen, Mark Antony, and a man called Lucius Munatius Plancus, Mark Antony's co-consul, who accompanied him to Egypt. In Tiepolo's painting this figure, apart from his odd beard and red hair, was the spitting image of Smith. In fact everything about the painting — the setting, the subject, even the large size — smelled distinctly of Smith. Francesco would have guessed without the teasing portrait.

The painter allowed himself a wry smile. "Signor Smith has discovered that being the Consul is a very expensive business. He needs to sell now more than he needs to buy."

"I am *so* glad." Francesco was unable to hide his glee. He thought of the malicious way Smith had toyed with him and tried to get him to discount Tiepolo. In one sense, the Englishman had been right. There was nothing remotely historical about *The Banquet of Cleopatra*. From the Corinthian capitals on the columns to the unlikely golden shade of the queen's hair, every element in the picture was inaccurate. There were no Egyptian antiquities in it at all, or even Greek ones, which might have been acceptable. The watching crowd was transplanted, like a theatre troupe that moved from one town to another, from other paintings by Tiepolo. A few colourful characters, including a pied greyhound, had drifted over from works by Veronese.

The whole picture was farcical, indefensible, *wrong*. By rights, Francesco should have rejected it on the spot. *The Banquet of Cleopatra* wasn't what he'd asked for; it wasn't even what he wanted. But it was what he needed. He loved its wrongness from the moment he laid eyes on it. He knew Smith must have felt the same way, despite his protests. The thought of how much it must have hurt the Englishman to renounce such a splendid painting gave Francesco added pleasure and made him want it all the more.

"How much would you like for it?"

Tiepolo named a sum: three hundred ducats. He could have demanded twice or even three times that amount and Francesco would have paid it. He ran back to Bonomo's to get the money.

The afternoon sun began to slant into the salon, sliding its radiance across the surface of the painting. The two brothers lingered on. Bonomo had the servant bring another bottle of prosecco. His wife Vittoria soon came in along with some jolly friends of hers and they all joined the celebration. Snacks appeared on trays. Word got out and neighbours popped in. The afternoon turned into a party with Cleopatra and her retinue as the guests of honour.

"She is fabulous," Vittoria said, squinting at the painting, her little nose almost touching the strokes of paint. "Why don't we have a banquet?"

Francesco was feeling tipsy and content. It remained for him to write to Count Brühl, the king's minister, and explain why, when he was sent to Venice to commission serious history paintings from Tiepolo, he was sending back this bit of theatrical whimsy instead. He didn't think it would be a problem; he knew he could describe the painting in such a way that *The Banquet of Cleopatra* would come across as a work of pure pictorial scholarship. And of course once King Augustus actually saw it he would simply fall in love, as Francesco had done, and there would be no more discussion. The problem would be sending the painting away. No doubt he would feel as bereft as Smith must feel. And then, poor Bonomo.

"That's it. I'm keeping her," his brother declared to the room full of people. "I don't give a damn about your king. Let him get his own. This one is mine. Mine, mine, mine." He ran his hand over the canvas. "Oh, I can feel the brushstrokes," he said, closing his eyes. "I've always wanted to do this."

It struck Francesco that it was Frederick, austere Frederick, not Augustus or Bonomo, who needed this Tiepolo most. On the spot, he made up his mind to write to the king and tell him this in the plainest terms, no flourishes, no flattery, no Latin. He would suggest that Frederick commission Tiepolo to fresco all the ceilings of the new palace he was building on the outskirts of Berlin, Sanssouci. He'd offer to work up a dramatic pictorial programme for him: Virtues and Victories romping in the heavens, Frederick flown to Olympus by squads of burly angels, Reason and the Arts, arrayed — nothing historical, nothing that needed too much explanation, just a framework for the Mystery to shine through. And of course there would be a Venus — there had to be a Venus — stretching out her grand, blond, heavy beauty full length on a comfortable cloud, making herself at home. Frederick had to say yes to this plan, Francesco thought giddily, it was imperative that he did so. He — they — needed Tiepolo: only Tiepolo had the skill to fill Frederick's cold northern rooms with golden Venetian light and transform them into a heaven where both reason and feeling could flourish together. Once the artist had worked his magic, Francesco and Frederick would be able to live together happily. They could lie side by side on the floor, looking up at Tiepolo's heavens for the rest of their lives, and laughing.

PART FIVE

Lorenzo Tiepolo
Venice–Würzburg, 1752

Venice-Würzburg, 1752

Lorenzo Tiepolo tried not to hear his parents arguing but the sound of their voices rose into his room through the floorboards, his father's low-pitched like the thrum of a faraway crowd, his mother's higher, louder, like angry music. She seemed to be doing most of the talking — or shouting. Lorenzo couldn't make out all the words. Sometimes his mother sounded as though she were crying.

One thing he knew for certain: the argument was about him. Certain words and phrases came though intelligibly: *Lorenzo, Enzo.* He put his fingers in his ears, then thought better of it and took them out again. *I'm asking you just to think about it for one minute!* They were deciding something. *It depends on how long...* It occurred to him that he should go out on the stairs and eavesdrop properly, to get the jump on them, to be prepared for whatever they were about to do to him. *And what if that doesn't happen? What if...?* That's what his sisters would do — Elena, Angela: they were shameless about spying. They were probably out there now sitting on the step, gripping a stair rod in each hand, taking it all in. They all knew it was necessary. His parents were crafty and unpredictable. *It would be disastrous. For him or you? I'm thinking of him.* They could surprise you with the things they decided. If you weren't careful, you could be the last to know.

Lorenzo rolled over and stretched out his legs under the sheet. It was a warm night. He had the bed, the room, all to himself and it was seductively comfortable. His parents sounded as if they were set to argue until dawn: they were capable of that; they seemed to enjoy a good fight. He came to the conclusion it was pointless to worry about it. In the morning, he could ask one of his sisters what she knew. Anna Maria, despite her air of superiority, was the nosiest. She would have all the details.

He drifted off to sleep with the sound of their voices murmuring, quieter now, continuous, like the sound of a river. In the early hours of the morning, he half woke, conscious of someone sitting down on the edge of the bed. He knew without opening his eyes it was his mother. She stroked his hair and then did something she hadn't done since he was very small. She lay down beside him and drew him to her with one arm, fitting the tops of her small, cool feet beneath the soles of his warm ones. Nestling back into her solidity, Lorenzo sank into sleep again. When he woke in the morning, she was gone.

His father spread out the long document on the worktable. "If you go over this carefully," he said. "You'll know all you need to know."

"Do I have to?" Lorenzo looked at the document with dread. It was closely written in a professional clerk's hand; it ran to several pages and had official seals and signatures dotted around. Overall, it looked like what it was, one of his father's very important work papers. That meant it would be fatally dull and that he'd have to remember all of it. Lorenzo squinted at the crowded lines of writing, packed with slanting letters. He didn't usually have to read this sort of thing. His father or Domenico usually just told him what such documents said — or he guessed from the kind of work they had him do.

His father gave him a fierce look. "What did you say?"

"I just mean, why do I have to read this contract now? It is a contract, isn't it? Why do I have to read a contract all of a sudden?"

"Don't you ask me why, boy," his father said angrily. "It's not your place to ask me why."

"Yes sir." Lorenzo stared sullenly down at the page.

"You're getting too big for your britches, Lorenzo. You need to watch yourself."

"Yes sir. I'm sorry."

"That's more like it." His father smoothed the paper with his hand. "But since you asked, there's a very good reason why. It's time you learned more about the business side of things. It's not all about drawing and painting, you know. Someday you'll have your own studio and then you'll need to know how to deal with clients, how to follow a brief, how to negotiate. This," his father laid his hand flat on the document, "is where jobs begin. And this is a very interesting job."

Now Lorenzo knew what his parent's fight had been about. "Does this mean I'm definitely going with you and Domenico to Würzburg?"

His father answered dismissively. "Of course you are. Why wouldn't you go with us? It's a big job and it might get bigger. We're going to need all the help we can get. Now sit down and read the contract."

Lorenzo obeyed. It took him most of a morning to wade though all the pages, sitting miserably at a table in the studio while all around him his father and brother and the assistants went about doing the real, normal work of painting. The document was a proposal for a series of frescoes to be done in the residence of someone called Prince-Bishop Grieffenclau, in a city called Würzburg, in a country called Bavaria. In painstaking, painful detail, it set out the programme for allegorical and historical scenes the Prince-Bishop, whoever he might be, wished Giambattista Tiepolo to apply to the ceiling of his Imperial Hall.

The contract's language was legalistic and high-falutin'. It contained pedantic instructions about the type, nature and position of the figures, including a host of imaginary beings — muses, nymphs, and spirits — as well as historical characters, such as Barbarossa and Beatrice of Burgundy. There were requirements about which pigments to use, in what quantity, for what price. There were strict rules and schedules for payment, completion dates and statements about the right of the Prince-Bishop (what *was* a Prince-Bishop?) to withhold money in the event the work was not finished on time, to his satisfaction. And so on. And on.

Lorenzo groaned out loud. As he read, there were times he thought he actually might die of boredom. By the time he had finished, he no longer wanted to go to Würzburg, clearly the source and origin of all tedium. But it wasn't up to him, of course.

His mother caught hold of him on a Sunday afternoon. "You need a haircut," she told him. She steered him into the kitchen and made him sit on a stool with a cloth around his shoulders. "No point in taking you to the barber," she said. "Unless you need a shave already. Do you need a shave?" She laughed. She knew very well he didn't.

"You have such beautiful hair," she sighed as she undid the tie that held it in a ponytail at the nape of his neck. Lorenzo grimaced. His hair was blond and fell in girlish ringlets if he didn't tie it up. His sisters always said they wished they had his hair; he would have been very happy to give it to them.

"Cut it short," he told his mother. "Cut it all off."

"Oh no!" she cried, running her fingers along his skull. Her smooth nails dragged deliciously against his scalp. "It's your crowning glory. That would be such a shame. Anyway, people would think you had lice. I'll just neaten it up for you. It won't take long."

She combed his hair briskly, working through the tangles with a practised hand. Then she used her little pair of silver sewing scissors shaped like a crane to cut the ends off. The locks fell onto the cloth spread over him like a tent and Lorenzo watched them slide down the slope into his lap. His mother made him keep them there until she finished. After, she pretended to throw them into the courtyard but Lorenzo saw how she hid them in one of her pockets. Later, he discovered them tied up with a ribbon in a carved wooden box in her bedroom.

All the sisters came down to the studio on the day they left, supposedly to help them pack. Of course they weren't any use. Mostly they milled around, their wide skirts getting in the way, watching the assistants haul bundles and trunks through the workroom and onto the campo in preparation for transfer to the boat. Elena cried a little — she had recently got married and was extra-emotional — but Angela and Orsola kept reasonably calm. Typically, Anna Maria took a practical interest in the trip. Where exactly did the road cross the Alps? she wanted to know. Was it true they would have to dismantle the coach and carry it over the pass in pieces?

She asked so many questions that their father got impatient with her. "If I stop to answer all these questions, my dove, we will never get to Bavaria." He always called the girls *my dove* when they got on his nerves. "I'll write you a letter about the journey when we get there. If we get there." They all crossed themselves.

"I don't think he knows the answers," Anna Maria said to Angela and sniffed. Lorenzo guessed she felt left out. *She* would never cross the Alps, and, of all of them, she would have liked it most.

His mother still hadn't appeared and this made Lorenzo apprehensive. He wondered if she'd come down at all to say good-bye and, if she did, whether she'd cry, intolerably. She'd spent much of the last few days in her room so anything was possible. He guessed she was working up to something big. The Tiepolo men had been on work trips before this, of course, but those were only for a few weeks at a time, a couple of months at most. This time, they'd be gone for much longer, maybe as much as a year. And they were travelling beyond the frontiers of the Venetian Republic for the first time. His mother's display of grief would have to be bigger and louder to match. Would she rend her garments like ladies in the Bible? Would she cling to their father like Armida, in his father's paintings, clung to Rinaldo? That would be mortifying. Would her theatrics make them miss their boat? That really could be a problem, Lorenzo thought. He couldn't imagine his father leaving while his mother was that upset.

He didn't have much time to worry. He was running around frantically, doing last-minute things for Domenico. His brother was in charge of the equipment list and Lorenzo could tell he was feeling the pressure because he was barking orders at the men and striding around with frown on his face that made him look like a Hun. All he needs is a whip, Lorenzo thought. And then: thank God Domenico doesn't have a whip.

His father was mainly concerned with the drawings. Lorenzo watched him get down on his knees to pull a rolled sheaf of them out of one of the leather tubes they'd been stored in for the journey and begin leafing through the pages. When he found what he was looking for, he grunted, reassured, then rolled the drawings up again and slid them back into the tube. He caught Lorenzo looking at him. "It's not as if we can come back for anything," he said, getting up stiffly.

"She could send it to us," Lorenzo said, wanting to appear confident. "If it's really important."

"Yes I suppose she could." His father smiled, looking tired even before they'd set out. The packing process had taken weeks. While that went on, the studio had been working nonstop to complete all its commissions before they left. They'd almost managed it.

Lorenzo's priest brother Giuseppe arrived at that moment, wearing his black cassock and looking glum as usual. "All ready to go, then?" he said, when it must have been obvious even to him they were far from ready.

"I could ask you the same question." Domenico stopped long enough to joke. "You're the one who'll be left here trying to control this pack of she-wolves." He tilted his chin in the direction of his sisters. "Honestly, I think I'd rather have my throat slit by bandits."

"You may well get your preference," Anna Maria said, throwing back her head. "I hear the roads across the Alps are thick with them."

Giuseppe looked uncomfortable. As the only male Tiepolo remaining behind, he would be in charge of the household while they were away, at least officially. There had been endless discussion about this, endless concern, since everyone knew Giuseppe lacked any trace of common sense. That was why their parents had made a priest of him. Fortunately, their mother knew how to do everything. Giuseppe only had to sign the documents. "I pray for guidance," he said mechanically, but Domenico had already hurried off.

Grinning, Lorenzo answered. "You're going to need it!" All at once he felt happy to be going away. He looked at Giuseppe and his sisters, standing in the studio with empty hands, no idea what to do. It would be so much worse to be one of them, one of the stay-at-homes. Instead, Lorenzo was a traveller at the centre of the drama. To demonstrate his importance, he picked up a large crate of materials and began to stagger with it toward the door.

His mother appeared in the studio just as they prepared to go. Lorenzo had begun to worry that she would make them all troop up to her room to say goodbye to her as she lay in her big bed, too heartbroken to get up. When she finally materialised, radiant and composed in a gown of sky-coloured silk, Lorenzo felt relieved. She didn't even look as though she'd been crying; she looked as though she'd been doing her hair. She had one of the maids in tow, her arms laden with packages. Lorenzo saw Domenico's face freeze when he saw this: more weight, he was thinking, more volume — Domenico was obsessed with balancing the load on the carriage. His mother caught his look.

"No need to panic," she said to Domenico. "It's just a few little things. You'll be glad to have them when you're far from home."

Far from home. Lorenzo had never really tried to imagine what life would be like once they were in Würzburg. Now he pictured the Venice studio, transferred to a mountainous land. Visible from the windows were dark green trees, canals that curved and resolved into rivers. *Far.* He understood then why they were taking so much of their own equipment with them. None of them knew for sure what they would find when they got to Würzburg, not even his father. The contract, despite its length and complexity, really gave them no idea what was waiting for them at the end of their journey.

His mother came over to Lorenzo first and placed his package in his hands.

"I expect you to make good use of this," she said.

"What is it?"

"Something you'll need." The moment had arrived. She put her arms around him and held him to her in an embrace that emphasised his smallness, her height. The top of his head came just to her breastbone, his nose pressed into the crêpey skin of

her bosom. He inhaled her smell of pepper and lavender, laced
with a whiff of warm sweat, an undertone of kitchen ash. Lorenzo
felt a little flutter of anxiety, communicated from his mother. He
suddenly thought of all the things that were *not* packed in their
trunks. Whatever was in the parting gift she'd given him, it was
too little to make a difference. They were going away.

The hug had lasted too long; it had marked him out from
his father and brother. He squirmed against her strong dou-
ble-armed grip but she paid no attention. She held him as long as
she wanted to and released him when she felt like it. He turned
quickly away, unable to look her in the eye.

"Now me, Signora," his father said.

He watched his parents hold one another. His father buried his
face for a moment in his mother's neck. His mother kept her dry,
dark eyes fixed on a point somewhere in the sky.

They opened their packages later that day, in the carriage.
His father's contained a box of the expensive cigars he loved so
much: thin, dark, tightly wrapped, no longer than your middle
finger. Domenico's present was a hairdressing set with flowers
painted on the ivory handles of the brushes. It was a gift for a girl,
but he seemed pleased with it: Domenico was very vain.

Lorenzo's package contained a disappointment. He opened
it to find a writing set in its own special box: a tiny penknife,
ink, an inkwell, a sand shaker. His father whistled when he saw
it. "Now that's fancy," he said. Domenico said it was too good for
a boy. Lorenzo felt annoyed: his mother's gift was manipulative,
plainly intended to make him write letters to her. He would have
preferred chocolate or a chess set or at least a much bigger knife
— and she knew it.

But then, beneath the box containing the writing set, he discovered a carton full of marzipan sweets coloured and shaped
like little fruits. He began to eat them immediately, one after an-

other, and went on shoving them in his mouth until they were all gone. Neither his father nor his brother tried to stop him.

Despite the fact that they were getting a late start for a journey over the Alps they took a detour to visit the village where his mother's family came from. Mastellina made an inconvenient dogleg that added two days to their journey and Domenico groused all the way, partly because it was already November and snow could close the pass any day and partly because Domenico despised all Guardis and Mastellina was their source

"They're all useless," he declared, glowering out the window of the coach. "Lazy, louche, spongers."

Lorenzo took a different view of his mother's relations. He loved his three Guardi uncles, Antonio, Nicolò, and Francesco, all painters by trade, none of them successful. Unlike the Tiepolos, they didn't work for noble families or pay taxes or belong to the professional association. His uncle Antonio, who lived rent-free in the house of one of his clients, liked to say they were "relieved from the burdens of prominence". Lorenzo rarely saw any of them actually painting, but they seemed to enjoy life. When Tiepolo and Domenico were out of town, his mother liked to invite his uncles over for meals. She claimed to be keeping them from dying of hunger, but Lorenzo sat with them as they ate and drank in the kitchen and saw how hard she laughed when she was with them. They were probably there right now, he thought, breaking into his father's second-best wine and performing conjuring tricks on the table with napkins and bits of straw.

If Tiepolo suspected this, he didn't seem concerned. He sat across from Lorenzo smoking one of his cigars as they jolted along in the coach, heading for the foothills. His father caught his eye and winked at him through the smoke. Lorenzo guessed that he didn't want to make the trip to Mastellina any more than Domenico did and it was his mother who had imposed it as some kind of a condition.

Mastellina was a tiny village of stone houses strung out beside a lively mountain stream, the Noce. The Tiepolos climbed the last stretch to the village on foot, since no carriage could go there. Everything about the place was on a slope, one end pointing down toward the green lowlands of the Veneto, the other up toward the high peaks. Smack in the middle of the cluster of houses stood a church with a sharp stone steeple, like a pointed fulcrum. When they arrived, rounding the last bend of the path, word of their coming had already spread. Almost immediately people swarmed out of the houses and ran down from the fields to greet them.

Lorenzo found that Mastellina was populated almost exclusively by Guardi relations, shock-haired men who resembled Lorenzo's uncles and handsome women who resembled his mother and Maria, his family's oldest servant. It was very strange. As the villagers pressed in around them, their similarity to one another reminded Lorenzo of scenes in his father's paintings where they had used the same model in several places, posed in different attitudes and wearing different costumes, to populate a large crowd. In paintings, you hardly noticed the repetitions; in life, their effect was disconcerting, especially for a boy used to the physical variety of Venetians. Lorenzo seemed to see a single face in several places at once, or identical features — ears, noses, eyebrows — cropping up on a variety of faces. At one point, he stopped short, arrested by the sight of a boy who looked too much like himself.

Even more unnerving was the fact that these similar strangers seemed to know all about him and the other Tiepolos when he knew nothing about them. It seemed his mother and uncles wrote to their relations in Mastellina, a thing he hadn't realised. His uncle Antonio even owned some property in the village: the locals showed them a house. Lorenzo was sceptical. He thought it was unlikely that Antonio, who was so proud of conniving to sleep rent-free in the palazzo of one of his patrons, owned property anywhere.

You couldn't fault the hospitality extended by the Guardis and sub-Guardis of Mastellina. They had made the day a holiday just for the Tiepolos, treating them first to a little tour of the town, including the church where Antonio had painted some hazy frescoes. Later, they reviewed the livestock: flop-eared sheep, pale grey cows with long bodies and heads shaped like equilateral triangles. Then there was a lunch party in a house with a stone portico where, they were told, Cecilia's father had been born.

This meant nothing to Lorenzo. He had never met this grandfather or indeed any grandfather — they were both dead before he came along. The lunch dragged on for hours and he sat kicking his heels on a chair with a hard seat. The food the mountain Guardis served was unfamiliar and they produced it with a flourish that meant you couldn't say no. As he had feared, there were speeches. His father was forced to get up and say something nice about Mastellina; Domenico spoke, too. Then a man who seemed to be the leader of the village delivered a long address in an accent Lorenzo struggled to understand. The meal seemed endless.

Fortunately, Lorenzo was rescued by several children who must have been his cousins, among them the boy who looked too much like him. They led him up a flight of rickety stairs to the attic and gave him beer to drink while they grilled him about life in Venice, a place they had heard about the way Lorenzo had heard about the New World. He quickly realised that he could tell these cousins anything he wanted, but telling them the truth was easiest and more than enough to impress them. Yes, he said, Venice had streets made of water and buildings so big you could fit their whole village into them. Yes, there were merchants from foreign places and you might meet anyone, of any colour, in the marketplace, buying and selling anything, speaking one of a hundred languages. Yes, it was true what Antonio Guardi had told them, that you could get paid a fortune just for painting pictures, an absolute fortune. Lorenzo named sums with authority, exaggerating only a little. His mountain cousins were silent with awe.

By the time lunch was finished, the last rays of the sun were lighting up the peaks that towered above the village, dyeing their white caps a hot shade of pink. Lorenzo stood and stared. He thought he knew these mountains. He had seen them many times from the roofs of high buildings in Venice, but he had never imagined what it would be like to stand in their cold shadow. In an offhand way, one of his cousins remarked that the snow would very soon reach down to where they stood, burying the village and cutting it off from the valley below. Now it was Lorenzo's turn to be impressed. Sensing this, the cousin began to speak excitedly of its coming, like someone expecting an invasion. The snow could be higher than a man's head, he told him, higher than buildings, and it could crash down unexpectedly, swallowing whole villages. People could be lost in snow and only found again when their bodies emerged like Pasqueflowers with the thaw. That had happened to someone they knew: his cousin named the dead man.

This image seized Lorenzo's imagination and didn't let go. He knew what it was to live in an island city with streets of water. People died from falling into the canals of Venice; sailors died on the sea around it. But to die in the snow, to have the snow *come for you*, seemed at once beautiful and terrifying to him. He shuddered with something like pleasure.

"You'll see for yourself," one of the boys said with a knowing nod. "You'll be right up there. If you're not leaving it too late."

The boy's words were true. From the moment they left Mastellina, the snow seemed to pursue the Tiepolos. Their guide over the mountains said the weather was much worse than usual for the time of year. They crossed the pass at the last possible moment, marching alongside the bearers and the horses in a blizzard that filled their footprints and closed the route behind them. At the foot of the pass, with the carriage reassembled, they proceeded toward Würzburg and the freezing weather came with them like an extra passenger. They huddled in the icy confines of their carriage, wrapped in every piece of clothing they had, blankets spread over their knees. All three of them fell ill. Domenico hacked endlessly. Tiepolo's nose was bright red, poking out from between a thick neck scarf and a large bonnet made of fur. His gout flared up, swelling the toes of his right foot until he cried in pain. Only Lorenzo was well enough to take in sights along the road, peeking through a chink in the leather curtain when the falling snow and mist didn't completely obliterate the view.

Their carriage finally rolled through the gates of the Prince-Bishop's palace one night in late November. The headman took one look at the state of the imported Venetian painters and called in a nurse.

While Tiepolo and Domenico were confined to bed, Lorenzo used the time to explore. Without asking permission from his father, who was too sick to worry about him anyway, he climbed out of a window in one of their rooms and began the process of becoming an expert in this new world.

He started by measuring the palace. He had no particular reason for doing this but measuring was a sort of habit with him, something he'd been doing all his life. He measured reflexively, almost without thinking, because it was fundamentally informative, a way of understanding anything you came across. Also, you just never knew when a good solid set of proportions might come in handy.

Beginning at one corner of the long rear façade, Lorenzo used his footprints as markers in the slushy snow and paced out the distance to the far corner of the building. On his way he passed a team of gardeners grubbing up a length of dead box hedging in the formal garden and two women with besom brooms sweeping snow off the terrace. He raised a hand to these strangers but didn't try to speak to them, not sure which language to use, not wanting to break his concentration. When he reached the corner of the palace, he spun ninety degrees on his heel and paced out the length of building's shorter side. He stopped then and did a quick calculation in his head. The result made him smile, feeling the tautness of his cold cheeks.

The length of the Residence's short side was a little longer than half that of the long one, suggesting the building's ground plan was based on the Golden Rectangle. This was good news in Lorenzo's view. Back in Venice, the extreme fussiness of the Prince-Bishop's contract had made him picture the client's palace as a complicated place, a mess of needless wings, turrets, arcades, dungeons, towers, cloisters, tunnels, keeps and battlements. Instead, he found it to be a modern structure ruled by sane geometry. He took that as a good sign. The rationality of the Residence pleased Lorenzo, and he was pleased with himself for discovering its key.

Up until that moment, the sky had been covered by a pale

sheet of cloud. Now the low winter sun broke through a thin parting and Lorenzo became conscious that he was standing on the brink of a vast open space. To his left stretched the front façade of the Residence, its golden stone and glazed windows sparkling in the sudden light. Ahead of him, at some distance, lay the town of Würzburg, a jumble of brown and yellow buildings with cobbled streets sloping downwards toward the brown, glinting column of a river. Hills rose on the other side of the water, striped grey with leafless vineyards. On top of the highest hill sat a square fortress, staring across the river valley at the town it protected.

Directly before Lorenzo there was an enormous piazza, bigger than San Marco, evenly covered in snow like a canvas freshly prepared with white gesso. Their carriage must have crossed this square the night they arrived — he saw that its surface was neatly scalloped by two curving brown tracks that came from the different sides and converged at the palace gates — but it had been dark then and Lorenzo hadn't seen the square or sensed it.

The sight of it now made him feel like yelling for no reason at all. Forgetting his measuring project, he started to run into the open space like a madman, relishing sound of his feet crunching against icy crust of snow. Though ragged and dirty around the edges where people and animals had tramped, the snow at the centre of the square was clean and smooth and it sparkled in the sun like crushed diamonds. Lorenzo headed for one of the clean patches, wanting to claim it, to mark it for the first time. But he'd only taken a few strides when he felt something hard and wet explode against his shoulder. He stopped and turned and was hit again, this time in the chest, the snow spattering into his face and eyes.

Now he saw the boys, three of them, their bodies silhouetted against the field of snow, a big red dog leaping around them. One of the boys bent down and took a scoop of snow and shaped it between his hands before throwing it, fast and straight, at Lorenzo. Seeing it coming, he ducked, then crouched near the ground to make his body a smaller target. Taking a fistful of snow in his bare hands, he copied the boy, passing it back and forth between his palms, compressing it into a solid projectile. It felt surprising natural, as though he had done it a thousand times. Squinting acoss the snowfield, he estimated the distance — measuring proved a useful skill in so many circumstances — stood up and let fly, hitting the boy squarely in the head. Then the dog began barking and leaping up and all three boys began throwing at him at once. In a hail of snowballs, Lorenzo ran toward them, whooping with aggression and wild joy.

Lorenzo was freer that first winter in Würzburg than he had been for years. Work was easy. He and his father and brother had nothing more to do than set up their studio in the suite of five groundfloor rooms that had been allocated for their use. They sourced materials, assembled equipment, fiddled with the designs they had brought with them from Venice. Tiepolo and Domenico were still having long discussions with the Prince-Bishop and his people, too. The elderly aristocrat was still very nervous about the project, and for good reason. He'd been swindled the previous year by a conman who took his money and ran off without putting down so much as a stroke of paint. Before that, there had been another artist, a young German, who produced a promising set of designs — then promptly died before he could begin to execute them. As a consequence, the older Tiepolos spent a good part of the cold months reassuring their client in a comical mix of Italian, French, Latin, a few words of cod German. The fact was they were all just waiting for the weather to warm up so the real work could begin.

This left Lorenzo with nothing much to do. Every day, he managed to get out of the palace for a few hours. No one asked where he was going. Sometimes he went looking for the town boys with their red dog, who was called Raus. Sometimes he came out of the Residence to find the three of them already there on the snowy piazza, waiting for him but pretending not to. They'd turn and start walking away as he approached and he would fall into step, exactly as if he'd been walking with them all the time. They'd taken him in.

The four of them didn't talk much. Instead, the boys took Lorenzo all over the town and down to the river, the Main, with its edges of ice, its black barges that had to be dragged by horses upstream but slid smoothly downstream with the current. Together, they crossed the bridge and climbed the steep hill to the fortress where they sat in the winter sun at the foot of a high wall and looked back at the Residence riding above the city like a thick bracket. Sketching in the snow with a stick, Lorenzo showed his friends how its shape was constructed of a square extended twice by a precise geometric process involving a compass. The boys found this interesting: they studied geometry, too. Afterwards they took him to a frozen pond in the woods that was almost perfectly round. The dog chased a duck onto the ice and went sprawling, four paws pointing in the four cardinal directions like a red compass rose. They laughed until they fell over and had to stuff their mouths with snow.

Lorenzo's mother sent him a letter. "Are you going to Mass every day?" she wanted to know. "Are you working hard for your Papa? Are you in good health? Write to your Mama with your lovely new pen. The man who sold me the set promised it would produce a fine line but perhaps he was lying? I am longing to see how well it works." His father sat Lorenzo down and told him to write a note on the tail end of one of his own letters, but he couldn't think of a thing to say. It crossed his mind to tell his mother how the town boys had taught him to write in the snow with hot piss, like an engraver etching lines with acid on a copper plate. He had only managed his initials: LBT. Lorenzo Baldissera Tiepolo was too long a name for anyone to write in piss, even with a full bladder.

Lorenzo knew his mother would laugh if he told her this in person, but he wasn't sure if she'd like reading about it in a letter. Letters were for polite words. "I am going to Mass often," he wrote instead. "I am working hard: you can ask Papa. My health is fine but the food here is not good. There are too many potatoes." He wanted to tell her more — about the snow, about the boys, about the fun he was having — but it was too complicated and he worried it might make her feel sadder because he was enjoying life so much apart from her. He simply wrote, "The pen works very well, as you can see. My handwriting is beautiful because of it. No blots on this page." Then he carefully drew a blot, to be funny. "Your loving son, LBT."

Lorenzo's freedom ended with the first hint of spring. As soon as the weather was warm enough to set plaster, he and his father and brother went to live on top of a tower of scaffolding in the Imperial Hall, the throne room of the Prince-Bishop. They worked all day up there in the hot air under the cupola; they worked and ate and pissed into a bucket and drank water from goatskins, like sailors, without ever coming down. They only descended after it was too dark to see and on Sundays when they had to go to Mass.

Lorenzo's father set the pace, driving them all to finish the work at breakneck speed, starting with the largest fresco at the centre of the ceiling. The first job was to spread fine finishing plaster over the vault's rough underplaster. This had to be done very carefully, since they were working inside elaborate frames already set in position by the stuccoist, Antonio Bossi. The size of the plastered area had to be precisely calculated, too, because the colour could only be applied while the plaster was still wet. If they miscalculated and the plaster dried before they finished painting they had to chisel it out and begin all over again. Lorenzo's father himself smoothed the plaster on the first two or three areas of the ceiling, to see how the timing went.

Soon the three of them established a working rhythm. When the wet plaster was applied, they tacked up large-scale drawings on paper and incised the outlines using brush handles. Peeling these away, they began applying the colour: pure pigment suspended in plain water. This had to be done very quickly and so the jobs were shared out. While his father and Domenico painted, Lorenzo kept the buckets organised and full, made certain that the colours were properly mixed. He fetched new brushes when the corrosive lime had eaten the bristles of the old ones. He kept track of the measuring tools, chalk lines, straight edges, mahlsticks, pieces of charcoal, plumb bobs, stepladders, notes on paper, jars of pigment, trowels, plaster hawks, sacks of slaked lime and sand. He fetched their lunch from the palace kitchens and carried it up the scaffold in a leather satchel. It was his job to climb all the way down and retrieve dropped things. This was his most hated duty and he performed it about one hundred times per day until he was as wiry and agile as a monkey and could have done the climb blindfolded in the dark. He wondered if any of his new friends could have managed it. He wondered what they were doing with their summer.

The snow had misled Lorenzo: the summer in Würzburg was surprisingly warm. Fleeing the heat, the Prince-Bishop and his staff retreated to his other palace in the hills while the Tiepolos stayed behind, painting in the oven-like conditions beneath the cupola. They never saw the real summer sky. For several months, the only sky they knew was slopped out of a pail, blue pigment and fermenting water. Their only sun was Tiepolo's figure of Apollo, driving his chariot across the parti-coloured heaven that bloomed from their brushes. The air trapped under the vault was stifling. The damp plaster guzzled the paint like a thirsty animal. It sucked all the moisture from their bodies, too: they were always parched, always drinking water, like men crossing the desert. The light bouncing around the curved surfaces of the ceiling played tricks with their eyes, making it impossible to judge distances, to get bearings. Some days were slapstick comedies of dropped gear and kicked-over buckets; knuckles, foreheads, elbows rammed into wet plaster. Then Venetian oaths rang out in the empty palace with no one to hear or understand them. On other days, the Tiepolos performed together like clockwork. On those days Lorenzo felt like part of a fine machine and the painting seemed to grow with a life of its own. He had never worked so hard in his life.

They finished the first fresco by July, *Apollo Conducting Beatrice of Burgundy to the Genius of Empire.* The picture was simpler than it sounded: on the one side of the scene a blond lady flew across the sky in a golden coach pulled by four horses, their big bellies shining white as they surged forward across the clouds. On the other, a youthful king sat on a blocklike throne surrounded by his retinue. In the sky around these two, putti flipped, flags flapped, hours hovered on butterfly wings, river gods perched on the rim of the plaster moulding that framed the fresco. Lorenzo's father had worked closely with the stucco artist, Bossi, to arrange for the fresco to break out of this frame and spill partway down the ceiling. This created the illusion that the top of the room had been lifted away like the lid of a jar to reveal the real sky. Lorenzo thought the result looked good and so did the Prince-Bishop.

Lorenzo was in the room when the clergyman aristocrat saw his fresco for the first time and it was a satisfying moment. The carpenters had removed the scaffold boards so that the client could get a clear view. The old man came into the great hall with his sister and a couple of his ministers and at first he seemed hesitant even to look up, as though he were afraid of what he might see there. But when he finally did — Lorenzo had to laugh — the Prince-Bishop almost lost his wig! It was funny to see an elderly dignitary so delighted, like a child with a new toy. He rushed around the oval room, stopping first here, then there, lifting his eyes, and then coming to a halt and gazing at the ceiling from every possible angle. He placed himself in the doorway so he could see the fresco as a guest would see it when he first arrived. He called for a chair, sat down in it to get an idea of what it would be like for people eating dinner. When this dance was done, he went over and embraced Tiepolo. Lorenzo thought he might kiss him. "We need to have a celebration," the old man said.

There was no question the party slowed down their progress. The scaffold had to be dismantled and stored away, all their gear had to be shifted back to the studio. The servants moved in and set up a long table and chairs, food was brought up from the kitchens, musicians arrived. But it was worth it, Lorenzo thought, to see the Prince-Bishop's guests come mincing up the steps of the grand staircase in full court dress and walk into the throne room for the first time. Lorenzo's father and brother were at the party. They had washed the plaster out of their hair, dug the pigment from underneath their nails, and put on their best Venetian suits. Lorenzo passed the evening with the servants in the White Room, which served as a sort of ante-room for the hall, watching his brother and his father receive praise for their work. Domenico looked happy for an opportunity to preen and peek down the necklines of the ladies. His father looked silly in his wig, but Lorenzo could tell he was relieved that things were going so well.

Late in the evening, Lorenzo spotted Tiepolo slipping out of the party. He followed him, thinking he was returning to their rooms to go to bed. Instead, Tiepolo made his way out onto the gallery of the Staircase Hall, the enormous room that formed part of the suite of staterooms leading to the Imperial Hall. As the name suggested, it had nothing in it but a big staircase spanned by an enormous vault. The Tiepolos came up this staircase every day on their way to work in the Imperial Hall and they went down it every night on their way back to their rooms. Lorenzo thought of it as a kind of grand passageway: despite its enormous size, he hardly noticed it any more.

Now he watched his father pause to light a cigar in the flames of a standing candelabra before strolling very slowly all the way to the far end of the Staircase Hall gallery, disappearing into the shadows.

Unseen, Lorenzo waited for him. What could his father be doing there all alone in the dark? Was he sad? Had something happened?

The noise from the Prince-Bishop's party echoed in the space under the vault, but he and his father were alone in the vast hall. Between them, the stairwell lay like a rectangular pool of inky black, deeper and more intense than the surrounding darkness. Across this pool of shadows, Lorenzo watched the little red point made by the ember of his father's cigar. It rose and fell as Tiepolo brought it to his lips and lowered it again. Even without seeing him, Lorenzo knew what his father looked like at that moment, his big eyes darting back and forth as he watched his own thoughts, the smoke pouring from his mouth as though his heart were on fire. Much later, remembering this moment, he realised what his father must have been thinking as he stood and smoked, imagining he was alone. He was thinking about the vault. He was already starting to plan what he would paint there. That was the moment when everything changed for them.

Because Domenico had a hangover, Lorenzo was forced to spend the whole morning copying the Madonna in red chalk. He was working from an original by his father, which he had copied several times before. He should have been able to do it in his sleep, but the drawing was causing him trouble. The soft folds of the Virgin's veil weren't coming out right. There was something distinctly strange about the shape of the Infant Christ.

Lorenzo cursed his brother. Domenico had spent the previous night in the *Hofbräu* and reeled into their rooms in the small hours, knocking over the easels in the dark. In the morning he dragged himself out of bed early and went straight to work in an effort to show their father that the life he was leading had no effect on him. He put Lorenzo to work, too, and Lorenzo knew very well why: his brother couldn't control himself, so he was controlling him, Lorenzo. Their father didn't seem to notice the injustice.

"It won't do you any harm to do some drawing practice," he said when Lorenzo complained. He went off with Bossi after breakfast and left Lorenzo at Domenico's mercy. To make things worse, it was snowing. From where he sat, Lorenzo could see light, lacy flakes falling diagonally past the window. His friends would be out in it now, sledging on the hill below the fortress. The thought of this was pure torture to Lorenzo. His muscles twitched with latent energy.

"I'm finished," he said loudly. He looked around. Domenico was standing beside a little desk, pretending to consult a book.

He didn't respond. "Did you hear me?"

"I heard you," he said without raising his glassy eyes from the page. "But I know you're not really finished."

Lorenzo struggled to control his frustration. "At least take a look."

Domenico closed the book with a growl and sidled over to where Lorenzo perched on a stool. He was bundled up in his new Bavarian coat with sable around the collar. It was warm in the room but Domenico was always cold — it was his excuse to buy expensive clothes and take a carriage for the short journey into town, a distance Lorenzo could sprint in exactly three minutes.

Domenico looked at the drawing and laughed in a nasty way. "For pity's sake. What do you call that?"

Lorenzo saw instantly what he meant. The Madonna's shoulder, even hidden by drapery, seemed detached from her body. The torso of the baby Jesus was too long. He looked like a composite of two different babies sewn together.

"I should make you do the whole thing over again," Domenico said, venting irritation that even Lorenzo could see had its origins somewhere other than in his drawing. As his brother bent over him he could smell the traces of alcohol lingering on his breath. His curly russet hair smelled of barmaids' armpits.

"Do you know what your real problem is," Domenico said. "You spent too much time with Mother and the girls always telling you how precious you are, how funny and clever you are. Dribbling and kissing all over itsy bitsy little Enzo. Who's a hootchie coo?" He pinched Lorenzo's cheek viciously. "It's made you useless."

Lorenzo batted his hand away. "Why are you bothering with me if I'm so useless? Why didn't you just leave me at home?" Angrily, he flipped his chalk across the table.

Without warning, Domenico slapped him on the back of the skull so hard that his head flew forward and he tumbled off his stool.

"Pick it up." Domenico said, slightly breathless. Sullenly, Lorenzo got up and fetched the chalk and returned to his stool.

Domenico spoke calmly; this was his lecture voice. "Have you ever thought what might happen to you if you don't have a trade, Lorenzo? I'll tell you what will happen. You will starve. Your children will starve. Father and Mother will be dead by then and you'd better believe that I won't lift a finger to help you. This," he pushed his finger at Lorenzo's drawing, "is all the help you are getting from me." He broke off suddenly, looking pale and sick. A film of sweat bathed his face. He moaned. "Oh mercy."

"You don't look very good," said Lorenzo, just managing to suppress a smile. "Do you want me to call Frau Knell?" Lorenzo wasn't sure what the maid could do for Domenico, but he knew you should call a woman when someone was sick and Frau Knell was the only woman they had to call.

"You mind your own business," Domenico said, belching. He showed him how to correct the Madonna by restructuring the highlighting on her cloak. The baby Jesus was a loss; to put it right Lorenzo would have to start the whole drawing again from scratch. Domenico wasn't going to make him do this because, as he explained, he was sick of the whole business of trying to teach Lorenzo anything.

Domenico went back to his book and Lorenzo made a few reluctant swipes at the paper with his red chalk. Domenico was right about the highlighting, he found. When he reworked it, it looked all right; the Virgin's shoulder joined with her body.

An intense quiet pervaded the room, broken only by the small murmurings of the morning fire burning down in the tall ceramic stove. Outside, the snow continued to fall. The light was yellow: storm light. Lorenzo's mind drifted into speculation about the texture and depth of this new snowfall. It might be wet and soft, like a frozen dessert, or dry and light as talc. Snow had so many moods, so many possibilities.

"Done," he announced.

Domenico dragged himself to his feet and came back to the table. He picked up the drawing and looked at it. "If you were my apprentice, I'd throw you out on the street," he said without much conviction. "It's lucky for you you're my brother."

That depends on how you define luck, Lorenzo thought.

"However," Domenico said. "The feet aren't bad. Her knees are in the right places. Altogether," he paused for effect, "it's not the worst drawing I've ever seen."

"So I can go now?" Lorenzo said joyfully, hopping off the stool.

"Not so fast." Domenico looked at him with a crafty expression. "Take this to Father," he said, handing the drawing back to him.

"You said it was all right!"

"I said it wasn't the worst drawing I had ever seen. What part of that sounded like I thought it was all right?"

Lorenzo took the sheet of paper. Now he was worried. His father wasn't brutal like Domenico, but in his way he was more exacting. Tiepolo just didn't understand how it was possible for a person to draw an awkward line or put shadows where no shadows should go. He blinked at a bad drawing with sadness and disbelief, as though it were a child with a deformity, and then he made you do it over as many times as necessary to get it right. This could mean he'd be stuck inside for the whole afternoon.

Searching for a way out, Lorenzo thought of trying to fool his father. For his exercise he had used a scrap of blue-grey paper he found lying on the shelf under a pile of drawings. On one side was his Madonna and her faulty Baby Jesus, on the other was series of drawings of hands and forearms in pen and wash: hands holding spears, hands outstretched, fingers pointing. They were dexterous little sketches. Lorenzo guessed they were his father's, but they might have been Domenico's or even the work of one of the two local painters they had hired. It was hard to tell. Lorenzo thought of showing these to his father instead of his own drawing, but realised there was no way Tiepolo, of all people, would mistake any of them for his youngest son's work.

He sighed. "Can I go out after that?"

"I'm not your keeper. Talk about it with Father."

"Where is Father?" he asked, resigned. There was no getting out of it.

"He's where he always is," Domenico said and went back to the desk.

Lorenzo got ready to sprint as soon as he stepped out into the corridor. One of the good things about living in a palace was that there was plenty of space for running, as long as no one who mattered caught you at it. Lorenzo rolled his drawing into a neat tube, grasped in his fist like a baton. He selected his route; after a year, he knew the palace as well as he had his old neighbourhood in Venice. He could go via the network of narrow back corridors the servants used to get from room to room. Or he could take an outside way that led through the garden, circling around the building and re-entering through the front door. That would be an opportunity to put his boots in the snow for a few minutes at least, but it was too risky. He was liable just to keep running once he got outside into the sharp, cold air, and then there really would be trouble. Instead, he chose the most direct route to the Staircase Hall. This led through the palace's wide public corridors where the polished stone floors were ideal for racing and sliding.

Lorenzo guessed he was safe; the Prince-Bishop and his retinue were out of town and there were no important visitors at the moment. With a sense of release, clutching his rolled up drawing, he began to run. He loped down a short stretch of hallway, turned the corner, gathering speed — and collided with the bulky form of Frau Knell.

"Oh oh!" Laundry flew in the air. "Master Lorenzo! Be careful!"

Lorenzo clutched at the housekeeper to keep her from toppling over, steadying Frau Knell on her feet. She was a sturdy lady in her forties with a plait of thick blond hair she wore wound up and over a bony masculine brow. Day in and day out, her uniform was a plain brown dress with a white collar. A tiny silver cross rested on her horizontal bosom.

Lorenzo didn't apologize for barreling into Frau Knell but he bent to help her pick up the scattered clothing.

"Now I'll have to do these all over again," she said.

"No you don't," Lorenzo said, shifting into Bavarian dialect, which was the only language the housekeeper spoke. He wondered why Frau Knell bothered washing their work clothes at all. They always ended up covered with filth — paint, plaster, blood, stain, size, pigment, dust, glue, sweat. She might as well leave them as they were and burn them when the job was done. That's what his mother did, as he told Frau Knell, trying to ease her housekeeping burden. Frau Knell didn't seem to understand what he was saying.

"Hold these," she commanded, thrusting more laundry onto his arms. She had been with them since the previous summer, replacing a constantly changing series of servants who found it easy to ignore the Venetians when no one was watching. Before she came, they'd lived in carefree squalor, their suite of five rooms transformed into one continuous disorderly studio. None of the Tiepolos would have admitted to minding the mess, and none of them said anything when Frau Knell materialised and cleaned it away. By unspoken agreement, none of the Tiepolos thanked her for her devotion to duty.

THE MERCHANTS OF LIGHT

"This way." She led him back to the studio and pushed through the door. The room appeared empty. "He is here, Herr your brother?"

"He was here a second ago."

Frau Knell peered through the doorway into the next room. "Huh!" she said. "During the day!" They could just see the soles of Domenico's shoes hanging off the end of the sofa. He was sound asleep. Frau Knell shot Lorenzo a look to show him Domenico's behaviour was just what she would have expected. She had a low opinion of him, because he was disrespectful and picked on her Bavarian obsession with cleanliness. He teased her, saying he would take her to Venice where she would have a field day scrubbing the slime off the canal walls, boiling the gondolas, scouring the tarts with lye. And yet it was Domenico who got the most satisfaction from Frau Knell's rage for order. He was the first to complain if the sheets weren't clean or the fires hot enough.

Frau Knell motioned for Lorenzo to put the pile of clothes down on an unmade bed and he did so. As he passed her, she sniffed him, reminding him of an affectionate dog.

"Hoo! You need a wash!" she said with a smile, showing the gap in her teeth. She had very fresh skin, like that of a young girl. Lorenzo knew Frau Knell had a daughter and he wondered what she looked like.

"I had one the other day," he lied. He put his nose down his collar. His body had recently begun giving off an unfamiliar odour, a bit like raw meat.

"You're not a little boy anymore, you know." Frau Knell said with a knowing nod. She cast her eyes around the tumbled room and sighed profoundly over the havoc. She had once admitted to Lorenzo that she saw her assignment to them as a kind of penance meted out by the Prince-Bishop. She must be atoning for some enormous sin, she reasoned, but she still wasn't sure what it was. Sometimes, especially after a night when Tiepolo and some of the assistants sat up late playing cards and drinking wine, Lorenzo surprised Frau Knell sobbing alone in the face of the chaos they left behind.

Released at last, Lorenzo ran. He ran to find his father, ran just to move. He ran at top speed past maids with buckets, a manservant carrying a large basket of linen, a pair of roughnecks hauling a heavy armoire down a passageway. Some of them hailed him by name — they all knew him. Some looked scandalised by his breakneck pace, but none of them tried to stop him. To him they were mere obstacles, nothing more. Using fancy footwork, he danced around them and kept moving.

Underfoot, the palace floors were a chessboard of black and white flagstones. Taking long strides, his feet fell on every fourth slab, white, then black, then white again. He sped down the broad corridor, passing window after tall window. The winter air cascaded down from the glass, making currents of cold that lapped against his ankles. Beyond the thick glass, the snow fell a finger's breadth away.

He turned a corner. The next passage, with its white walls, made Lorenzo think of a snow tunnel. His mind raced as fast as his legs. Could you build a tunnel of this size through snow? Could you build a palace all of snow? One of his town friends had heard of a tribe who lived in domed houses constructed of nothing but snow. You couldn't have a fire in a snow fireplace or take a bath in a snow tub. You couldn't paint pictures on snow walls or snow ceilings. No. You'd have to decorate them in cast snow, Lorenzo reasoned, the way Bossi embellished plaster walls with shapes made of plaster. He'd made the White Room that way, the anteroom to the Imperial Hall. It looked as if it were made of snow and decorated with snow, the walls alive with cold white tendrils, fronds, ferns, scalloped shells, ghost trophies of pallid helmets, spars and shields, albino dragons, ladies, and lizards. A snow boneyard, bleached by frost. It was beautiful. It was the opposite of what he and his father did with colour.

Lorenzo leaped down a short flight of stairs, thinking that snow was the main thing he had learned in Würzburg. He was supposed to be mastering fresco painting, but he'd known about that already. This was new: this was his apprenticeship in snow. By the time they went home again next summer, he'd be a full-fledged master in the art. He'd teach his Venice friends about it; they would be amazed. Maybe he'd lead them on trips into the mountains and show them the places where the snow would *come for you.*

Running along the corridor, Lorenzo slid though another turn, hitting the far wall and rebounding off flexed wrists. Then he dashed down another long hallway, picking up speed as he went, trailing his new, meaty smell through the chilled air.

Suddenly, he burst into the open vestibule, a wide room huddled under a shallow dome. Slender, paired columns stood like young birch trees around a circular floor designed for turning coaches. Today, the large double doors stood open admitting a freezing wind that struck Lorenzo full in the face as he skidded to a halt. A carpet of muddy slush trailed through the door and over the flagstones to a waggon pulled by a pair of draught horses with dirty blond manes. Workmen milled around the waggon, unlashing a snow-dusted cargo of planks and poles. The dome rang with their shouts and with the knock and bang of the lumber as it was shunted off onto the shoulders of bearers.

Lorenzo spotted the foreman standing by the tailgate and went over, stuffing his rolled up drawing into the band of his trousers as he went.

The foreman looked up and saw him coming. "Well, look who's

here. Our little Maestro," he said, the German consonants ringing loudly under the dome. "Our little Tiepolino, the genius of
our time. Where are big Tiepolo and medium-sized Tiepoletto
today?"

Lorenzo tried to smile. *Tiepolino.* Who had taught the Bavarian
workers this insulting Italian diminutive? It had to be the stuc-
coists, who came from Lugano. They had been in Würzburg for a
decade and had been infected by the heavy local sense of humour.

"If they were here, we'd have the whole set!" the foreman bellowed. He was a fat man with short legs and a fair moustache. He
wore a hunter's cap with earflaps. It was wet with melted snow.
"Oh, I am funny."

Lorenzo ignored this. "I'm going up," he said, indicating the
staircase with his chin. "I'll take something."

The foreman goggled. "Tiepolino!" he cried. "You surprise me!
You think you can carry one of these by yourself. Your precious
hands will be crushed and what would the Prince-Bishop say then,
eh? Or Tiepolo, or Tiepoletto? They'd skin me alive. No, no. We
can't have that."

Lorenzo gritted his teeth. Rather than arguing, he went to the
tailgate of the waggon and waited for the next piece of wood to
be handed down. It was a rough pole as thick as his leg and three
times the length of his body. It was so heavy that the weight of it
made him stagger.

"Careful now!" called the foreman, not joking anymore. "I
mean it, son. You'll have a rupture. At least let's ask Herr your
father."

"I'll ask him at the top," Lorenzo grunted. With difficulty, he
balanced the pole on his shoulder. Bowing under its weight, he
shuffled toward the staircase, struggling to keep the long piece
of wood from tilting and swinging at either end. Suddenly he felt
the weight ease and steady. Looking behind him, he saw a big

labourer with a red moustache placing the other end of the pole on his massive shoulder.

"I can do it myself," Lorenzo said sullenly, because that was the idea. "Let go."

"The foreman said," Red Moustache replied and stood waiting. He was very tall, almost a giant, and the pole made a steep downward diagonal between his massive shoulder and Lorenzo's slight one.

"I don't need any help," Lorenzo said.

"The foreman said," the worker repeated. Other labourers hurried past them up the stairs, carrying planks and poles on their shoulders. Turning in disgust, Lorenzo began to climb the staircase.

Even with the big worker supporting the other end, the pole was heavy and pressed painfully on the muscles of his shoulder. For the thousandth time since he'd started working in the palace, Lorenzo was glad for the strange design of the staircase risers. They were oddly shallow and wide and they forced you to take small, incremental steps that looked ridiculous but made climbing easier. Balthasar Neumann, the architect, had designed them for the convenience of old Bavarian noblemen wearing long robes, but the steps were also ideal if you had to carry things up them, like buckets of plaster, or sacks of sand, or scaffold poles.

He reached the first landing without breaking a sweat. He was a lot stronger than he had been a year ago, that was one good thing about this job. He could have easily kept going past the second landing, too, except the labourer carrying the other end of the pole was lagging. Easing the pole off his sore shoulder, Lorenzo turned and waited, observing his helper critically. Red Moustache was plodding up, flat footed, taking his time. He had his head thrown right back and the tips of his moustache dangled down the sides of his cheeks. His mouth hung wide open, as though his jaw muscles weren't working properly. Lorenzo wondered if the man were actually an idiot. Then he realised.

"I see it's the first time you've been in here," he said with a smile.

The man stumbled on the last step and his scared eyes met Lorenzo's. He nodded numbly. "I came to town on the barge, with the lumber," he said. "I've seen the outside of the Residence before. But…"

His big eyes rolled up and over the vault, which seemed to expand overhead like a buff-coloured sky. Lorenzo hadn't quite forgotten the sensation of walking up these stairs for the first time. On that day more than a year before, he'd been mostly interested in beating Domenico to the top, taking the low steps four, five at once. He'd ignored the vault. But now he was an insider, an expert. And they'd all started thinking differently about the vault since last summer when the Prince-Bishop first suggested they paint it.

"I can tell you its measurements," he boasted to Red Moustache. His father was so enamored with its dimensions that he had drilled them into both his sons like a catechism: 32 metres by 19, with a 5.5-metre rise.

The labourer, clearly overwhelmed, wasn't interested in numbers. Crossing himself with his free hand, he wanted to know how in God's name such a monstrous thing stayed up.

Lorenzo was enjoying this. "That's something no one understands," he said mysteriously, "except maybe the Prince-Bishop. You know he says special prayers every night to make the angels come and prop it up. But you never know. There could be other forces at work."

The labourer crossed himself again. Looking up the final flight of stairs, Lorenzo caught sight of his father sitting on the edge of the gallery with Bossi. Their legs dangled down into the stairwell.

"My father and I are going to paint that vault," he declared. His words had the desired effect on Red Moustache.

"You?" the man said, his mouth still slack with wonder. "Impossible. How do you expect to get all the way up there?"

County bumpkin, thought Lorenzo. He felt sorry for the man, who was too ignorant to realise that the pole he was carrying on his shoulder was a support for scaffolding. He undoubtedly lived in a tiny cottage where his head hit the roof beams every time he stood up and had no conception of how to manage large buildings. Lorenzo thought of taking the man through to the Imperial Hall to show him the scaffold tower standing there, self-explanatory, waiting for painting work to recommence the spring. But he couldn't resist the temptation to have some fun.

"Oh," he said, "we fly."

"People don't fly," the man said, more horrified than ever.

"Venetians do." His tone was deadpan. "Everyone knows that. That's why they hire us."

The Bavarian looked sick and crossed himself again. He stared at Lorenzo and then up at the vault. When they'd deposited the pole at the top, he practically ran down the stairs. He couldn't get away from the demonic foreign boy fast enough.

B ossi saw him first as he approached them across the gallery. "Ask Lorenzo," he said, gesturing toward him. "He'll know the answer."

Tiepolo turned toward him and Lorenzo could see his father was in a playful mood. He loved Neumann's vault; just being under it seemed to make him feel jolly. He liked consulting with Bossi, too. The two men sat next to one another on the brink of the drop into the stairwell as companionably as a pair of Sunday fishermen cooling their feet in a lake.

"The answer to what?"

"Don't think about this too much, son: Titans or nymphs?"

"To mark the corners of the cornice." Bossi pointed. A plain horizontal pediment ran around the room above the tall windows, marking the point where the straight walls stopped and the curved vault began. "Two figures in each corner: boom-boom, boom-boom."

"Titans," Lorenzo said, absolutely certain.

Bossi clapped his hands together. "You see! What did I tell you? Domenico would have wanted nymphs."

"He's twenty-five. Of course he wants nymphs." Tiepolo hunched up his shoulders and laughed.

"Titans will be much better. Bigger, stronger." Bossi spoke Italian with a strange accent after being in Bavaria too long. With his hands he sculpted massive volumes in the air, and then paused, lost for words. "Just the thing."

He shook his dark, shaggy head violently like a dog climbing out of a river. It was the kind of unexpected gesture that startled Lorenzo when he first met Bossi, but he was used to these tics now.

"Titans then," Tiepolo said. He never seemed to notice Bossi's spasms. "Seated back to back on the cornice. A leg or two dangling right down. Like so." He transferred the cold stub of his cigar from his hand to his mouth, then shifted his back until he was leaning against Bossi. He thrust both legs out over the void below.

"Very graceful," Bossi commented with a secret smile for Lorenzo. His diminutive father looked more like a churchman slipping on the ice than a reclining giant. "They can be leaning on some kind of device: a shield, a scallop shell."

"Life-sized?" Tiepolo mused, shifting his cigar to the other side of his mouth, changing the angle of his legs slightly but keeping them raised. Labourers were still bringing pieces of lumber up the stairs. Lorenzo saw them glance up curiously at Tiepolo's waving legs. Lorenzo imagined Red Moustache running out of the vestibule door and all the way back to the mountains, crossing himself in fear of flying Venetians.

"Bigger," Bossi said. "They're Titans."

"Good point." Tiepolo let his legs swing down and drummed his heels against the wall excitedly. "That was too easy. You make my life too easy. What's wrong with you, Bossi? Can't you be more difficult?"

"As long as he's happy," Bossi said bashfully. He leaned forward over the void, turning his tricorn hat in his hands. When any of them talked about "he" they always meant the client.

Tiepolo shrugged. "If he doesn't like it we can always change it. That's why we do modelli, so he can fiddle with them to his little heart's content. Once he sees what he doesn't want, then he knows for sure what he does."

"And that is the definition of a client," Bossi said sagely. "When does he want it?"

"Oh, sometime in the spring. April."

"Better get cracking," Bossi said with a shudder Tiepolo didn't see because he was looking the other way. Sometimes Lorenzo wondered what went on in Bossi's head that made his body jerk around this way. He had seen the stuccoist fly into sudden screaming rages when the plaster mix was too wet or a cast was too rough. But when this happened he'd get himself off the scaffolding and out of the room and not come back until he'd calmed down. He never struck anyone and no one ever got fired. He was a man full of contradictions.

Bossi and Tiepolo stood up stiffly and embraced, the Luganese enveloping the smaller painter in the folds of his yellow cloak. Without thinking about it, Lorenzo put out an arm between them and the drop. He and his father stood on the lip of the stairwell and watched the stuccoist walk down the stairs, seeming to sink away into the darkness. It gave Lorenzo a funny feeling to see their friend swallowed up by shadows.

"I saw you hauling that lumber, young Titan," his father said to him, still staring after Bossi. "You should get paid for that." He reached out and felt Lorenzo's biceps. "Well, well."

Lorenzo remembered the drawing tucked in his waistband. He'd have to produce it sooner or later, but there was no harm in stalling a little. It was rare to catch his father alone. "So we're definitely doing this room, then?"

Tiepolo slid him a look. "Let's hope so. Do you think he likes us enough?"

"No, he's figured out we're crooks."

"That's right. Let's take the money and run off to Milan."

"I'll start packing right away."

"Good boy. Come over here." Tiepolo moved away from the edge of the gallery and found a place near the windows, where the light was brighter. Lorenzo followed. He watched his father fish a piece of charcoal out of his pocket as he knelt down stiffly on the flagstones. He drew a large rectangle across the pale grey stone surface.

"Here is the vault," he said. "There's the north end, there's the south end. There are the two long sides." Tiepolo drew a little compass rose next to the rectangle, indicating the cardinal directions. "We have Bossi's Titans here and here at the corners." He roughed in pairs of masculine figures. "And here, looking relaxed. We don't want raging Titans on our vault. Not this time." He sat back and looked at his sketch. "There we have a sort of frame. Of course, it's not really a frame. You won't ever be able to see the whole span at once. You'll see part of it from the first flight stairs, a different part from the second flight, from the gallery…"

Lorenzo suddenly had a thought. "Oh no!"

"What is it?"

"I hope the Prince-Bishop's not going to do one of those briefs for us, like he did before. That was terrible."

Tiepolo ran the charcoal once more around the rectangle. "No, there's not going to be a brief this time. We know what he wants. *You* know what he wants."

Lorenzo thought for a second. "One like his cousin's."

"One like his cousin's," Tiepolo confirmed. "Only better."

In the autumn, the Prince-Bishop sent all three Tiepolos out to Schloss Weissenstein in Pommersfelden, a day's carriage ride away. This palace belonged to his cousin and was smaller and less imposing than the Residence, but in many ways it was similar. It had its own Imperial Hall and a Staircase Hall with a vault frescoed by a painter called Byss. This is what the Prince-Bishop had sent them to see.

None of them had wanted to make the trip. Tiepolo was in a bad mood all the way there and Lorenzo guessed he resented being commanded to look at another man's work. Byss had been dead for ten years but the Prince-Bishop still sang his praises, giving the impression that he would have hired him instead of Tiepolo if he were still alive.

As soon as they walked into the Staircase Hall at Pommersfelden, however, they all felt much better. The first thing they noticed was how cramped it looked in comparison to the one at the Residence. The problem wasn't the size, it was the design. The Staircase Hall in the Residence was a huge, rectangular room with a wide gallery reached by a single, central staircase. Everything about it was designed to showcase the unbroken span of the vault. Pommersfelden's hall was smaller, square, with three sets of arcaded galleries stacked one atop the other and two flights of stairs zigzagging up. This overabundance of architecture created a sort of narrow well at the centre of the room that hemmed in the little vault at the top. Far above sat Byss' fresco looking very small and remote, like a swatch of sky glimpsed from the bottom of a mineshaft.

When Tiepolo saw this, he smiled.

To give Byss credit, he had obviously seen the problem and tried to find solutions. First, he attempted to bump up the fresco's impact by using overpowering colours — intense blues and bruised, aching lavenders, all swirling around a yolk of acid yellow. Then, he'd absolutely *stuffed* his painted heaven with celestial and allegorical beings. Every god in the pantheon was present, jostling for a seat on clouds arranged in an unnatural rectangle, kicking at the heads of the earthly beings below. These terrestrial figures were lined up along the four sides of the cornice. Supposedly they were allegorical representations of the four continents, Asia, Africa, America, and Europe, but Byss had painted them as a motley throng, pressing against a painted balustrade, gesturing and gaping like punters watching a horserace.

No one said it out loud, but all the Tiepolos were delighted with the many ways Byss' fresco failed. They had travelled back to Würzburg in high spirits, stopping for a good lunch at an inn by the river. Lorenzo remembered it as one of their very best days.

He sat down beside his father and looked at his sketch. "Does Domenico know what we're doing yet?"

"He *thinks* he knows," Tiepolo said. He switched the stub of a cigar from one side of his mouth to the other. "But you're the first one I'm telling."

Lorenzo felt a flush of pride. "Whatever we do, he'll say it's his idea."

"Yes, he will." Tiepolo sounded serious. "Let's not destroy his dreams. Take a look at this." He put his index finger on a point near the centre of the rectangle. "We start here at the south end right at the top with a big god, let's say Apollo. He's holding up a lamp, or something, there are other gods, Zeus, Mars, a big juicy Venus over here on a comfortable cloud — lovely — putti here and there, some nice hours wearing pretty, pretty butterfly wings…" Tiepolo's hand moved as rapidly as he spoke, the line of charcoal tracing the figures loosely on the smooth stone.

"It'll need more gods," Lorenzo suggested. "But not too many." He thought of Byss' overcrowded heaven. "You don't want it to look like a tenement."

"A few more gods, in the distance," Tiepolo agreed. "Don't forget we still have the whole other end. We'll have to set some good gods aside for that." Sketched figures and clouds cascaded down from the centre of the rectangle toward one of its ends. "You'll see this section best from the bottom of the stairs," he said and lifted his hand and paused, turning to look at Lorenzo. "What comes now?"

Here we go, he thought. Every conversation with his father and brother always ended up in some kind of test. "One of the continents, I guess."

"Which one?"

"Does it matter? Is there a certain order?"

"No."

"America, then." America was the newest part of the world and it interested Lorenzo the most.

Tiepolo seemed to consider and accept. "Tell me what you know about America."

"It's over that-a-way," Lorenzo said, pointing west-ish.

"You know what I mean," Tiepolo said.

Lorenzo tried to look serious. He knew what his father was after: the iconography for America as described in Cesare Ripa's book. He had studied this reference from the earliest days of his apprenticeship and they had brought it with them to Würzburg.

But it was still packed away in one of the trunks. It had been more than a year since Lorenzo had looked at it.

Closing his eyes, he tried to reconstruct the illustration that carried the visual codes meaning America. "A naked woman in a feathered helmet carrying a bow and arrows. Next to her there's a big lizard. She has her foot resting on a — on a human head with an arrow through it." Lorenzo felt a pang of doubt. "Is that right?"

"Not bad." Tiepolo's charcoal was already moving over the stone floor. He started sketching America's head first, turned to one side, then the fan of her plumed headdress, then the a pair of wrestler's shoulders, a pointing arm, one flat, circular breast. He drew in the lines for a muscular leg with a tapering foot. Perpendicular to the figure and just beneath it, Tiepolo began to draw a rough outline of a long, cylindrical body with a sharp snout and a curving tail. He added back-turned lizard legs with claws and finished the drawing to show that the naked woman savage was riding the monster. Lorenzo suddenly remembered that in America they called this creature an *alligator*.

"But I've seen one of those!" he exclaimed. "Back home. Uncle Ambrosio took us."

"What?" Tiepolo's hand never stopped moving. Now he was scratching in a kind of saddle for the giantess on the alligator's back. "What are you telling me?"

"Really." Lorenzo became very animated. Here was something he could offer. "One of uncle Ambrosio's friends brought it back from America. They had it in a kind of tent on the campo and charged us to see it, but less than other people, because of Ambrosio."

"Sweet Maria! Where was I when this happened? Your mother let you go?"

"Oh, Mama came with us. You know she likes that kind of

thing." He squinted at his father's drawing, comparing it to the dark object in the shadowy tent. "It was smaller than that," he advised. "And much flatter." Lorenzo held out his two hands indicating the thickness.

Tiepolo frowned down at the drawing. "Flatter you say? But definitely alive?"

Lorenzo paused, uncertain. "I'm not sure if it was *alive*. Elena knocked her fist on it and said it felt like a board. The man told her off. It had vicious teeth." Lorenzo demonstrated by baring his own.

His father looked thoughtful. "This alligator you saw came all the way from America?"

"Definitely. Or that's what he said."

"Do you think the sailors might have taken out the insides to keep it from stinking on the way home? Like a codfish?"

This made sudden, disappointing sense to Lorenzo. For years he had enjoyed imagining a wilderness where flat but lethal predators glided over the ground like rigid shadows.

"So maybe he wasn't so flat originally," Lorenzo admitted. "I think yours needs a few more teeth, though. They come up from below like this."

His father added more teeth and began drawing a little pile of human heads at the feet of the alligator.

"What are those for?" Lorenzo asked.

"You remember." Tiepolo drew the line of an arrow through one of the heads. "Cannibalism."

Lorenzo took this in. "Is the Prince-Bishop really going to let us put cannibalism on his vault?"

"Why not?" Tiepolo said. "It's part of America. They're always eating people over there."

"But he's a bishop. I thought they didn't approve."

"He is a bishop, yes. And he's a prince, and he's curious about new discoveries, like some princes are. He likes to read books by people who've actually travelled to these places. He gave me a few to look at and, do you know, they were interesting."

Tiepolo was on his hands and knees, moving around his sketched rectangle, looking at it from one angle, then another. He lowered his head until the tip of his cigar almost touched the floor and squinted one big blue eye, then he swiveled his head around and looked up into the vault.

"What's the animal for Africa?" he said with his head turned backwards, like an owl.

Lorenzo was ready for it. "A lion."

"Asia?"

"Come on: a camel. And Europe's a horse."

"A horse or — ?"

"You must think I'm really dumb. A horse or a bull."

"Just checking. Even I sometimes forget."

No you don't, Lorenzo thought irritably. You never forget. There's nothing in your mind but pictures. Lorenzo rubbed his arms. He made a policy of never wearing a coat indoors, to improve his hardiness, but it was very cold in the Staircase Hall, and very quiet. The stairs were empty now. Lorenzo listened for the sounds of the men downstairs in the vestibule, but heard nothing. He guessed they had finished unloading the waggon and were taking it back to the port on the river Main to fetch another load of lumber.

"So all this extra wood is for the scaffolding in here?"

Tiepolo went on sketching. "We'll re-use the wood from the tower in the Imperial Hall, of course."

"Did we get everything we asked for?"

"Every last stick, or we're not going up there," his father said. "And don't look so disappointed. We're painters, Lorenzo, not acrobats."

Lorenzo *was* disappointed. There had been a struggle over the plans for scaffolding the Staircase Hall. They discovered that the Bavarians, in other ways so generous, were stingy when it came to providing wood. The Prince-Bishop's ministers claimed there was a shortage and baulked at the expense of scaffolding the huge hall properly. Then some clever court engineer suggested the Tiepolos work from free-swinging cradles suspended from iron rings drilled into the roof trusses. Tiepolo was appalled by this plan. He put his foot down and almost threatened to quit.

"I still think it could have been fun," Lorenzo said. Idly, he looked up and tried to gauge the distance from one side of the great hall to the other and from the cornice to the apex of the vault. The scaffolding was going to be a major construction, like a palace of wood going up inside the palace of stone. It would have to carry them, he estimated, higher than they had ever worked before. By way of measurement, he traced the trajectory of a falling body from the imaginary scaffold's platform down to the bottom of the stairwell. He estimated the fall time with his own heartbeats. One, he counted, two. Three at the very most, before the body hit the steps of the lowest flight of stairs.

His rolled-up drawing dug into his hip, reminding him of why he had come to find his father in the first place.

"Father?"

"Yes?" He was roughing out more and more figures.

"Do you need me this afternoon?"

"I always need you." Tiepolo didn't say things like that to him except when they were alone and not working, which was almost never. His words made Lorenzo feel like a baby. Tiepolo sat back on his heels and looked down at his drawing. "Tell me what you think."

Tiepolo had hashed out designs along all four sides of the frame. The drawing was very rough, like a tray of tangled black wire, but Lorenzo could clearly read the scheme. In the centre of the frame, dotted here and there were the celestial figures, randomly spaced, no more than threadlike scribbles on the pale stone floor. On each of the four sides of the rectangle there were bigger, more massive figures advancing along the horizontal in an irregular line. At the centre of each procession was a giantess mounted on a huge animal.

"That's good. Too bad you did it on the floor and not on paper."

"That lion is too small," his father said. He reached out and rubbed away a whole line of figures with the ham of his hand, obliterating Africa, her lion and her retinue. He started to sketch again.

Lorenzo tilted his head sideways and studied the drawing. Even in this rough form, he could see its ambition. He estimated there might be more than a hundred figures in his father's sketch so far. He turned and looked up at the vault, parsing its space into days of work, time per figure, time for the open sky and clouds, which were quicker to paint. Involuntarily, he gave a Bossi-like shudder. "That's going to take us a long time."

"Not necessarily." His father looked up at the vault and drew a breath. He thought for a moment. "We've got the Imperial Hall still to finish, the figures of the virtues in the lunettes, one or two little overdoors — your brother is taking charge of those — and some figures on the cornice, all fairly straightforward. While we're polishing off those bits, they can scaffold the south end in here and by midsummer we should be able to start painting. That would leave us half a season to fresco this end of the vault," he held up his hand, marking out the area in his sightline, "another whole season for the other two-thirds. If we can get three or four good teams together — plasterer, painter, assistant, all working at a good clip — we could be finished in two or three years," he concluded cheerily.

Lorenzo tried not to look surprised. "That long," he said.

"If everything goes to plan. If it doesn't… well, then it's as long as it takes. We're in God's hands."

The boy nodded at the floor. He'd bragged to Red Moustache that he and his father would be painting the Staircase Hall vault, yet he hadn't really thought about what that meant. Time was the issue. One year had seemed the right amount of time to be away on a proper man's adventure, and one year was how long the Imperial Hall was supposed to take them. Lorenzo had always imagined that they would return to Venice at the end of the coming summer but now he realised the truth: frescoing the Staircase Hall had always been part of his father's plan. Tiepolo, Domenico, and even his mother had known they would get the work — it was never in doubt. Before they even set out for Würzburg, they all knew that the men would be staying away from home for years and years. They just hadn't told Lorenzo.

Now he understood why his mother had fought so energetically with his father before they went. He'd always assumed she was trying to browbeat Tiepolo into leaving Lorenzo, her baby, her last one, at home with her. Now, sitting on the cold stone floor with his father, Lorenzo realised that it was just as possible that she had been trying to force his father to take him along. If he hadn't come, he'd have lost his chance to finish his apprenticeship. Had she won the argument, or had she lost it?

Either way, his mother had said goodbye to him knowing he would be gone for years. He thought of the way she stole his hair, his childish hair, now tied up in a ribbon in a box in her room in Venice. Now his hair was different, darker, thicker. She had known this would happen, too. Why hadn't she warned him? She had sent him away, knowing that he'd be a completely different person by the time he returned — if he returned — and she hadn't said a word.

His father said. "I know it's going to be hard work. But it's good work, a real opportunity."

Lorenzo said quickly. "I don't mind the work."

"So your brother is wrong about you." His father was teasing him.

"He's wrong about everything," Lorenzo managed to say. There was a pause during which he kept his eyes trained on his father's drawing, fighting stupid tears that seemed to come from nowhere. He reached behind him and extracted the rolled-up drawing from the waistband of his trousers. He smoothed the curled paper on a flagstone next to his father's knee. "I'm supposed to show you this."

Tiepolo reached out to anchor the drawing with one hand on the top of the page, another on the bottom. He studied it for some moments without saying anything.

"I know the baby is no good," Lorenzo said, glad for something to say. "Domenico told me all about it."

Tiepolo agreed. "Next time, go at the two figures as if they're one thing. I know I've said this a hundred times before. Think of them as a unit, a kind of bundle. Otherwise, it's all right. Her feet are excellent."

"That's what Domenico said."

"You see, even he recognises native genius." This was the term his father had learned from their friend Algarotti. Lorenzo had no idea what it meant and neither, he suspected, did his father. It made him think of the images he had seen of life in America. *Native.*

"Your brother has his own faults when it comes to drawing, you know. His heads are always too flat at the back. You can tell him I said so next time he criticises you."

Lorenzo started to feel better. He sensed that his father was prepared to be lenient about the drawing and seized his opportunity. "Does that mean I can go out?"

Tiepolo looked at the windows. The snow was still falling stead-ily. There was no wind. "I can't see the harm. Where are you going?"

Lorenzo shrugged. "Just out."

"Into the storm." His father's gaze wandered down to the draw-ing on the floor again. "Be sure to wear your coat," he said vaguely.

Lorenzo was already on his feet and heading for the stairs. He bounded down them four or five at a time and reached the vesti-bule to find the waggon driving in through the double doors with another load of lumber. Red Moustache marched behind it, his boots covered in snow, the white flakes caught in the wings of his facial hair. He looked at Lorenzo with alarm as the boy sped past, perhaps wondering if he might take off and sail into the swirling air. Lorenzo flew beyond him out the door, losing himself in the smooth, unknowable beauty of the snow.

PART SIX

Domenico Tiepolo
Zianigo, the Veneto, 1774

Zianigo, the Veneto, 1774

It was almost nightfall when Domenico finally arrived at the gates of the family villa at Zianigo. He'd been late getting the boat from Venice and, though a servant had met him promptly with his horse at the dock, he had dawdled on the last leg of the journey, riding slowly through the flat agricultural landscape of the Veneto. It was a warm night in late September and the breeze smelled of drying fruit. Little green frogs sang their last songs in the drainage ditches beside the road. He breathed deeply, savouring the calm before the storm that was waiting for him at home.

"Thank God you've finally come," his brother Giuseppe said when he opened the door. His thin, irregular face was pale against the black of his peasant's tunic. He looked scared.

Domenico eyed his younger brother while the servant lifted his dusty riding cloak off his shoulders. "You look awful, Giuseppe. From your face a man would guess someone had died."

"What makes you say that?" He crossed himself with the casual precision of an ex-priest. "Did my note give you that impression?"

"It's what your message didn't say that concerns me," Domenico muttered. "I suppose the girls are here already, waiting to pounce on me? Or did you draw the short straw this time? Do you have to face the dragon all alone?"

"Angela and Orsola are waiting for you in the salon. Elena says she'll come over tomorrow."

"It's a team effort, then. It must be worse than last time." Domenico laughed. "Where's Mother?"

"In her room. She hasn't been out in two days, except to go to chapel. It's not good, Domenico." Giuseppe bit his upper lip with his lower teeth, an unattractive expression he assumed when he was especially nervous. Domenico felt sorry for him. Giuseppe took things so to heart.

"Come on, Beppo. What can an old lady like her have done? Betrayed state secrets? It can't be as bad as all that." Giuseppe opened his mouth to say something, but Domenico stopped him. "After I've eaten," he said.

His siblings let him eat in peace, sitting alone at the kitchen table, the way he liked to do when he arrived at the villa late at night. No fuss, no fancy cooking. Just well prepared rice and beans and the game pie he especially favoured, seasoned with thyme. He savoured the cool red wine, served from a clay jug, drunk from a plain clay cup, its rim rough against his lip, tasting of the soil. Then bread with plenty of salt. Domenico liked salt. Figs, walnuts, and honey for dessert, washed down with a glass of sweet Spanish sherry.

He was happy to be there in the kitchen at the back of the villa, alone with the silent old cook. His father had always insisted on a quiet transition into the house after a day of work. When he became head of the family, Domenico had fought to preserve the right to a tiny interval of calm before the demands began. The kind old cook, Bettina, had been with the Tiepolos for decades and knew just what was wanted. She placed the food before him and shuffled away to wait like a sentinel with her back to the door, effectively barring it against other family members.

Domenico sighed with contentment, chewing the figs and walnuts together in a mouthful, mingling the flavours, sweet and bitter, on his tongue. He wasn't really annoyed by his brother's summons. On the contrary, he was always looking for a pretext to get away from the studio and come over to the mainland for a few days. He loved Zianigo for reasons that seemed obvious to him. It was his family's house, one of the tangible symbols of their success. The villa was sizeable, but not ostentatious, with two symmetrical wings flanking a two-storey central section. It had its own minute chapel, a pillared gate and drive, a kitchen garden, an orchard, and plenty of land. There was nothing very fancy about the house, but Domenico always associated it with the splendid golden heaven they had painted onto the vault in Würzburg. Tiepolo had bought it in 1757 with the gold he — they — had earned there. The house was a solid investment, a sign of arrival, but it was the sky and the flat, fertile earth of the Veneto, stretching all around it, that made it precious. Zianigo gave the Tiepolos what all Ventians craved, what Venice could never give them: open space and terra firma.

He welcomed the excuse to come out to the villa, especially at this time of year, in the interval between the harvest and the onset of winter. It was a peaceful period of bright days and fields furred with stubble, an abundance of good food and a mood of achievement among the country people: summer's work was done, the barns and granaries and larders were full. The air was fresh at night, but not cold. The cook had the habit of keeping the door to the garden open as long as possible into the autumn, until the frosts forced her to close up. There were a few dried leaves scattered on the terracotta tiles by the door and the sweet smell of the fields met the smoky, rich smell of the kitchen. Nudging a leaf with the toe of his boot, Domenico wondered if he would have time to arrange a little hunting trip with the farm manager. He sighed again. There was no point in putting the inevitable off any longer.

"Thank you, Bettina," he said, pushing himself heavily away

from the table. He rose to find Giuseppe and his sisters and hear his mother's crimes.

When Domenico came into the room, Giuseppe was standing in front of the fire, poking the flames with a long stick, frowning like a magistrate. Orsola and Angela were sitting side by side on a low sofa, their wide skirts obscuring the furniture so it looked as though they were floating. All three jumped when Domenico came in.

His sisters rose to kiss him. Orsola came first. "We're so glad you're here," she murmured. "We know you'll know what to do."

"Don't speak too soon," Domenico said, giving her a peck on the cheek. She was the most beautiful of all his sisters, which was to say she looked the most like Cecilia, the least like his father. She must have been forty, and was now quite stout, like Cecilia and like Domenico himself, but she still carried her head high on a long neck, the line of her jaw was clear. She had married a lawyer.

"How are Giovanni and the children?"

"Well. Maria Cecilia has eczema after all," Orsola sighed.

"Is that all it was? I thought she had leprosy."

Orsola slapped him on the shoulder and laughed.

"Is that funny?" Giuseppe interjected sanctimoniously. "I'm not sure that's funny."

Domenico turned to kiss his other sister. Angela was his oldest surviving sister and she had never married. She had taken over the role of companion to Cecilia when Anna Maria died five years previously. It suited her much better than it had her older, more acerbic sister. With no husband and no children to worry about, Angela, was the most carefree person Domenico knew. She and Cecilia were a popular pair in their circle, frequently invited, generous, dedicated hostesses. Angela was useless as a chaperone, however.

He held her at arms' length and glared at her. "Here's the one to blame. So what have you been letting Mother get up to?" She was almost as tall as he was, slimmer than Orsola, with a hint of Tiepolo's nose, but still obviously recognisable as Cecilia's daughter. She wriggled in his grasp.

"What do you expect me to do, tie her down?"

Domenico released his sister and planted himself in a comfortable cushioned chair near the fire. Orsola poured him a glass of yellow wine from a jug on the sideboard and placed it on the little table next to him. He clamped his hands over his kneecaps and faced his siblings, who stood in a little group like naughty children expecting to be punished. "Right," he said. "I'm ready to hear it. Who's first?"

Both women looked at Giuseppe. "I wasn't even there!" he protested.

"But you're so good at explaining," said Angela.

"That's right," Domenico put in. "If Angela or Orsola does it, all I'll hear about is what everyone was wearing."

"You're still not taking this seriously," said Orsola.

"I still don't know what it is!"

"All right," Giuseppe began. "If it will help move things along, I'll tell him even though I had nothing *whatsoever* to do with it."

"We all know you never do," said Domenico. "Now get on with it." Of all the Tiepolos, Giuseppe was the slowest and had the scantiest sense of humour. He'd been an awkward boy, not athletic and not bookish either. His career in the priesthood had been untroubled by piety, scandal, or brilliance. Now, since their mother had bought him out of his order, he spent his time in the little orchard growing fruit — quinces, plums, greengages, damsons, apricots, pears, peaches — so much fruit that the family couldn't consume it all and had to give bushels away to neighbours. Pruning was Giuseppe's sole passion. Domenico frequently found himself finishing his brother's sentences, but he trusted him to tell the truth.

Giuseppe came and sat down on a small footstool on the edge of the hearth. "It was last Wednesday," he began.

"That's right," said Angela supportively. "I remember because the coffee and chocolate delivery arrived that very morning. We were out of everything."

Giuseppe continued. "I understand from Angela that she and mother were invited to Don Fulgenzio's for the evening. They were to play cards and have supper."

Domenico broke in. "As usual, as has happened a hundred thousand times before without the slightest variation in the formula for the last, what? Fifteen years. And what did you wear, Angela?"

"My green silk dress with the yellow stripes," Angela said brightly.

"And what did mother wear?"

"Her nice lavender one, with little shell buttons and lace on the sleeves."

"I wore a dark blue gown. And a toque," said Orsola.

"How lovely. You went too?"

"I did. I was staying here and the invitation extended to me, naturally. They are old friends, always more than happy to see us."

"And what did you wear, Giuseppe?" Domenico said sarcastically. "A bright yellow coat with purple breeches?"

The sisters tittered at the idea of Giuseppe dressed like a pimp. "I told you," he said grumpily, "I was not there. Do you want to tell the story or not?"

"I just wanted to get the wardrobe choices over with," said Domenico with a wink to Orsola. "So I can visualise the scene."

"Oh, you are so hilarious," pouted Angela. "I thought you'd come to help."

"Me? I just come for the hunting." He made a silly pantomime of shooting a rifle. He was aware that he was stalling but wasn't sure why.

Giuseppe heaved a sigh and ran a thin hand over his face. "Last Wednesday," he repeated, "Mother, Angela, and Orsola *in their finery* all went in the carriage over to Don Fulgenzio's for supper and cards. He had a number of guests, from what they tell me, just like he normally does. Some of them you'd know. The doctor and his wife, the Ambrosinis, the notary and some others, it doesn't matter. But among them was a man Mother and the girls had never met before, a nobleman, by the name of the Chevalier de Shinygold."

"De Seingalt," Orsola corrected, stressing the T. "It was such a funny name I made a mental note. Foreign, I would have guessed. But the odd thing was that he was Venetian. Or he said he was."

"He was very handsome and charming," Angela put in with a nod.

"Well, that *proves* he was Venetian," Domenico said.

"We were all simply dying with laughter at the things he said. The most outrageous things! At one point Mother popped a button on her bodice and I had to discreetly look for it on the floor."

"I'm sure you were most discreet," smiled Domenico. "I can see you now scrabbling around Signor Fulgenzio's carpet on your hands and knees."

"He had a strange way of talking, I have to say," mused Orsola. "Venetian definitely somewhere in the mix but with other accents sort of layered on top. I guess if you were being kind you'd say he sounded cosmopolitan, a bit like dear old Algarotti. Do you remember how we used to laugh at his Frenchified accent?"

At the mention of Algarotti, Domenico felt a residual sadness. The family friend and patron had died eight years before in Pisa, where he had retired after a career spent at Frederick the Great's court in Berlin. Domenico and his father and brother were working in Madrid when the news reached them. Tiepolo cried when he heard it. At the time Domenico had taken these unusual tears as sign of his father's increasing fragility.

Angela defended their old friend. "Poor Francesco sounded much better than this Chevalier person. His voice was pure music."

"He was the sweetest man," Orsola agreed.

"This one spoke like — well, I couldn't quite put my finger on it. Like an actor who couldn't decide what character he was playing that night, so he played them all at once. Still he was fascinating. There wasn't any subject he couldn't converse on, was there Orsola? Famous people, music, poetry — "

"Not one. He even knew about necromancy. You could tell he had been in all the great courts of Europe."

"He made it seem like we were in the middle of a wonderful salon, even though we were only sitting in Signor Fulgenzio's little front room with the blue curtains. It was the most fun I've ever had at his house."

"I agree!" Orsola cried placing a hand on her breast.

"So what the devil was this astonishing person doing at Don Fulgenzio's way out in the middle of nowhere?"

The two women looked at one another sheepishly.

Giuseppe made a derisory noise. "We can only wish Mother and the girls had asked themselves that obvious question. Or that Don Fulgenzio had," he said sanctimoniously, "before they started playing cards."

"Oh no," said Domenico, not at all surprised. This is exactly what he had been expecting. "Don't tell me this. Not again."

"To make a long story short, Mother sat down to play with this Chevalier."

"And lost," Domenico put in.

"Naturally. If she had won you wouldn't need to be here, would you?"

"What did they play?" Domenico asked, already knowing the answer. There was only one game his mother really loved and only one game she lost at disastrously.

"Faro," said Orsola in a small voice, cringing a little as if she thought her brother might hit her.

Domenico shut his eyes for a moment, trying to remember the specific threats he had made the last time this happened. Had he said he would suspend their allowances, confine them to Venice, cut back on their silk budget? He couldn't remember so he took a breath and began in a general vein.

"This is like a bad dream!" he shouted, pounding his fist against the arm of his chair. His sisters quailed. "What do I have to do to get it through your heads that you CANNOT PERMIT MOTHER TO PLAY FARO!"

"She can hear you, you know," whispered Angela. "Her room is right above us."

"Good, I want her to hear me. Did you catch that, Mother?" he boomed at the beamed ceiling. "Bezique, all right. Piquet, as long as the wagers are in two digits, maximum." He poked his fingers at the ceiling. "Two! But never, never, never faro. What the devil were you thinking? That Mother is luckier than every other punter in the world? She's not. I hope you're listening, Mother. We have ample proof that you are no more fortunate than ordinary mortals!"

Four loud bangs sounded on the ceiling. All four siblings looked up, waiting. Silence followed during which the only sounds were the crackling of the fire and the scrape of crickets outside in the garden.

"At least she's paying attention," said Giuseppe after a pause. "It may save time."

"Please give us a chance to explain, Domenico. We were powerless to stop her," said Orsola weakly. "You know how she gets."

"Did you even try?" Domenico bellowed. "No, you did not try. What you did was to sit down beside her and start playing yourselves, like a couple of tame monkeys, giggling your heads off, never once thinking of what could happen. Remember last time? Do you? No, you probably don't because YOU didn't have to clean up the mess afterwards. YOU didn't reach into your own pockets to pay Mother's debts."

"We did try, Domenico!" cried Angela tearfully. "When we couldn't get her to leave, we sent for Giuseppe immediately. What else could we do? Drag her out by her hair? It would have made a terrible scene."

"I came as quickly as I could," Giuseppe said. "But by the time I got there, it was too late. You had only to look at Mother to see she had lost significantly. Losing a few coins puts her in a terrible mood, but losing large amounts… She was flushed and laughing as though she were drunk, gay as a young girl. When I took her arm I could feel her heart beating like a drum. I just brought her home as quickly as I could."

Domenico knew exactly what Giuseppe meant. Cecilia after a bad losing streak was radiant with excitement. Winning, she took in her stride. "How much?" He judged it was time to expose the kernel. None of his siblings responded. He repeated the question in a louder voice. "How much?"

"We don't know," Orsola said in a timid voice. "After a while Angela and I went outside to wait for Giuseppe. We think that's when it must have happened."

"You *think*."

"And ever since we've been trying to get her to tell us, and

Giuseppe's been trying, but she won't say a word," Angela said in a whisper. "She just clamps her mouth shut and locks the door and writes letters. You know how stubborn she is when she's in the wrong."

"What does Fulgenzio say? I assume you've been to see him."

Giuseppe answered. "I went to him the next day. It seems he was playing at another table and has no idea what went on between his guest and Mother."

"The old fool. Did you talk to this Chevalier person?"

"He was out when I called. Fulgenzio hardly knows him at all. When I heard that, I began to worry. Who knows what kind of character we're dealing with here? That's when we sent for you."

"And who do I send for?" Domenico cried dramatically. "Who helps me fix this family's problems?"

"The lawyer, usually," Angela said. Domenico looked at her sharply and saw she meant this sincerely, as a helpful suggestion. "He was wonderful when Elena contested Papa's will, wasn't he?"

At the mention of this painful past episode in the family's history, Giuseppe shifted uncomfortably on his footstool. "No lawyer can help with this situation," he said tersely.

"I've been praying to Saint Cayetano," piped up Orsola, brightening. "He's the patron saint of gamblers."

"Well! I hadn't thought of that," said Angela, taking her sister's hand in hers. "That's the best idea I've heard so far. I shall do the same." Both women settled back on the sofa and gazed at their oldest brother with faces full of relief and trust.

"Sweet Maria, give me strength." Domenico groaned loudly and hung his head in his hands. This was for their benefit. He was not as worried as he was pretending to be. He was disgusted with his sisters and, by association, with Giuseppe, for being weak and disorganised and failing to control the crafty Cecilia. But how much could an old lady have lost in a penny ante game at Don

Fulgenzio's? Not that much, in the broad scheme of things. Still, as head of the family he wanted to impress on all of them the importance of keeping Cecilia in check, so he wouldn't have to. The truth was, the debts hadn't been all that significant the last time, a handful of ducats, really. Cecilia had sold a few pieces of jewelry to pay her creditor, and the whole matter was settled with a minimum of fuss.

Domenico regretted that now. Perhaps because of the easy resolution, the lesson hadn't sunk in. He should have stormed more, made it harder for everybody. He determined that this time there would be no question of a repeat of this problem. He sat there for some time, staring at his own well-made shoes and new stockings, thinking of what to do.

"Right," he said lifting his head and peering around at his siblings. He could feel the tension in the room as his brother and sisters, and probably his mother listening upstairs, waited for him to come up with a brilliant plan.

"Here's how it is going to be," he began, feeling for the right line. "Mother's gambling is never going to be a problem in the future."

"Oh, that's a relief!" said Orsola. Both his sisters looked pleased by this optimistic statement. His brother stared at him, waiting.

"And why won't it be a problem?" he coached them.

"Because Mother is old and will eventually," Orsola dropped her voice, "pass away?"

"You goose, I mean while she's alive!" They looked at him blankly and he pressed on. "It's because from now on you — and I mean everyone in this household," he pointed a finger around the room, "will not allow Mother to so much as BREATHE on a deck of cards for as long as she lives. This especially goes for you, Angela, since you are with her all the time."

Angela nodded enthusiastically. "No cards, ever again. I'll burn the ones we have in the house. I think there are only ten or twelve decks."

"Ten or twelve!"

"We entertain, too, you know. We need them, for parties, for guests."

"And get rid of the dice while you're at it," added Giuseppe.

"There are only a few sets of those. Mother isn't really interested in dice, is she Orsola?"

Orsola concurred. "She doesn't find any sport in them. Maybe if they were coloured, you know, prettier. Black on white is so tedious."

Angela looked serious. "But, Domenico, let's say there is no gambling at our house. That's fairly easy to arrange. But how do we keep Mother from doing it when we go out? If we're sitting around in company and the host puts cards on the table, then what?"

"Then you make your excuses," Domenico said. "You get up, collect your fan or whatever and call your carriage. You simply come home."

Angela looked downcast. "That's going to make all our lives unbelievably dull. Especially mine." Orsola reached out and patted her sister's knee consolingly.

"If you had done that last Wednesday, we wouldn't be here now having this conversation." Domenico said, feeling that at last his message was beginning to sink in. "There's one more thing."

"We all have to wear black and cover our heads with ugly veils, like Turks," grumbled Orsola.

"No. You two, Angela and Orsola, have to pay half of whatever Mother lost at Don Fulgenzio's."

The two women leapt up, crying out against this edict. Angela shouted that it was unfair. Orsola argued that her husband would have a fit. They railed against their brother. Domenico sat impassively until the noise died down. He glanced over at Giuseppe, who sat in a withdrawn posture. Domenico imagined he was contemplating the afterlife, or rather, looking forward to it. Eventually, the two sat women down again, panting with rage.

"Now that's over with," Domenico drew a breath. "I'll say this: if this ever happens again, if Mother ever manages to lose money at cards, ever, anywhere, even if you are not with her, the rest of you will pay the whole cost of her debts. And I include Elena in this, because I know she's in on it, too. Not because it's fair, but because then you'll understand what the consequences are for letting her act this way. " He felt good. Now he had the root of the situation in hand, the cause. This was a step farther in his discipline. What worked with his apprentices often worked just as well with his family. They wouldn't forget their duty this time, he was sure, especially Angela. His sister showed how well she understood by getting up and dashing out of the room in tears, followed by Orsola, who shot Domenico an evil look as she went.

"That was a little bit harsh, don't you think?" Giuseppe said. "It wasn't really their fault."

Domenico was surprised. "What are you talking about? It's clearly their fault."

"Have you ever actually tried to pry Mother away from a gaming table? I have. She's like a demon. She curses you, very quietly so no one can hear, in language you can't believe could come out of her mouth. Then, when she gets home, she takes revenge."

"What kind of revenge could Mother take!"

"She burned down my chicken coop, once."

"Nonsense." Domenico assumed Giuseppe was exaggerating. "I just think it's time the girls took some responsibility for what happens around here. They encourage Mother. Anyway, I doubt the money involved will be that much. How much could Mother really have lost at a card game at Fulgenzio's?"

Giuseppe pulled a pained face, like a man who has bitten into a bad fruit. "I guess we'll find out soon enough. When are you planning to speak to her?"

"It's late. Maybe I'll wait until tomorrow. Do you want a glass of wine?" He got up and poured himself another one from the jug.

Giuseppe shook his head. "I think you'd better do it tonight."

"Is that your spiritual guidance for me, Father Giuseppe? What could Mother tell me that I don't already know?"

"I just think you should find out exactly what happened as soon as possible. She wouldn't talk to me. I take that as a bad sign."

"Seeing that the two of you are so very close," Domenico said pointedly.

"We are close," Giuseppe affirmed mildly. "By necessity and by design. It wasn't my own choosing."

What he said was true. Giuseppe had been left in charge of the Tiepolo household during the eight years Domenico, his father and Lorenzo had been away, working in Madrid. It was never a good plan: Giuseppe was shy and unworldly and obviously dominated by his strong-willed mother. This meant that for eight solid years Cecilia did whatever she liked with the family money while Giuseppe hid in his orchard, coming in now and then to put his signature wherever his mother told him to put it. With no restraints upon her, Cecilia had embarked on a frenzy of property speculation, buying up every townhouse, barn, cottage, vacant lot, shack, hovel and warehouse that came up for sale in Venice or the mainland. This empire building went on unchecked — ducats flying out of the door, deeds accumulating in the cupboards — until Tiepolo died and Domenico returned to Venice.

"It could just as well have been you in my shoes, Domenico," Giuseppe said. "Think of it. If the first Domenico had lived, you'd be the second son. You'd have been sent to the priesthood instead of me. You'd have been left in charge of Mother."

It was an unpleasant thought. Domenico couldn't think of a life he'd less rather have. "And you'd be brother number three," he said spitefully, "scraping out a living doing little genre pictures in Madrid like poor old Lorenzo. You're probably a better draughtsman than him anyway."

"And where would Lorenzo be then?" Giuseppe said.

"He'd be a lawyer, of course. Mother always wanted one of us to go into the law."

The idea drew a tight smile from Giuseppe. "I can't see it being Lorenzo. Antonio might have been capable. He was a bright boy." Giuseppe was the only one besides Cecilia who ever mentioned Antonio. Domenico hardly remembered him. He came along among the flurry of Tiepolo babies, after Giuseppe but before Lorenzo, while Domenico was in the midst of his apprenticeship. His early death of a burst appendix quickly made him irrelevant.

"Even so, it's worked out all right," Domenico said, easing back into his chair. "We worked it out. We shouldn't complain. Nobody is going to starve." Once he had untangled the alarming knot Cecilia had made of their affairs, Domenico had found that the family was richer than ever. In the end they made money on most of his mother's rogue deals, a fact he was still trying to conceal from her. There would be no living with her if she ever found out.

"No, that's true. We're very fortunate," Giuseppe, said, his eyes shifting back and forth as he watched the flames. *Especially you.*

Domenico knew this was what Giuseppe must be thinking even though he didn't say the words aloud. He had made superhuman efforts to carry out the division of property fairly after his father's death but it was impossible to satisfy everyone. As the oldest son, he got the lion's share: Zianigo, the Venice house, the studio and the business. The rest, and there was plenty of it, was divided equally between the siblings. Cecilia received a small portion for herself. In any case, it was done. He had done his best.

"We're all still here," he said out loud. "We're all still on speaking terms. This will blow over." Domenico stretched out his legs toward the fire and took a sip of his wine. "It always does."

It was very late when Domenico finally went up to Cecilia's room. He half hoped that she would have fallen asleep, but she answered his knock at once.

"Come in Domenico darling," she said. Cecilia always knew which one of her children was on the other side of any closed door.

Pushing open the door, he entered the large room and found his mother sitting in her special chair in front of her own little fire. The chair was made of dark wood and decorated with bright silver fittings that shone in the low light. Cecilia's back was to the door, and she didn't turn as he came in quietly, almost stealthily. Suddenly, he felt abashed. It was one thing to imagine his mother in the abstract, as a force or a mere principle, a thump on the ceiling, but to deal with her face to face was always another matter. She was venerable now, and she looked every inch the respectable dowager from the top of her head, capped in white lace, to her little feet, shod in slippers of pink silk. She was wrapped in a pale blue robe of quilted satin and had a light blanket spread over her knees. A black and white pied dog slept on her lap. The animal raised his head as Domenico came to stand before his mother, regarding him with protuberant eyes, shiny and black as the wing cases of certain beetles.

"Be a love and put a bit more wood on the fire," Cecilia said. "Sabina has gone to bed and I don't want to disturb the dog. He's been having such nice dog dreams." She stroked its ears and the little animal lay his head down with a satisfied grunt.

"It's like an oven in here." Domenico stooped to the basket

that held a small pile of neatly sawn logs. He reminded himself to have a look at the fuel bills before he left. "Do you keep this fire burning all night long?"

"I get the heat rising from downstairs in this room, too," Cecilia said. "It's lovely. I like it hot." She snuggled voluptuously into her chair.

"Just like the Queen of Sheba."

She smiled. That was the family's nickname for Cecilia. "Is Sheba really a place?" she asked. "I've been thinking about it recently. Is it very hot there?"

"Not hotter than in this room."

"Seriously. Where is Sheba?"

"It's in the Holy Land, I suppose. You'd have to ask Giuseppe about it."

"Elena's been telling me that Levant ladies go to hot rooms made of marble where they spend all day scrubbing themselves and putting red henna in their hair. They go in all together, the way we go to church, except stark naked. Can you imagine that?"

"I'm trying very hard not to," said Domenico placidly.

She smiled. "Naughty boy. I think I'd quite like a hot marble room."

"I'll call the builders first thing in the morning."

"You are sweet."

She's nervous about this conversation, he thought to himself. Her little diversionary speech seemed to indicate it. Yet as Domenico pulled up a chair and settled himself at some distance from the heat of the fire, he observed that Cecilia seemed a picture of calm. Perhaps things weren't as bad as Giuseppe feared.

"It's late," he began when she showed no sign of speaking. "You must be tired."

"I'm never tired, darling," Cecilia said. "I used to be such a good sleeper but I seem to have lost the knack." She turned her gaze from the little dog to her son. Her dark eyes glittered. "You're the one who is tired. Look at you. Bags under your eyes, needing a decent shave. You look awful. I can always tell when you've been sleeping in the studio. When are you going to finally marry that Mocenigo girl of yours and set up a proper home?"

"You know exactly when, Mother. You were there when we signed the contract. It's next year. I know you haven't forgotten."

"The sooner the better. If you don't mind my saying so. Forty-seven is too old for a man to be single. Being busy is no excuse."

"I never said I was too busy to get married. You said that."

"That's what you tell yourself. You've been telling yourself that for years and years," she said. "You might as well say you were too busy to pray."

Cecilia was uncannily correct; this is exactly what Domenico had said to himself throughout his twenties, thirties, and most of his forties. Working alongside his father left Domenico, by his own calculations, enough time for love affairs but not enough for marriage. His professional life amounted to a continuous series of projects, one painting after another, one villa after another, one church after another. His love life was the same, a series of affairs completed to the satisfaction of both parties (more or less) then left behind. Domenico preferred married women with complacent husbands or pragmatic young widows who understood the art of avoiding pregnancy. Maria Mocenigo, his fiancée, was something of an afterthought. She came from one of the old patrician families and his courtship started out as a kind of experiment. Would a girl from a family like hers actually consider a proposal from a painter? To his surprise, the answer was yes, as long as her groom was the last remaining Tiepolo, the richest and most famous painter in Venice.

"Maria is such a lovely person," Cecilia said dreamily. "You shouldn't make her wait so long."

"She's in no particular hurry," Domenico said. "She has her own wing in her father's house; three servants, her own gondola."

"That girl is not spoiled! Maria has a wonderful, sweet, loyal disposition."

"What I'm saying is that I can't blame her for not rushing to move in with me."

"I want to see my grandchildren before I die. Who knows how much time I've got left?"

"You're in your prime, Mother. You're not going to die any time soon."

"I bet that's what you told your poor father and look at what happened to him."

Nothing had happened to Tiepolo. His mother knew this very well. His father had died in Madrid without warning and without drama. He was perfectly well in the evening, smoking his little cigars and talking about the altarpiece he was painting. When they went to wake him the next morning, he was stiff and cold between the sheets. It was so sudden that, four years later, Domenico still had to remind himself that his father was really gone.

"Mother, you know why I'm here. It's not to talk about your health."

Cecilia shifted in her chair. "They called you unnecessarily," she said. "Your brother and sisters need to learn to stop pestering you with every little household problem. I learned that being married to your father. He had other things to do besides sorting out the house. He counted on me to do that. And he could, very confidently. I was good at running things. No one gives me credit for that now."

"Of course we give you credit," Domenico soothed. "We all know how it was."

"Was. That's the crux of it. Now I'm not the problem-solver, I'm the problem-maker. Just another one of those annoying domestic distractions." She dabbed at her eyes with the lace on her sleeve. Her tone was bitter.

"Please, just tell me what happened at Don Fulgenzio's. I won't get angry."

"What's the point? You heard the rest of them. I have nothing more to add to their detailed account of my appalling behaviour. I'm such an embarrassment to you."

"I'd like to hear your side." This was a tactic Cecilia herself had always used with the children to get them to confess whatever they had done wrong. The approach promised sympathy; the effect was to dig out the truth in order to enable punishment.

She laughed coldly. "But I have no side! I have no defence! I have been very, very bad and I must be punished. That's what you're here for, admit it."

"I'm here to help," Domenico was beginning to feel that he had lost the high ground somehow. That was easy to do with his mother. He tried again, gently. "Between us, we worked everything out last time. You and me. It wasn't so bad, really."

"Last time!" Cecilia snorted. "Last time! Trust me, this is not exactly like last time."

Hearing his mother say this, Domenico felt a twinge of genuine concern. He struggled to suppress it. "I take that to mean you lost more to this Chevalier person that you did to Signora Zen. I guessed that already. They told me as much."

Cecilia sat up straight and rolled her eyes toward the ceiling like a saint in agony. "I am such an idiot!" she wailed, sounding more angry than repentant. "Actually, I am not such an idiot. It was going well most of the night. I had good reason to feel I might win. The girls were egging me on. Don't you believe them if they say they weren't."

"I never do."

Cecilia swivelled her head and stared into the fire. "It was a lucky night, I could feel it. All the way to Fulgenzio's I felt so happy. We were all in such a good mood, even Orsola who can be so ill tempered, my little bear. It felt like a charmed night, perfect for a nice game of cards. You know that feeling."

"Of course." The truth was he'd sooner throw his coins in a canal than put them on a number. The loss was over quicker and you didn't feel cheated.

His mother caught him in his lie. "But you *don't*, Domenico. You hardly play games, let alone bet like you mean it. You're a tightwad, like your father, not the least bit interested in chance or fortune or luck. No, you like things you can control. You've been the same since you were little."

"What's so bad about that? My work is hard enough to control. Not to mention this family. It's all the excitement we can take." Domenico occasionally caught himself using "we" as though his father were still alive, as though he still had a partner.

"Perhaps," Cecilia said. "Still, I do think you miss something if you never sit down with a deck of cards and a pocket full of money you are prepared to lose. There's beauty in it, a special thrill. There are things about life you'll never understand, son, because you refuse to gamble."

How like his mother to turn her vice into a virtue before his eyes. "We still haven't arrived at Fulgenzio's," he said. "I'm eager to meet this mysterious Chevalier."

"Oh, him. They told you about him, did they? He was really something. A piece of work. It's rare that you meet a man like him around here, especially at Fulgenzio's. My goodness, he livened the old place up no end! Donna Lugarezia was all over him! He took liberties and I'll tell you something, she *loved* it."

"Who was the first to suggest playing faro? Was it him?"

"You know how it is. It's the obvious thing to do." Cecilia dropped her eyes to her lap. With one knotty finger she caressed her many rings so they clicked like coins, bringing the sound of the gaming table into the room. "He didn't cheat me, if that's what you're thinking. That would have been impossible."

"Why impossible? Even a good player can fall victim to a fraud. I assume he kept the bank. That provides all kinds of opportunities for cheating."

"That's just it," she looked straight at him. "I was the one who kept the bank."

Domenico stared at his mother. Only members of the aristocracy were allowed to keep the bank when faro was played. The law prohibited ordinary citizens from doing it.

"I've done it before," she said in a casual tone. "Don't look at me like that. I'm quite good at it. Everyone says." He heard the pride in her voice. Being banker at faro usually meant that you were the richest person in the room.

She began to narrate the game then, hand for hand, in tedious detail: how the players bent their cards this way, crooked up the corners that way, how patterns of winning cards emerged, how the odds went up. Soon, Domenico stopped following his mother's account and listened only to the tone of her voice. He had imagined this conversation as a sort of confession: Cecilia would admit her transgression and he would find a penance for her. Instead, his mother was reliving the excitement of the night at Don Fulgenzio's, throwing around French terms like *paix paroli* and *trente-et-le-va* with the enthusiasm only an obsessive gambler feels for the arcane vocabulary of the game. He saw that she was pleased to have the opportunity even to talk about playing faro. The obvious lust in her voice — there was no other word for it — made him feel sick.

For the first time, he began to worry in earnest. Two words kept ringing in his head like the two tones of a big bell: how much? How much? From the way his mother was talking, he knew that it would be more than he had expected. There were aristocrats working as stable hands because they lost fortunes on the turn of one card in faro. There were duchesses selling their bodies in the alleys behind the casinos for the price of one more wager. These ruined souls undoubtedly talked about the game that destroyed their lives in the sensual way his mother was talking about it now.

"The Chevalier was calm and cool as anything," she said. "When the queen came up that time, his hand was solid as a rock, not so much as a tremor. He congratulated me. 'You are a gallant lady,' he said. But that didn't stop him."

How much? How much?

"And so I turned up the six on the banker's side. And then, on the punter's side, wouldn't you know it, here came the *seven*. Can you beat that? I've never liked sevens, they're very tricky."

Domenico felt his own heart pounding.

"And that was that," Cecilia concluded.

"Let's see if I understand you," Domenico said. "I think what you're saying is that on that evening in Fulgenzio's salon, while Orsola and Angela looked on and did nothing to stop you, you lost thirty times the stake the Chevalier laid on his card." His voice quavered a little.

"No, no!" Cecilia held up her hand, impatient. "You haven't been paying attention. It was *soixante-et-le-va*: I lost *sixty-three* times his stake."

"Mother," Domenico almost sobbed. "I cannot multiply anything by sixty-three. I'm not that good at mathematics."

"I know that about you, darling," she said consolingly. "You have other gifts."

"Help me, with your famous head for figures. How much are we talking about? Some multiple of sixty-three amounting to, what? Two hundred ducats?" He said this knowing this wasn't the answer. That was roughly the amount she'd lost last time.

She cleared her throat. "A bit more than that."

"Five hundred? Don't make me play guessing games."

Cecilia screwed up her mouth as though trying to prevent something from escaping. One thing was certain, Domenico thought, she knows this number down to the last zecchino.

"One thousand ducats? Or, by some divine miracle might it be less?"

Cecilia hesitated. "It's not — less."

"More than a thousand ducats? My God!"

"Don't shout so, Domenico. And don't use oaths. You'll wake the others."

"No one in this house is asleep tonight," shouted Domenico. "And from the way things are going, no one is going to get any sleep. Ever. You lost over a thousand ducats to this man?"

"Yes," she said, her eyes shifting toward the shadows beyond the glow of the fire. "And no."

"For the love of God, Mother! Put me out of my misery."

Cecilia sniffed. "The amount is no longer important, Domenico. What I've been trying to tell you is that I've already taken care of it. There are many ways of settling debts, you know."

Domenico saw a glimmer of hope. "Oh good, you're giving him Angela. Shall we send her over there right now in her best nightie?"

"Don't be foul, Domenico. The important thing is that it's not a question of money at this point. The Chevalier and I have come to an understanding."

"I'm very relieved to hear that. Speaking confidentially, I don't think you have anything like a thousand ducats to your name. Not any more."

"That's just it. I don't," she said. She looked at him with hauteur, chin tilted up in a pose so often used by his father to depict Venus or Juno. "But it's not a problem. It's all settled. I have just received a letter from the Chevalier this afternoon and he has accepted a settlement. He is, after all, a chevalier. He understands how delicate these matters can be, for a lady." Her hand, as she recommenced stroking the dog's back, trembled a little.

"Let me see his letter at once," Domenico demanded.

"That won't be necessary. I'll tell you what it says. But before I tell you, I want to put it on record that, no matter what you think about this situation, I know your father would have backed me up. He would not have questioned my decision in this or stood in my way. He trusted my judgement in money matters and he respected me, above all. That's all I ask from you: respect. I'm your mother. I deserve it. And if your blessed father were here tonight, he would insist on it."

"If Father were here," Domenico muttered, "you wouldn't be swanning around the neighbourhood showering shady chevaliers with what's left of the family fortune."

"There you go, Domenico. Disrespectful. That's exactly what I was referring to." Sensing Cecilia's annoyance, the little spaniel jumped down from her lap to the footstool and then to the floor. It came and sniffed Domenico's shoe, then went and sat on the hearth, blinking its great beady eyes at the embers of the fire.

"I'm sorry," Domenico said. She was in the wrong, but he was sorry. It was inevitable. What she said about Tiepolo was absolutely true, however. His father's greed had been for work, not for money. He had left day-to-day affairs in Cecilia's hands entirely.

Domenico wasn't inclined to be so trusting with his mother, or anyone else. At least the division of the family property meant that she was only able to get her hands on her own share. Come what may, she couldn't touch his. The thought calmed him somewhat.

"You know I will always look after you, Mother," he said. His own filial loyalty brought tears to his eyes. She was his mother and he would look after her; the thought touched him.

"You are a good son, Domenico, but you can be terribly pompous. Of course you'll look after me. What else would you do? Oh, let's get this over with." She waved her hand. "The letter is in the top drawer of the desk by the window. You can read it if you like, but the settlement is quite straightforward, quite rational. And I have committed myself to it."

Domenico hauled himself out of his chair and hurried to the desk. In the top drawer he found a letter in an elegant, elongated hand, written in Italian. He scanned it rapidly, sifting through its literary niceties and compliments to find the kernel of meaning, the way he did with contracts. There were many flourishes and tropes to wade through — the Chevalier was practised in the art of flattery — but when he finally identified the gist, Domenico gasped aloud.

"I don't understand," Domenico said, although the letter's meaning was clear. "He seems to be saying he'll accept Zianigo in lieu of cash."

"That's right." Cecilia looked at him with a matter-of-fact expression, as though the solution should be obvious to anyone of reasonable intelligence. "We paid four thousand ducats for this place when we bought it in '57. It's probably worth at least five now, with the land. It's a fair settlement, I think. He could demand more, but he likes the area. He knows it, you see, from holidays when he was a boy."

Domenico heard a loud rushing sound his head. His doctor had told him to cut down on the salt because it enlivened the blood and made it move faster. He felt dizzy and steadied himself on the little feminine desk on spindly legs. The china ornaments on it rocked.

"You can't do this," he said, his mind racing as fast as his pulse.

"But I have no choice," said his mother cheerfully, holding out her hands and letting them drop in a gesture of helplessness. "*We* have no choice. The debt has to be settled one way or another. This is the moment when it would help if you were a gambler yourself. It wouldn't be so hard to make you understand."

"I mean," he swallowed, struggling to remain coherent, "you really cannot do this, Mother. Legally. Zianigo belongs to me. According to the terms of the will. You can't give away what isn't yours."

"Well, obviously, darling, that's why I asked Giuseppe to send for you! I need your signature."

Domenico imagined hitting his mother. He was a powerful man and he could almost feel what it would be like to send her flying across the room. The old lady would break into a dozen pieces, like a china ornament.

As if reading his thoughts she said, "Darling, don't be angry. You need to remember that we only have Zianigo because of me. You imagine your father made all our money, but it was me, investing your father's earnings, that made us rich. Your father had the power to turn paint into gold but I was the one who turned the gold into something even more valuable: property."

Domenico still didn't trust himself to speak. *She's ruined us at last*, he thought. *It was only a matter of time.* He had other houses, one in Venice, another not far away, in Sceltanigo. But none of them were Zianigo. He loved this villa. The very first money he earned from his own work was sunk into this house. On days when he felt especially weary, he imagined himself retiring there, pruning the orchard with Giuseppe and spending long winter afternoons trapping ducks in the estuary. There were blank walls and ceilings and small rooms all over the house where he could paint little murals just for his own amusement — or leave them blank if he felt like it.

His silence was obviously unnerving his mother. He wasn't shouting at her, and so she began to make her case, running too rapidly through all the arguments she had prepared for him in advance. He kept missing his cues, but it didn't seem to matter to Cecilia. There were several threads to her rationale, and each was worked out to a fine level of detail. She started with the many reasons why it was her right to give away Zianigo as a forfeit for her gambling, even though it might seem, under the law, to belong to her oldest son. That was a mere formality, she said. Everyone knew that it was really meant to belong to her until her death. Then she moved on to the complete normality of losing such a huge sum of money at cards. Simply everyone did it, everyone who was anyone. It was a sign of wealth that the family of his fiancée, the noble Mocenigos, could only admire and comprehend. Finally she worked her way around to the position that giving up Zianigo was just the thing to benefit the whole family. It would save them money in the long run; it would light a fire under those lazy girls and make them be more independent. She'd spend more time in Venice and they would all see one another more often.

Domenico let Cecilia go on. It didn't matter what she said now. His breathing was returning to normal, his blood subsiding. Using the discipline he had developed from years of dealing with difficult, even mad, clients, he mastered himself. Feeling his whole big body relax into weariness, he returned to his seat and went on listening, saying almost nothing. The Chevalier's letter drooped between his fingers. He planned to take it with him when he went to bed, to study it more carefully.

Meanwhile, his mother was running down like a clockwork toy. The righteousness that had powered the first part of her monologue had given way to a kind of sweet pleading.

"I am your mother, after all," she said. This was the final figure on the balance sheet, the profit that wiped out all the losses. She smiled at him uncertainly. "Aren't you going to say anything?" She had always mistaken silence for compliance, Domenico thought.

This is one reason why her children had got away with so much mischief.

"There's nothing to say. I'll go and see this Chevalier first thing tomorrow. That is, today."

"That's fine," she said. "Be polite. He's been very reasonable." She smiled again and held out her arms to Domenico. "You stubborn mule. I knew you'd agree to do what was best. Eventually."

Domenico approached and bent down to kiss her, feeling her frail arms encircle his neck. The skin of her cheek was silky and cool. He thanked God that he hadn't given into the evil impulse to strike her. What kind of a man does a thing like that? He rested his chin for a moment on the white lace cap on the top of her head.

"Will you sleep now?" he asked.

"Not after all this excitement," the old lady said, settling back into her chair and closing her eyes. By the time Domenico had reached the door, he could hear her snoring quietly.

Domenico's travelling clothes released clouds of road dust as he removed them in his room. The maid had left a pitcher of water for him and he washed himself halfheartedly in the basin before lying down naked on the bed. It felt wonderful to get the weight off his feet. His bad shoulder throbbed the way it always did when he was tired. As he put his head down on the pillow, he heard the very first notes of birdsong. He lay there for an hour, staring at the dark beams of the ceiling. There was a brown stain on the plaster in one corner where a cracked roof tile had let water in two years before. The repair was temporary, and every time Domenico came into the room and saw the stain, he wondered if he should call the roofer and get the whole house seen to. As he lay there, his mind travelled the customary path — stain, repair, new roof — before he stopped himself. He might never have to call the roofer for Zianigo. Soon even this stain might belong to another man. The idea was unbearable. He sat up and called out for his servant.

Two hours later, Domenico's horse was saddled and he was setting off to ride the short distance to Don Fulgenzio's house. It was far too early for a social call, but he couldn't wait any longer. Only the servants were awake when he left and he felt that was for the good. Riding out of the gate onto the lane, he turned and looked at the prosperous middle-class facade of Zianigo. He half expected to see his mother standing on the little balcony at the front of the house to see him off, but she did not appear.

It was a crisp, hazy morning. Fingers of mist stretched across the harvested fields. The road to Fulgenzio's was straight as a rod. There was little traffic at this hour, a farm cart or two, four women walking with bundles of brushwood slung across their backs. One raised a hand to Domenico and he nodded down at them. If he carried on in this direction for half a day, he'd arrive on the banks of the Brenta canal where the villas of the Venetian nobility sat strung like Palladian beads along the sluggish channel of water. It was Cecilia who had calculated that Zianigo lay about halfway between Venice and those villas, where he and his father had done some of their best work. When they bought the house, Tiepolo joked that it was like a wolf making its den where it could stroll out and enjoy a view of flocks of sheep.

In the inner pocket of his coat Domenico carried the letter from the Chevalier. In his head, he bore a list of things he might offer this man in place of his home. He had decided it was impossible to challenge the settlement for legal reasons. He might win his villa back in court, but the case would make the family look ridiculous, him especially. He could give the Chevalier paintings, of course, or execute frescoes for him. He had other properties he'd be prepared to offer, thought none of them was as attractive as Zianigo. He felt no special attachment to his other country villa or to any of the many smaller farms, shacks, animal pens and hovels the family still possessed. This stranger might take a fancy to some of them, however, and be willing to make a trade. You never knew.

He could see Don Fulgenzio's house for a long time before he reached it. It was a pink villa, a little larger than Zianigo, nestling among large trees. He had been worried about waking up the household by arriving so early, but a servant appeared to take his horse and another opened the door to him even before he rang. They knew him as a neighbour and they led him into the main salon on the first floor. He waited only a few minutes before Fulgenzio came hurrying in.

"My dear Don Domenico," he said, taking Domenico's hand in his and holding onto it, his watery blue eyes full of concern. "I am so very, very sorry. Call me naive, but I had no idea such a thing could happen in my own home." Don Fulgenzio was a small man in his late fifties with a thin face and a broad belly emphasised by the folds of his luxurious dressing gown of green Chinese silk. He was from a line of successful cloth merchants and he had married the only daughter of his best client. They were very wealthy and childless. They had been friends and neighbours of the Tiepolos since the family bought Zianigo.

"I feel this is all my fault," he said, sounding heartbroken. He cast his eyes down at his own feet as if to draw attention to his embroidered slippers. They were very beautiful, Domenico observed, and they made Fulgenzio look like a pantomime pasha.

He reassured his neighbour. "Nobody forced Mother to play." Domenico did blame Fulgenzio. The man was compulsively social, seeming not to be able to bear an empty house. This meant he invited all kinds of people without knowing anything about

them. In the past his compulsion had saddled him with seduc-
ers, tramps, frauds and the worst kind of freeloaders. Cardsharps,
however, were a new development.

"If there's anything I can do to help." Fulgenzio waved his
chubby pink hands in the air.

"Tell me something about the Chevalier. I will need to speak to
him, of course."

"Naturally. This is so unfortunate! My Lugarezia is very upset.
It was she who was first introduced to him in Padua. She blames
herself. But the Chevalier is so very charming. You'll see when
you meet him. He's close to the Memmos, you know, and the
Zaguris; nobility. Lugarezia couldn't quite believe her luck when
she found he was at a loose end. She simply wasn't able to resist
inviting him."

All this, Domenico could have guessed. He pressed on. "He's
called de Seingalt. That name doesn't ring a bell at all. What else
do you know about him?"

Fulgenzio pursed his lips and arched his eyebrows. "Dear Don
Domenico, we never ask for references when we invite guests into
our home. You know how we love to welcome friends."

Domenico felt a twinge of annoyance. "You are very hospitable,
Don Fulgenzio. It does you credit."

The old man bowed his head modestly. "I only hope we can
resolve this to everyone's satisfaction. We are all civilised people,
aren't we?"

"Let's hope so," Domenico said.

A servant showed him to the Chevalier's room and knocked on
the door for him.

"Come through!" a deep male voice called in response. "I'm
on the terrace."

Domenico stepped into Don Fulgenzio's best guest room, a large corner chamber with double doors opening onto the garden. The walls were cream coloured; the windows were over-dressed with a set of lustrous, embroidered silk curtains that cascaded to the floor — there was never any shortage of expensive fabric at Fulgenzio's. The Chevalier sat outside on a small private terrace. He was perched on a stool in his dressing gown, peering at himself in a hand mirror while a hairdresser, an elfin young man, busied himself with his hair.

"You'll forgive me for calling on you so early, Chevalier," Domenico said standing in the doorway, crowded by the curtains. "I've interrupted your toilette."

"Not at all." The Chevalier reached out sideways to offer Domenico his hand without turning towards him. Domenico stepped forward to take it. "Excuse me if I let this boy carry on. If I send him away now I won't see him until noon. Shall I order some chocolate for you? Don Fulgenzio's cook makes excellent chocolate. She has a special way of whipping it into a froth."

Domenico declined. He saw the Chevalier's eyes studying him in the mirror, dark, wary eyes in a swarthy, pocked face. He sat presenting his profile to Domenico, like man who hopes one day to be emperor and see his likeness on a coin. He had a domed forehead, a large beaky nose and a chin that he carried proudly to compensate for its relative weakness. Domenico guessed that de Seingalt was about his own age but well preserved by a fop's life-long servitude to good looks. His hair, it was clear at close range, was a short chestnut-brown wig. The room smelled of sweet almond-scented lotion.

The Chevalier went on studying him in the mirror. "But you undoubtedly know all about the quality of Don Fulgenzio's chocolate. You are an old friend of the family. In fact, I can tell you more about yourself. You are Domenico Tiepolo, son of

Giambattista Tiepolo and the exquisite Signora Cecilia Guardi Tiepolo. You are the premier painter in Venice, current president of the painter's academy, patronised by princes and kings. Shall I go on?"

"You are well informed." Domenico gave a little bow. Fulgenzio must have briefed him. "I'm embarrassed to say that I know much less about you."

"Is that true?" The Chevalier's eyes sought Domenico's in the mirror. "Don't you recognise me? Think back."

Domenico was taken off guard. It was true; there was something familiar about the Chevalier, the rounded shape of his head, his way of sitting with his shoulders thrown back. He racked his memory of minor noblemen he had met — there must have been thousands over the years — but came up with nothing.

"Forgive me," he said. "I have no memory for faces unless I've had to draw them."

The Chevalier laughed loudly. "That is an excellent excuse if I ever heard one. I'll have to recommend it to my brother, Francesco. He's a painter too and could make good use of it because he never remembers anything or anybody. He's a bit of an idiot. But you are certainly no idiot, sir. I'm sure you can remember me."

For the first time the Chevalier turned to face Domenico. Rather, he swivelled around and presented his face with a theatrical flourish of his arms. The hairdresser had to leap back to avoid being hit.

"Here I am, full on. Do you know me now?" He turned his face this way and that, as though selling it. "You sat straight across from me."

"I'm sorry…"

The Chevalier mimed eating, tearing off a hunk of something with his teeth, chewing it in an exaggerated fashion. "I was very

THE MERCHANTS OF LIGHT

hungry that night. No doubt I ate like a labourer. Now?"

Domenico shook his head, at a loss. The Chevalier looked annoyed.

"All right then, I will tell you: five years ago in Madrid, at the Venetian Embassy, I sat across the table from you with Rafael Mengs. Ambassador Mocenigo introduced us."

Suddenly, Domenico did remember. "Signor Casanova," he mouthed automatically, trying not to choke. "What a complete and utter — delightful — surprise."

"You had no idea did you? You never guessed?" Casanova smiled at him. "I wish you could see yourself. Here, take a look: *The Astonished Man*. Caravaggio couldn't do it better."

He held his mirror up to Domenico's face. In it, Domenico saw a pale, rigid visage, suffused with horror, much like the face of a man who is about to lose his beautiful house to a notorious swindler.

He had met Casanova at the table of Sebastian Mocenigo, the Venetian Ambassador to Spain for part of the period when the Tiepolos were working there. Though the painters weren't really part of the Venetian expatriate social scene, they had been invited to dine at the embassy now and again as a courtesy. Domenico remembered that he went to that dinner alone. Lorenzo was off somewhere with his Spanish sweetheart and Tiepolo, feeling tired, stayed home in their townhouse in San Martín. There were various Venetians present, a few freethinking Spaniards, and Rafael Mengs, the official court painter, a Roman. It was Mengs who had brought Casanova.

When he realised who Casanova was, Domenico's first impulse was to alert Ambassador Mocenigo and have the rogue thrown out. Casanova was a heretic, a fugitive from the law, a black magician, a Freemason. Everyone knew he had escaped from the Doge's prison and gone on a rampage across Europe, giving

Venetians a bad name wherever he went. Surely the ambassador didn't realise who he had sitting at his table, Domenico thought. Surely Mengs had no idea the kind of person he had living in his house, for it emerged that Casanova was actually lodging with the painter.

He had said nothing right away, and it was a good thing he hadn't. Over the course of the evening, Domenico learned that the Ambassador knew perfectly well who Casanova was and so did Mengs. He knew the Ambassador had a patchy reputation himself — he had once been imprisoned in the very same prison Casanova had escaped from, for pederasty — but it astonished him that Mengs, a reputable, religious, and ferociously ambitious man, could have brought such a criminal to dinner.

Out of politeness and having no wish to seem to be a ridiculous prig, Domenico said nothing. It was a waste of time to try to peer into the motivations of gentlemen like the Ambassador or Mengs anyway. As his father always said, it was wiser to treat all gentlemen as clients, which meant there was no need to understand them. "All you really need to know about a client," Tiepolo liked to say, "is what they want." And eventually they are certain to tell you because it is in the nature of all clients, and all gentlemen, to get the things they desire.

In the crowd around the Ambassador's table that night, there had been nothing about Casanova that marked him out as an adventurer. He was well spoken, beautifully dressed and mannerly — the sort of person that made Domenico feel his lack of training in the arts of being a gentleman. He presented himself as a literary lion, a writer, *bel esprit* and friend of Voltaire. Mengs and he were great chums. The two had sat next to one another at table, relishing a conversation about verisimilitude in art, or some such hooey. At one point, Mengs had reached across the table and tried to draw Domenico in, but he had kept quiet —

they wouldn't have liked his opinion in any case — and gone home as soon as he could.

"I'm speechless," he said, trying to recover. "But how could I have guessed? You must be travelling incognito, Signor Casanova. No one here has the slightest clue who you are."

"Why, I am the Chevalier de Seingalt, dear Signor Tiepolo. It's really my title. A noble friend gave it to me and it's very useful. I didn't use it in Madrid, among my old Venetian friends. Who would I be there but Casanova? It's my father's name. Sometimes I use my mother's name, Farussi. Oh, I am rich in names if nothing else. All the best people have an assortment of them. Kings and queens have eight or nine. Like topcoats or hairpieces, we put them on to suit the occasion. But it's different for you." Casanova looked thoughtful. "You are Tiepolo. Only and always. You share that one name with your father and your brother. You take it with you wherever you go. That seems to work for you."

Domenico didn't know how to reply. "It is our name."

"And what a famous name it is. I was so thrilled to meet you in Madrid. I regretted your father wasn't with you. He was unwell, if I recall."

"He was an old man even then and didn't relish late nights. He died just a few months later."

Casanova frowned. "I hope he didn't suffer too much. It's so awful when they linger."

"Thank you. My father died in his sleep after working all day. We should all be so fortunate."

"You must miss him." Casanova regarded Domenico with tragic eyes. Watching his face was like watching a theatrical production in miniature, constantly changing, the mood and intensity shifting. No wonder Domenico hadn't been able to remember it. With no wish to discuss his feelings for his father, he made a silent gesture of assent and hoped Casanova would let the matter drop.

Casanova seemed to take his cue. "You are not here to talk about the past, Signor Tiepolo," he said. "You are here to talk about the future."

Rising from the chair on the terrace, he dismissed the hairdresser with a wave of his hand. The young man gathered his tools quickly and made his exit, shooting one curious glance at Casanova as he went. The instant that hairdresser stepped out the door, Domenico reflected, everybody in the house would know who the Chevalier really was. In two hours, the farmhands working in the fields around the house would have heard the news and, by afternoon, the local police would probably be battering on Fulgenzio's door. The idea pleased Domenico. Perhaps settling Cecilia's debt was going to be simpler than he feared.

Casanova didn't seem worried. He floated into the room, the hem of his long dressing gown brushing the doorsill, patting his wig into place as he came. He carefully closed the French doors behind him, indicating that Domenico should sit down in one of the chairs upholstered in pale yellow silk.

"It's a pretty room," Casanova remarked. "A little pokey, but I've stayed in worse. Were you aware that the Spanish locked me up in the Buen Retiro prison on a trumped-up firearms charge? That was a disgusting experience, I can tell you: twenty men in a cell and not even one bucket. Not a misfortune you've shared, I'd guess."

"Thankfully, no," said Domenico coldly. He was not a touchy man, but the suggestion that he might have seen the inside of any prison made him bristle. He wondered if Casanova was baiting him.

"That whole city is a police state." Casanova sat down in the chair opposite and put his feet up on a low table. "Crawling with spies and the lowest kind of informers. You couldn't fart without being denounced in Madrid. But you must know all this better than I do. How long did you say you were there?"

"Eight years in all."

"Eight years!" Casanova shook his head in disbelief. "My sympathies, if only for the weather. I have never been so cold anywhere as on a December day in Madrid. The frosts left me with an abscess the size of a melon. What the devil kept you there so long?"

"We had several commissions in the palace and El Escorial. Some altarpieces for various churches, a little teaching. My younger brother Lorenzo is still there. He married a local girl."

"Now that I can believe. Spanish women are beautiful, far more intelligent than the men. They can be delightful — provided they keep themselves reasonably clean."

Domenico couldn't suppress a smile. Casanova was crude, but accurate. The Spanish girls he had known, though lively and attractive, were not outstanding for their personal hygiene. Not that he was fussy. "My sister-in-law's the daughter of a bookseller," he offered. "A very cultured girl."

"Well that *is* fine," Casanova said, clearly thinking of something else. "Lovely." He leaned his head in his hand and gazed into space. There was a long pause.

"I trust Don Fulgenzio has made you more welcome than the Spanish authorities anyway," Domenico said, after an interval.

Casanova sighed sadly, swiveling his eyes until they rested on Domenico. "The good Don Fulgenzio and Donna Lugarezia have been very kind to me. But, truthfully, I've been bored out of my skull. I'm glad you're finally here."

Domenico was nonplussed. "Were you waiting for me? If I'd known it was urgent I would have come sooner."

"Ah, now I understand the source of the delay. It's down to your extraordinary mother. Any other woman would have run to you in floods of tears the day she lost to me. Instead Signora Tiepolo keeps her cool, she tries every last thing she can think of — and she tried everything, I promise you — and she only calls you in when she's out of ideas. What spirit! She's a wonderful woman, Signor Tiepolo. Very clever and still a beauty, even at her age, if you don't mind my saying so. She lives up to her reputation, like all the Tiepolos I've had the pleasure to meet. It's a family trait, it seems to me. Not to disappoint."

"You flatter us," Domenico said awkwardly. It was proving difficult to get to the point with Casanova. If he were nastier, more triumphant, it would be far easier. Domenico decided it was up to him to push on. "I wondered if we could begin by discussing your last letter to my mother," Domenico extracted the folded piece of paper from his pocket.

"Oh, we're ready for the brass tacks, are we? So soon?" Casanova sat up straight, eyes shining. "Go on. You have my full attention."

"This is your letter, dated yesterday?"

"It certainly looks like my letter. What does it say?"

"Surely you know what it says." Is he really going to make me spell it all out? wondered Domenico, guessing this was some kind of a negotiating tactic.

"Signor Tiepolo, I have a lively epistolary life. I write dozens of letters every day. I can hardly remember what I put into all of them. Your mother and I did quite a lot of vigourous negotiating over the past week. Back and forth, back and forth. It's a proper correspondence. Someday it should be published. If you'd kindly remind me."

"It says you will accept our villa at Zianigo as a settlement for her debt."

"That's right! Now I remember. Thank you."

Domenico was beginning to get angry. Casanova noticed.

"Well?" said Casanova. "Don't just sit there looking as though you want to murder me. Say something."

"I'm trying to find a polite way to say this, but I can't, sir. Zianigo belongs to me. It may be my mother's home, but it isn't hers to give away."

"Oh, that sly little lady! She didn't tell me *that*," Casanova said with a secretive smile. He picked up a little round pillow and began plumping it. "So what will the Tiepolos do now?"

"We will make you another offer. Hopefully there is something else that will satisfy you. We have land, we have other property, furniture, jewelry. And of course we have paintings, etchings, drawings, books. You're a scholar, if I recall. The books might interest you."

"Go on."

"We could arrange to do a fresco for you. Something to your taste, tailored to a decorative programme set by you."

Casanova interrupted. "And where would I put a fresco since I have no house? On the clear blue sky? On the side of my trunk? I am a homeless wanderer."

"A suite of smaller oil paintings, then. They are portable. We put them on hinged stretchers and you can just fold them up and take them with you."

"Now there's an image."

"Or why not a portrait? Do you have a good portrait of yourself?"

Casanova looked thoughtful. "Only tiny miniatures and I tend to give them away to ladies."

"There you go. A gentleman should have at least one proper portrait." Domenico was overreaching himself slightly now. His studio didn't take portrait commissions as a rule. If Casanova accepted, he'd have to draft in his friend Pietro Longhi or another portraitist.

"Forgive me for saying so, Signor Tiepolo, but I think you take me for some kind of a bumpkin. You talk as if I have no idea what your work is worth. My brother Francesco is a painter, as I said. Not a very good one, it's true. He has a line in sea battles, lots of dark green water and white froth, ships sinking, that sort of thing. Their main selling point is size; they're huge, as big as that wall there. And they are truly, truly awful. Not the sort of thing a person of taste would have in their home at all, but there is a market for them and I know what Francesco charges per square metre. Now, even if I were to multiply my brother's pathetic prices by a factor of ten or twenty to get into Tiepolo range, Signora Tiepolo must owe me the equivalent of a gallery full of paintings. No." He put the little pillow decisively to one side. "It just won't do." He stood up then and bowed to Domenico as though ending the conversation.

Domenico stood up automatically. "I acknowledge my mother's debt to you, Signor Casanova. But I can't agree to give you Zianigo. If you insist, we'll end up in court and it will cost us both a fortune."

"Well, that was powerful." Casanova looked surprised. He dropped down onto on the chair again. "Now I need to sit back down. You too," he gestured to Domenico.

Domenico remained standing. He was so furious now that the blood was hissing in his ears. How had he arrived at this humiliating position, to be bargaining with a scoundrel over the ownership of his home? He foresaw a legal struggle lasting years, costing thousands. He'd win, eventually. But Zianigo would be spoiled. He could never enjoy it again.

"I think our negotiations are over," he said. "My lawyer will be in touch."

"Oh sit down, Signor Tiepolo. I see I've gone too far."

"You're making a fool of me, Signor Casanova, and I don't appreciate it."

"Here," Casanova said, holding out his hand. "Give me that letter. Give it to me!"

Domenico handed the letter to him. He watched as Casanova

tore it into several pieces and threw them into the air. Domenco watched them flutter down like confetti.

"There. You see, I was only joking."

"*Joking?*"

"I told you I was bored. And dear Signora Tiepolo was so enjoying the drama of it all. She's bored too! If I had thought she was really distressed, I promise you I would have stopped."

"Are you telling me you don't want Zianigo?"

"Of course I *want* it. A nice villa in the Veneto, even way out here, would be the perfect retreat for a man of my age. We must be almost exactly the same age." He squinted at Domenico. "How would you like to be staring at fifty with not so much as a square inch of property to your name and no family money behind you? It's not reassuring, I can tell you."

Domenico sat down. "Nobody gave us our money, Signor Casanova. We earned it."

"That's perfectly true. And a remarkable job you've made of it, too. That's why we can have this frank conversation, as two men who have had to earn our living. I've published books, plays, essays. I'd bet you didn't even know that. I'm working on a verse translation of *The Iliad* right now. I never stop working and what good has it done me? When I sat down to gamble with your mother, I had two hundred ducats to my name. That's the sum of my worldly wealth and I put it all on the seven. I may be lucky at the table, but believe me I'm not lucky in any other way, Signor Tiepolo. Patrons have never liked me, for long. Fame has never found me."

"You can't say you don't have fame," Domenico said, aware that he was being provocative.

"But it's not the kind of fame a man hopes for, is it?" Casanova gave him a sharp look as though he was deciding whether to take offence. "I won't deny it. My reputation is mixed. Yet the infamous can be honourable, Signor Tiepolo. They just never get the credit. You were a friend of Francesco Algarotti, if I'm not mistaken."

"He was a family friend," Domenico said. "And a longtime client."

"That astonishing polymath, that captivating, beautiful genius," said Casanova, rolling his eyes. "I heard Frederick the Great put up a huge marble monument to him in Pisa. The king of the Prussians even penned the epitaph himself. How did it go?"

"*Algarottus non omnis,*" Domenico quoted. A friend had sent him an etching of Algarotti's beautiful tomb of carved Carrara marble.

"'Algarotti, but not all'. What a perfect tribute from a king: manly, succinct, classical. How typical of Algarotti, charmed in life, charmed in death. Do you know when I was twenty I wanted to *be* Algarotti? He was my hero. I even once plucked up the courage to speak to him on the street outside the Ridotto. He looked at me like I was nothing."

"That doesn't sound like Algarotti at all. I never saw him be rude even to a servant."

"I didn't say he wasn't polite," Casanova said acidly. "In any case, instead of being known for my writing, like your lucky friend Algarotti, my claim to fame, as you well know, is being a fugitive from Venetian justice. Since nobody reads my books and I can't play the fiddle or paint sea battles, even bad ones, or make kings fall in love with me (though I have tried) I sing it for my supper at dinner parties all over Europe telling the story of my escape from the Doge's prison. I'm like a regular theatre troupe, all by myself. I can perform my tale in Italian, French, Latin, and German, take your pick. It takes a good two hours to tell it properly, with all the voices, but the audience sits through it with their mouths agape. I tell you, Signor Tiepolo, I know exactly how Homer must have felt."

"I seem to remember hearing you tell part of it in Madrid," Domenico said, his memory stirring suddenly. "The company was amazed."

"They always are. You remember that, do you? It's a great story if I say so myself." Casanova smiled bashfully, then let his face fall. "And yet it's my curse. It brands me, it strips me of protection. It means than anyone who wants can throw me into prison whenever they wish. That's what happened in Madrid. They hardly need a pretext."

"If it causes so much trouble for you, why do you broadcast it?"

Casanova looked at him fiercely. "Because a poor man needs a calling card, something to offer. You offer your art. The story of my escape is all I have to give. My life is one great irony: being imprisoned so young ruined me absolutely — and it gave me everything I now possess. It made me what I am." Casanova folded his hands together behind his head and looked at the ceiling. "The funny thing is that the most important thing about my story to *me* is just what everyone else overlooks. I wonder if you remarked it? People remember the squalor of the cell, the infamy of my gaoler, the flight by night over the roof of the Doge's palace and the buffoon of a partner I had, the defrocked priest, Balbi. Everyone loves Balbi."

Domenico had no recollection of any of these details. He remembered watching Casanova speak and thinking he was effeminate and untrustworthy, wondering how he could cut the evening short and get home to his comfortable bed.

"They quote these things back to me in my own words. I hear people retelling my story to others, passing it on. But no one picks up on the single detail that still haunts me. I suspect it's too technical."

"What is it?"

Casanova leaned forward and looked at him intently. "Will

you understand if I tell you? You are a painfully respectable man, Signor Tiepolo. I'm sure the police have never so much as knocked on your door. You can't even imagine what it would be like to be arrested."

"I'm not sure I can imagine it," Domenico answered. He wondered if he should gather up the torn up pieces of the letter so that the servants couldn't put them together again and read what it said. Casanova, he was sure, would never think of this precaution. "But I'm interested in what you have to say."

"A free thinker, are you? A libertine? What I tell you might be radical, outrageous. You're not a Mason by any chance?" Casanova leaned toward him and peered intently into his eyes.

Domenico felt the blood rush to his face. "Certainly not! Who says so?"

Casanova laughed loudly. "Don't worry. I never thought for a second you were. I'm joking again, Signor Tiepolo. I can see you have a hard time knowing when I'm joking. Your mother was more ready to see my humour. Your sisters, bless them, just laugh at everything. It must be jolly to have such sisters."

"I may not understand your humour, but I am listening to you," Domenico said with an edge of threat to his voice.

"That's good of you. All right then." Casanova leaned forward even further, reached out his left hand and rested the tips of his fingers on Domenico's knee. The intimacy of this gesture unnerved him. Male friends might take your arm or even embrace you, but strangers didn't touch your knee. He fought the impulse to bat Casanova's hand away. He wondered if he should just hit the man in the face and get it over with. But he made himself sit still and continue to meet the other man's gaze.

"Go on." Casanova's eyes were very large and set deep beneath the bone of his prominent brow. They seemed to be pleading. One thing was certain, Domenico would never forget his face again. He would be able to draw it from memory.

"They never told me why they put me in prison," Casanova said. "I was never charged with any crime, I never had a trial, I never received a sentence. To this day, I still don't know why I was sent to prison or how long I would have had to stay if I hadn't escaped." He sat back now, and observed the effect of his words.

Domenico was affronted. "But that's impossible. There are procedures in Venice, processes. You must have done something — "

"You see!" Casanova snapped his fingers in the air. "It's exactly as I said. You're too respectable to understand how such a thing can happen in your own city. Yet things like that happen all the time, and to better people than me. It's enough to make a man bitter, and I was bitter for a long time. But now I'm over it. I grew out of my rage." He ran a hand over his face in an unself-conscious gesture. "And so did Venice. We both got tired of our lovers' spat."

"You're not being very clear, Signor Casanova."

"They've granted me a pardon. After twenty years. That's why I'm here in the Veneto. I am going home." To Domenico's surprise he saw Casanova's dark eyes brimming with tears.

Domenico tried to weigh up what this might mean for himself and his mother and the gambling debt. He decided it was probably a good thing. If Casanova really was interested in turning over a new leaf, he wouldn't want to enter Venice with the enmity of the Tiepolos hanging over his head.

He said, "But this is wonderful news. After twenty years! Say what you will, there's no place on earth that compares to our Venice."

"Oh, I don't know." Casanova dabbed his eyes unashamedly with his sleeve. "Constantinople has more impressive churches. The fashion is better in Paris and the gaols in Holland are tip-top." Casanova brought his fingers to his mouth and kissed them.

"You're joking again. I got it that time. Still, I am happy for you. Really. I hope your return goes well. I'm sure you must still have many friends in Venice."

The little clock on Don Fulgenzio's mantelpiece said it was an hour until lunchtime and Domenico's stomach was growling. If he set off now he could bring the good news to his mother, eat a big meal at home and have a nice long sleep to smooth the previous night away. He didn't need to be back in the city for two more days and the weather was fine. He might stroll to the coffeehouse in the village afterwards and get an iced lime drink.

"Not enough friends, Signor Tiepolo." Casanova looked sad. "Several of my most devoted ones have died in the last few years. It's a colder city than the one I left behind. The truth is I could use a few more friends. It would be safer for me."

Domenico realised that his negotiation with Casanova wasn't over yet. *Eventually you find out what they want.* "You seem to think your lovers' quarrel with Venice isn't quite finished."

"That's one way of putting it. I fear it may be a trap. Or they may change their minds. For all I know they'll arrest me the instant I set foot in the city."

Domenico opened his mouth to say the Council would never do something so underhanded, but he knew what Casanova would say.

"In that case," he said, "I suppose you would need respectable friends."

"Don't look so worried, Signor Tiepolo! I'm not asking you to adopt me. What I need is someone who will speak up for me if I'm denounced, who'll look for me in the cells if I disappear. I'm too old to escape over the rooftops now."

Domenico felt a sense of revulsion. "I think you overestimate my influence. I'm just a painter. I don't have that much clout."

"Maybe not, but you're of good standing, aren't you? And

you owe me. I wouldn't dream of taking your villa, but you can't expect me to leave here empty handed."

Domenico studied him. "I'm not sure I understand you."

"It's very simple. I want someone who'll come for me if they put me in prison again. If that happens, someone will need to pay for my food and basic comforts while I am locked up, since I have no money, and probably that person will need to fork out to get me released. That's the way it works. However much it might cost you, I promise you it won't be anything like the sum your mother lost at cards."

"And if they don't arrest you?"

"Then I will go about my business and we won't meet again, unless we bump into one another on the street, in which case you can turn the other way and pretend not to know me. I won't take offence. And I won't pester you for money, you can be sure of that. I'm able to make my own living if left in peace. I just need some backing if things go wrong." A grim look passed across his features like a shadow.

"That sounds too good to be true. Are you saying you don't want anything from me now, up front?"

"Am I saying that? No." Casanova looked thoughtful. "I'm not saying that. Taking absolutely nothing wouldn't be honourable, would it? Given that I beat your mother fair and square. I have to carry something away with me, a trophy of sorts, a memento of my adventure with your dear mother, the daring Signora Tiepolo. And now that I reflect on it, I think I know the perfect thing."

Casanova told Domenico what he had in mind. His tone was playful — he was obviously charmed by a sense that he was acting magnanimously, with a poetic flair. He spoke for some time about things that seemed to Domenico to have nothing to do with the business at hand. One minute he was talking about Venice, the next about Venus and how one embodies the other.

He talked about time and advancing age and homecomings. It took Domenico some time to understand what he was actually asking for. When he finally managed to do this, his reaction was utter bafflement. "A portrait of your lovely mother painted by your gifted father. That's all."

Domenico deliberately took his time riding back to Zianigo. He let his horse amble in the sunshine stopping from time to time to crop weeds by the roadside. The idea was to let his mother and sisters stew a while longer before delivering the good news that the Chevalier (as they thought of him) was letting them off the hook. He imagined them huddled together in the salon with the shutters closed, silent and tense, anxiously awaiting his return. The thought of their worry gave him some comfort. Let them wait, he thought. Let them simmer.

He came home to find his mother and all three sisters had gone out. Donna Elena had arrived shortly after breakfast, the maid explained, and taken all the ladies to town in her carriage for the morning. Don Giuseppe was in the orchard clearing brush.

Domenico considered getting back on his horse and tracking the female Tiepolos down in town and dragging them back to face the music, but he felt too tired. Instead, he went upstairs to his room and stripped off his clothes. The servant brought up a cold lunch and he ate it stretched naked between clean sheets — bread and tomato and salty, thin-sliced ham — letting the crumbs gather in his greying chest hair. He was still chewing sleepily when he heard Elena's carriage return. His mother's voice floated up to him from the drive. "He's back already?" he heard her say. Someone came quietly up the stairs and he heard the door to his room open just before falling into a deep sleep.

Domenico awoke feeling wonderful, his limbs light and melting. It was afternoon, and the sun had moved to the far edge of the window frame. In this light, the stain on the ceiling looked like a mackerel, the most beautiful of all fish. Domenico contemplated it affectionately: Zianigo would remain his.

He gave thanks for the vulnerability that meant Casanova needed allies more than he needed property. Now that he had no reason to fear him, he indulged in pity for the man — imagine existing the way he did for so many years, homeless, stateless, without a family or profession or even the rudiments of faith? It was Domenico's idea of a living hell.

Even sadder, in his infamy Casanova still craved respect. The last thing he said as he and Domenico parted was, "If anyone asks, tell them I behaved honourably." But nobody would ever ask. Domenico would do everything in his power to make sure nobody ever heard about this disaster.

He turned his thoughts to Casanova's two strange requests. Both of them were perverse, both intrusive in a way that made Domenico feel like a conspirator. Strictly speaking, he didn't have to fulfill either of them: once they were back in Venice, Casanova would have no power over him. Even so, Domenico felt bound to give the man what he asked for. He wasn't quite sure how he would react if a call for help ever came from the cells. If he could send money anonymously, with no risk to himself, he would probably do it. If not, he wouldn't.

As for the portrait, that was trickier. Casanova obviously thought his request was whimsical and modest. He imagined the Tiepolos' house littered with likenesses of Cecilia Tiepolo painted by Giambattista Tiepolo. This told Domenico that, despite having a brother who was a sort of painter (sea battles!), Casanova knew nothing about the way painters lived. The idea that his father might have had the time to sit around doing little portraits of his own wife was ridiculous; professionals like him didn't get paid for immortalising family members. Instead of painting pictures of their wives and children, they painted pictures *for* them, producing likenesses of other people's loved ones so their own could eat. In any case, Tiepolo only did portraits grudgingly. The sitters, invariably vain, were never satisfied with the way they looked on canvas. Their finicky demands for adjustments to noses, mouths, hair- and waistlines had the effect of destroying all traces of semblance between themselves and the image. "Portraits," Tiepolo liked to say, "are just paintings of people with something wrong about the eyes."

Domenico decided not to tell Casanova that he had asked for something that didn't exist. He had spent most of his life trying to satisfy the irrational whims of the gentry; Casanova's request was no more impossible than most. He set about fulfilling it with a sense of professional obligation.

He rose, washed and put on clean clothes. Out on the landing, he stood for a moment, listening. The Tiepolo women were in the salon and the sounds of their voices rose up the staircase to him. He made out Elena's laugh, Orsola's throaty reproach, the yap of Cecilia's little dog. A servant came out of the kitchen, spotted him at the railing and gave a questioning look. Domenico shooed him away with both hands. Once he was sure the he'd gone, he edged carefully along the corridor and dodged into his mother's room.

The room was empty and tidy, the green damask bedcover smooth, the fireplace cleaned of ash. Domenico's eyes scanned the walls, passing over a beautiful oil painting of the Madonna and a smaller picture of San Rocco, both gifts to his mother from his father. On another wall, hung in two rows of six, were twelve small oil paintings, also by his father, depicting the Stations of the Cross. Casanova was a known heretic; there was no chance he would want any of these.

Domenico went next to a pair of small pictures hanging side by side over a little table by the bed. They were matching pastel portraits of his parents done by Lorenzo shortly before they all left for Madrid in 1762. Domenico leaned close and scrutinised them critically. They were of uneven quality, like everything Lorenzo did. The portrait of Tiepolo was a complete failure. The nose was out of kilter, the cheeks were boneless, and the head was buried in the sort of cascading formal wig Tiepolo never wore. The result was almost a caricature. Lorenzo's excuse had been that Tiepolo would never sit still long enough to be drawn properly, but Domenico had painted Tiepolo's head himself more than once. His father's face had strong individual traits that made it easy to reproduce: scooped divots at the temples, a flat, vertical brow, and eyes that sat loosely in their sockets like an egg in the palm of a hand. Lorenzo, typically, had overlooked all of these way-markers and then tried to hide his incompetence under a hairpiece.

The likeness of Cecilia was a little better and this is what Domenico had come to evaluate. Even he had to admit that Lorenzo had nicely captured the shape of their mother's head and the set of her skull on her neck. Doubtless, he took his time over it, the two of them sitting together for days, chatting while Lorenzo rubbed at the oily pastel with his thumbs; he was never in a hurry and Cecilia could never get enough of her youngest son's company. She had dressed up for him, choosing to wear her best lace along with her favourite jewelry — a diamond brooch shaped like a bow with a pendant cross, a pearl bracelet. The irony of this suddenly struck Domenico: these were the very pieces he made his mother sell to meet her last set of gambling debts. Maybe their likeness would serve to clear her current ones.

As he reached for the pastel portrait, intending to take it from its hook on the wall, Domenico heard a little scream behind him. He turned to find his mother standing in the doorway holding her hand over her heart. "You scared me to death!" she said. "What are you doing in here?"

He ignored her question and instead turned back to the portrait. "Do you think anyone would take this for father's work?"

"That's a funny thing to be asking. Why didn't you come down? What happened at Fulgenzio's?" She moved a few steps into the room with a limping gait: her knees troubled her. "Did you come to terms with the Chevalier?"

"Terms? Now what terms are you talking about?" He looked at her with an enigmatic expression. It was cruel; he could feel the pent-up tension radiating off her. In it was a ferocity that always seemed out of place in an old woman, giving the lie to her lace cap, her demure silk dress, the anemic smell of roses that came with her into the room. Hovering near him, she reminded Domenico of a little sparrowhawk, pausing in the air just before stooping to the kill. He had never liked this avidity in his mother and he wanted to torment it. He lifted his other eyebrow. "Terms…"

Her patience snapped and down she came. "Don't just stand there making monkey faces at me! How can you be so offhand? You must know I've spent the whole day worrying. I could hardly eat my lunch." Despite what she said, his mother appeared alert and fresh, not at all like a lady who had missed her lunch.

"It doesn't look like that to me," Domenico said. "I got back here to find you'd all swanned off to town, Tra-la. We're not in debt. We're not going to lose our house. We don't have a care in the world. Tra-la."

"It wasn't like that." She hobbled a few steps closer. "We needed some things. The girls wanted to take my mind off it."

"I'm sure they did."

"They meant well. Please tell me what happened." She twisted her hands together and Domenico relented. Briefly, he told

Cecilia what had passed between him and the Chevalier, leaving out the part where he promised to support Casanova if he were imprisoned. As he spoke, he fully expected his mother to throw his arms around his neck and kiss him. Instead, he watched her face cloud over with disappointment.

"But I thought he and I had reached an understanding," she said, her dark eyes darting around the room in confusion. "I was entirely prepared to go through with it. Why would he give up his claim? Did he explain himself?"

"What a way to take good news," Domenico said, irritated. "I imagined you'd be pleased at the way I saved Zianigo. Stupid me."

"I am pleased," she said too quickly. "But are you sure you understood him correctly? You're sure he's satisfied? We don't want him spreading rumours that the Tiepolos don't live up to their obligations."

Clearly, it distressed Cecilia to give up the fantasy of losing Zianigo at cards. Deliverance was not the outcome she'd expected. Perhaps it was not even the one she wanted.

"I can't believe this," Domenico said angrily. "You should thank God it's worked out so well. And then you should thank me."

She looked at him resentfully, a sparrowhawk who had missed her kill. "Thank you, Domenico. What should I tell the others?"

"Don't tell them anything. It's not as though they know the true extent of the problem, is it? Only you and I and the Chevalier know that and I'm absolutely sure he won't say anything about it."

"He's a true gentleman," she sighed. "I knew he was." Domenico wasn't about to correct her. His mother would find out the Chevalier's true identity as soon as they returned to Venice. When she did she would have the satisfaction of being thrilled all over again: trounced at cards by a known criminal! For now, Domenico saw the sense in deflating his mother's sense of drama.

"If you really don't want people to talk about us, just keep this to yourself."

"Can't I even tell Angela?"

"Especially not Angela or any of the other girls. I forbid it." He watched his mother set her mouth in a hard line. He was bossing her around now, and her instinct was to resist. She gave a little sniff, regrouping. She came up next to him and looked at Lorenzo's portrait.

"So the plan is to give him my one and only portrait? Well I guess that will teach me a valuable lesson. It's worse for me than giving up the house, you know, since it's the only thing I have of Lorenzo's."

"Don't start that again, Mother. You know he's fine in Madrid. Maybe a little too fine."

"But I'll never meet his wife." she almost sobbed. "I'll never hold my grandchildren in my arms. They'll grow up speaking *Spanish*."

"Don't worry, it's the same as Italian, only louder." Domenico continued to study the portrait. Why did Lorenzo insist on working in pastel? It was a weak, bleary, girly medium. Everyone knew Tiepolo despised it and never used it. Someone in Venice was sure to point this out to Casanova.

"It won't do anyway," he said finally. "We'll have to find something else. Are you sure there aren't any more portraits tucked away somewhere?"

"What a question. You know perfectly well your father refused to paint me, even though I asked him time and again. I was thinking of you children, something to remember me by. And do you know what he said every time? He said he'd rather paint forty-five gods, fifteen angels, a dozen putti and a brace of parrots than do a single portrait of me."

Domenico had to smile. "He must have thought you were too ugly."

"Oh, you're as bad as he was, big funny man. Do you know what else he said? He said it wasn't personal! He'd give me a little kiss right here and say it wasn't personal. His very words, and I'm his wife! There were things I just had to accept about your father. He had bizarre ways sometimes." She did her best to look severe and long-suffering.

"So you're saying we have nothing to pay off your creditor, Mother," Domenico said. "Maybe we'll just have to give him the house after all."

"He obviously doesn't want the house." His mother pursed her lips and frowned. "It must be too small for a man of his position. But why on earth would he want a portrait of me instead? He must be a very strange sort of man. Unless..."

"Unless what?"

"Unless he really doesn't care what we give him." She nodded to herself. "I have an idea."

She led the way down the long corridor, past his sister's room to a door at the far end. When she pushed it open, its bottom edge scraped uncooperatively along the floor making a sound that set Domenico's teeth on edge. The room they entered seemed abandoned. It was bare of ornament, like a monk's cell, except for a wooden crucifix on the wall above the big wooden bedstead, its mattress covered with a piece of rough canvas to keep out the dust. There were no pictures on the walls, no personal knick-knacks, no other signs of occupancy. Beneath the window, a few dead bluebottles lay curled up on the floorboards.

Domenico couldn't remember the last time he'd been in this room. The family always referred to it as their father's bedroom, but Tiepolo had rarely come to Zianigo and, when he did, he preferred to sleep in his wife's room. These days his old room occasionally served as a place to accommodate extra guests and small nieces and nephews when the house was full. On damp days the maids strung lines from the ceiling beams and hung up the wet linen there.

"It's stuffy in here." His mother crossed the room, rolling on her bad knees like a ship at sea, to open a window. Cool evening air flooded in, bringing with it the smell of smoke. "Giuseppe's having another one of his bonfires," she commented, peering out the window. "For a man of the cloth, he certainly loves burning things." She nodded toward a heavy bookcase standing in an alcove by the bed. "There they are," she said. "Just where he left them."

Domenico went over and stood in front of the bookcase. It held a series of about twenty tall, thick volumes identically bound in leather. Their titles were tooled in gold letters on their spines: *Figures for Ceilings, Volume 1*; *Children, Dogs and Dwarves*; *The Holy Family*; *Philosophers and Magicians*; *Various Ideas and Thoughts*. Selecting a volume at random — *Standing Male Figures* — Domenico slid it from between its companions. The leather cover felt buttery and plump in his hands.

Domenico opened the album to a page at random. On it was a picture of a fat man wearing a Turkish robe. On the next page a lanky soldier leaned on his spear. Here was a bishop with his hand outstretched, a bearded saint, a boy carrying a shield. Each drawing had been carefully cut from its original sheet of paper and pasted into the book. Sometimes a single page accommodated a pair of smaller sketches. The medium varied — red chalk, pen and wash, black crayon — but the images were all familiar to Domenico. He had copied these drawings, adapted them, chopped, recombined and recycled them for use in various projects over the years. He and his assistants used such drawings every day for reference. Filed away in loose folders at his studio, there were several versions of the same leaning soldier, the same Turkish gentleman, the same pensive boy, ready for use in an altarpiece, a ceiling fresco, a history painting, as needed. The drawings were tools to Domenico, as vital to his trade as brushes and pigment. They were also the source of the studio's stylistic identity: they were what made Tiepolo paintings look like Tiepolo paintings.

"I'd forgotten all about these," Domenico said. He felt the warmth of his mother's body at his elbow. She slipped her hand around his biceps and squeezed.

"You see, they're in perfect condition," she said. "Just like the day your father put them here. I still don't know what he thought they were good for. The quality of the binding is nice, though."

He turned the thick, creamy pages. There was one important difference between those working drawings and the ones so carefully bound in these volumes. The drawings in the studio files might be by anyone: Tiepolo or Domenico or Lorenzo or various assistants, apprentices, jobbing painters, students. The drawings in the bound volumes were all by his father.

This fact was obvious to Domenico as he leafed through the book. The signs that identified these as being Tiepolo's drawings were subtle, and they might have escaped someone who wasn't Tiepolo's son. But Domenico had been compelled to absorb his father's idiosyncrasies into his own technique, so he knew them better than anyone. It was said, perhaps too often, that it was impossible to tell the difference between his work and his father's. In the final years of their partnership, as Tiepolo's vigour faded, their success had rested on this illusion of seamless continuity; when you hired one Tiepolo, you got the value of two or even three — Lorenzo was an incalculable part of the bargain. However, Domenico could easily tell the difference between a drawing he had done and one by his father. So could Tiepolo.

Domenico said, "I remember him collecting them up before we went to Madrid. He told me he was doing it, but I was too busy to ask why."

When the summons came from the Spanish king, they had had only a few weeks to wind up a number of commissions, pack up the whole studio and make preparations for the journey. Instead of helping with this work, Tiepolo spent his energy trying to get out of the obligation to go, writing plaintive letters to the Doge and the Spanish ambassador, begging to be let off the hook. In the meantime, Domenico was left to make all the arrangements for a journey he knew to be inevitable. Privately he approved of the idea. Commissions were drying up in Venice. The Seven Years' War had throttled trade with northern Europe and brought an end to the time when new clients swarmed over the Alps and arrived in town with their purses already open, gasping for art. They had Algarotti's martial friend, Frederick the Great, to thank for that.

The Venetian government eventually forced Tiepolo to accept the king's commission. It would have been a diplomatic disaster to refuse. It was at that point that his father began combing the studio files and sketchbooks, rifling through the cabinets and cubbyholes and drawers to extract all his old drawings — only his — in order to furnish these volumes.

"He never told me why," Domenico said out loud.

His mother squeezed his arm again. "Your poor darling father always knew he was going to die in Madrid." Her voice was perfectly steady. Domenico turned and stared at her. It was so horrible when she said out loud what he was thinking. "We often talked about it."

He tried to brush her words off. "That's ridiculous. He never said anything like that to me."

"But he wouldn't, would he? Not to you." She took another volume from the bookshelf. "Have a look at this one. It might do the trick."

He opened the volume, *Female Figures*, and began flipping rapidly through the pages. As with the drawings in the first volume, he knew these images intimately, recognising the figures of women, girls, goddesses — standing, seated, lying down, airborne — as elements he had used in his own work. But he now found he was looking for one in particular, a half-remembered drawing, one he hadn't seen in years or maybe one he had never seen and only heard of or guessed existed. He turned the pages with increasing impatience, worrying that his memory was playing tricks on him. Then he found it.

The drawing showed a young girl sitting on a chair with her naked back to the artist, her face turned in profile. Her torso was powerful, almost masculine, her arms were the arms of a stone-cutter, but her features were fresh and tender and achingly lovely. She had strands of pearls wound into her fair hair. A length of plain cloth fell from one shoulder to the floor, crossing her back and skimming her plush hips, her knee, one rounded thigh. A single foot peeked out from the hem of her robe.

"Will you look at that?" His mother chuckled in his ear. "That drawing must be fifty years old. I tell you your father never threw a single thing away."

Domenico tilted his head and examined the drawing. It was carefully done, its line meticulous, almost fussy. Domenico recognised his father's exacting youthful style, taught to him by his first master, Lazzarini. Suddenly he remembered copying the drawing himself in the early years of his apprenticeship — he might have been nine or ten. The key to the figure, he recalled, was the set of the rounded shoulders and the drape of the cloak across her back. The ear, just exposed by the girl's upswept hairstyle, had posed problems for him. First, he had drawn it too small, then he had drawn it too big. Finally his father had made him draw the girl's ear all by itself, just the ear, alone, framed in fine tendrils of hair.

As a result of all this drawing and re-drawing, the troublesome ear was burned in Domenico's memory forever. Yet he never once thought of it as belonging to his mother. Now, in the darkening room, he stole a glance at the side of her head. There was no doubt about it: the ears were the same. Any variance was easily explained by the difference in age between the young girl in the sheet and the elderly lady in the dress of French silk: elderly cartilage went on growing, soft, old lobes drooped down like withered plums. Domenico felt as though he had failed to notice something important that had been staring him in the face all his life.

"Is that you?" He felt embarrassed to pose such a patently stupid question to a woman as clever as his mother.

"Don't be silly, darling, of course it's not *me*. When did I ever go around wearing a sheet? You know who that is. It's Campaspe. But we can tell the Chevalier it's me if you want. I think we can make him believe it."

Domenico turned the page and found another early drawing of the same young woman, a girl almost, sitting on a chair facing the artist. She wore the sheet again, this time clipped modestly over her shoulders. Her face, staring straight out of the image, was a youthful blank.

His mother chuckled. "Your father thought that old sheet looked classical, can you imagine?" she said. "To me it just looks like I have nothing to wear but the bedding. But then Tiepolo would have liked that notion. He was a sort of savage. He never saw the point of clothes."

She reached out across Domenico's body and turned the next page with her own hand, revealing another drawing. This one was of the same young girl seated on the ground, looking up. Her face was in profile, her hand upraised in a gentle gesture of reproach. It was a study for the figure of Rachel for one of his father's earliest works in fresco. On her knee leaned a small child looking straight out at the artist.

"Will you look at him!" Cecilia cried. "Who's that beautiful boy? My beautiful little boy with all that curly blond hair. Now look at you. So big, so famous. With less hair." She ran a hand over the crown of his head, laughing at her own joke. "How the time goes." Domenico suddenly understood why his father had wanted to compile these particular drawings. Unlike the studio drawings, these originals were linked to specific moments in Tiepolo's life. They contained the seeds of the work he had done subsequently, his first thoughts, the place where his mind touched the material. Obviously, the bound volumes were never intended for sale: clients didn't care about the origins of things, they cared only about products. No, the volumes were records only another painter would appreciate: *Tiepolo, but not all.*

It flashed through Domenico's mind that it might not be Zianigo or even the business that was the most precious part of his patrimony but these sketches, overlooked for so long. It was an absurd thought which couldn't survive long in the climate of his mind. No sooner had it formed than it began to slip away, leaving eddies of uncertainty behind it. When faced with doubt, Domenico did what he usually did: he fell back on business.

"We'll give him this," he said decisively. He guessed Casanova would be charmed by the album. The rogue Venetian, more than his customary clients, would be capable of appreciating the intimate, informal nature of the sketches. Freethinkers and Masons valued that kind of thing. "I think we can confidently tell him it's you in the drawings. He'll have no choice but to believe us. And then we'll be done with it."

"If it's the best we can do," Cecilia said, drawing a sigh. "I still don't understand why he doesn't want the villa. It's a very nice villa." She reached out and laid her hand on the page. Her many rings glittered in the last light from the window. Domenico brushed his mother's hand aside and closed the volume with a snap.

"It's settled, then," he said, tucking the book beneath his arm. Anger surged up in him again — it was always there, waiting. Why? He should have felt relieved, even triumphant. He'd found a clever, cost-free solution to a potentially expensive problem. Getting Casanova to accept a volume of studio drawings in place of their villa was an excellent outcome. Yet Domenico felt cheated. It was as though Casanova were making off with his most valuable possession while his mother stood by applauding the theft.

With the book clamped in his armpit, he prepared to leave the room. Cecilia held him back. "Is it settled?" she said. "You don't seem happy. You're still angry with me."

Domenico denied it. "I want to send this off to Fulgenzio's tonight. We don't want the Chevalier changing his mind."

"Who is changing his mind, Domenico? Not the Chevalier. Clearly he doesn't care what he gets as a forfeit. It's you. I know you. You're thinking we're losing out, that we haven't got enough to give this one piffling little sketchbook away. But I'm telling you, and I know what I'm talking about, we have plenty."

"You behave as if our wealth is inexhaustible, Mother. It's not. It all comes from somewhere and it can all be spent if we're not careful."

"Careful!" she cried. "Who do you think made our wealth? Who do you think is responsible for all this? Think about it for one minute. Your father and I did it together and all from scratch, from nothing. We didn't inherit, or steal or beg to get here. We *made* things together: paintings, money, children — you, my darling son. That's the wonderful thing about being *us* and not the sort of people who have to wait around for other people to give us things. We just make them ourselves, between us, don't you see? Once you do that and you see how possible it is, you stop worrying about giving away too much or losing what you have. That's what you have to remember, Domenico, when you feel as though things are slipping through your fingers. And you do feel that, don't you? You need to have more confidence that you can make things for yourself." She put her arms around him and laid her head on his chest. "Your new wife will help you. Then you'll know."

Just then they heard a voice calling from the corridor. Angela stuck her head around the edge of the door. "There you both are! We wondered what had happened to you." She stood in the doorway with her wide skirt filling the frame. "It's so dark in here. We hope you're done killing Mother so we can have dinner."

Domenico stood still as his mother held him in a grip that was too powerful for an old lady.

"Oh good," she said, releasing him and moving toward the door. "I'm starving."

PART SEVEN

Lieutenant John D. Skilton Jr.
Würzburg, Germany, 1945

Würzburg, Germany, 1945

Lieutenant John D. Skilton stood aboard a log raft floating down the river Main. The morning was unseasonably cold for July. A light rain stippled the fast-flowing surface of the water and turned the pine forest black. Skilton was chilled and tired — he had been up since before dawn bargaining with the lumbermen. His pockets were empty; the canny Bavarians had all but cleaned him out. But he wasn't sorry. On the contrary, as he rode the current downstream toward Würzburg, Skilton felt like Huck Finn. He felt like he was getting away with it.

If they could see me now, he thought. He had in mind his friends back home. How surprised they would be to see him swashbuckling like this, with a star on his shoulder and a helmet on his head, riding into a ruined city on a crude raft of hand-hewn logs, surrounded by men who had only weeks before been his mortal enemies. Skilton was surprised too. When he had signed up to be a Monuments Specialist Officer, he'd thought the job would entail the wearing of white gloves. In fact it meant transforming himself into a pirate, a fixer, a scrounger, a carpetbagger and a thief. He was rather enjoying it.

Then the outskirts of Würzburg came into view and Skilton felt a sense of urgency return. Suddenly, he remembered that it wasn't a raft he was standing on, it was salvation: the raw material destined for the roof that could save the Residence.

Skilton had never wanted to be a soldier. From an early age, he wanted to be a conservator, one of the careful, attentive people who preserve the artifacts of human existence. It was not a glorious calling in the eyes of the world. Mostly, the work was invisible, taking place in quiet, well lit work rooms, far from the public gaze. It involved careful attention, good record keeping, a sharp eye for detail and a way with philanthropic donors. It did not normally involve lumberjacks or engineers or sawmills. It did not call for stealth or brinkmanship or deception. It was a clean, honest profession and Skilton would have been happy to follow it all his life if it hadn't been for the war.

Skilton's commitment to conservation was cemented during his student days. He had studied Art History at Yale with a specialism in pre-Revolutionary American prints. Yale was a joyful time for him; it brought him a sense of community, not only with his fellow students but also with the past. Every time he took a 200-year-old engraving in his hands he thought about all the people across the centuries who had made it possible for him to do this. He imagined them literally as a line of determined individuals, passing the delicate paper carefully from hand to hand — a sort of cultural bucket brigade — until they were able to place it gently into his. The world was a destructive place — Skilton felt it even in the safety of the university. Fragile works of art only survived if people took pains to preserve them. What did survive was a testament to the individuals who took the time to think about the future and prepare for it.

When war was officially declared, Skilton found himself living in a faux-French chateau in the Blue Ridge Mountains of North Carolina with only a green parrot for company. Seeing what was unfolding in Europe, the trustees of the National Gallery had decided to crate up their greatest treasures and send them out of the target zone of the nation's capital. They shipped them to

Biltmore House, George Washington Vanderbilt II's grand pile, which lay empty just outside of the town of Asheville, North Carolina. As a junior member of staff, Skilton took his turn as their guardian, travelling down to the South and installing himself in a nearby vicarage. There were 250 rooms at the chateau, he learned, but not one that could be used by the staff.

It was a lonely vigil, with no one to talk to but a pair of local security guards and the parrot, who also lived at the vicarage but didn't seem to belong to the owner. The parrot was emerald green, like the hills around Asheville, with a black beak and feet that looked like new-laid asphalt. He took a liking to Skilton and soon became part of the daily routine. Skilton would get up in the morning and bravely face the plate of oily grits his landlady prepared for him every single day. When that was over, he'd find the parrot and put it on his shoulder. Together they'd walk the mile to Biltmore House through the steamy green lanes. It was very, very quiet in North Carolina, except for the screeching cicadas and the frogs throbbing in the ditches. There were days when Skilton never saw another soul on the road. And if it was quiet in the open, inside Biltmore House the atmosphere was like a tomb.

When he was first given the assignment, Skilton imagined himself making use of the time to put himself on intimate terms with the artworks. These included all the most important treasures of the newly formed national collection: Titians, Rembrandts, Vermeers, Giottos, and Goyas. It was a unique opportunity for a young conservator to get to know these works by heart. Skilton imagined himself spending voluptuous days with the canvases, touching their brushstrokes with clean fingers, sniffing the varnish, sketching the figures — he was a competent draughtsman — examining the backs of the frames for clues a thousand other pairs of eyes had missed, tracing the signatures over and over. He fantasised about making some small discovery that would revolutionise the scholarship on one of the paintings. He would write it up when he returned to Washington; it would make his name. He smiled at the thought of giving co-author credit to the parrot.

So he was crestfallen to find that all the works were to be kept prisoner in their bulky pine crates. Intimacy with them was impossible. They were housed in temperature-controlled ballrooms that were darkened by heavy brown blackout curtains and looked more like warehouses than places to dance. All through the sultry, still days of that southern autumn, Skilton wandered through the deserted chateau with the grumbling, clacking parrot riding on his right shoulder. His main job was checking the humidity and temperature controls in each of the rooms. The imposed darkness, the square, ugly profiles of the crates — the denial of life and light — made him reflect on the fall of empires, the end of his hopes for civilisation and his own loneliness.

The news from Europe was terrible. Even in this remote corner of the American South, it reached Skilton and it shocked him. He was appalled by the reports of killing, the ruthless aggression that was driving Hitler's progress. And there was another level of worry, specific to people of Skilton's calling. Rumours had begun to circulate in the museum community about priceless art collections abandoned as their owners, many of them Jews, fled for their lives from the Nazi war machine. It was becoming clear that Hitler was systematically stripping the treasures of occupied nations and dragging them back to Germany as the spoils of war.

When Skilton heard about this, he imagined a wild animal dragging its kill back to its cave to chew on the bones at leisure. The idea disgusted him — the brute selfishness of it. He looked at the crates in the ballroom and imagined the great castles of Europe stuffed with similar crates ready to be shipped to the land of the victors (it was a vision that later proved prescient). And these, he knew, were the objects that were safely out of danger.

Even as he stood there helplessly, there were the others that were not safe, others being destroyed by the fighting on both sides. These were losses that couldn't be calculated until the war ended, if it was ever going to end.

When he heard about the Monuments Specialist Service, some time after he returned from exile in Asheville, Skilton felt he had been called. Being a Monuments Specialist Officer seemed to offer a way to serve not only his country, but also the cause of art. He envisioned himself painstakingly wrapping and crating and tagging, storing objects in safe places where they were in no danger from the fighting. In his imagination, he was always wearing white gloves while he did this good work, a symbol of his pure intent.

By the time he reached Würzburg, Skilton knew that white gloves were never going to come into it. For the past year, most of his energy had been spent trying to explain to various commanding officers what he was doing in the theatre of war. None of them had ever heard of the Monuments Specialist Service and they didn't know what the hell to do with a dapper, cultivated but stubborn soldier who kept claiming to belong to that outfit. Did he have orders? He did, but they were always lagging one step behind him as he was swept northwards through France, riding the wave of the Allied invasion. Since no one knew what Skilton's brief was, he was constantly being roped into work that was not his. He washed dishes, he buried the corpses of soldiers from both sides, he incinerated the bodies of horses that were decomposing on the battlefields. The German army had used a surprising number of horses. Their large bodies burned with a damp, reluctant flame.

Eventually, someone realised that Skilton spoke French and he was put to work as an interpreter. This meant he had to carry out what he still believed was his real mission on his own time, sneaking out after curfew to collect the fragments of a shattered shrine or furtively boarding up a chapel against looters. The local inhabitants had a clearer understanding of Skilton's purpose than his officers did and they helped him when they could. In the blasted towns of Brittany, a wheelbarrow was his most useful tool.

It was only when he reached Germany that Skilton's orders finally caught up with him. He was summoned to Paris to receive his commission and assigned to the Military Government Section. Within a few days he found himself back in Germany, reunited with James Rorimer, his senior officer in the Monuments Specialist Service. Rorimer was another American curator turned soldier, and he and Skilton had become friends during their training stint in England. He hadn't seen Rorimer since he'd sailed for Normandy and the mere sight of his colleague cheered Skilton up. Rorimer brought authority and clarity to Skilton's mission. He also brought intelligence about where the Nazis had hidden stolen artworks. With the arrival of Rorimer, Skilton's life became, for a brief period, a thrilling treasure hunt.

Their first mission together was Heilbronn where Rorimer's sources told him that the Nazis had hidden a large cache of stolen artworks in the tunnels of a salt mine. Outside the occupied town, they stood in a field of rubble at the mouth of the mine while Rorimer quizzed the mine manager through an interpreter.

"What's he saying?" Skilton asked. The mine manager was talking at great speed and volume, waving his hands at the mine entrance. Despite this activity, it was clear he wasn't cooperating.

"He says the soldiers dynamited the entrance. The tunnels that run under the river are flooded." Rorimer put his hands on his hips, thinking. "He says there's nothing down there anyway."

"But you don't believe him." Skilton studied the mine manager, thinking of all the compromises a man like him had to make during a war, all the lies he had to tell just to get through it.

"I believe Rose," said Rorimer. "She's been right so far."

Rose Valland was a curator at the Jeu de Pomme in Paris and Rorimer's key source of information about stolen art. While continuing her job at the museum during the Nazi occupation, she secretly documented their systematic looting. Her information had led Rorimer to finds at Altaussee, another salt mine, where Hitler had stored a huge number of stolen artworks as well as some works from Viennese museums. In the mine at Merkers they found most of Germany's gold reserves and hastily hidden art from German collections. At Bernterode they found a ghastly subterranean reliquary containing the coffins of the three greatest political heroes of the Third Reich — Field Marshal von Hindenburg, King Friedrich Wilhelm and Frederick the Great, King of Prussia — all jammed into a common chamber and draped with black and red Nazi regalia. Frederick the Great's coffin was made of solid steel and literally weighed a ton; it took fifteen men an entire day to extract from its sepulchre deep in the mine.

"She's right this time too," Skilton said. "Look at this. I found it in the rubble." He handed Rorimer a piece of broken glass. It was about the size of a large stamp with three straight sides and one ragged broken corner. Even before he'd picked it up, Skilton had recognised the familiar form of a photographic slide such as those used to catalogue museum collections.

Holding it between his thumb and forefinger, Rorimer raised the fragment up to the pale sun and squinted through it. "Well, well," he said. "That certainly changes things." On the broken slide was the image of a painting of an old man sitting on a bed in a cell. Skilton had identified Rembrandt's *Saint Paul in Prison* at once and so had Rorimer. "Are there others?" he asked.

"Lots. I think someone must have dropped the whole catalogue. Poor fellow," he added. Skilton visualised the German soldier stumbling in the rubble as he hurried toward the mine open-ing, the box falling from his hands, the slides fanning out as they fell, shattering against the tailings. Skilton had managed to drop a box of slides once at Yale and never managed to live it down.

"Let's get the pumps going," Rorimer said.

Neuschwanstein was next. Skilton had visited Mad King Ludwig's folly before the war. Then, he had found it magi-cal, frivolous and extravagant, and he was eager to go back. But, as he and Rorimer drove toward it up the deserted mountain road, the castle's sharp turrets looked sinister, like missiles. And it contained a sinister hoard. As Valland had promised, the castle was stuffed to the rafters with the looted wealth of France's richest families. They found room after lofty room crammed with furni-ture, paintings, tapestries, prints, books, silverware, rugs, jewelry and porcelain. They were carefully crated, numbered and tagged or stamped with the initials of the Third Reich's official looting agency, the ERR, the *Einsatzstab Reichsleiter Rosenberg*.

Neuschwanstein reminded Skilton of Biltmore House, his own deserted castle full of crates. It engendered in him the same feel-ing of desolation. There is nothing lonelier, he concluded, than beautiful objects, which are made to be seen and touched and enjoyed by human beings, hidden away in the dark.

Nearby, hiding out in a nursing home, they found two ERR officials who had been in charge of the castle's cache of art. As Rorimer questioned the men through a translator, Skilton found himself wondering where they stood in the brotherhood of care-takers. He had seen for himself their painstaking inventories, their neat indexing system, their scholarly library of reference books, their little sets of rubber stamps for categorising the col-lection. It was the sort of cataloguing he would have done himself if this had been his collection to look after. What was the difference between the Nazi conservators and himself? In their place, offered the riches of the world to care for, would he have acted any differently?

Any trace of sympathy Skilton felt for the men evaporated as the interrogation went on. It became clear during questioning that both men were committed Nazis with senior positions in the ERR. They showed themselves to be irritated by the Allies rather than frightened of them. They were entirely unrepentant. But the worst thing in Skilton's eyes was their total lack of concern about the fate of their collection. They had run away at the first hint of danger, making no provisions for guarding it, and now they appeared indifferent to its future. From the beginning, all they were interested in was ensuring their own survival.

When the interrogation was drawing to a close, Skilton took the arm of the interpreter. "Please tell them," he said, "that their excellent records will make it practically effortless for us to return the stolen goods to their rightful owners. Use that word: effortless. Make sure they understand how much we appreciate their assistance."

He watched the men's faces while the interpreter translated. It took longer to say things in German than it did in English and Skilton had plenty of time to observe their reaction as they realised they were being taunted. One of them muttered a phrase and shrugged angrily.

"What was that?"

The translator looked uncomfortable. "He says, more or less, that helping you was never their intention."

Skilton smiled. "But still you've helped," he said, looking into the eyes of the ERR man. "Thank you so very much for all your hard work."

After Neuschwanstein, things changed quickly. Rorimer moved on to other discoveries, following the intelligence passed to him by Rose Valland, and Skilton went alone to Würzburg with a scribbled list of priorities in his breast pocket.

At Würzburg he would find no hidden caches of art, no stolen gems to rescue and return, just a small German city devastated by Allied bombs. His work with Rorimer had been an adventure, a hero's quest for restitution. Würzburg was very different: there was no glory to be won in that city, no glittering prizes to unearth and take away. Here, Skilton's side was responsible for most of the damage. Here, he knew as soon as he saw the extent of the bombing, nothing would be recovered in one piece. At best, Skilton could hope to protect some of what remained, and even that looked doubtful when he saw the scale of the work at hand.

Where the Residence was concerned, protection took a literal form: without roofs to shield them from the elements, the vaults carrying Tiepolo's frescoes would shortly collapse. Skilton's mission became constructing four great roofs to cover the four main parts of the Residence before winter came. From the moment Skilton arrived in Würzburg, his life stopped being about art and became all about lumber.

Skilton shortly discovered that all the wood and every sawmill in the Occupation Zone around Würzburg were under the control of the Army Corps of Engineers. When he showed up in their tent with his request for material to fix the palace roof he innocently expected their cooperation — they were on the same side after all. But the engineers stared at Skilton as though he were a madman and rudely informed him that their orders were to provide a million board feet of wood for military construction only, not for anything else. And then, there were the homeless Germans to worry about, they added as an afterthought. Winter was coming and shelters of some kind would need to be built for them.

All this made perfect sense to Skilton, yet he had his own orders and he intended to carry them out. He *was* a kind of madman, he supposed. As the engineers shooed him out of their tent, he embraced his desperation. That was the moment he stopped trying to do things through the proper channels and began to do things his own way.

The rain continued. There was no time to lose. After some initial confusion about who was in charge, Hauser settled down to a role as right hand man and proved an indispensible ally. He drove the Jeep when Skilton commandeered tarpaulins from an army store. He went with him out to the displaced person's camp on the edge of town where they hired a clutch of German adolescents, put buckets and brooms in their hands and stationed them on top of the Residence with orders to sweep the water away from the vault and bail it off the parapets. The boys worked with a will in any weather and were happy for a chance to earn something, to do something. It gave Skilton hope to see them moving against the sky, alive and laughing among the Residence's battered statuary. As the storms continued to roll over the roofless palace, there were days when he felt the boys were the only ones doing anything useful to save the building.

As for Skilton, he was hunting wood. Every day, through the labyrinth of military government bureaucracy, through the rubble-strewn streets of the city and out into the sodden summer countryside, Skilton chased logs, planks, trees, tumbledown barns, bundles of twigs, old fencing, anything he could beg, buy or salvage to slap on the roof of the Residence. He had a small team of helpers: Hauser, the youths, then Albert Bosslet, a local architect who knew the building well, and several other German civilians who lent their energy and expertise to the salvage project. Skilton drew them all into his obsession with wood. Through them word went out that this slight, mannerly dervish of a lieutenant had cash to pay and would take as much of any kind of timber, lumber, kindling or driftwood as a supplier could provide. While Hauser manned the office, Skilton scoured the countryside in vehicles he cadged from sympathetic individuals or those not quick-witted enough to see him coming. Through local sources he heard of a large cache of logs jammed upriver in a secret bend of the Main. Up he shot and bought them on the spot, then he rode them downstream in triumph. When they reached the city, the Army Corps of Engineers tried to commandeer his precious cargo but Skilton fought them off with guile and diplomacy, bartering his logs for an equal amount of milled timber and thus saving himself a step in preparing them for use on the roof.

His German improved daily. *Stillstand*: logjam; tugboat: *Schlepper*. Soon they had enough lumber to begin roofing and he went back to the camp and hired a bigger team of German labourers: *Arbeiter*. While they went to work on the roof, he went out again looking for more materials. *Beton*: concrete; tarpaper: *Dachpappe*. When he needed a sawmill in a hurry, he reached into his own pocket and paid to get a disused one up and running. Sawmill: *Sägewerk*. There was no time to lose. Skilton knew the vagaries of military posting: he might be re-assigned at any time with no warning. Once he left, he knew the work would slow to a crawl, perhaps stop entirely. Who else would be crazy enough to take it on? Then winter would come. If by some miracle the vaults were still standing by then, the snow would finish the job of pulling them down.

The thought of the destruction of the beautiful building and the paintings on the vaults drove Skilton. He worked every hour he could and slept without dreaming, starting awake when he heard any kind of sound, believing the vaults were caving in. He skipped meals, and the weight dropped from his already slight form so that his uniform hung on his bones; he paid a private who had been a tailor to take it in. He didn't want to look like a wreck. If he was dressed neatly, kept his hands groomed and shaved his face carefully, he figured, people would be less likely to take him for a nut. Many already thought he was deranged, obsessed by art and blind to the reality around him. Military men accused him of being pro-Kraut; Germans cursed him as a looter; Red Cross medics told him he had no sense of priorities, that he lacked a basic sensitivity to human suffering.

Was any of it true? The accusations reminded Skilton of that old ethical chestnut: the museum fire. He had first heard it in an art history lecture at Yale and it went like this: there is a fire raging in a museum. You have to choose between saving the Mona Lisa or rescuing an old lady. If you choose the old lady, the painting will be destroyed. If you choose the painting, the old lady dies.

In his class at Yale, the students were all for letting the old lady burn. She was old, they pointed out, she would die soon anyway, but the painting was "eternal". That was the word someone used; the professor approved it and no one argued. Skilton kept quiet in that discussion — he usually kept his own counsel. But it haunted him for years afterwards. The decision wasn't hard for him: he would save the old lady. He pictured himself lifting her in his arms, light as a bundle of twigs, wearing a little handbag on her arm. He'd make his way through the smoke-filled hall away from the Da Vinci's smirking matron, speaking soothing words as the painting behind them caught fire. Skilton had never liked the Mona Lisa anyway, but that wasn't why he made this choice. It was because he knew the old lady would feel abandoned in the flames — she would feel — and the painting would not. It was just canvas and pigment, and it was nothing like eternal, despite what his classmates argued. And even if the old lady died of a heart attack in his arms on the way out of the building, at least she would know that someone was there, trying to help her when she needed help.

Now Skilton had seen burned museums for real. And burned churches, burned libraries; burned hospitals, homes, factories; burned palaces. From the things the survivors told him, there were no choices to be made when the flames swept through. The reality was much simpler than any theory: old ladies caught in the conflagration died and the artwork went up in smoke. The question was no longer what could be rescued from the fire, but who would bother to pick through the ashes. Skilton wasn't too proud to do this. Why, he thought, should all the good be destroyed? Why should we let them do that to us?

"There. Exactly there." The German youth pointed enthusiastically. "See?"

Skilton leaned in and shone his flashlight into the space where the youth was pointing, directing its beam behind the knee of one of the plaster Titans. He and the young German were standing atop their only scaffold tower in one corner of the Staircase Hall. The tower was a flimsy metal thing that nobody else in the US Army trusted enough to use. One of Skilton's people had salvaged or stolen it from a junk pile and it was missing bolts and cross braces so it shook and swayed whenever they shifted their weight. Skilton did his best to avoid climbing it. Today he'd come at the request of some of his young workers who reported that they had found something interesting lying on top of the cornice while they were doing a survey of the damage to the plasterwork.

As he directed the beam of his flashlight into the darkness, Skilton saw only the rough back of the plaster cast and a moonscape of thick ash and dust coating the top of the cornice. "Are you sure it was here?" he said, trying to control the trembling in his knees. What, after all, could be so exciting? A sack of gold, a box of jewels? The only thing that would have really thrilled

Skilton was the discovery of a hidden lumberyard.

"Yes. Here, here," the boy insisted. He pressed his face near Skilton's to peer into the space. "See?" The youth reached out a finger and carefully brushed at a ridge in the grey dust.

Skilton saw what it was and laughed. "Well, I'll be."

He reached in and picked the object up, drawing it out carefully. He cradled it in his palm and he and the boy looked at it together. "See?" the boy repeated. He saw: in his hand he held a small cigar, like the Cuban panatellas he so loved to smoke at home. When he blew the fine dust off it, it was clear that it had been partially smoked.

"Did one of you boys put this there?" he said. "Are you fooling with me?"

"No, no," the boy said, grinning. His name was Toby. "It is cigarette of Tiepolo."

Skilton shook his head in wonder. Could it be true? Surely it was more likely that some worker had left it there in the centuries since Tiepolo and his sons had painted the vault. Could rolled tobacco leaves really survive for 200 years? He blew a little more dust from the cigar. Only the tip was charred. It was easy to imagine someone lighting it, then being called away and stashing it up there, planning to come back for it later.

Skilton lifted his eyes and let them play across the painted surface of the vault. It was a bright day, and they had removed a few of the boards from the windows so they could see well enough to conduct the survey. Skilton rarely allowed himself to look at the paintings — when he did he felt overwhelmed by the responsibility of saving them — but he looked at them now: the wild processions of cloaked and naked human figures marching along the cornices, the serene gods lounging among the clouds, the exotic animals, the many species of bird. It didn't take much illumination to bring the frescoes to life. Balthasar Neumann's vault seemed to gather and intensify even the most fleeting glimmers of light, turning them into stage lights for Tiepolo's theatre of life.

His eyes sought out the portraits of Tiepolo and his son Domenico. They were painted on the wall dedicated to the continent of Europe, in a corner above another set of rangy Titans leaning on a shield. Tiepolo was the older man in a workman's cap and the young, fresh-faced dandy in a blue coat and a white wig was Domenico, his son and partner. Bosslet, the architect, had told Skilton all of this and there were times when Skilton wished he hadn't. Personalising the frescoes made it harder for him. It made him feel how much there was at stake.

But now, holding the relic of the cigar in his hand, Skilton felt unaccountably happy. It was such a blessedly ordinary thing: a man stealing a smoke on the job. A man interrupted in his quiet moment, getting sidetracked by a thousand different tasks and decisions, damping the end of his cigar and parking it there on the cornice, intending to come back for it. The scaffold structure would have been shifted on down the hall as the job moved forward, the cigar was left behind. Skilton felt close to Tiepolo at that moment, a comrade and colleague, a fellow smoker. Two hundred years was the blink of an eye. The past was only a smoke away.

"Shall I?" he joked, pretending to hold the antique cigar to his lips.

"Yes, smoke it!" The boy laughed, shaking the rickety scaffold tower.

Skilton touched the cigar to his lips and tasted dust.

Skilton kept up appearances. He hung on to his manners even when his patience was tried to the limit and he was so tired he felt like weeping. He prayed daily for help in his task, for the goodwill of his fellow soldiers and the German populace and he got both, in some measure. He prayed for the strength of Neumann's vaults and they held. Though he wasn't in the habit of bothering God about trivialities, he prayed passionately for the rain to stop.

It didn't. One day a dark patch appeared on the vault in the Staircase Hall. Skilton's eyes scanned its painted heaven and stopped at what he first wanted to believe was a dark cloud, part of the picture. It was no cloud; it was a wet stain spreading near the reclining figure of Venus. The sight of this leak made him feel sick; it was like looking at an open sore. Here, he knew, was the weak point, the place where utter ruin would begin.

Skilton envisioned Tiepolo's perfect heaven opening up just there, where the dark stain touched Venus' pink shoulder. The rain would insinuate its way into the plaster and, gradually at first, the vault would crumble inward, revealing a sliver of the imperfect, real sky. Then the rain would establish its dominion, sending individual drops to slide down the inner curve of the vault, tracing the path from its apex to the floor of the staircase. In short order, the vault would begin to come down. The figure of Venus would fall first, riding her cloud through Neumann's sublime space like a pin-up girl painted on a bomb. The next to go would be the cluster of distant gods to her right, then the chariot of the sun, all peeling loose from the vault's supporting iron ribs and raining down like paratroopers onto the switchback staircase. After that, there would be no stopping the destruction. The integrity of the vault lost, the chaos would spread down the walls. The continents would dissolve into rubble, their dark heavy bodies, their outflung hands, their wild, beautiful heads, sloping forward as they peeled free of the underlayer, pitching headlong into space to land on the floor. Skilton imagined the sound they would make as they fell: a series of wet, defeated thuds.

There were ominous changes in the palace rooms as the weeks went by. Try as he would, Skilton couldn't ignore them. It wasn't just the Staircase Hall that was the problem. In the Imperial Hall mould grew on the surface of the frescoes, dimming their radiance. Water filtering though the plaster began leaching minerals into the paint layer. Red and green curls of mineral pigment drifted down into the layer of dust and ash coating the checkered marble floor. Terrible colours, ones Tiepolo never chose, began to appear across the surface like a rash. Pus yellow, gunmetal grey, vomit pink blurred the complexion of blond Beatrice of Burgundy in her white chariot, her sweet blond vacancy, her pearls.

Skilton found the White Room the most pathetic of all. This square chamber stood between the Staircase Hall and the Imperial Hall and was a kind of anteroom for the throne room. In contrast to the rooms nearby, its décor was a monochrome confection of stark white stucco. Antonio Bossi, the artist, had created an intricate masterpiece of delicate Rococo frond and shell-forms around the vault and finely crafted trophy reliefs over the doorways.

Of all the rooms of the Residence, the White Room was Skilton's secret favourite. He admired Tiepolo's virtuosity and would do anything to save his works, but Skilton was a twentieth century man and the fact was that the convulsions of the high Baroque left him feeling a little queasy. Bossi's fantasy in white was more to his taste, providing a sort of caesura, a breathing space, between the two lushly decorated staterooms. Skilton found it entrancing — or he would have, if the White Room's delicacy of style hadn't been proving so literal. Rain had already brought down a section of the ceiling, reducing Bossi's exquisite plaster creations to damp piles of chalk dust. Skilton had begged a second scaffold tower from a sympathetic engineering unit and used it to prop up the weakest part of what remained. Every day, the humidity in the air dissolved more of the stucco bonds and sent calcified fronds, curls, fractal segments and minute spinal columns of plaster skittering down the walls. The room rattled constantly with these tiny, incremental losses, punctuated by louder crashes when a whole stucco shield or a bough of tracery gave way.

Skilton's heart literally ached whenever he thought about the White Room. It was a reminder of all that was teetering on the brink of being lost and all that was already beyond recovery. The bombing had destroyed so much of the palace outright: the Spiegelkabinett, a room made entirely of gold and mirrors, also decorated by Bossi; the Court Chapel with paintings by the Swiss artist Rudolf Byss; the Green Lacquer Room, with its walls of viridian enameled over silver. Boards were nailed across the passageways to keep the sickness of annihilation from spreading from these dead limbs to the parts of the Residence that were still alive. And this was the least of it. In the city at large, the list of losses was endless: the municipal museum, most of the Cathedral of St. Killian, and thousands of men, women and children burned beyond recognition and buried in the mass grave just beyond the city limits. And still that wasn't all. Bomber pilots, foot soldiers, both German and American, all dead: irrecoverable. Germany as it had been before the war, a place Skilton had known and admired: gone forever.

Skilton lived with this knowledge. But if he thought about the losses too much, it slowed him down. He tended to hurry through the White Room from the Staircase Hall, which still looked strong even with its spreading wet patch, to the Imperial Hall, which, despite the flowering mould, he still believed they could save.

He almost admitted his fears to Ingrid Bergman. It was a moment of weakness. Her lovely face was so open, her gaze so absorbent. She seemed to drink in every word he said, looking at him with eyes as blue as a patch of azurite sky. He had been lonely. He couldn't confess his fears to his colleagues or his workers or his superiors or his antagonists in the Army Corps of Engineers. But he thought, for a just a moment, that Ingrid Bergman would understand.

Skilton was on the riverbank when it started, supervising the delivery of a barge full of lumber. Captain Hauser came running down the muddy track, shouting his name. *It's happened*, Skilton thought, bracing himself. *The vault has come down*. Skilton wondered how many were injured, who was dead. He stood still and waited for Hauser to reach him. The captain grabbed him by the shoulders.

"You have to come right away," he said in a terrified voice. "Ingrid Bergman is asking for a tour."

"Very funny." Skilton felt his whole body relax. He thought Hauser was pulling his leg. He knew the USO had arrived in Würzburg only because the brass had asked his permission to set up a stage on the square in front of the Residence. He said yes, on condition they filled the biggest bomb craters and afterwards gave him the lumber they used to build the stage. They agreed, and he quickly forgot all about it.

"What about Jack Benny?" he said, turning back to watch the men hefting planks off the barge. "I suppose he wants one too?"

Hauser was beside himself. Skilton had never seen the placid captain so excited. His dark eyes were wild and his hair, usually so sleek and supine, was standing at attention. "I'm not kidding, Lieutenant. I've been looking for you all over. She's really waiting for you. You personally. She's really Ingrid Bergman."

Skilton had to laugh. "I've got to get this unloaded, Captain.

Why don't you give her a tour?"

"No, no, no." Hauser looked stricken. "I couldn't. I wouldn't know what to say. I'd just stand there with my mouth open, looking at her. You should see her. It's really, really her."

When they reached the Residence, they found the actress standing at the entrance surrounded by a clutch of moonstruck Military Government officers. What Hauser said was true: she was waiting for Skilton.

"There you are, Lieutenant," she said in her soft unidentifiable accent, taking his hand like an old friend. "They were afraid they wouldn't be able to find you, but I had a feeling you wouldn't have gone too far away from your project. Will you show me what you are doing here? I would be so grateful."

The young actress wore an elegant dark skirt and a jacket with wide lace cuffs that belled out over her slender wrists and fluttered when she moved her hands. Her light brown hair was covered with a silk scarf — Hermés, Skilton observed with pleasure. Without any formality, she took Skilton's arm and he escorted her inside, the entourage of Allied officers trailing after them jealously. Many of them had never taken the time to come see the work in the Residence before and Skilton was grateful to Miss Bergman for luring them there. As she walked at his side, he picked out the notes of her perfume: tuberose, vanilla with an undertone of — yes, he wasn't mistaken — leather. As they moved at the head of the group of uniformed men, Skilton noticed them breathing in her smell like beached fish gasping for oxygen. The others might think she smelled of sex, but Skilton knew better: Ingrid Bergman smelled of civilisation.

"You're a dark horse, Skilton," Hauser said later, eyeing him with a new respect. "How come you didn't tell me you already knew her?"

"I didn't. I never met her before today," Skilton replied.

Hauser studied him closely. "It seemed like you knew her, or she knew you. She seemed to like you anyway. What's your secret?"

"She liked the Residence. She liked the fact that we're trying to save it. Look around you, Hauser. Look at this city. Think of all the other cities she's seen on the way here. She liked seeing something good happening for a change. There's nothing strange about that."

He saw that Hauser looked doubtful and tried again.

"Let me put it another way. Here you are in this bombed-out country. There's death all around. Everything is ruined, destroyed, kaput. You like seeing Miss Bergman, don't you?"

"What the hell are you talking about, Lieutenant?"

She had seemed to enjoy her tour. Skilton steered her across the vestibule and up the staircase, narrating the main points as they went. It had been a long time since he'd had the pleasure of acting as someone's guide and a long time since he'd had the pleasure of a having the company of a cultivated young woman. He'd been spending his time talking rigging and coverage and cubic board feet. He had to reach deep inside to wake up the part of himself that knew how to talk about art and architecture. Once he warmed up, he discovered he had learned a great deal about the building since he had arrived, especially from the local architects, Bosslet and Dr. Erik Berger, who were funds of knowledge. Now he was able to speak confidently about Neumann, the man who had designed the building, and point out the reclining figure in the southern frieze that was reputed to be Tiepolo's portrait of him. He showed her the figure of the stucco artist Antonio Bossi in his voluminous yellow cloak, looking straight out of the painting with an unnerving intensity that seemed to presage his eventual descent into madness. Finally, he told her what he knew of the Venetian painters, Giambattista and Domenico Tiepolo, and showed her their portraits, father painted by son, son by father, placed like a pair of signatures at the edge of the Europe frieze.

"They look so much like real people," the young actress exclaimed. "Like men you would know. And look at their eyes, so full of spirit and intelligence and fun. They are most definitely Italians." She laughed then and Skilton heard a sort of collective sigh pass through the group of officers.

Miss Bergman gave a little gasp when she stepped into the Imperial Hall. Of all the staterooms, this one preserved most of its former splendour. Every inch of it was decorated and, even stripped of furniture or chandeliers, its impact was almost overwhelming. Subalterns had removed the boards from the windows for the star's visit and, as the rare sunshine came flooding in, the room seemed to pulse with colour. Fluted columns of purple, pink and white marble rose upwards to a soaring dome that was pierced with round windows and sunken lunettes in the shape of paraboli. The Baroque stucco work was battered by the bombing, its gilding dulled with dust and smoke, but what had survived was lavish and endlessly inventive. There were shields and fronds and leaves and garlands, gambolling putti, powerful caryatids, and capitols that looked like they were formed of jungle plants. Stucco frames delineated Tiepolo frescoes that opened like windows into other worlds. High on the walls at either end of the oval room, false stucco hangings were pulled back like theatre curtains to reveal huge scenes. On the ceiling, the Venetian and his son had frescoed the heroic scene of a handsome blond girl riding through the sky in a chariot drawn by white horses. Apollo, in a halo of radiance, lights her way. *Fruity* was the word Hauser always used to describe it.

Skilton lent the actress his binoculars to examine the ceiling. He imagined she would take a quick look, ask a few questions, then hand them back and return to her makeshift dressing room to get ready for her show. There was a rhythm to tourism, and Skilton knew it well. But the young actress stood for a long time with the field glasses pressed into her eye sockets, studying the ceiling in silence. The officers who had come in with them grew bored and began to talk about other things, their masculine voices echoing in the vault. While he waited, Skilton was aware of another sound, too. From the roof came the noise of hammering as the labourers fixed reclaimed slates to the cupola. It crossed his mind to draw Miss Bergman's attention to this sound, since it was to him the sweetest music in the world, the melody of salvation, but she seemed lost in thought. Awkwardly, he stood near her, trying to ignore the impatient murmuring of the officers. One of them caught his attention and tapped the face of his watch.

When she finally handed the binoculars back to him, Skilton saw the inner rims of the eyepieces were wet. Quickly, before any of the others noticed, he handed her a clean handkerchief.

"It's just so joyful," she whispered to him, a catch in her voice. Taking a deep breath she furtively dabbed her eyes then handed the handkerchief back. "So playful."

"Yes it is," Skilton mumbled, folding his handkerchief neatly before putting it back in his pocket. "That's exactly what it is."

This was the moment when Skilton was tempted to confess to her. She had revealed her sorrow to him, only to him, dropping just for a moment the official mask of the USO trooper. It was a privilege, and it made Skilton want to be honest in return. He had only to open his mouth and it would all come flooding out: the anger, the pain, the hopeless feelings of futility he'd been struggling with since he'd arrived in Würzburg. What was he doing there? What were they doing there? How could life ever be normal again?

When he told this story in later years — and it was one of only a few war stories Skilton loved to tell — he left this part out because he found it too difficult to explain. Instead, he identified an emotion he thought everyone would understand and he substituted that for what he really felt when he stood next to Ingrid Bergman in the Imperial Hall. What he said was that, at that moment, he felt as though he were falling in love with her. In person, he informed his listeners, her charm was far more powerful than it was on screen. But what won him, and what surprised him, he said, was her intelligence and sensitivity.

"She appreciated what we were doing," he said. "I was — touched, I suppose, because, for much of the time, no one else did." He claimed to have preserved the handkerchief she'd wept into but he never actually produced it.

This story was a fabrication, a good forgery or a careful restoration of something that never happened. It was, as these things so often are, an improvement on reality. In fact, Ingrid Bergman left no room for confession. She pulled herself together before he could say a word. He saw her give herself a little shake and square her shoulders, take a breath. Then, turning on her heel, she got back to business, saying in a loud voice, "Now I want you to tell me all about this picture. It intrigues me. It looks like a wedding."

The four roofs over the Residence were completed by the end of September. On the 24th, they held a *Richtfest*, or topping ceremony, to mark the milestone. Skilton stood in the rutted palace garden with a crowd of workers and a few soldiers and watched a team of boys fix a small pine tree to the ridge of the cupola. The weather was hot and sunny and the colourful strips of rag tied to the tree's branches lifted in the breeze and streamed against the sky, which was as blue and limpid as any Tiepolo had painted. It was as if the promise of the frescoes had been fulfilled. By saving them, Skilton thought irrationally, they had somehow saved the real sky. The men clapped and whistled. They were all exhausted, especially Skilton. It was a day none of them had believed would ever come.

By special dispensation, they held the celebration in the Residence. Skilton wanted to use the Imperial Hall for the *Richtfest*, but, even with its new roof, the room was too fragile to fill with sixty-five beer-drinking men and boys. Instead, they set up trestle tables and benches in the Garden Room, a chamber on the ground floor with doors opening into the palace gardens.

The Garden Room had sustained little damage during the bombing, which Skilton thought was ironic; it was his least fa-vourite room in the Residence. Under its dark, slightly sinister frescoes of nymphs and shepherds — not painted by Tiepolo but the work of an artist called Zick — the German workers gath-ered to eat the bread and liverwurst Skilton had begged from the monks at a nearby monastery and drink beer from rented steins.

Skilton stood up and gave a short speech in German. It was the sort of thing he hated doing, and only the challenge of de-livering it in German gave him any satisfaction. In simple phras-es, he thanked the workers for their efforts and reminded them that this work was done for themselves, for Würzburg, and for the future. Afterwards, Bosslet rose and gave a much longer speech that ended with three cheers for Skilton. Listening to the male voices bark out the hoorahs, Skilton knew there was resentment and disdain and even hatred mixed with the sounds of praise. That was only natural; he was the occupier. It was what he would have expected. Hauser, sitting next to Skilton, socked him in the shoulder and he tried his best to smile.

Only later did Skilton relax. Thank God for beer, he thought, lifting the heavy stein to his mouth. The day had descended into a golden evening, with low sun streaming through the open doors and lighting up the tanned faces of the workers as they sat nursing their beer — there wasn't that much of it — and talking. How long it had been since any of them had enjoyed an evening like this one? It felt wrong in many ways to sit idly and do nothing, to sit together after all that had happened. And it felt good.

Still later, when the men linked arms and began to sing, Skilton sang with them. He didn't know all the words to the German songs, but he lent his fine tenor voice to the melody and the sound soared upwards to the roof they had built together and beyond, to the open sky.

THE END

Main Characters

John D. Skilton Art historian, museum curator, US soldier. Serves as a Monuments Specialist Officer in Würzburg, Germany during World War II.

The Guardis
Cecilia Guardi, daughter of Domenico Guardi, a painter, deceased, and Claudia Guardi. Both are immigrants to Venice from the Treviso.
Antonio Guardi, her eldest brother, a painter
Claudia Guardi, her mother, a widow
Francesco Guardi, her middle brother
Nicolò Guardi, her youngest brother

The Tiepolos
Giambattista Tiepolo, a Venetian painter
Cecilia Tiepolo, his wife, born Cecilia Guardi
Orsetta Tiepolo, Giambattista's mother, a widow
Zuane, a servant

The Tiepolo children
Elena Tiepolo, daughter, dies of smallpox in infancy
Anna Maria Tiepolo, daughter
Domenico Tiepolo, son, dies of smallpox in infancy
Elena Tiepolo
Domenico Tiepolo, son, a painter, becomes Tiepolo's partner
Orsola Tiepolo, daughter
Angela Tiepolo, daughter
Antonio Tiepolo, son, dies in childhood
Giuseppe Tiepolo, son, a priest
Lorenzo Tiepolo, son, a painter, works with Tiepolo

Francesco Algarotti Second son of a wealthy family of Venetian merchants. Scientist, art expert, world traveller, friend of King Frederick the Great of Prussia and author of *Newton for Ladies*.

Bonomo Algarotti A merchant and art-lover, Francesco's older brother.

Joseph Smith English merchant and longtime resident in Venice, ultimately English Consul. Collects and deals in art and antiquities.

Giacomo Casanova Venetian author, poet, playwright, professional gambler, one-time priest, Freemason, necromancer and fugitive from the law. Also known as Giacomo Farussi, Chevalier de Seingalt.

The majority of characters in this novel are based on historical figures and as such they lead two distinct lives: the one they live in my story, and the much more ample one they lived in reality. To learn more about the history behind the characters, please see my website: www.martamaretich.com

Acknowledgments

Every novel has a life of its own and creates a sort of atmosphere around itself even as it's being written. From the first, *The Merchants of Light* was a happy, fortunate project that attracted kindness and generosity from everyone who came into contact with it. I put this down not to any special quality of mine, but to the novel somehow channeling the joyful, playful, witty spirit of the Tiepolo paintings that inspired it.

I'd first like to thank the trustees of the Eastern Frontiers Educational Foundation whose timely award of a residency on Norton Island allowed me the freedom to do the risky early explorations for the book and even hash out some paintings of my own.

Several prominent Tiepolo scholars gave me the benefit of their expertise during the writing of this novel: Beverly Brown showed me why Tiepolo's oil sketches are more revealing than his finished work. Catherine Whistler shed light on the little-examined period the Tiepolos spent in Spain. Svetlana Alpers graciously put me in touch with her colleagues and received this fan's effusive emails with kindness and interest. I am extremely grateful to them all — and delighted to have shared part of this journey with such brilliant companions. Any factual errors or lapses in taste are my own and have nothing to do with them.

My special thanks go to my earliest and most dedicated readers: Catherine Temma, who saw many versions of this book without losing her love for it; Carolyn Tipton, who showed me what it means to bring the discipline of words to visual art; and Libby Mosier who brought clarity and faith to my project, without which I might well have failed to complete it.

Thanks to Sojourner Jones, Susan Foster and Henry Acland, all of whom read and offered valuable feedback on early drafts. Theresa Sanminiatelli helped me capture the spirit of Venice in these pages. *Grazie!* Jo Swinnerton held my hand through the difficult early stages of turning a manuscript into a book and helped me come up with the perfect title. Alan Ogden gave me the benefit of his sage advice at several key moments. I'm indebted to all of them.

My heartfelt thanks go to my brother Mike Maretich for doing such a good job of taking care of our parents, thus freeing me to write this novel.

I am grateful to our production team who went beyond the call of duty to make this book both readable and beautiful: Di Steeds for brilliant copy-editing, Guy Eaglesfield for scintillating design and formatting and Kim Glyder for a luminous cover worthy of Tiepolo.

Thanks to the team at Nine Elms for believing in this project and helping me bring the vibrant world of the Tiepolos to a wider readership.

Above all, thanks to my family who remain the true inspiration for this novel and for all my other creative works. Without them, none of it would be possible — or worth it.

Research Notes

The Merchants of Light is primarily inspired by the paintings, frescoes and drawings of Giambattista Tiepolo. These were my touchstones and my prime sources at every step of the creative process, yet the writing of the book was also fuelled by research.

The research process turned out to be a voyage of discovery that took me into some of the world's best archives and museums and exposed me to the work of wonderful scholars, dramatists, historians, artists and critics, past and present. The experience was thrilling. Given the chance, I would do it all over again and I would highly recommend further exploration to anyone still eager to learn more about the Tiepolos and their fascinating times.

Here are some resources I found useful:

Giambattista Tiepolo: The paintings and drawings are the place to start with Tiepolo who, despite his fame during his lifetime, left few personal traces behind him. There are many, many books on the subject of Tiepolo's works but the best general introduction is the comprehensive *Giambattista Tiepolo: His Life and Art,* by Michael Levey.

Cecilia Tiepolo and the Tiepolo and Guardi families: Biographical information for Cecilia Tiepolo and both the Tiepolo and Guardi families is scant and what there is tends to be buried deep in archives.

During the writing of this book I leaned heavily on the findings of art historians who came before me, including George Knox, Pompero Molmenti, Federico Montecuccoli degli Erri and Catherine Whistler, among others. They did the painstaking work of identifying Tiepolo wills, letters, marriage registers and court proceedings and from these piecing together a rough picture of their lives and family dynamics. Information about Cecilia Tiepolo's early life and the Guardi family draws on a remarkably detailed dissertation by Alice Binion: *Antonio and Francesco Guardi: Their Life and Milieu.*

Life in 18th Century Venice: Books about the history of 18th century Venice are plentiful, but there are few sources that record the details of ordinary life at this time. To get a flavour of the times, I turned to one of the era's most notorious figures: Giacomo Casanova. His 12-volume autobiography, *History of My Life*, is much more than a criminally entertaining account of his sexual conquests (though it certainly is that). It's a compendium of contemporary manners, habits, attitudes, customs and tastes, written by a native Venetian who travelled ceaselessly around Europe and mixed with all levels of society, from kings to beggars, in many countries.

Casanova's books became my go-to source for information about what people wore, what they ate, how they travelled, what they did for fun — all the details of ordinary life none of his more staid contemporaries bothered to record. Reading these books completely changed my view of this controversial writer who, it now seems to me, is remembered for the wrong things. To those looking for an introduction to Casanova, I recommend Ian Kelly's accessible biography: *Casanova*.

Other key sources for things mundane and human were the works of the Venetian playwright Carlo Goldoni, especially his trio of plays set during the summer vacation in the Veneto, *The Holiday Trilogy* (*La Villeggiatura*) and his autobiography, *Memoirs*. Andrea di Robilant's nonfiction books about Venice, notably *A Venetian Affair*, were not only gripping but useful for helping me establish a sense of context. Finally, I discovered many telling details in the paintings of Pietro Longhi who, unlike Tiepolo, painted ordinary Venetians in their homes and about town, as well as in the early works of Giovanni Antonio Canal — Canaletto — who painted the working class neighbourhoods of Venice at the beginning of his career.

Francesco Algarotti: Algarotti is the best-documented historical character in the novel apart from Casanova. A prominent figure of the Enlightenment and a prolific writer, he speaks for himself through a significant body of correspondence and criticism — and of course his charming introduction to the science of optics, *Newton for Ladies*. Biographies of Frederick the Great include further information about Algarotti, however the nature of their relationship remains a matter of controversy and discomfort for historians. I have come to my own conclusions based on reading the correspondence between Algarotti and Frederick, which is, amazingly, available online through a digital project from the library of the University of Trier.

Some details about Algarotti's commissions for Tiepolo are drawn from Jaynie Anderson's detailed study, *Tiepolo's Cleopatra*. Two further books were essential for understanding the Tiepolos' professional context and the art market of Venice during the latter part of the 18th century: *Patrons and Painters: Art and Society in Baroque Italy*, by Francis Haskell and *Painting for Profit: The Economic Lives of Seventeenth-Century Italian Painters* by Richard E. Spear and Philip Sohm.

John D. Skilton: Like Algarotti, John D. Skilton left his own record of his experiences, including his work in Würzburg: *Memoirs of a Monuments Officer* by John D. Skilton Jr. Although I ran across fleeting references to him early on in my research, it wasn't until I actually went to Würzburg and visited an exhibition about the wartime damage to the Residence that I finally discovered his name. In a world where other Monuments Men have become cultural heroes, thanks to Robert M. Edsel's good work, Skilton's name should be better known.

For details about the bombing of Würzburg and its aftermath, I turned to an account written by one of its survivors: *To Destroy a City: Strategic Bombing and its Human Consequences in World War II* by Hermann Knell. Knell provides useful background on the wartime history of Würzburg as well as a moving account of what happened to his family during and after the bombing. He also delivers a damning analysis of the history and strategic value of the kind of area bombing that was responsible for the devastation of Würzburg. The Tiepolos' long-suffering housekeeper, Frau Knell, is named in the author's honour.

The Tiepolos in Würzburg: There are several wonderful reference works on the Tiepolos' work in Würzburg, which are now part of a UNESCO World Heritage site. *Heaven On Earth: Tiepolo Masterpieces of the Würzburg Years* by Peter O. Krückmann is beautifully illustrated and provides a useful overview. *Tiepolo's World: The Ceiling Fresco in the Staircase Hall of the Würzburg Residence* by Werner Hamburger and Matthias Staschull gives an account of the recent restoration of the frescoes and makes informative reading with regards to technical aspects of the painting.

However, for real insight into the Tiepolos' extraordinary achievement, I looked to the lyrical, groundbreaking book by Svetlana Alpers and Michael Baxandall: *Tiepolo and the Pictorial Intelligence*. This book reads like a labour of love and, more than any other I ran across, it literally shines a light on what is unique about Giambattista Tiepolo's genius. It served me as a constant reminder of what really drives visual artists: not stories — those are the preoccupation of writers — but pictures. Always pictures.

Topics for reading group discussion

"After what Skilton had witnessed since he landed on Omaha Beach almost a year earlier, he could see how it was possible that nature, or even God, might want to scour Europe clean and simply start again. And yet it was his job to pick through its ruins, to see what could be saved." How does the character of John Skilton serve as our introduction into the Tiepolo story? How do his reactions help us understand what's at stake?

The narrative takes a big leap in time from the 20th century to the 18th. There are also long breaks in the story during the fifty years it covers in the life of the Tiepolo family. How do these breaks affect the way the story unfolds? What is the advantage of telling the story this way?

"Cecilia glimpsed the old Antonio again, funny and easygoing. It was like seeing a close friend after a long absence. If they were just a little bit richer, she thought, Antonio could go back to being that way again. It wouldn't matter that he wasn't serious about work. No one would expect him to keep them all alive or blame him for not being more successful." How does Cecilia's relationship with her brother Antonio influence her decision to marry Giambattista Tiepolo?

Cecilia believes that "talent is a form of power". What does she mean by this? Why is talent so vital in her world?

Cecilia is surrounded by male artists and knowledgeable about painting, but she doesn't seem to feel the need to create art herself. Is this only a reflection of traditional women's roles or does it say something about Cecilia? What does it suggest about Cecilia's view of painting?

What do the personal family histories of Cecilia, Antonio and Tiepolo tell us about the lives and status of painters and artisans at this time?

When Cecilia goes to see Tiepolo at the Palazzo Sandi, she recognises her own likeness in his fresco. At this moment, she realises that she has "become one of her husband's tools". Why is this insight important both to their marriage and to Tiepolo's future career?

"Petition T's muse" Francesco Algarotti writes in a note to himself, referring to Cecilia. Then he reconsiders because, "he'd been called a muse
himself while he was living with Frederick and he didn't care for the title.
Muses, he well knew, were never taken seriously." What makes Cecilia more
than a muse to Tiepolo? Why does Algarotti want to reject the role of
muse?

"The English can appreciate Tiepolo's talent," says the art collector Joseph
Smith to Francesco Algarotti, "but they'd prefer he exercised it in a more
rational manner. They're all in love with Reason these days." How are
reason and imagination at play in the work of Tiepolo? Why is this inter-
play so important — and troubling — for Algarotti?

"Had she won the argument, or had she lost it?" Accompanying his father
and brother to Würzburg changes Lorenzo's life and his relationship with
Cecilia. Do you think she argued for Tiepolo to take the boy, or for him to
leave him behind with her?

Cecilia is an enthusiastic gambler and gambling plays a part in the action
at different points in the story. What does Cecilia's love of gambling reveal
about her character and her abilities? Is it in keeping or in conflict with
her role as a devoted wife and mother?

"The idea that his father might have had the time to sit around doing little
portraits of his own wife was ridiculous; professionals like him didn't get
paid for immortalising family members." We know that Tiepolo often used
his wife Cecilia and other family members and friends as models. Yet the
story makes a distinction between portraits and the likenesses that Tiepolo
incorporates into his paintings. Does this change your view of the relationship between models and painters? Does it change your ideas about the
process of painting?

Throughout the novel, there's a tension between the printed word — stories — and visual representation. Much of Tiepolo's work involves depicting scenes from history, the Bible, or classical mythology, yet he is often

frustrated by the way his clients insist on using printed texts as a way to communicate what they want in their commissions. What does this tell us about the way Tiepolo approaches the process of painting? Does he tell stories in paint?

In Tiepolo's time, painters were considered to be artisans, not artists in the sense we understand them today. They worked on commission and produced paintings that met the specifications of individual clients. Personal vision, creative drive and inspiration, though they may have been present, weren't thought strictly necessary qualities for artists and didn't form part of the bargain. Does this make the art they created less moving, less authentic or less successful? Is it really art if it doesn't come from the heart?

At the end of the novel, we learn that Tiepolo stayed in Madrid for eight years and died before he could return home to Venice. What do you think this says about his relations with Cecilia later in life? What do you think it says about his commitment to his work?

"Ingrid Bergman smelled of civilisation." What do you think Skilton means by this? What does this statement reveal about him?

There are five different narrators in the book but we never get the point of view of Giambattista Tiepolo, arguably the character at the epicentre of the story. Why do you think the author adopted this strategy? How does it make you see the character of Tiepolo?

The author has said elsewhere that the subject of her novel is "creativity in its many forms". What do you think she means by that? Do you agree that different kinds of creativity are represented in the story? Which characters practice alternative forms of creativity?

By the same author

THE POSSIBILITY OF LIONS
Marta Maretich

GemmaMedia 2011
Paperback and e-book
ISBN: 978-1-936846-02-3
USA: $10.00

www.martamaretich.com

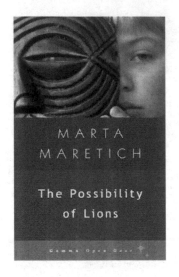

The Possibility of Lions tells the story of an American family forced to flee their home in Nigeria at the outbreak of the Biafran war. They wash up in a small town in California, a "safe" place where nobody has ever heard of Nigeria or the war that cost them their home.

For a while the children and their fragile mother find comfort in the belief that one day they'll be able to return to Africa. Their father, a man who's experienced war up close, knows better.

As the truth sinks in, mother and children fall under the spell of another lost African, a former big-game hunter from the Congo. His grandiose dream — to establish a wild animal park on the dusty outskirts of town — seems to offer hope that the two worlds can be brought together in one place. But can what's lost ever really be found again? And can they convince the cautious locals to embrace the possibility of lions?

"Maretich writes in a clear, sharp voice edged with humour and compassion. She knows what it means to be displaced, and understands the unexpected friendships forged between the lost."
Catherine Temma, author of *The Priest Fainted*